The Potent Solution

By Ashley Nova

For the former gifted and talented kids.

My name is Charlotte Elizabeth Price, and on the 16th of October 1834, I was at the Palace of Westminster when it burned to the ground.

October 8th, 1834
The Peculiar Case of Timothy Waters

Chapter 1

I was late.

Worse than that, I didn't even know if I was late. "Off with the faeries," my father would always say when I was deep in my thoughts. I'd popped into the Turkish café across the street from the shop where I apprenticed, intent on enjoying a quick cup of coffee before starting my day. Instead, more than an hour had passed, and I found myself engrossed in a rather fascinating book on the subject of lycanthropy. The coffee was cold, the hustle and bustle of Carnaby Street was beginning to build outside, and I was none the wiser—it was no small wonder I made it to work at all.

I'd like to tell you I wasn't usually so scatter-brained, but I'd be lying. Lateness came to me as easily as breathing. I could recite the names and key properties of all the known chemical elements, I memorised the hieroglyphs of Nicholas Flamel, and I could calculate daily, weekly, and monthly finances with mental arithmetic alone—just don't ask me to do any of that on any kind of regular schedule. It wasn't so much that I was forgetful—I had a very good memory, in fact. Forgetting and remembering just aren't the right words for it. Instead, it's more like losing something, and not knowing you've lost it until all of a sudden you need to run out into the rain and your umbrella is nowhere to be found. Then, someone helpfully points out that it's in the umbrella stand, exactly where it should be, and you have nothing to do but hide your shame.

It was pure chance—or dumb luck—that when a cat darted onto the street outside, it spooked a cart horse and caused such an enormous ruckus that I almost jumped out of my skin. When the animal part of my brain finally accepted there was no immediate danger, I looked out the window and spotted an old lady crossing the street and walking straight up to the front door of my place of employment.

"Fuck, I'm so done for." I downed the remaining dregs in my cup—I never waste good coffee—and practically sprinted for the door.

Carnaby Street had been completely ripped up in the 1820s—all part of the rejuvenation works around the new Regent Street to the west—and a purpose-built shopping street was designed and constructed under the supervision of noted architect, John Nash. The new market consisted of two picturesque terraces of three- and four-storey houses, each with a shop on the ground floor, and it quickly attracted an array of clientele from bakers and butchers to couturiers and umbrella makers. Having grown up in the back streets of Camden Town—where one would be more likely to find a brothel than a bookshop—Soho always seemed something of a juxtaposition of upper-class opulence and working-class grime.

The shop where I worked was, even by Carnaby Street's standards, eclectic. The tall picture-frame windows were stuffed floor to ceiling with colourful poultices, bottled ointments and remedies, and signage that proclaimed relief from all life's ailments. Whether it was joint pain, a weak stomach, migraines, or *marital problems*, one substance or another could be found within the jumble of wares. The brickwork, window frames, and door of the shop were all painted in a deep shade of green, above which a sign was boldly styled in gold paint:

The Potent Solution
J. Morton

Despite looking like a bizarre apothecary's or pharmacy, the Solution was far more than meets the eye. If you knew what you were looking for, you would note the small window above the door, styled with a geometric symbol known as The Squared Circle. It was the calling card of an Alchemist, someone who studies the boundaries of the Arcane and Mundane, a brewer of potions and transmuter of the elements. My employer, Jennifer Morton, was one such person.

The old woman I'd spotted was standing on the doorstep, alternating between ringing the bell and knocking on the door. Odd, I'd expected Jennifer to open up with or without me, but the closed sign was still hanging in the window. What was she up to? More importantly, could I get away with being late?

"Morning, ma'am, sorry to keep you waiting." I stepped up beside the woman and brandished the keys to the door.

"Half an hour I've been here," she lied. She was bundled up in more coats than I could count and had a pale face covered in liver spots.

"Of course, please accept my deepest apologies." I had no interest in arguing with a septuagenarian before nine o'clock—or really any time of day, as grandmothers always have an unending supply of complaints—so I simply unlocked the door and showed her inside. "What can we do for you today?"

She moved to answer but was taken aback by the haphazard arrangement of tables and display cabinets, which could only be justified as a form of organised chaos. "I've been having trouble sleeping, young lady. Mr Parsons over on Dean Street recommended your… establishment," she said after collecting herself.

"Well, whatever your problem, we have The Potent Solution," I said with a pained smile. "I would recommend our lavender ointment; we also have oil of valerian—though that should only be used short term—as well as a poppy seed extract that's quite effective for some people. Or perhaps you were looking for something more specialist?"

"Specialist, dear?"

"Potions, decoctions, that sort of thing. If you need something Arcane in nature, we offer individual commissions at very competitive prices." Competitive prices were easy because we were the only Alchemy shop in London.

She gave me a puzzled look, and then one of disdain. "Oh, you aren't one of them, are you?"

"One of what?" I sighed.

"Witches."

Witches. It wasn't the worst thing I'd been called, but

quite possibly one of the most out of date. Nobody referred to the magically gifted as witches anymore. "No," I said, stifling a sharp laugh, "we aren't *mages*. Or sorcerers, or wizards, or druids. We're alchemists."

"What's the difference?" she asked, impertinent. "I don't want nothing to do with anything illegal." I sighed to myself—no matter how enlightened society had apparently become, some people refused to leave the 16th century. When you spend every day surrounded by magic, you sometimes have to stop and remember that most people don't know or care one lick about it—excepting, of course, a few who get nostalgic about the witch trials.

"Well," I paused to gather my thoughts, "technically speaking, mages cast spells by channelling energy from the Arcane Aether, made possible by an unexplainable personal connection to the magical world." The customer stared at me with a blank face—babbling Arcane nonsense was a trick I'd picked up from Jen to deal with difficult situations. "Anyone can do Alchemy—with the right knowledge and training. Besides, magic is perfectly legal."

That wasn't entirely true—mages faced tight restrictions when it came to magic and employment—but no one was hanged or burned at the stake anymore. Alchemy enjoyed something of a legal exemption from those restrictions, having historical popularity among the ruling classes came with certain benefits.

I smiled again at the woman, but this time in a more impatient—*are we done here because I'd like to get back to my book*—kind of way.

"I'll just take the lavender ointment," the old lady said after a moment's pause.

"Coming right up, ma'am." I collected the bottle from the shelf, took the payment, and noted everything down in the ledger. Once the customer had left, I sat down and pulled out my book. A job well done, and I'd managed to avoid Jennifer's notice.

Or so I thought. A bang came from the stockroom behind

me, muffled by the wall. "You're late," Jennifer called a second later. "Something for you on the cash desk."

"Dammit," I said quietly, followed by, "I know, I'm sorry," much louder. Jennifer had left a box of small bottles on the desk, along with a blank chalkboard sign—all of which I'd somehow failed to notice. "What's all this?"

"Things that should have been in the window an hour ago," she responded. She was moving around in the stockroom, making a hell of a racket. "Flu remedies. I want them next to the cough syrup."

The glamourous life of an apprentice alchemist, stocking shelves and arranging window displays. "Right, there's a lot here, do I need to clear anything out?" Evidently, she didn't hear me.

There was a loud crash, a panicked sound, and a sigh of relief. "I'm going to be in a lab all morning, and it's important I'm not disturbed."

I made a sound of understanding, then went to look at the displays in the window. The cough syrups were stuffed into the corner of one shelf, with no space around them for the new bottles. I could've removed the laudanum to make room for the flu remedies—but that was one of our best-selling products—the shelf above had a line of incredibly popular smelling salts—below was a range of chewing tobacco. Any one of those choices would have been perfectly reasonable—but which did Jennifer think was the right one? "Jen, I could use a little more to go on."

It was like talking to a brick wall, and Jennifer just kept going on her train of thought. "The experiment is really delicate, Charlotte. Just make sure I'm not disturbed."

I went back to the cash desk and looked again at the box of remedies and grew even more puzzled. "I got that, Jen, but if you could just…" I was interrupted by the sound of a door opening and turned to see Jennifer's legs as she disappeared up the stairs. A moment later the door to the lab on the first floor closed heavily. "…and she's gone."

Here's the thing about working in a shop; most of the time, it's bloody boring. It wasn't long before I found my attention inexorably drawn in a thousand directions. It was hard enough for me to stay focussed at the best of times, but nothing shut down my ability to act more than being told to do something without clear instructions. No matter how much I willed myself to get to work, I simply found myself stuck at the juncture of near-infinite possibilities on *how* to get to work. There were times where I considered Jen to be the finest mentor I could have asked for; this was not one of them.

I must have spent an hour oscillating between the box of remedies and the open pages of *The Complete Taxonomy of Werewolves and their Kin* before I finally decided where to put the display. It was right then—in a tragic twist of irony, I'm sure you'll agree—that I was interrupted by the doorbell. The silhouette of a man appeared against the bright morning light. His swallowtail coat and top hat made for an unmistakable and increasingly common sight across the city: an officer of the London Metropolitan Police.

Chapter 2

"You must be—" he began, in a considered East London accent, "no, no, don't tell me. Catherine?" I shook my head, and he corrected himself with a triumphant snap of his fingers. "Charlotte! That's it. Ms Morton has been speaking about you, a promising student I hear." He chuckled and ran a hand through his thinning ginger hair. I was struck by his cheerful demeanour, unlike any I'd encountered amongst officers of the law—they weren't called Peel's Bloody Gang for nothing.

"That's right," I responded, a little off guard, "Charlotte Price, and you are?"

The officer stuck out a meaty hand, which I regretted taking as soon as he locked my fingers into a vice like grip. "Inspector Baker, ma'am, Metropolitan Police, Stepney Division."

It was a long way from Stepney to Soho, I dreaded to think what bought him across the city. In the two years or so that I'd worked for Jennifer, she'd been a consultant on a score of cases for the Met that had unexplained magical elements—not that she ever included me in those activities. But she'd always been invited by letter—Inspector Baker's presence implied unusual urgency.

"Stepney, eh?" I asked while rubbing my sore hand. "I assume you didn't come all this way to sample our collection of sleeping remedies?"

"Quite right, Miss. Is Ms Morton around? The matter is in fact quite serious and requires her unique attention," Inspector Baker explained, straightening up and putting his arms behind his back. *Quite serious,* of course, being British English for *Really, incredibly, deadly serious*—myinterest was most-assuredly piqued.

"She's in the lab at the moment and was very specific about not being disturbed. I can take a message, if you like," I said, but before Baker could respond, the familiar slamming of the heavy lab door echoed from the first floor. Footsteps on the stairs followed, and soon the tall, lithe figure of my mentor stepped out in a swagger.

Jen was never the sort of person to simply walk into a room—that would be far too pedestrian—no, when she entered, she swooped. A day hadn't gone by since she found me huddled over a makeshift alembic that I hadn't been floored by her outrageously dashing looks. She was unashamedly contrarian, endlessly confident, and utterly brilliant—and somehow made it all look effortless. If you told me that she'd rolled out of bed and flirted her way into an audience with the King, I would believe you, no question. Needless to say, I forgot all about being annoyed at her.

"No need to take a message, Charlotte, the inspector's voice can be heard clear across the street." She punctuated the sentence by dropping her lead-lined apron onto the cash desk. There was a note of hoarseness in her voice from inhaling a few too many fumes in the lab, and a mixture of iridescent powder and ash had been smeared across her face. "Baker, good to see you. Something serious needs my attention?" She was grinning with an unnerving curiosity.

"A body's been found ma'am, foul play is suspected, but the cause of death is," he paused, searching for the right word, "peculiar."

Jennifer frowned and responded, "I'm going to need a little more than peculiar to go on, Inspector. I've got plenty of peculiar right here."

"Rude," I interjected, coyly. Jen gave me a look that said about a thousand different versions of "really?"

"Burned, Ms Morton, alive for certain," the inspector said a moment later, a slight hesitation in his voice. "Strange thing is, he's the only thing that did burn. No other victims, no damage to the property. We've got nothing."

The cogs and gears in my mind kicked into motion for the first time since I woke up, and I couldn't help but speculate. There had been very few recorded cases of death by magic—whether due to a reluctance on those reporting or otherwise,

I can't say—but Baker wouldn't have come all this way to one of the cities foremost experts on the subject if he didn't suspect the Arcane. There were probably a few thousand mages in London at the time, but most had little to no formal ability to manipulate the Arcane—let alone with enough skill to burn someone alive. Magic was responsible, but the kind of magic, and its source—that was the mystery.

"Peculiar indeed." Jennifer's strange grin was back, and she sprang into motion, grabbing her dark brown riding coat and stuffing a myriad of objects into the dozen pockets she'd sewn onto the inside: notebook, pencils, a few vials of liquid, magnifying glass and several little boxes of raw alchemical supplies. She stopped for a moment and looked at me, quizzical. "Charlotte, have you set up the new display I asked for?"

"Yes," I lied—either I was a better liar than I thought, or Jen wasn't all that interested in the truth.

"Perfect, get your coat and the keys, I'd like you to come too." She didn't even glance at Baker for approval before striding toward the door. I shared a puzzled look with the Inspector before he shrugged and gestured for me to follow.

I collected my things and by the time I'd stepped out into an unseasonable autumn heat and locked up the shop, Jennifer and Inspector Baker were climbing into a cab. I'd have gone right after them, but of course I'd left the small "open" sign hanging in the window. I cursed before heading back inside to correct my mistake. Then, as a deep sense of unease and uncertainty settled into my gut, I headed down the street.

"Stepney, Driver. St John The Evangelist," the Inspector called once we'd all settled in the cab.

I sat silently next to Jennifer, unsure what role she expected me to take on. Was I to be the attentive student, the plucky sidekick, or a knowledgeable colleague? I knew next to nothing about her life outside of the shop and my alchemical studies. Between client confidentiality and need-to-know information, she didn't talk much about her sleuthing. In fact, in all the time I'd been working for her, Inspector Baker was the first person I'd met who knew her as a private detective first, not an alchemist.

Thoughts and questions came to my mind like long-forgotten melodies, wordless and half-formed, and I tried to focus on not looking at all agitated by the sudden change of plans.

"How are you keeping, Anthony?" Jennifer asked. I was surprised that they were on a first name basis, given that the Inspector's formal attitude. His posture seemed to loosen at the question, like a tightly wound rope given a little slack.

"Well as can be, Jen, all things considered. Yourself?"

"Busy, as always," Jennifer sighed. "I was in the middle of a rather delicate experiment before you arrived. Had you been any earlier, your booming voice might have set off quite the reaction." The inspector's face paled, and Jen let out a wicked chuckle. "Joking! Of course, it wasn't explosive. This time."

"Quite right," Baker said, letting out a nervous laugh. "And you, Miss Price, I hope we aren't pulling you away from anything too important?"

My mind screeched to a halt at the suggestion that I was in fact present in the moment, and not just watching from afar. "Oh, sorry, what?" I asked, despite having heard the Inspector quite clearly.

"Are you well, Miss?" he asked, and my mind finally caught up with the conversation.

"Yes, quite well, thank you."

Baker smiled, and a little more of the tension he was holding onto eased away. "I'm surprised it's taken so long for us to meet. When Jen said she was taking on an apprentice, I figured you'd be working cases together right away."

Truth be told, I didn't know what to say—the idea of learning the investigative trade had never been raised—I'd been more than content with my potions. But, now the seed of learning more—of doing something new, something that mattered—had been well and truly planted. Why had she kept this from me?

Probably sensing my apprehension, she put a reassuring hand on my knee, "Charlotte is a prodigy in the lab, Baker, her alchemical studies have taken precedent. Now seems like a good time to get her up to speed. Besides, there hasn't been anything interesting enough to bring her along to lately." She gave the inspector a snide look, and he rolled his eyes.

"What about the Whitechapel hauntings?" Baker asked.

"Boring. It was a pair of sprites causing trouble."

"Or when London Docks froze over, in July."

"Some idiot dropped a crate of Svalbard Sapphires off a ship."

"The Gargoyle at St Paul's—"

"Which turned out to be a disgruntled actor with a flair for illusions. What I'm saying is, when was the last time you bought me a murder, or a grand robbery, or a vanished viscountess?"

The Inspector chortled. "You have very particular tastes, Jen. You best be careful around this one, Miss Charlotte, she'll have you on all sorts of misadventures."

"I'll keep that in mind," I said, giving Jennifer a healthy dose of side-eye. As odd a pair as they seemed, I got a strong feeling that their relationship was more than professional. "How long have you two been working together?"

Jen clicked her tongue, "Fifteen years, I think? Baker here was the first officer I worked with, back when he was a Bow Street Runner," Jennifer said as she leaned over to me, pushing up against my shoulder. "It was before I'd opened the Solution, but as it turns out, I already had something of a reputation for problem solving."

Baker laughed like a booming cannon. "Reputation is one way to put it, Ma'am. I caught her snooping around the scene of a bank robbery and thought she'd committed it," he said to me. "Wasn't till after the banker explained that he hired Jen that I took the cuffs off her."

"Not the last time he had me in cuffs, either," Jennifer whispered. Definitely more than professional, then.

"What?!" Baker turned an almost scarlet shade of red and straightened up like a flagpole, and Jen shot me a wicked grin.

"What? Nothing. Anyway, the bank robbery, that was an interesting case. Nobody could work out how the robbers had entered the vault, just that there was a huge hole in the wall that wasn't there before," Jennifer explained—she always gesticulated wildly when telling stories, and spoke with barely contained excitement at her own brilliance. "My first suspicion, of course, was explosives, but there was no debris at the scene. I was about to give up when I made a startling discovery; the robbers didn't realise they had left something quite telling behind."

"Shit," Baker said, bluntly. "Nasty pile of droppings that smelled like sulphur, a few yards down a side street by the bank."

"It turned out someone had smuggled in a salamander from Central America that vomited an acidic bile so potent that it burned right through the stone. Of course, since then I've identified upwards of two dozen bizarre animals illegally imported from the Americas, and it's become quite old hat."

The two of them laughed, and I joined in, in that awkward way you do when old friends are sharing jokes. "What happened to the salamander?"

Jennifer thought for a second. "You know, I think it ended up in London Zoo?"

"Aye, it did, though I think it may have died last year," Baker answered—I'm surprised he didn't get whiplash from the way he kept straightening and relaxing. Jennifer leaned backwards, their eyes met, and she smiled brightly.

"Sounds like you have quite the history, then." Something else crept across the Inspector's face, a sad and longing expression. His professional instincts must have taken over and he sat up straight, looking proper. Jen sighed and turned to look out the window. I sat in the silence that followed, slowly turning as red as a lobster in a boiling pot. "Oh, shit—" ("Language," Jen quipped, which didn't help), "—it seems I touched a nerve. I'm sorry. You're just so… Comfortable together."

Jennifer put a hand on my knee and sighed again. "No, Charlotte, it's quite alright. History is the right word for it. Anthony and I parted on good terms." She was smiling at him, genuine and warm. The smile then turned wicked again. She jabbed me with her elbow and said, with a heavy dose of sarcasm, "Work and sex never mix."

And she had the audacity to tell me to watch my language! I was too stunned for words, but the Inspector just chuckled and shook the remark off. Jennifer had little in the way of a filter between her brain and her mouth. She spoke from the heart, told people how she felt and what she was thinking. It was endearing, if you could get past the occasional stinging comment.

The mood in the cab shifted. Jennifer took out a handkerchief and started wiping off the iridescent powder that had been so perfectly highlighting her cheeks. She then opened her battered old notebook and found an empty page. "So, Inspector, tell me about our victim."

"Right, of course," Baker said, shuffling to find his own notes. "Male, early forties. Went by the name Timothy Waters. He had been staying at a flophouse, not too far from where he worked at West India Docks." Jennifer was noting down what the Inspector said, and he waited for her to finish. "He arrived at the flophouse at around midnight, according to the landlord, possibly having been drinking."

"Every landlord thinks every person who sleeps in a doss house is also a drunkard," Jen noted.

"Precisely," agreed the Inspector. "The witness reports we have agreed that around two am, a fire started in the room where Waters had been sleeping, no one saw how it started, and in the commotion to clear out, no one got a good look at what happened."

"How long did he burn for?"

"A couple minutes at most."

"And no one else was injured?"

"None."

I wasn't entirely present in the conversation; my focus having blurred over the rapid back and forth. I'd been watching the ships and boats move on the river when a thought crystalised in my mind. "What was he like?" I asked, interrupting whatever was being said.

"Pardon?" Baker asked.

"Timothy Waters? What was he like?" Jennifer and the Inspector had been speaking as if the victim was just that, and not a person with a life, as squalid as that life might have been. But he must have been more than just a man who burned to death.

It took the Inspector a few seconds to catch onto my thinking. "Ah, right you are. Let me see." He flicked through a few pages of witness interviews. "A few labourers he worked with were staying at the same tenement. Here we are. 'Waters was a quiet man. Kept to himself. Hard worker who always finished quicker than you'd expect. Sang to himself all the time.'"

"Sang to himself?" Jennifer said in a puzzled tone, her middle-class upbringing on show.

I cocked my eyebrow. "Working songs, Jen. Helps with the monotony of hard labour. Sea shanties and folk music. Right, Inspector?"

Baker nodded, "Most likely, Miss Charlotte. Though I don't see how any of this helps."

Jen shrugged and said, "don't be so sure, Anthony, it is important to have the full context. Good thinking, Charlotte." There was nothing I could do to hide the smug grin on my face, so I awkwardly looked out the window. Not content to let me have my moment, Jennifer cleared her throat. "There is something I need to ask you, Charlotte, before we get there."

"What's that?" I replied, suddenly much more anxious.

"Have you ever seen a dead body?"

Chapter 3

I had never seen a dead body—not up close anyway—and nothing Jennifer told me in those last few minutes of our journey could have prepared me for what was coming.

The cab pulled up outside a run-down, four-story tenement building made from red brick. The windows were shuttered, and dark clouds crept over the rooftops. Two constables stood by the door, coats buttoned and truncheons at their waist. A crowd of people in ragged clothing huddled outside, muttering to themselves and pleading for information. Like the building itself, they were run-down; the sort of folk who were one bad day away from life in the workhouses.

Baker led the way, buttoning his coat as he walked. He tipped his hat to the constables when we reached the top of the stone stairs at the entrance. "Morning lads, any trouble?"

"No sir, though I hope we can get moving 'fore the rain starts, these folks won't be none too happy about waitin' outside much longer," replied the older of the two officers, a man with dark skin and a salt and pepper beard. His partner was no older than twenty and had a nervous energy about him; his eyes darted between the inspector and the crowd of people—I couldn't tell if he was ready to fly, or fight.

"Very well, we'll try to be fast. Ms Morton and her apprentice are experts in this kind of thing. They'll have us home in time for lunch."

"Hear that, Charlotte, Baker thinks you're an expert," Jennifer japed, which did little to settle my mind.

Inside it was dank and musty, with possibly a decade or more of human occupation rubbed into every surface. The floorboards were scuffed, and the stairs worn down so much that some of the steps could have been paper in places. Stuttering orange light from the nearly burned-out candles cast fuzzy shadows all over. An aura of oppression and suffocation permeated the space, as if by design.

Baker led us through the building, walking softly for such a big man. We climbed a tight staircase that opened onto a long corridor with half a dozen doors on each side. The hairs on the back of my neck stood on end as the Inspector reached one of the rooms and asked, "Ready?" Jennifer nodded. She may have been ready, but I wasn't.

Baker opened the door and the smell hit me like a tidal wave. Burned flesh, burned hair, burned shit, and burned cloth. The foul air caught in my throat and turned my stomach so hard that I vomited beside the door. When I steadied myself enough to look inside the room, a new, fresh horror laid out before me.

Twelve or so beds lined the walls of the room—a luxury one could afford for fourpence or fivepence a night if you didn't mind sharing. A room like that would have slept up to seventy, with most sleeping on the floor. As bad as it was to sleep in a crowded dosshouse, it was no doubt better than sleeping on the streets or toiling in a workhouse. Sacks and piles of people's belongings, abandoned in their flight, were strewn around the edges of the room. Fresh drag marks on the floorboards suggested a hurry to move things away from the tragedy that was unfolding, and I couldn't blame them.

Sometimes, I still have nightmares about the thing that lay in the centre of that room. As I stood and stared at the mangled corpse, the image of horror forever burned in my mind—a thousand photograms that not only captured the detail, but the stench, and the dry itchiness of the air, and the putrid colours of death.

What was left of the man's body lay a few yards from the doorway. His limbs were contorted into inhuman angles, his right arm twisted up around his neck and face, and his left wrenched away from his body, hand outstretched as if he was grasping for something. His legs were tucked up, foetal in position, but a flash of pale bone indicated fractures along his shins. His face, spared from the worst of the flames, was locked in a never-ending scream—eyes screwed tight in an otherworldly grimace.

This wasn't just peculiar; it was fucking inhuman.

Baker was gently rubbing my back when Jennifer called from inside the room, "Charlotte, are you alright?" She had already walked in while I was transfixed on the corpse, strangely calm.

"Just peachy, Jennifer, I didn't enjoy my breakfast, anyway."

"Good, you should come in here."

I should have stayed back at the shop, I should have stayed in the damn café—but despite my weak stomach and sense of sheer horror, I steeped toward the corpse. Jennifer was kneeling over it—as focussed as a sunbeam through a magnifying glass.

"Tell me what you see," she said, in a voice as soft and reassuring as it was firm and commanding, "As much as you can."

Tell her what I saw—what on earth was she playing at? "Right… this man is clearly dead." As I stumbled over the words, Jennifer started scribbling in an empty notebook. "What are you doing?"

"Just keep going. He's dead, yes, how?"

Something strange happened to me then, as I looked closer at the blood curdling figure before me—all the fear, disgust and panic I felt faded away, replaced by a morbid curiosity. It wasn't a dead body in front of me, but a puzzle—a puzzle with an answer. Without my realising it, my mind had already begun to sort the thousands of tiny details.

"Well, cause of death is immolation—his torso is completely blackened, which suggests the fire must have been incredibly intense. All the flesh from half-way down his chest to the furrow at his pelvis has burned away. His major organs have been completely incinerated, with only ash and bone remaining." The words flowed from my tongue with an ease I'd rarely known.

"Good. Keep going."

"His ribcage looks like it was cracked open, and the ribs themselves are split down the length. Actually, all of the bone here is, the spine, what's visible of the hips." Jennifer made some noises of agreement, but I'd almost tuned her out. The fog that clouded out the world so often for me was

21

now working to my advantage. "What I don't understand is why his chest and abdomen are burned down so much, but his extremities are intact. His shoulders and hips are charred, but the flesh hasn't burned away, and down the arms and legs there's a kind of gradient."

Jennifer's cutting voice reached me. "Gradient, what do you mean?"

"How much they've… cooked? Cooked isn't a word I want to use, but the black charred flesh changes to almost caramelised browns, then blistered reds and his hands… His hands are almost untouched." More and more became apparent to me as I spoke. I could see connections between the details I could scarcely have imagined—dare I say it, I was excited by it. "Here, along the upper biceps, the flesh has split open, and—" I got down closer to look "—yes, the bone is split open too, almost as if his bone marrow was lantern oil or coal. I can even trace a darker burn down to his elbow before it fades."

"Exactly what I thought. What the about the floor?" Jennifer said, gesturing around the corpse.

"I, the floor…" The momentum I had faltered, but it only took a few seconds for me to get back up to speed. "There's nothing, the floor's bare, it's… it's not burned. Baker said as much, but I didn't quite believe it. But it's… not burned? How does a man incinerate from the inside, but leave his limbs gently roasted and the floor around him unscathed!? Magic, obviously, but…" My rambling thoughts had suddenly taken a tumble down a mountainside, every syllable a rock that added to my frustration at not knowing what really happened.

Jennifer grinned at me, then turned to the doorway. "Peculiar indeed, Inspector."

"What's the verdict, Jennifer? Are we reporting this a murder or a suicide?" he asked bluntly.

"Murder implies a perpetrator, while suicide implies intent. I don't believe there's evidence of either," Jennifer responded matter-of-factly.

"You can't mean this was an accident?" Baker asked, almost indignant at the suggestion. "People don't just burst into flames."

"Not ordinary people, anyway," I said out loud, without really realising it. The Inspector said something in reply, but I was already off with the faeries. I'd always been fascinated by magic, ever since I was a child, but it wasn't until my days studying chemistry in Cambridge that I saw it with my own eyes. One summer, I had a brief tryst with a young Romani woman; a performer in a travelling circus—her name was Femi, and she was stunningly beautiful, but that's beside the point— what matters, is that she could breathe fire. Now, I know what you're thinking; that's a pretty standard circus trick, all it takes is some high proof alcohol and a lot of guts. But, not for her—this wasn't a trick—it was magic, real magic. She sang—the melody and the words had long been lost to my memory—and the flames danced, as if she was breathing her very life into them.

I was lost in my mind, tracing the lines of her body when, like a bolt of lightning, it hit me. Timothy Waters hadn't been a fan of the odd sea shanty, he wasn't killed, and he wasn't trying to kill himself. He was trying to save himself, that was why nothing else had burned—whatever he'd done to bring forth the flames, he'd been aware enough to control them as he died. "It's not singing," I said, finally.

"What's not singing?" Baker asked, but I was too focussed to answer.

I squatted next to the corpse, gently lifted the man's left arm, and turned it over. It was stiff, but a joint or a bone cracked slightly, and I was able to see what was left on the inside of his forearm.

"He's a mage." Emblazoned across his skin, undeniable and exact, was a wine stain birth mark that stretched from elbow to wrist, marking the space between the bones of the forearm with subtly shifting colours that almost looked alive. *The Brand*, as it had come to be known, was the only thing that told apart mages and everyone else. It used to be that people thought it was a curse or mark of the devil—unless you were rich or lucky, chances are you'd have been slaughtered in the crib if you had it. Enlightened minds prevailed at the turn of the last century, and the Brand is now understood to be scar tissue of some sort, from exposure to the Arcane in the womb.

I sat back on my haunches and took a deep breath to settle myself. "He wasn't singing like the witnesses said. It was Worker's Cant."

"Worker's what?" the Inspector said.

"Cant; it's a kind of improvised spell casting. Poorer mages like it because it's subtle and easy to learn; traditional magic is how folk get nicked by your lot and fined for unauthorised magical labour. No offence."

Baker's lips curled into a sly grin. "None taken. Know something about avoiding my lot, eh?"

"You learn certain things growing up where I did." It took every ounce of my willpower not to wink at the Inspector. "Where was I? Right, Cant isn't all that different from other kinds of spell casting. According to George Starkey's *Introduction of Arcane Chymistry*, magic is all about resonance and symbolic meanings, and—" I stopped myself before I spent half an hour rambling about Arcane theory. "The music makes the magic happen."

Jennifer was clapping. "Nicely done, Charlotte. Nicely done. So, our victim was a mage, a spell gone wrong, perhaps. Magical spontaneous combustion. No perpetrator, no clear intent," Jennifer explained.

"Magical. Spont…" Baker was starting to say, when Jennifer cut him off.

"Spontaneous combustion, he caught fire out of nowhere. Well, not nowhere. The question is where did all of the energy come from—it normally takes a lot of skill to manipulate the Arcane like this, and spells are more likely to fizzle than go bang."

I'd taken a few steps back, taking in the whole scene, imagining the man, still alive, surrounded by people. He didn't die quickly—the witnesses had enough time to move their belongings and escape—he must have understood what was happening on some level. He was reaching for something, in what might have been a last desperate attempt to save himself.

Baker and Jennifer started talking, part banter and part business, but I was already off in my own thoughts again.

Belongings and bedding had been pushed to the edges of the room, away from the burning man. I walked in the direction the corpse was facing to the pile of blankets and bags. I pushed past the gross smell of body odour, and worse, and began rifling through what had been left behind. Clothes, some bags of food and valuables, some books, and then I found what I was looking for.

A small oilskin pouch nestled among the belongings, which had been singed on one side. Nothing else had burned, so the only way the pouch could have been caught was if the victim had been holding it. He must have dropped it before the panic started, only for it to be moved away from him with everything else. It felt like it was full of sand, or maybe flour, certainly a powder of sorts. It had a cord pulled tight to keep it sealed, with a bronze clasp stamped with a maritime seal. "Jennifer, I think this belonged to our victim," I said as I walked over and handed her the pouch.

She looked at it curiously, and after a moment, she nodded in agreement. "Whatever was so important that you still need it in death?" She opened the pouch and dipped a finger inside, and it came out with a coating of a very fine black powder. "Interesting."

"What is it?" I asked. But before she could answer, Jennifer let out a yelp of pain and wiped the powder off her finger. "Jen?"

"It burned me. Damnation, it can't be, can it?" Her finger was bright red and starting to swell. She quickly pulled the cord shut and then fished out a mason jar from her coat and stuffed the pouch inside.

"Jen?" Inspector Baker said, softly.

Jennifer stood up and held the jar up for us to see. "This is our culprit, that's for certain. Black Ember. It's a drug, derived from opium, but it's laced with several compounds with specific Arcane resonances. It's dangerous, incredibly addictive. I didn't know it travelled to Europe. I thought it was only used in East Asia."

Baker stepped up to Jennifer and looked at the jar. "Where did he get it from then? If this Black Ember stuff can immolate folk, we need to track the source. This man's death may well have been an accident, but what if something worse happens?"

"My thoughts exactly, Baker. Charlotte, let's get back to the shop," Jennifer set off without waiting for either of us to respond. The Inspector tried to say something, but just stammered and shrugged toward me.

I began to catch up and called back to the Inspector, "I assume you know what she's playing at. Nice meeting you!" and we were gone.

Chapter 4

I took a long, deep breath when we walked back out onto the street. Once we had started 'working,' the distractions around me faded from view. But in the brief moment of respite that followed, all those things held back by a wall of focus came crashing back. The ashy air clung to my lungs like tar, and the stench had sunk into my clothes.

My one relief was that the rain had started. I took some time to breathe in the fresh, earthy scents of the just dampened ground. I wanted the rain to wash the sight of poor Timothy Waters from my eyes, to cleanse my mind of the horror I'd got so close to. The calm was needed, a few short minutes without speaking, without thinking, without death.

"Charlotte," Jennifer's voice cut through the fogginess in my mind like a knife. She was stood with one foot in a four-wheeler, waving to me.

"Sorry, off with the faeries," I said, shaking off my daze.

She chuckled. "I've told you before, if you were off with the faeries, you'd come back with no ears and a belly full of cockroaches."

"Sometimes I really do wonder whether you're joking or not," I said, but Jennifer just winked at me before climbing the rest of the way into the cab.

"Here," she said when I settled next to her, "take this." She handed me the notebook she was writing in. It was a pretty little thing, with long thin pages so it would fit inside a coat pocket, a leather cover that was dyed a shade of royal blue and high-quality paper which had that delightful fresh and new smell. Jennifer had written down, in detail, all the things I'd said and even left some helpful notes in the margins. "Always write down everything you see at a scene. You never know when you need to look back, and it's better than trying to remember things when explaining your conclusion to a magistrate."

"Thank you," I said, so stunned it was all I could think of. She was smiling at me, full of pride so infectious I could feel it welling up inside me too. I'd always struggled to fit into the patterns of life that society had deemed correct ("difficult, unfocused, malingering, impulsive; full of useless facts and little else," one professor had opined), but I saw it as struggling against myself just as much. I could never take any real joy in my successes when the simplest things in life—like showing up to work on time—proved to be so hard.

"Are you crying?" Jennifer asked.

"No!" I was.

"Oh gosh, you are crying."

"I am not!"

"If you're going to cry each time I say you did a good job, you'll have to bring a dozen handkerchiefs everywhere we go."

"Shut up!"

"You were brilliant, Charlotte, truly. I knew I could count on you."

"Now you're just trying to make me cry." She laughed, which made me laugh. I wiped away the tears of joy from my face and said through a beaming smile, "brilliant, eh?"

"Absolutely. A brilliant deduction. What prompted you to think of Worker's Cant?" she asked.

I told her about the memory of the circus performer. "Honestly, it just jumped out at me. Baker said Waters liked to sing and…" I trailed off.

"You just made the connection. Great work." She grinned at me, expecting another flood of tears.

"Be serious, will you? That was fucked up," I exclaimed.

"'Be serious' she says, 'Fuck fucking fuckety fucked' she says. Is that really how they teach you to talk in your ends?"

I stared blankly back Jennifer, her stupid grin taunting me. I'm happy to report I did not rise to it, this time. While I won't deny that I have a foul mouth, it was hardly the foulest I knew, given I grew up opposite a brothel. Still, I learned to talk all proper-like when the circumstances call for it.

"Yes, he was 'fucked up'," Jen said after a moment, making little air quotes around my words. "Haven't the foggiest how. I only know a little about Black Ember, it's something I learned of from a colleague in Hongkong."

"Is it alchemical?" I asked.

"Yes, I believe so, though that would depend on your definition. Typically, it's considered bad form for an alchemist to experiment with narcotics and psychoactive compounds. But this is a rare exception," she said. She sat back into her seat and assumed a more professorial tone and affect. "You see, it's best to avoid anything that might exaggerate mental side effects, and absolutely avoid anything that may have addictive consequences."

"I'm not sure I follow."

"It's a matter of safety, for the most part. The problem lies, ultimately, in the lack of a coherent way to predict side effects in certain combinations of ingredients. Take mercury, for example. When used in a formula that increases reflex speed, what might the side effects be?"

I thought for a minute, trying to dig up the information from my studies. "Temporary tachycardia and hypertension?"

"Precisely," Jennifer responded. "But combine it with rose water and produce a tincture that focuses and refines the sense of smell?"

"Joint pain. No, anosmia. Why is it so variable, though?"

"That's the issue, we don't know. The science hasn't caught up yet. Mostly we work these thigs out through trial and error."

"So, with the Black Ember, while you might just expect a bad opium hang over, it could do something much worse?" I asked.

"Precisely. Memory loss, long-term fatigue, chronic pain, hallucinations. All side effects that have happened when an unsuspecting alchemist has messed with things that already mess with your head. Of course, if you plan accordingly..." she trailed off. "Never mind, not important right now."

"What are the effects of this Black Ember, then? I tried opium once and I did not have a good time one bit. I can't imagine what you might try and do with it alchemically."

"I have no idea," Jennifer said. There was a moment of pause in her voice, broken by a low rumble of thunder in the distance. "But I know someone who might. We'll need to move fast, though, he'll go to ground if word gets out."

"Right, so what do we do now?"

"That depends, where are we?" she asked, looking out the window.

"Blackfriars, there's the bridge."

"Perfect. Driver!" she yelled, and before the cab had even pulled over, she was hopping out onto the street. "Take her along to Carnaby, I've business here," she said by way of an explanation to the perplexed cabman. "Charlotte, I won't be back till late, so head on home after closing and I'll see you in the morning!"

"What? Where are you—Jennifer!" I cried to no avail. She was off spraying water from puddles as she jogged down the street.

"She usually that mad?" the driver asked.

I let out an exasperated sigh. "This is actually a fairly mellow day."

"Right you are, miss."

It was around two in the afternoon when I finally arrived back at the shop, and the turn in the weather had driven away any hope of custom for the rest of the day. I went inside and dried myself off in the back room, before turning over the open sign in vain, and sitting by the cash desk. I was almost going to go through the notes Jennifer had written for me, but then I found the book I'd been reading that morning in the café.

So, despite the eventful morning and having plenty to think about, I spent the next few hours researching were-wolves. As promised, Jennifer didn't come back before the end of the day. I'm not sure what I expected. She had a habit of disappearing like that on occasion, only to come back with wounds in need of stitching and an inflated ego. I just wished she'd told me what she had planned.

About a half hour after I locked up and flipped the sign to closed, there came a rapping on the window. I was stood in the storeroom at the time, desperate to find something to do—other than the dreaded display of flu remedies—as an excuse to stay longer. Befuddled, and more than a little annoyed, that anyone would come knocking when the shop was clearly shut up, I went to give whoever it was a piece of my mind.

It was dark, except for the small lamp I carried with me, and the soft orange glow of the gas-fired streetlights outside. I called out to the visitor, "I'm sorry, but we're—" then stopped dead in my tracks, the words utterly lost at the sheer impossibility of who I saw—it simply can't have been.

And yet…

I knew that face as well as my own reflection. At least, I had known it. The last time I'd seen that face was through the window of a coach leaving Cambridge for London, and even through the rain spattered front door I could see how different it was. In a hundred ways the lines and details had changed. It'd been nearly two years since we last saw each other, and in that time the person I remembered may as well have become a ghost.

My heart couldn't decide if it wanted to stop or beat at nineteen to the dozen and settled into a staccato rhythm in my ears. The ghost of who *she* was faded from my mind, and I found myself somewhere more unexpected than anywhere else I'd been that day—not relieved to see her, or anguished by the way I'd left—I was swooning, like some teenage damsel in a romance novel. She'd always been cute—in a *trying hard not to look too boyish or too girlish to draw attention*, sort of way—but I never imagined I think of her as…

I stopped myself from imagining anything of the sort when she furrowed her brow and nodded at the lock. How long had I been staring? Did I even want to know? The world started to spin again, and I let her inside.

"Hey—", I started, cutting myself off before I put my foot in it. That wasn't her name, not anymore. My jaw hung on its hinges, and she had the good graces to rescue me before I made even more of a fool of myself.

"Eloise. Well, Elly. I like Elly. It's good to see you". There was a silvery note in her voice that hadn't been there before, but the juxtaposed mix of Cornish tang and Cambridge sophistication was undeniable.

"Elly?" The name felt so new, yet so fitting. "I like it too."

Her face flushed as red as her freckles, and the way she smiled—dear God, I'd never seen her smile so wide and so true—if I could formulate and bottle that kind of happiness, I'd be the richest alchemist in the world.

She'd grown out her chestnut hair, it dropped down to her shoulders in dainty ringlets, and she wore a floral day dress under a frock coat that had just the right amount of petticoats to be fashionable but not ridiculous. Of the few things that hadn't changed, it was her eyes that stood out the most—sky-blue, with a dark ring like lapis around the edge—she fluttered her eyelashes, as if she was trying to put me in even more of a fluster.

A few words managed to stammer out of my mouth, "I didn't know you were back in town. I haven't seen you…"

Elly finished the sentence. "Since you left Cambridge." That was a kind way to say it, she couldn't have known how much that kindness would hurt. All the promises I made were laid bare in the things she didn't say—to visit, to write, to invite her to stay, and to tell her that I was doing all right—none of which I kept.

On the writing desk by my bed, under a pile of papers and half read books, precisely two-inches from the left edge, was the start of a letter that simply said "Dear…" and the name Elly no longer used, which I'd forgotten existed for eighteen months until that exact moment.

"Elly, I'm so sorry…"

She gave me the briefest smile, then said in a forlorn tone, "You had your reasons, and—truth be told—I needed the space." Before I could ask what she meant, she gasped and took my hand—and closed the distance between us at last. "Space in general, I mean, it's not that I wanted you to leave, or that I didn't want you around," she rambled—honestly, I should have stopped her, but I was too busy squeezing her hand to check it was real—Elly shook her head, the curls in her hair bounced around softly. "It's just that when you were there, I was always occupied trying to manage your…" she trailed off.

"The College Mistress called it a 'diseased faculty of attention'. Seemed a rather apt way to put it," I said with a roll of my eyes.

Elly nodded, but she didn't say anything else on the subject. She didn't need to. I was as much a distraction as I was distracted, and as harsh as I was on myself about the way I behaved, a small part of me could see that leaving had been for the best.

We both stood there, silently, for a moment that felt like an age. A soft sigh escaped through Elly's lips, and she said, "Maybe I shouldn't have come."

"Don't say that. I'm glad you're here." There was so much I wanted to say to her—stories to tell, memories to reminisce over, feelings to share—I wanted to tell her all about Jennifer, alchemy, and the anything-but-peculiar death of Timothy Waters. But the instant she smiled at me again, every coherent thought melted from my brain—the only incoherent thoughts left amounted to, *girl pretty*—and I said, "You look—"

"—different?"

"Happy." I took a step back to take all of her in, but I didn't let go of her hand. "And beautiful, if I may say so."

She scoffed and slapped my hand away playfully. With her mouth, she said, "You can keep your flirtatious wiles to yourself," but the blush across her cheeks said otherwise. The clock at the back of the shop floor chimed seven times, and Elly pulled a pocket watch from her coat. "I'm afraid I must go."

"You only just got here."

"I only meant to drop in, but I'll come by again," Elly said—my heart dived into the pit of my stomach, then lurched back up a second later. "Not tomorrow, the day after, maybe? Perhaps we could take lunch together."

"Lunch sounds good," was all I managed to say.

I watched Elly leave, my face burned with the warmth of a new crush—or it may have been a very old one, kindled anew—and when the door clicked shut, I was alone again, with only a flickering candle for company. In the silence that followed, my stomach churned the longing I felt into something much less hopeful. What the hell was I doing fawning over her like that?

My head swam with a dozen trains of thought as I made my way back to my father's house in Camden—it hadn't taken long for Jennifer and Timothy Waters to return to the forefront of my mind. When I finally drifted up to my bed, it was in a haze of exhaustion and cheap gin.

<u>October 9th, 1834</u>

An Interview with the Viscount's Son

Chapter 5

I woke to the sound of rain on the window, unsure when I'd managed to fall asleep. For a few blissful minutes I'd forgotten all about Timothy Waters until the smell of bacon wafted up from the kitchen. My stomach turned as the sheer inhumanity of the scene reformed in my mind, and I only became more unsettled at the odd sense of curiosity came with it. Something had driven Waters to his limits, something worth dying for.

I stumbled down to the kitchen in my nightshirt and found my old man pottering about. He wasn't the sort you'd expect to find in front of a stove—standing just over six-foot-tall. Father was a stocky, strong man—he was a cabinet maker by trade. His ruddy brown eyes were like varnished oak behind his little round glasses, and he was greying and balding in random patches.

"Mornin' poppet," he said, all too chipper for the early hour.

"Hello, Old Man," I yawned in reply.

He set two plates on the table—eggs fried to within an inch of edibility accompanied the bacon—and sat across from me. "Heard you tossing and turning all night, something on your mind?"

As much as I appreciated Father's concern, I didn't want to spoil breakfast with the lurid details of incinerated mages or admit to any untoward thoughts about a certain recently returned friend. "It's nothing, just work stuff." Unfortunately for me, parents in general develop some kind of uncanny ability to tell when "nothing" is not actually nothing.

He folded his arms and sat back in his chair. "Balderdash. Out with it, what's got your head all in a knot?"

I huffed and sat forward with my elbows on the table. "Jennifer has a new kind of job for me," I said, my voice uncertain—maybe if I was vague enough, he would stop worrying about me. "It's really interesting and challenging, but also kind of disturbing? And she just kind of dropped it on me out of nowhere, and I can't really work out what she wants me to do."

No matter how old I got, he never could stop looking at me like I was a kid. The extra lines on his face just made it even more patronising. "She's your boss, Charlotte, you do what she says."

"You're not—I mean what does she want me to *do*," I said, with a pause where the words, *listening to me,* should have gone. I waved my arms around—to some effect, I don't know what effect, but to something. "I'm not apprenticing to a blacksmith, or a baker, or a cabinet maker." Frustrated that I couldn't articulate my point, I sat back in a huff. "I don't know."

"That's three words you say an awful lot that you very rarely mean." He sat forward, adopting the universal posture of dads telling you how it is. "It's not about what Ms Morton wants. What do you want to do?"

What did I want to do? When I was a kid, I wanted to be a pirate—I know, I know, I would have been an amazing pirate, but I get awfully seasick. In that moment, all I wanted to do was run and hide in the lab. "I don't know."

"There you go again; I think you do know. You've always been driven by something."

Something. I have to hand it to the old man; he did have a certain way with words—not that I ever listened to what he meant. "I want to know what I want. Does that answer the question?"

He smiled, and despite all the lines and wrinkles of age, he still had that same glint in his eyes. "Don't take too long, you don't want to be late or anything."

I slapped the table and gave him a conspiratorial look. "Why would I be late? What do you know?"

The old man guffawed and started clearing the table. "Oh, my medicines running low, think you can fix me some more today or tomorrow?"

"No problem," I said between mouthfuls of egg.

"And if you're planning on working late again, just send a note and stay at the shop."

"Uh huh." I rolled my eyes; did he think I was still sixteen?

I finished up my breakfast as Father fussed around the kitchen, got dressed in some plain work clothes, and headed out.

***

Carnaby was quiet, and the shop was just as I'd left it the night before. There was no evidence of Jennifer's return, not that I was expecting there would be. There was still half an hour till opening, so I made myself some tea and went about some tidying. I thought about giving Jennifer a piece of my mind when she eventually decided to show her face again, but I was hardly one to talk when it came to reliability.

I couldn't help but feel frustrated and restless all morning, with a dozen things I wanted or needed to do, none of which I had the will or enthusiasm to start. When I wasn't occupied with what Jennifer was up to, or the circumstances of Timothy Waters, I thought about Elly. In fact, I thought about Elly a lot. Every time the door opened, I looked up, excitedly expecting to see her, only for my hopes to be dashed in an instant. There was a flutter in my chest as I wondered where to take her for lunch— the patisserie down the road, or the pie and mash shop I found in Holborn—and for a brief, terrible moment, I even considered changing into something more presentable.

Every now and then, a little voice in my head would chime in and inform me of how much of a fool I was. Elly wasn't interested in me like that. I'd known her for nearly twenty years, and she'd never expressed any sort of desire for more than just friendship. But neither had I, and there I was daydreaming about her.

The next thing I knew—between a smattering of regular customers and an excessive amount of thumb twiddling—half a day had gone by in a blur. Dread and guilt slowly replaced the wistful thoughts in my head with every minute that I wasted. There was nothing that needed doing that I couldn't do in a heartbeat, but the weight of it all seemed to pin me

39

in the chair by the cash desk.

The cherry on top of it all, was that just as I was finally, actually, honestly, definitely about to restock some shelves; a very wet, very muddy, and very smug-looking Jennifer walked in the front door.

"I've done it!" she proudly proclaimed, striking a triumphant pose with her arms akimbo, and head turned to the sky. I wasn't in the mood for her shenanigans, so I just stared at her blanky. A full thirty seconds after her exclamation, she stopped looking to the heavens and asked, "aren't you going to ask me what I've done?"

"No, I figured you'd tell me anyway," I sighed, my annoyance laced thought every word. She knew damn well that I didn't do well by myself. I wanted to tell her how much I hated how useless I felt without her. I wanted to tell her how lost I felt.

I wanted it to be her fault.

But the want didn't form into words, and instead I just looked at her and screwed up my lips.

"You're no fun. I have been to every public house, brothel, opium den and soup kitchen in Camden, and I have found who we are looking for," she said proudly.

The nerve—the audacity, even—to go gallivanting around my part of town, while I sat on my arse. "Camden!? Did you forget that I live in Camden before you ran off yesterday? Who was so important to find that you couldn't at least tell me about it first?" True, I hadn't spent as much time there since I started working at the Solution, but I still knew those streets like the back of my hand.

"My dear, there's no need to get all worked up."

Worked up? Oh, I wanted to show her worked up. She wouldn't have believed how worked up I could be. Except, then she shot me her diamond smile, and I was powerless against it.

She continued, "Camden is where the students at London University go to get pissed, and we're looking for a student with a propensity for getting very pissed. Well, former student."

Jen had flipped the window sign to closed when she entered and was now perched on the side of the cash desk. She had her coat balled up around her arms and an infectious grin on her face. I had a weakness for her charms, and she knew it. She was just so damn dashing; it frankly wasn't fair how she could walk in after apparently gallivanting around the city in the rain for a day and a night and look like a fucking painting. It was almost like every wet strand of hair and smear of grime was deliberately placed on her face. As much as I tried not to, I eventually gave in, and accepted that I didn't have the energy to stay mad at her.

Besides, two can play at her game.

"Jen. If you wanted to ask me out for drinks, you didn't have to put on such a show; you could have just done that," I said, dropping my voice into a smouldering register. "People might say things, though, what with you being ten years my senior and my employer." Jen's jaw dropped and she slipped off the desk.

She narrowed her eyes at me, then slowly and deliberately brushed one of the wet hairs from her cheek behind her ear. "You don't want to play this game because I would win. I've been wrapping people round my fingers since before you could count all of yours," and just as I felt my knees start to weaken, she added, "Pumpkin."

"Pumpkin!?" I repeated back at the top of my voice, damn near falling out of my chair.

"Too much?"

"Too much, you made it weird."

"It was already weird."

"You're weird!"

There was an awkward pause, broken by Jennifer slapping her knee. "Right, let's get sorted. I need to change into some dry clothes."

"What should I do?" I asked, puzzled.

Jennifer was already heading off to her apartment on the second floor. She stopped at the door to the stairs and said, "Oh, umm. Can you grab the pistols from the lab?" and then jogged up the stairs.

"Pistols!?" I questioned, but I don't think she heard me. Jen had been teaching me to shoot for a few months, but I'd convinced myself along the way that it was just for sport—but nothing Jen does is *just* anything.

That should have been the moment I questioned what she was up to, it was the first in a list of opportunities to nip all the unfortunate business to follow in the bud. I could have said no—maybe I felt like I had something to prove, maybe I was running from making my own choices, maybe I was desperate for her approval—but I headed to the laboratory, where the pistols were kept, and tried to keep myself from imagining why we needed them at all.

The lab smelt like some combination of earthy tones, punchy spices, metallic tangs, and a pungent fishy odour that I never tracked down. There were shelves of substances used in alchemical transmutations filling the room, from flowers, metals and animal parts to all sorts of different magical oddities. Salts precipitated from elementally active ethanol, organs from Arcane creatures—including, but not limited to: salamander gall bladders, chimera tail barbs, basilisk eyes, the lungs of a Long-Haired German Troll and the heart of a Bandersnatch—crystals in a dozen different colours, and knucklebones used in scrying.

I took a deep breath as I strolled through the room—it was my favourite place to be. Within those four walls, magic happened, literally. This was where Jennifer and I tinkered away, breaking down the barriers between the Mundane world and that of the Arcane. I would spend hours there, when time allowed, fussing at the formula for a potion, or studying a new ingredient. Every new detail learned, every transmutation completed, every question about the universe answered—only made me want to learn more.

In the centre of the room was a hexagonal table about five feet wide, and tall enough to work at while standing. It was solid oak almost eight inches thick, which had been carved from a single horizontal slice of what I imagined must have been an enormous tree. Everything about it was precisely crafted to focus, direct, and combine ambient magical energies, and even the frame it stood upon was infused with cold iron that grounded it and prevented any explosive feedback loops.

Tucked away at the bottom of a cupboard on the far end of the room was a wooden case that was heavier than it looked and had a little silver clasp that kept it shut. Inside were a pair of exquisite duelling pistols and several pouches of paper cartridges. The pouches were made of leather and lined with sealskin that kept the water out and were satisfyingly soft to the touch.

When I emerged back onto the shop floor, Jennifer was waiting for me—posing in a rather dapper suit. "You look like a dandy," I said, looking her up and down. The flash of blue was from her jacket, which tapered at a cinched waist. She had an extravagantly tied silk cravat around her neck and sported a pair of dark pantaloons. The look was topped off, literally, with a top hat in the same colour as the suit jacket.

"Charlotte, my dear. There are few things in life that command as much respect and adoration as a woman in a well-tailored suit," she said, grinning.

"If by respect and adoration you mean angry glances and fragile masculinity, then sure," I responded. I'd always admired Jennifer's fashion sense, but rarely was I able to pull off anything more stylish than back-alley couture. It was not without trying—I'd bought an eclectic array of clothes over the years—but I'd eventually get bored with any new style and slip back into my well-worn shirts.

I put the gun box on the cash desk beside her and asked, as non-committal as I could, "Are you sure we need these?"

"Just in case we run into trouble, not that I'm expecting any," she said, the latter statement added quickly after she saw the look on my face. "It never hurts to be prepared." With the care and attention one might use when handling priceless heirlooms, Jennifer opened the case and gently brushed her fingers across the matched set of pistols. After a moment of admiration, she lifted one off the cushion, twirled it in her hand and held it out to me, "Remember what I showed you?"

For a second, but no more, I hesitated. The long-barrelled pistol had a reassuring weight, and the wooden grip had little platinum inlays when my fingers fell. The hammer made a satisfying click as I pulled it into the half-cock position, which revealed the unique innovation Jennifer had devised. The flintlock mechanism had been replaced by a pair of yellowish crystals, one clamped between the jaws on the hammer, and the other set flush with the barrel. Arcane in origin, the stones created an arc of electricity that replaced the need for priming powder with every shot, saving precious time when reloading.

At one point, Jennifer had called them "bolt locks," but she stopped when I told her how close that was to "bollocks." I finished my inspection of the pistol and looked at Jennifer expectantly. She smiled, and said, "Good work, but don't neglect to check the barrel for obstructions. We don't want any misfires, do we?" My brain unhelpfully added, *you moron*, to the end of her question. I shook my head and held the pistol flat in my hands. "Now, I know these make you uncomfortable, but you really are a natural shot."

It wasn't the pistols themselves that made me uncomfortable, but what they represented. Power over life and death, in the palm of my hand, and how tempting it was to accept it. "Shooting at a target is an entirely different prospect to shooting at a person."

"Well…" Jennifer said, as though she was about to give out a reassuring pearl of wisdom. "Never mind. We'll be heading to The King's Arms—wonderfully unique name—in Camden. We're looking for a man named Bryce Rosehouse. He was, until recently, a student at London University, and he's the son of a rather influential member of the House of Lords. I've got it on good authority he'll be there this evening, and he has something of a reputation for indulging in certain substances."

Thankful for the change of subject, I set the pistol down and leaned against the cash desk. "You think he'll know about the Black Ember?"

"If he doesn't, he'll know who does. We just have to get him talking."

"Find some aristocrat in a pub, in a dangerous part of the city, and just get him talking? With guns, just in case?" Did she even have a plan? My pulse picked up, and I had to fight the urge to fidget with something—was it nerves, or excitement, or both? I wasn't sure. "Are you sure this is a good idea?" I asked, in the hope it would prompt the right conclusion.

"Of course, I do this sort of thing all the time, don't worry about it." She headed for the door and picked up an umbrella on the way. "Come along then, we'll try and wave down a cab."

I threw on my coat and—against my better judgment—slipped the pistol into the deep inside pocket. We walked at pace through the rain to the busy thoroughfare at the end of Carnaby when all of a sudden Jennifer stopped in her tracks and grabbed my arm. "Oh, before I forget, this is important: Bryce is a mage," and as quickly as she stopped, she nonchalantly set off again, as if she just reminded me to grab eggs on the way home.

Chapter 6

The smell of roasted fowl and beef stew wafted through the small public house from the kitchen. A fire burned in the hearth, drenching the room in dancing orange light, near to where Jennifer and I had found a table to dry off from the now torrential rain. We drank a dark bitter ale, which Jennifer assured me had undertones of cinnamon and nutmeg. To me it just tasted like a dark bitter ale.

Before long the pub began to fill with an assorted clientele. Most appeared to be the sort you'd associate with students, young men, and a few women, dressed fashionably and speaking in haughty tones about the big questions in life. Such was the apparent excitement of their intellectual duels, that you might have been forgiven to think that they were the next Aristotle or Newton. Unless, of course, you actually listened to what they said and realised that none of it was really new. I knew that from the moment they started, because it's exactly what I did in their place.

"It's nothing more than a way to enrich the landowners at the expense of the working man. Any person should have an automatic right to relief, can't you see that?" challenged a young man with a chinstrap beard and trimmed brown hair.

"Simply absurd! The rural workers had become too complacent. The Poor Law Amendment makes it possible to move those workers, who aren't producing anything of value, into the cities. It's a revolution of industry that's driving us forward after all," argued another.

"By pushing them into workhouses run by the rich, for the rich."

It went on like that for some time, with other members of the group chiming in, and none of the interlocutors ever changing their minds. All the while as I watched them, I found myself back in the dark, dingy student pubs in Cambridge, where the air tasted of pipe smoke and the ale was light and crisp. I'd spent so many nights intellectually jousting with my peers, always to my own frustration in the end. Elly had always chided me for that—and she was always right, to be fair. Eventually the noise died away and the gaggle of students sat down, laughed, drank, and soon kicked off another "debate" on a completely unrelated topic.

Jen's voice came through the haze. "Something on your mind, Charlotte?" She lounged back and glanced across the bar. "You're being unusually quiet."

Sometimes I hated how easily she could read me. There was something on my mind, but I wasn't sure if it was something I wanted to admit to Jen. I hadn't told her about Elly's unexpected arrival back in town, but reminded as I was about my days in Cambridge, it was all I could think about. "It's nothing."

"Oh, come on, we have some time to kill," Jen said. "Unless you want me to deduce it out of you?"

Faced with the possibility of one of Jennifer's scarily accurate predictions, I tried my best to steer the conversation to somewhere less awkward. "Fine…" I started, before I took a gulp of ale. "Suppose—hypothetically, of course—that someone you knew from earlier in your life—someone important that you haven't spoken to in quite a while—just happens to show up out of the blue—and that this someone might be a someone that you might have possibly had… complicated feelings for."

Jennifer furrowed her brow. It was strange to see her so visibly confused, for once. "Good God, Charlotte," she said after a moment's pause. "You aren't talking about Baker?"

I choked on a mouthful of ale and cough out, "What? No, not at all!"

"Because I thought we were both quite clear that there's nothing going on between us anymore."

"This isn't about Inspector—" I said, before Jennifer, who now sat with her legs crossed and her hands linked behind her neck, cut me off."Anthony is a very nice man, but there's just no way—".

I rapped my fist against the table to get her attention back, and said, rather desperately, "I wasn't talking about you and Baker, I was talking about me and…"

The confusion vanished from Jennifer's face, replaced by a delighted grin. "Oh? I see. This is about the one you went to university with—the Chynoweth lad, right?"

"No—I mean, yes, but—it's complicated. She—" Jennifer cocked an eyebrow at the choice of pronoun, so I said it again for good measure, "She is back in London, and we're having lunch tomorrow—if it's all right for me to leave you with the shop, of course, and…" I must have looked like an absolute fool. My cheeks were red hot, and I'd slumped so far forward on my elbows that my arms were flat on the table. Jen gave me a pitying look and I straightened up and refused to look her in the eyes.

"This is very inconvenient timing for you to be lovesick," she said, checking her fob watch.

"I am not lovesick, I…" With a sigh, I slouched back in my chair. "You brought this up, I didn't want to talk about it."

She looked at me very seriously for a moment, and said, "I need you to focus now, Charlotte. Mr Rosehouse will be here soon, and when he arrives, I want you to go to the bar and order a drink. Try to strike up conversation with him." Jennifer lifted her tankard and took a sip, expectantly.

"Me? Why do you want me to talk to him? I thought you said he was some kind of aristocrat?" I was protesting much too hard, and a sinking feeling in my gut told me that the hole had already been dug for me.

"Second son of The Viscount Kidderminster. Disgraced, but not yet disowned, as I understand it," she explained. "That's not important though—he's young, a former student, an outcast. If I try to talk to him, he'll see a middle-aged, middle-class woman in the wrong kind of establishment. He'll suspect something."

Wherever she was going with this, I didn't like it. "And I'm, what? A university drop out from the arse end of Camden?" I thought up about half a dozen other ways to deprecate myself, but Jen simply put a hand on mine and looked at me with soft, kind eyes that hid the coming wave of sarcasm perfectly.

"You, my dear, are brilliant, and your experience at Cambridge is exactly why he'll take an interest in you." There was a pause, for effect, of course, before she sat back in her chair. "Besides, you're also very pretty."

She winked at me. She fucking *winked* at me.

Fuck. As sudden as a volcanic eruption, my face burned, and I was much too flustered to argue back. All the good it would have done, however, as a moment later the door opened and a tall man in his mid-twenties with a dishevelled look about him sauntered into the pub. Without a care for precision, he dropped his umbrella *next* to the stand beside the door, then hung up his coat and hat. I must have had this idea of what aristocrats looked like in my head—all haughty and snobbish, dressed in only the finest fabrics, and some flavour of dashing, handsome, or suave—Mr Rosehouse was none of those things. His suit was not dissimilar in style to Jennifer's, but less fitted and duller in colour, and had a bad case of five o'clock shadow. The bar maid soured the moment he sat down and murmured something in her general direction.

"You're up. Don't give too much away. I want to get him back to the shop, if we can," Jennifer said, and I reluctantly walked over to the bar.

Chapter 7

I was never that good at outright lies, just the small ones I needed to cover up my mistakes; but I did my best to act nonchalant. I ordered the bitter ale that Jennifer enjoyed and sat a few stools down from my mark. Not entirely sure where to start, I drew upon all those nights I spent in dingy student pubs and stirred up those flirtatious wiles Elly said I should keep to myself.

"Is there anything worse than philosophy undergraduates?" I said, just loud enough to get his attention. He perked up and listened for a moment to the ongoing debate across the room—now a disagreement about the nature of consciousness—and let out a short chuckle.

"I take it you haven't met any theology students, then?" he responded, his voice like an ever so slightly untuned cello; deep, full-bodied, smoky, but taut and off kilter.

"I kept my distance on purpose, actually." A coy, half-smile and a wink came almost automatically to me, and I blushed as soon as I realised what I'd done.

Bryce, clearly more than a little inebriated already, didn't seem to notice my embarrassment. He regarded me, before asking, "Natural philosophy?"

"Chemistry, so close enough."

"Where did you study?"

"Cambridge, Newham College," I said. A small pang of shame hit me as I did. "I didn't finish, though." I really didn't want to dig into that part of my life with a stranger I was trying to get information out of, so I moved on as quick as I could. "I take it you're local. King's?"

"Formally of London University. Arcane Theory." As he spoke, I could almost see my own shame mirrored in him.

"Charlotte, by the way, Charlotte Price." I put out a hand and for a moment he looked puzzled, as if all his aristocratic upbringing never included shaking hands with a woman. When he finally did, I caught a glimpse of a curious tattoo around his wrist.

"Bryce," he said. "Tell me, Miss Price, how does a girl like you end up studying a Cambridge?"

"A girl like me?"

"A commoner. Oh no, don't look at me like that, I don't mean it negatively. Your accent is quite distinctive, not many people of small means go to university, much less women."

I had to blink the shock out of my system. He really had read me like a book. "I had help, a friend of my father's. Tuition, room and board all paid for, with a little extra from pulling pints on weekends."

"Your father must have very good friends."

I let out a soft, warm chuckle. "Yes, I suppose he does. All the better they never held my cock-ups against me."

"What was it like, Cambridge?" Bryce asked as he eyed me over his tankard. I couldn't tell if he was interested in me for my story or my looks, but in the moment I didn't much care.

"Quiet compared the London. Pretty, the people and the town. Stuck up, traditionalist," I answered. "I would have enjoyed it much more had there not been so many rules."

"Cheers to that." We tapped our drinks together, and I was struck by how easy the conversation felt. He was quite unlike any aristocrat I'd ever met, and he had the most curious eyes—past the tiredness, his eyes were a deep, complex shade of green, like an emerald that glistened in the candlelight. A part of me suspected that Bryce had a score of broken hearts behind him, and another part almost wanted to be one of them.

I caught myself before I could fall head over heels for a stranger in a pub, and remembered I had a job to do. "Arcane Theory, you said? I suppose that means you're a mage?"

Bryce rolled up his left sleeve to show off his intricately tattooed skin. A coiling serpent of some kind wrapped around his arm, framing the distinctive marking of the Brand in his flesh. "Guilty as charged, just don't rat me out to the witch-finder general," he joked. He covered his arm again before I could look closer at the tattoos that surrounded the brand, but I got a sense they were more than just ink.

"What kind of things did you study?"

His mood turned sullen, and he looked away from me. "I'd rather not talk about my studies, if it suits you."

"Of course," I said, cautious not to push too hard. I needed him to trust me. "For what it's worth, I understand. Academia is a torturous life, I'm much happier having left."

"Really? I actually took quite well to university; it was university that didn't take well to me."

Then—and I'm really quite proud of myself for this one—I asked, "And where does take well to you, Bryce?"

He pondered for a moment, as if all the layers of bullshit between us had been peeled away. "I think that might be the most fascinating question I've been asked in a pub."

"I'm full of fascinating questions."

We laughed together and it all felt so easy to be taken in by his charm. Bryce turned in his seat toward me and spoke softly, "I love a good gallery. Art is the language of the world. I feel I could go anywhere and learn all I need to know from the galleries."

"Really? I don't think I've ever been to a proper gallery."

"Perhaps I could take you to your first?" Bryce asked. I was in.

"I can think of somewhere else you could take me first," I said—frightfully, I might have actually wanted it.

Mr Rosehouse downed the last of his drink and tossed a few coins onto the bar. I went to fetch my coat and was surprised to find that Jennifer had vacated our table. Where had she got to this time? I was nervous enough about heading into the dark, stormy night with a stranger without having to calculate her next move. There was no other choice but to trust that she had a good plan.

We stood under his umbrella, the rain was torrential, and I was suddenly uncomfortably aware of the pistol slung on the inside of my coat. Bryce moved to pull me closer—entirely gentlemanly to save me from the rain—but I pulled away instinctively. "Oh, sorry, I was about to wrangle a cab for us, Mr Rosehouse."

Shit.

"How? How do you know that name?" he asked, and I froze. There was no way to salvage it now. I'd messed it all up and every fibre of my being was begging for a way to escape. All my bluster, all my flirtatious swagger, all my confidence left me in an instant and I stood there, desperate for an answer.

My breaths came short and fast, and I stammered out the words, "We just… we just needed to ask you some questions."

"Who's we?" Bryce said, his charm buried beneath a visage of anger.

A click came from behind him, and in the dim light of the streetlamps I saw Jennifer with her pistol levelled at his back. "I was really hoping you'd come quietly." She was soaked from head to toe from the driving rain. How long had she been waiting out there?

Bryce raised his hands slowly, still holding the umbrella, and Jennifer's posture relaxed. She couldn't see Bryce's face, though, and he didn't have a look of acquiescence. "You should put that down," he said. "One word and I could incinerate your friend."

"Jen, I would rather not be incinerated, please." I stepped back once more, all too conscious of the rain trickling down my back and the weight of the pistol at my side. "Can we all just calm down?"

Bryce started doing something doing something with free his hand, it looked almost like a nervous tick, dragging his thumbnails along the tips of his fingers. The rhythmic tapping echoed unnaturally around us, as if the sound were carried by the rain. He began to mutter something too quiet for me to hear, a repetitive mantra in time with the beat he made. Whatever he was doing, Jen didn't hesitate to stop it—in one fluid movement she wrapped her right arm around Bryce's neck and pressed her left palm against his jaw. There was a flash of metal from the sleeve of her coat that pierced the skin of his throat, so quick I almost missed it.

"We'll have none of that, Mr Rosehouse," Jen grunted as

Bryce struggled against her grip. The umbrella clattered to the ground, and I flinched at the sudden deluge of rain. Bryce went limp and slumped into Jennifer's arms, out cold. A sleeping draught? I pushed the urge to question the components used in the formula out of my mind and helped Jen with the dead weight of Bryce's body—he was heavier than he looked.

Jennifer was as calm as ever and slipped her pistol into its holster with her free hand, but my mind raced in vain as I tried to make sense of what had just happened. "He was doing magic; that was Worker's Cant," I said, puzzled. "Where would an aristocrat learn that?"

"Friends in low places, I suspect," Jen replied. She holstered her pistol and then looked across at me. "You did well, for the most part."

I was still in too much shock to process the compliment, not that I would have agreed, anyway. Good would have been avoiding a fight altogether. "What now?" I asked when my wits finally made it back to me.

"Get him back to the shop, ask him some questions." We hailed a cab, and after promising the driver that our new friend was simply sleeping, and not at all liable to vomit in his vehicle, made our way back once again to the Potent Solution.

Chapter 8

The old chaise-lounge that sat in the corner of Jennifer's crowded office was lumpy and smelled of musty clothes and spilt wine. The orange glow of candlelight slowly brightened through my eyelids, so I sat up straight and let out a shuddering breath. Jennifer walked around the room lighting candles, having ditched her coat and jacket. Her cravat hung untied around her neck over the damp shirt she still wore.

We'd dropped the sleeping Bryce onto an armchair in the centre of the room, across from a couch over a coffee table. None of the furniture matched, and all were worn and dusty. Bookshelves filled every inch of wall available, overflowing with tomes and manuscripts on every topic you could imagine. Huge, heavy curtains, the colour of a crimson sunset, hung closed over a bay window that looked out over the street below. The rain beat down on the glass, occasionally accompanied by a rumble of thunder.

With shaking hands, I pulled off my coat and hung it on the stand, and then carefully removed the gun from its holster. I held the heavy ornate pistol in both hands, staring into the distorted reflections and then to the man we'd apprehended.

Jennifer cleared her throat. "What happened back there?"

I took a deep breath and looked back at the pistol. "I don't know. I was nervous he'd notice this thing, and I had no idea where you were. What if things went wrong and you weren't there? What if I had to…?" I trailed off.

"I understand," she sighed and then wiped off the grime from her face with a towel. "I can't make your decisions, and I will never tell you to hurt someone against your wishes. All I can tell you, is to keep your eyes open," she punctuated each of those last words with a pause. "If you aren't looking for the truth, you'll never find it."

"I don't know how you were so calm, how you just did what you did."

"He was going to kill you, or at least try." I wasn't satisfied by the answer, and I think Jennifer knew it—she looked at me with steadfast eyes, wholly confident in what she had chosen to do.

I put the gun down on the coffee table, unwilling to get drawn into a philosophical debate with my mentor, and sat on the couch across from Mr Rosehouse. He was still out cold, and the small trail of blood from the pinprick on his neck had dried. With more light, I could now make out more detail from the tattoos along his forearms. I took out the little notebook Jennifer had given me and started scribbling my thoughts.

Tattoos line both arms and extend beyond the elbow under his sleeves

Left arm, main design appeared as a serpent at a distance, but clear now to be a wyrm or dragon. Its jaws open at the wrist.

Left arm, several smaller designs, each separate. A moon, a cloak and dagger, a mind's eye, can be seen.

Right arm, less designs but the ink looks fresher. A panther and a scythe take up the upper forearm, and a ring of chains loop the wrist.

The ink isn't black, but rather a deep blue, perhaps midnight or similar. It seems to be flecked with…

My notes from that night remained unfinished, but I remember the curiously white specs that appeared to move within the ink on Bryce's arms. I almost dropped my pencil while staring into them, because our guest awoke with a frightful start. "Where am I?" he yelped, his voice tremulous and uneven.

"Mr Rosehouse, welcome to The Potent Solution," Jennifer took a seat next to me on the couch, resting her elbows on her knees and interlocking her fingers.

"You can't do this! I'll go to the police… I'll sue—my father—"

"You and I both know that your father couldn't give a shit what happens to you, and you're here because the Metropolitan Police have requested our assistance in an investigation."

Mr Rosehouse dropped his shoulders like an insulted peacock. "What investigation? I assure you I have nothing to do with it."

"How would you know if we haven't told you anything about it yet?" I asked.

As if he hadn't known I was in the room, Bryce jumped a little and looked me up and down. "You? You should be careful how you speak to me. Just who are you anyway?" he asked of us both.

"Jennifer Morton. You met Charlotte, my apprentice," Jennifer answered.

"Apprentice? A little old, aren't you? What, you couldn't hack academia and now you're in the kidnapping business?"

"Fuck you." What little respect I had for Mr Rosehouse was quickly diminishing. In the soft, warm light of the public house he had an almost Mr Darcy-like air of mysteriousness, but now, among the stark shadows of Jennifer's study, he was a creature of pride and disdain.

"Charlotte, mind your language in front of our guest," Jennifer chided with furrowed eyebrows.

"Sorry. Fuck you, sir." I swear you could have bottled and distilled the sarcasm into a fine perfume.

He rolled his eyes, "Charming."

"Upper class prick," I shot back instinctively, and caught a light slap on the back of my head from Jennifer for it.

"Let's get this started, shall we?" Jennifer said after she gave me a stern look to ensure I would hold my tongue. She leaned back in her seat, licked the tip of her pen, and began to question our guest. "Name."

"To quote your little student, 'fuck you'," he responded, far too cocky for a man in his position.

Jennifer—not one to take stubborn refusal lying down—kicked the coffee table, knocking its contents to the floor and ramming it into Bryce's shin. "Name," she repeated, with as much force as her boot.

Bryce grimaced and, through gritted teeth, said "Bryce Alexander Rosehouse."

"Mr Rosehouse, you were a student at London University

studying Arcane Theory, correct?"

"Yes."

"You were expelled before the end of the spring semester, why?"

He shifted uncomfortably in his seat. "None of your business."

"Nothing to do with selling illicit narcotics and opiates to your classmates?"

"No comment," he said through gritted teeth, followed by a subvocal grumble in his throat.

Jennifer was completely detached in tone, as though the situation was no more serious than questioning a puppy about missing bacon. She wasn't even looking at him, just scribbling down notes. Bryce said nothing, but the rage on his face was palpable and rising—no doubt the exact reaction she'd been hoping for.

"Who supplied you?" she asked, pointedly. She looked up from her notes with an expression that was an open challenge, and one Bryce could no longer ignore.

"You clearly already know the damn answer! Why don't you get to the actual point of your ridiculous dance?" His voice cracked with the response; his face scrunched in a snarl.

"Who supplied you?"

"I've had enough of this." He moved to stand, but Jennifer leapt the coffee table like a pouncing tiger and drove him back into his seat. She straddled his lap and grabbed at a wad of hair on the back of his head. Bryce groaned and tried to twist out from under her, but that only made her pull harder. With her free hand, Jennifer produced a small glass vial from a pocket. It was filled with a pale liquid that she poured into Bryce's open mouth. The room momentarily filled with the calming scent of lilac and honey, before fading back to normal.

"You'll be done when I say so." At first, I thought Jennifer was angry, but the growing smirk told me that this was all part of the same game. She was doing everything she could to unbalance Rosehouse, even using her body to her advantage. Bryce wasn't the only one getting unbalanced, and I had to clear my throat because watching her hold the man down was turning my face a deeper shade of red with every passing second. Jennifer got up and walked around the back of the couch Bryce was sitting on.

Rosehouse coughed and scraped at his tongue. "What was that?"

"Truth serum, in a few moments, any lie you tell will accompanied with excruciating pain. So, try to answer honestly," she said. I raised an eyebrow, uncertain if I liked the game Jennifer was playing. "Oh, and you'll have a headache tomorrow morning."

"You're going to regret this," Bryce said.

"I'm sure," Jennifer said. "Now, who was your supplier when you were dealing to your classmates?"

"King Charles," Bryce said, but then grimaced and doubled over in pain. "Damn it all. Hawkins, I was working for a man named Hawkins. I never met him—I don't even know his real name." Jennifer nodded in satisfaction, as if she really did know all along.

"Who's Hawkins?" I asked.

Jennifer leaned towards me, "He's a criminal, runs a gang out of the docklands. I've been chasing him for a few years now and he always seems to melt away when I get close. Honestly, I don't even think he exists, just a strawman to scare away the Met."

"Can you get to the point already?" Rosehouse asked, wearily.

"Fine," Jennifer said, retaking her seat beside me. "A man burned to death last night in a tenement building in Stepney."

"So, people die all the time," he dismissed.

"Not like this, they don't. Timothy Waters, a mage living rough, working the docks, indulging in the wrong substances," she tilted her head, but Bryce barely reacted. "His corpse was found burned from the inside out. You see, his torso was utterly incinerated, and yet somehow the rest of his body was unevenly cooked like a bad roast dinner."

"That's impossible…"

"He had this with him." Jennifer reached into a pocket and produced the small pouch with its maritime clasp.

"It can't be…" Bryce started. His face turned to fear, and he looked away.

Jen leaned forward and opened the drawstring, revealing the opalescent powder inside. "Can't be what?"

"This is a trick. That can't be what I think it is."

"What is it, Mr Rosehouse?"

"I… I don't know." Bryce cried out and grabbed at his stomach, tears welling up in his eyes. "Poison is what it is. Black Ember. The foulest substance this side of the China sea. Wherever you found it, you should be rid of it before it's too late."

"Explain." Jen loomed over the table, like an alley cat playing with its food. She was going too far.

"No, don't make me look at it. Take it away, please," Bryce begged, he met Jennifer's piercing stare and it must have taken all of his resolve not to break.

Jen didn't relent. "Not until you tell me everything you know." I looked from her to Mr Rosehouse—should I stop her? Could I stop her?

"Look, I don't know what you think it going on, but I moved on from that part of my life. I don't want anything to do with that…." The young aristocrat's voice trembled, and his hands began to shake. Jennifer was pushing him too far; it was painful to watch.

"Talk, Mr Rosehouse, or you will discover just how far I am willing to go." She pushed against the pouch with a finger, the opalescent powder threatening to spill over the table.

"Jennifer," I said sternly, but she ignored me. Bryce was visibly distraught, and I decided I'd had enough—I grabbed up the pouch and closed it. "Jen. Stop, I don't like this side of you."

Her gaze snapped to me. There was a fire within her that I'd never seen before. For a moment, it felt like she was boring a hole through my chest directly into my soul. I stared her down defiantly, and she backed down. "My apologies, Mr Rosehouse."

Bryce mouthed the words "Thank you," at me. He watched carefully as Jennifer returned the pouch to her jacket pocket, then nervously fiddled with the buttons of his coat. "Black Ember is a drug derived from Opium," he said after collecting his thoughts. "In most people it just enhances the narcotic effect, but for mages it's much, much more."

"What does it do?" Jennifer asked. Her demeanour had changed again, a calmness had come over her and she was listening intently. All the while she scribbled in her notebook.

"It enhances our abilities, makes impossible things seem possible."

"Enhances?" I asked.

Bryce sat forward and was breathing heavily. He mopped the sweat from his brow and finally said, "Magic. Magic is like a river. Its source is the Arcane, and the Mundane the open ocean." He looked at the pictographs on his arms, tracing them with his fingers. "It flows through everything, the earth, animals, plants, objects. Even unbranded people. Imagine the river coursing through you, imagine that you are a lock."

"As in a door lock?" I puzzled.

"He means a canal lock, Charlotte," Jennifer interjected.

"Quite. Now, the natural flow of magic from Arcane to Mundane isn't enough to manifest any magical phenomena. But if you can close the lock gate to the Mundane you can fill the lock up with water from the river."

"Similar to how we focus magical energies in an alchemical formula," Jennifer interjected again.

"Do you want me to explain this?" Bryce asked, which warranted a shrug from Jennifer, and she sat back, miming out buttoning her lips. "Now, the thing with a lock is you can only open one door at a time. Open the door in the Arcane and nothing happens immediately; the lock fills with energy from the Arcane, but there's nowhere for it to go and there's no differential at the boundary. Open the Mundane, however, all of that energy rushes to escape." He snapped his fingers and a small flame, no bigger than that from a candle, appeared between them for a few short seconds.

"The sudden energy differential is what powers spells and such?" I asked.

"Precisely. Every mage has a limit. How much energy they can gather within themselves before releasing it, the height of the lock in our analogy."

"But then you have to start again? Once the spell is cast, there's no more energy. So, then, how does that change with Black Ember?" I pressed, getting a little impatient.

"Black ember opens both gates. Suddenly you don't have a lock anymore that takes time to fill and empty, but a weir or a waterfall, with free-flowing power crashing from the Arcane into the physical world without a care for who or what gets in the way. Just a small amount of the stuff can open up possibilities you couldn't ever have imagined before, and the more you use, the faster and stronger the current that flows through you." There was something wild in his expression, like a barely tamed circus lion eager to pounce.

Jennifer spoke, and the words crushed the wild spirit in an instant. "Then how did poor Timothy Waters end up looking like my last Christmas dinner?"

Bryce was sullen for a moment, contemplating his choice of words. "When the Ember wears off, the gates close. If you're in the middle of channelling a spell, it's, well, it's a paradox. An irresistible force meets an immovable object. Suddenly there's all this undifferentiated, wild Arcane energy, and the only thing holding it all together is a weak body made of flesh and bone." He punched a fist into his palm. "Some people can handle it—I would taper myself, smoking it allows for more control of the excess energy—or you need somewhere else to for the magic to go. Like a Ley Line or Arcane focus. But, at the end of the day, it sounds like your victim just lost his high and couldn't manage the drop."

I frowned and shook my head. "A man is dead, Mr Rosehouse. If this drug is so dangerous, why would anyone use it?"

Bryce scoffed, "why does anyone take any drug? To escape their troubles, to find some enjoyment or relief in a world with neither."

I rolled my eyes. "That's rich, coming from a member of the aristocracy. What were you escaping from? Daddy Viscount wouldn't buy you a fourth pony? What could you possibly know of troubles?"

"You have no idea what it's like to be a mage in this country," he snapped—I'll admit, righteous indignation was a much better look on him than pomposity. "No prospects, no voice—having to hide our talents to simply hold down a job—while people like you profit off magic freely. I may have been born to a privileged station, Miss Price, but there are hundreds like me who do not have that luxury."

Jennifer cut us both off and a snap of her fingers. "That's enough, both of you. You want to talk politics, then piss off back to the King's Head."

Silence filled the room. Bryce leaned back into his seat and crossed his arms. Despite his moment of fervour, he looked alone and afraid. Jennifer was writing a few things down but stopped mid-sentence to think.

I was uncomfortable, and desperate to break the unease that filled the room, I asked the next question, "Where did it come from? The Black Ember."

Bryce sighed, finally overcome by acquiescence. "There's a warehouse on the Isle of Dogs, about halfway down Stewart Street by the river. That's where I would pick up the goods to sell on. I was already hooked on the poppy by the time Hawkins' underlings roped me into selling. At first it was just opium, then a few months later he started bringing in Ember."

"Jennifer?" I looked over and she was pacing the office. The intensity had gone out of her and left in its place an uneasy calm. Neither I nor the downtrodden Mr Rosehouse spoke to interrupt her contemplation, lest we discover that calm to simply be the eye of the storm. Her notebook lay open on the table; she'd written twice as much as I had, but it was all in a code I couldn't decipher on the fly. No help in discerning what had her so wrapped up in thought.

She eventually sat at her desk, kicked her feet up onto its surface, and stared at the ceiling. "Thank you for your time, Mr Rosehouse. We won't keep you any longer." Bryce nodded, got up, and left without saying another word. Jennifer and I listened to his footsteps recede down the stairs, and after the doorbell rang Jen moved to the window and peered between the curtains. "What did you mean? What you said," she asked me.

"What part?"

"That you didn't like that side of me."

I sighed; I'd almost forgotten. Thoughts crowded in my mind; truths, half-truths, and lies. Jennifer may have been forthright and open about her feelings, but I didn't have her courage. I should have told her that the way she seemed to just turn off her emotions scared me. I didn't, and instead tried to deflect, "It was nothing. What do we do now? Do we go back to Baker?" I asked.

"Not yet. Hawkins has ears everywhere, even inside the Met. No, we need to move quickly before the evidence gets moved. Baker is a good man, and I doubt he'd approve, even if we did tell him. How are you feeling?"

"Agitated, unnerved, hungry,"—*concerned.*

Jennifer grinned, "You didn't say tired. Come on, get your things, we're going to Stewart Street. Tonight." There was a fire in her eyes, as though she delighted in calculating all the different possibilities and dangers we might run in to. I took no such pleasure, my mind once again full of half-formed thoughts. Jennifer must have sensed my apprehension, because she stopped her frantic preparations and sat beside me on the couch. "Charlotte, talk to me."

"You kind of threw me in the deep end, there. First thing I'm trying to have a conversation with this man, then you're pointing a gun at him, and he's threatening to incinerate me." I couldn't look her in the eyes, but I could feel her gaze on me. What did she want me to say? "You drugged him, Jen, against his will," I said, quiet as a mouse. "You crossed a line, and you made me part of it."

The air of confidence Jennifer exuded left her with a sigh, and a look of uncharacteristic resignation fell over her face. She was disappointed in me. *She* was disappointed in *me*—and for what? I should have been furious at her; part of me wanted-ed to scream that I had a right to be upset, but that part was drowned out by the knife in my heart. It was painful enough to meet her sharp, penetrating gaze, but that was nothing compared to the words that followed. "I may have misjudged how ready you were for all this."

My greatest weakness had always been being underestimated. Nothing motivated me more than the thought that someone I cared about—and I cared very deeply for Jennifer—might think that I was incapable. I pushed past the pain of letting Jen down and thought carefully about what I wanted to say. Sentences formed and picked themselves apart in my mind, and possible responses echoed after them. Which of my morals was I willing to compromise to prove myself to her?

"More people are going to die if we do nothing, won't they? Waters was just the first," I said after a pause that might have lasted a lifetime.

"Almost certainly," Jen said. She lifted my chin up—my knees went so weak that it was a good thing I was sitting—her touch was gentle and warm. "But I won't ask you to do anything you aren't comfortable with."

"I want to see this through," I said. Jennifer's eyes were like deep pools of amber, and I could feel my worries and concerns sinking away into them. If I hadn't looked away, I might have done anything she wanted, and it took every scrap of willpower I had to do it.

The sense of her lightly calloused fingers lingered for what felt like a century in seconds after she pulled away from me. "I'll get some supplies together and wrangle us a cab, I'll be downstairs when you're ready."

Chapter 9

A distant rumble of thunder accompanied the rattle of carriage wheels on the paved street outside the shop. How Jennifer had managed to get hold of a cab this late and in this weather, I had no idea. The driver was an older woman of Mediterranean descent; she greeted us sternly and grumbled about how far we wanted to travel until Jennifer offered to pay her double the usual rate.

Jennifer had a satchel with her, made of heavy canvas and reinforced with leather banding. She took out and cleaned one of the duelling pistols before handing it to me in a leather holster. "I don't know what we are going to find at Stewart Street, but I need you focussed and alert."

"I'll try," I said, not even trying to hide my nervousness. I took the pistol and wrapped the holster belt around my waist. The long barrel of the guns made them a little clumsy when worn like this, but Jennifer advocated for quick access over comfort.

"What if we can do better than try?" she asked, in a leading tone.

Words stumbled out of my mouth in a kind of curious and confused surprise. "I. Umm. Better? I don't. I'm not sure what. Huh?"

Jennifer produced a small brown glass bottle from her bag and held it up to the window, where the passing streetlamps revealed the clear liquid within. "This is a stimulant I've been working on, sulphur base with calcinated antimony and coca leaves, then dissolved in a mixture of aqua vitae and quinine."

A million questions battled for prominence in my head. I sat back and chewed my lip until one of them decided to form actual words. "You made this for me?" I said, finally.

She cocked her brow and gave me a healthy dose of side

eye. "I thought you'd question the use of sulphur instead of mercury first, to be honest." With an almost accusatory tone of voice, that was clearly less of a statement and more of a challenge. One that I was more than prepared to accept.

My riposte came with a flat, matter-of-fact tone, the vocal equivalent of yawning as you deflect your opponent's blade. "Well, mercury would be my first instinct in making anything that would act as a stimulant, but sulphur tends to produce longer lasting effects and has stronger meta-arcane connections to individual personality traits."

Jen was quick to press the attack. "Very good, but what role does the antimony play?"

"You're avoiding my question—" I pointed out, not missing a beat, then stated, "—the antimony is an Arcane catalyst, needed to overcome the notoriously high threshold for drawing out the magical properties of the coca. And before you ask, the aqua vitae is because I prefer potions over powders." My impending victory tasted sweet and left me utterly unprepared for the proverbial knife Jennifer had to my throat.

The pause Jennifer left in the air was just about long enough for me to realise my error. She asked, cool as could be, "The quinine?"

"The quinine—" I said, all too confidently. My mouth hung open, expecting words that would never come, because I hadn't the foggiest what the quinine was for. "Fine, you got me on that one."

"The quinine is experimental, but my intent is that it acts as a surrogate element of sorts. The less serious side effects will be drawn from the quinine as opposed to the coca, and yes, I did make it for you."

"Ah ha, you've fallen into my trap. Now I know that you've realised that I'm an unfocussed disaster of a human and will develop a complex about it," I joked. Kind of. It's not like there was a box of flu remedies still sitting ignored back at the shop, or anything.

It should have been obvious to me that Jennifer's real game plan hadn't been to quiz me on my alchemical knowledge, but to distract me from my looming anxiety. To her credit, she did a stellar job of it, and I'd gone a whole five minutes without fussing with the holster straps on my thigh. Whether this was pragmatism on her part, or out of a sense of compassion, I can't say.

Jennifer rolled her eyes, then very carefully uncorked the bottle so she could draw a small amount of the clear liquid into a pipette. "It should help you focus, and if I've done it right, you won't go out of your wits from the coca."

"If?" I asked, taking the dropper from her.

"If."

The potion was quite possibly one of the bitterest things I've ever tasted, more intense than the darkest Turkish coffee or eating an entire lemon peel. Jennifer was laughing at my futile attempts to entirely remove my tongue from my mouth, so I did the only thing I could in the moment and kicked her in the shin.

"OI!" she yelped. Satisfied that we were now both suffering, I joined in on the laughter.

Once the taste had faded, and it appeared Jennifer's leg stopped hurting, I said, "I don't feel any different."

"Give it some time. Come now, you must have more questions?"

"Oh, yes, I did. You said alchemists don't mess with psychoactive substances, yet here you are giving me a stimulant based on coca?" I asked, without hesitation.

"Quite right, recall that I said the reason for that is the unknown side effects. This formula attempts to combat that it two ways, firstly it's not arcane intensification that is so often attempted, but rather the magical effects are to pare down and consolidate only the positive effects. Second, as I mentioned, I added the quinine in an attempt to circumvent the psychological side effects."

"So, alchemists shouldn't make magic drugs, but you can because you're so clever?" I chided.

"Quite."

"What about the concoction you forced upon Rosehouse? The truth serum?"

She smirked knowingly but didn't answer.

"Not a real truth serum?"

No response, but a look that said, "carry on."

"When you opened it, there was a perfume. Floral and sweet, enticing."

"There was."

"Perfumes of course used to entice people into believing all sorts of wild fantasies. That potion didn't make him tell the truth, it just made him believe you when you said it was," I concluded.

"Nine out of ten marks for the young lady. I couldn't make him believe he had to tell the truth, but I could convince him that lying would be painful."

"The Arcane suggestion was strong enough to manifest real pain?"

"It seems so. The effects may have been enhanced by the fact that Bryce is a mage himself. There's not a lot of research into the interaction of alchemical formulae and branded individuals," Jennifer explained. "Feeling any different?"

Different was an understatement. Everything felt as clear as the first breath after a cold, like the first day of spring after a bitterly frigid winter. Instead of jumbling and jostling for prominence, my thoughts almost lined up to take their turns. But there was something else to it, a block of sorts that prevented my mind from wondering off course. "Yeah. I feel great, actually," I said, still shocked at my own lack of hesitation.

"Any jitters, upset stomach or… paranoid delusions?" I must have looked like a wide-eyed rabbit in the face of a hound; Jennifer grabbed my shoulder and said, "I'm kidding!"

"Not funny." I brushed her hand away and tried to hide the disconcerted look on my face. For the first time in my life, I could truly think clearly. There were butterflies in my stomach, I was unstoppable. But as wondrous as that felt, I was disquieted by the realisation that this might just have been *normal*. This might have been the way everybody else felt, every day of their lives, and it killed me a little.

Fuck, I was not going to start crying in front of Jennifer again, of that much, I was certain. Before I could apologise for being such a mess all the time, the carriage rolled to a stop and the driver knocked on the roof. "We're here," Jen said, and my attention snapped firmly back into the here and now.

'Here' turned out to be dirt and gravel street running north to south along the east bank of the Isle of Dogs, just wide enough for two carts to pass side by side. We stood at the north end of the street, under a gas lamp, with the Thames to our left behind a row of warehouses. The ever-present orange glow of gas light stopped abruptly a few feet ahead, and a foreboding darkness stretched out beyond it. There was a salty sea breeze that carried with it the soft sloshing sounds of the river and distant calls of sea birds. We'd been near the river long enough that I could barely pick up the foul stench of the waters, my nose instead filled with old smoke and the damp earth.

Jennifer paid the driver, who pulled around and left without another word. I stared into the darkness ahead as Jennifer fussed with an oil lamp she'd pulled from her satchel. The scratch and hiss of a match cut through the quiet of the night, and I was suddenly dazzled by the cone of light that flooded out ahead of us. Jen took the lead and said, "Should be down on the left."

Most of the buildings here were old and run down, some even looked abandoned with fallen in roofs and broken windows. A fitting sort of place for a secret drug smuggling operation, to be quite honest. The heavy rain had turned most of the road to mud; I had to step carefully to keep my footing, but as we moved to the dryer side of the road, I spotted something. "Jen, there's tracks here."

"Good catch. They must be fresh with all this rain."

"They aren't very deep," I posited. "Unladen?"

"Definitely, and a four-wheeler, I'd wager." Jennifer dropped into a squat and pointed between the tracks. "Now, look here, hoof prints. One horse, prints are in pairs."

"A trot? The driver must have been in a rush," I said, a little too chuffed with myself.

Jennifer turned the lamp to follow the tracks, which lead to a building about twenty or thirty yards further down the street. "Therefore; someone has a delivery coming."

The warehouse backed up onto the riverbank, and the

cart tracks ran to a huge pair of doors which were now shut. The walls were made up of about two yards high of brick, and another ten or so of sheet steel. The roof was slanted so that it sloped down toward the river. Unlike the rest of the street, this building was new—the brickwork hardly worn and not a speck of rust in the steel. Someone had gone through a lot of trouble to set up shop here, away from prying eyes. The wide double doors were open just a crack—a slither of light escaped onto the street—above which hung a faded sign that read, "Sparrow and Son's Trading Co."

Jennifer checked her pocket watch and said, "Nearly nine." She doused the lamp, and we waited a minute or so for our eyes to adjust. "Now, if I were a captain hoping to dock upriver after making a clandestine late night drop off, I'd want to be done before quarter past."

"Why's that?"

"West India and Millwall Docks close up at ten." There was a tight alleyway between the warehouse and the rundown building next door. Jennifer drew her pistol and quietly walked down the path. I followed suit, an uneasy calm settling over me. A side door halfway along the wall was slightly ajar. Jennifer moved right up next to it.

A raspy and dry voice came from inside that carried an air of authority. "Move those crates, I don't want anything to slow us down tonight. Marcus, make sure that horse is ready to go as soon as the cart's loaded." The voice continued giving orders for several more moments and then a bell tolled on the river. "That's the Hyacinth, prep the moorings!"

The shape of a shipping vessel drifted across the river through the gap between the buildings. "Should keep them busy?" I whispered. The little voice in the back of my head was very concerned by this, but I couldn't hear what she said.

"Perfect time for us to get in unnoticed." Even in the dark I could see the shape of her wry, chaotic smirk. She checked the door, and it creaked ever so quietly. "Hmm." The pistol in her hand slipped away into its holster, and then she thrust a heavy steel syringe into my hands. The glass barrel was about a quarter cup, filled with a faintly glowing blue liquid as thick as blood. The needle was a good three inches long, and without warning Jennifer pulled a second syringe from her bag and pushed the steel point two-thirds of the way into her biceps.

I picked my jaw up from the muddy floor and watched as a blue mist coalesced around the injection sight. Jennifer pushed the plunger all the way down and a deep bodily shudder to cascaded through her.

"What is that?" I asked.

The mist fully enveloped her left arm. Holding her fore-arm across her waist, then drawing it up over her torso and head, the mist soaked into her body. "Protection," she said. "Enough to stop a bullet if need be. You'll lose body tempera-ture regulation for a few hours when it wears off, so wrap up warm." She looked at me expectantly.

"Right, I'll just—" I fumbled with the syringe as I holstered my pistol and shrugged my coat off one shoulder. I took a breath to steady myself and pressed the cold metal tip against the exposed skin of my arm. No use turning back now. I drove the needle deep into the muscle and bit my lip so hard in the process that I tasted blood.

It took every ounce of willpower not to cry out at the pain. A wave of cold flooded across me as I pushed the plunger down, as though the potion had frozen my veins. My heart began to beat twice as fast and twice as hard to drive the Ar-cane fluid onwards. The mist had formed over my arm, and it felt like snowflakes falling on my skin.

The mist clung to my clothes and my skin as I drew my arm across my body—just as I'd watched Jennifer do—and formed a pristine layer of… magic something. The surface shimmered as it settled; the smooth, slick surface under my fingertips reminded me, strangely, of a sugar glaze on a cake. "This is something else, Jen. How did you…?"

"Another time, Charlotte." She opened the door before I could protest and stepped inside. The dim light of a hanging lantern illuminated a small stockroom. Shelves stacked with sacks and barrels lined the walls on either side of the entrance, with another door directly opposite that presumably opened into the warehouse proper. I stayed close to behind Jennifer as she moved around the edge of the room and traced her hand long the shelves. "Shanghai, Canton, Hongkong. These are all coming in from China."

"Any idea what's in them? Maybe there's a manifest or stock book we can look at." I said, quietly.

"Good idea, it's too dark to see any of the labels in here though." Suddenly, Jennifer bolted up straight against the wall and pulled me beside her. "Someone's coming." Footsteps approached from beyond the interior door, and a gruff voice with it. Jen put a finger to her lips. Not that I needed to be told to stay quiet.

"All right, all right, I'll check the supply room." The door opened and orange light washed into the room; Jennifer and I hid behind the open door. The man was tall and slim, wearing a sou'wester hat and rain mac. His face was bony, and he looked like he'd had some recent sun burn. I took all this in, and hoped he'd turn back the way he came, but in a flash of motion, Jennifer pushed the door shut and rushed the man. "What the?" he said, before Jen grabbed his head on one side, and with her other hand, pressed her palm up against his neck.

The man slumped to the ground, sound asleep, just as Mr Rosehouse had done earlier that evening. I caught Jen's hand and pulled back her sleeve to reveal a small contraption strapped to her wrist. There were three vials, secured in leather pouches, each with a retractable needle attached. Two of the vials were empty, presumably having contained the sleeping draughts, while the third was filled with a pale white liquid.

I let go of Jennifer's hand and said, "Nightshade or Valerian?" The question came faster than I could comprehend the events that just played out in front of me, as if automatic—it was one that had bugged me since The King's Head.

"Both, actually. He'll be out for an hour or two at least," she replied. Out of nowhere, a few moments later, she asked, "What's the matter? You're looking all pensive again."

My brow had contorted itself into a deep furrow and I'd

chewed my lip raw without realising it. Somewhere in the back of my mind, there was a frightened, visceral reaction to what had happened. "It's just…" My voice trailed off. I wondered just how often she carried around high-strength sedatives—and what sort of person keeps a ready supply for a night of wild vigilantism. But those thoughts stayed neatly tucked away, my focus stayed in the moment. "It's nothing, it can wait. We have a job to do, right?"

Jennifer put a reassuring hand on my shoulder. "These are dangerous people we're dealing with; I can't afford for you to hesitate."

In the dim light I could only just make out the contours of her face—fierce determination dominated her features, and there was just a hint of something eerily playful. I swallowed hard and said, "Just tell me what you need me to do."

Though she didn't say it out loud, Jennifer's eyes drifted to the firearm I held so tightly in my hand. I understood what she meant by it—she needed me to be ready to pull the trigger.

"Sounds like they've started unloading," said Jennifer at the heavy thuds coming from next room, "let's get a closer look." To my surprise, she opened the door, crouched low, and stepped quickly across the warehouse floor. I got a clear enough look at the riverbank end of the building to tell I could move unseen and followed in Jen's wake to where she crouched by a horse and cart.

The warehouse was cavernous, with rows upon rows of shelving that was suspiciously empty. A group of six or seven people moved big barrels and sacks off the ship via a gangplank. They all had sailors builds; lithe and wiry or burly and wide. The biggest one of them, wearing a long coat and tricorn hat, bellowed in a Greek accent. "How many more? We're on a tight schedule."

Another replied, "Almost done, cap'n."

"Good," the leader said. "You three, start moving things to the cart." The man pointed over in our direction. Jennifer and I shared a furtive glance.

"Follow my lead, this is where the fun begins." She winked

with that wicked grin of hers and then strolled out into the open like a god-damned fearless gladiator. "Evening lads, lasses. Good night for it?" Jennifer declared. Half a dozen heads snapped to her, almost too stunned to go for their weapons. Almost. Clubs and knives were drawn, and Jen whipped out her pistol. "Why doesn't everyone just relax?" she said casually. It was around about that moment that I began to suspect that Jennifer had gone completely mad. I moved up to her side—wondered if I, too, had gone completely mad—and tried to look as if I wasn't terrified.

"Who the hell are you?" their leader barked.

"Concerned citizens, curious what could be so important for a late-night delivery," Jennifer said. The wooden floorboards creaked as the workers took tentative steps towards us.

I was all too aware of how little distance there was between us, them, and death. A single bead of sweat ran down the side of my face as the silence permeated the warehouse. Everyone else in the room was coiling like vipers—I was more like a rabbit ready to run.

"How about you all put your weapons down, and we have a nice little conversation about your employers?" Jen asked. She had a wicked grin on her face—she was enjoying herself. Had she gone bat shit crazy? There were better ways to get your kicks than getting into a shoot-out.

"I was thinking the same thing," said the man in charge.

Jen clicked her tongue. "That's a shame." With that, she pulled back the hammer on her pistol.

The three sailors closest to us—each as burly as the next, bearing long knives—sprung forward. I stumbled backwards, but Jennifer moved with a predator's speed and grace. They had no time to react before her pistol went off. The deafening crack of black powder and thunder echoed off the steel walls and roof. One of the sailors fell to the ground with a ruined face where the bullet had gone right through his eye and out the back of his head. My stomach turned and I stumbled to my knees, but Jennifer didn't stop.

The second sailor dropped his bag and ran toward Jennifer,

moving off to the side. She had already reloaded her firearm at lightning speed, but the shot went wide. I watched and winced as she swung the butt of her pistol at the man's head, knocking him to the ground. "Charlotte, get down!" she called. I turned and the last of the three sailors came at me, brandishing his jagged knife above his head. I managed to duck below his swipe, and without thinking, I put the pistol to his gut and fired.

He fell down, dead, in front of me. I didn't have time to comprehend the lifeless eyes that stared up at me, or the blood that had sprayed across my face, because Jennifer's voice was already cutting through my mental fog to bring me back to focus.

At the other end of the warehouse, the other sailors had responded to the noise of the fight and gathered on the loading deck, armed with rifles, pistols and long naval knives. "Oh, you've done it now, ladies," challenged their leader.

Chapter 10

My heart rate doubled, and then almost tripled. My vision narrowed, my breath caught in my throat, and the pounding in my head muffled out the yells and heavy bootsteps around me. I was more focussed than ever before, but solely on exactly how fucked we were. There was a body at my feet, a dead man with a pool of blood growing around his stomach. I shot him, and now he was dead. But that didn't matter, it was insignificant in the face of my mortal terror.

The wooden floor panel in front of me shattered into a shower of splinters, and I fell back on my arse. Jennifer was yelling at me, her pistol aimed at the broken floorboard. "Charlotte. Pay attention. I need you to hold them off, lay down some cover fire. Can you do that?" Shaking, I looked past the crates and saw the group of workers rushing to find cover of their own, loading firearms as they moved. There were more of them, rushing down the gangplank of the ship at the sound of the commotion. Everything Jennifer had taught me about shooting emptied from my mind.

"I-I can't, I'll get shot to bits," I called back.

"No, you won't," Jennifer said, putting a hand on her arm where she'd injected the shield potion. "Just draw their attention. I need about a minute."

"To do what!?" I demanded. But before she could answer a shot went off, and a bullet flew over my head and embedded into the wall with a blast of dust.

"Charlotte, now! Remember, eyes open," Jennifer said, and I nodded.

I took shaky breaths to try to steady myself—I had to act fast. I put my back to the crate, and held up the pistol, walking through the steps in my mind. Hammer to half cock, jam a cartridge into the barrel with the ramrod, hammer to full cock, aim, breathe, then fire.

I planted my right foot and pivoted on my heel, then picked out the closest target. As soon as the pistol was level, I squeezed the trigger—there was a loud crack, and the pistol kicked back in my hand. The shot was good, and my target fell backwards with a hand on his shoulder. I pulled out another paper cartridge and started listing the steps in my head again.

Before I could finish loading, I felt a red hot, blistering pain in my shoulder and an incredible force that threw me backwards. I put a hand to my chest, but there was no blood. Instead, I found the bullet in my fingertips—hot to the touch—and a web of shattered pearlescent glass. The light danced with a myriad of reflections as the glass moved and coalesced. The shield evanesced from sight as the cracks closed, leaving no trace of its presence.

A rush of confidence and excitement surged within me—can you blame me? I was bulletproof, after all. I finished loading my pistol and took up my firing position again, and that same mischievous smirk that Jennifer so often wore found a home on my face. The man who just shot me dropped his powder horn when he saw me get up unwounded, scattering black powder across the wooden floor. I put a shot square in his chest, and I was so caught up in the moment that I didn't even blink when he fell.

Jennifer was gone, to who knows where, to do who knows what. I had my own problems to worry about, however—a shower of splinters sprayed across my face—my cover wasn't going to hold much longer. There was a storage platform to my left that looked to offer a good vantage point. I made a break, but before I could make it, I was hit again. A gut punch knocked the wind out of me, followed by a blow that took my left leg out from under me. My momentum carried me into an awkward roll, and I ended up on my back behind the platform. The Arcane shield regenerated, and two high calibre bullets rolled onto the floor. I chuckled, "That the best you got?"

Of course, I was taunting them—why the hell was I taunting them? Maybe Jen was a bad influence.

The leader of the group, the Mediterranean man, was dumbfounded, "What are you playing at!? Kill her and find the other one!"

Two more were coming toward me, but my motions were almost automatic by that point. I moved with the terrifying precision of an apex predator—though who it was more terrifying for, I couldn't say. My hands danced in perfect timing to load, cock and fire. A spray of blood painted the wall as a bullet tore through one of the sailor's jaws. The other, a lithe young woman, stopped and dropped down to check on the limp body beside her.

I was already jamming another cartridge into my firearm when I was blinded by a flash of powder in the corner of my vision. A bullet stopped less than an inch from my face—the Arcane glass shattering into a thousand fractal shards around my eye.

Pain flared in my skull, and then my neck as the force whipped me backwards—trust me, you do not want to get shot in the face—a moment later I came to my senses on the floor. The glittering refracted lights from the shield dazzled my sight as it regenerated. I managed to pull myself away from more incoming fire to try and catch my breath.

My ears rang like church bells, and there was blood running from my nose. How many were there? How many had we taken out? Four, maybe five? I tried to take another look, but a new hail of bullets and shrapnel pushed me back into cover. "Fuck. Now would be a good time!"

A thunderous crack echoed off the walls, like an answer from heavens. Jennifer leapt down from the catwalks above with the grace of a lynx, landing beside the body of the man she'd shot from above. My eyes must have been playing tricks because she somehow covered half the length of the warehouse in the time it took me to blink. She left a blurred trail behind her, like a badly timed stroboscope. She was like lightning unbottled, moving unpredictably and impossibly swiftly. From nowhere, steel flashed, and she was holding a small sword with an ornate hand guard. Without warning, she had closed the distance with the woman closest to her and drove the point of the blade into her throat. The woman coughed and sputtered before collapsing in a heap.

Watching her move and fight, it was like seeing a creature from another world. Was that why she'd hidden so much from me? Was she afraid of what I'd think of her, after seeing her mow down a room of people without breaking a sweat? Or was she afraid I'd want to join her? I stared unblinking as the trails of her movement hung in my vision—what I was more afraid of? All the times she'd disappeared and come back bloody—I figured she just took part in underground boxing fights like any normal person—is this what she was doing? Is this what she was training me to be?

A hail of gunfire snapped me back to the moment, filling the warehouse with an ear shattering noise and a billow of powder smoke. Half a dozen rounds must have found their mark on Jennifer, but she didn't even flinch. The shield held firm and for a moment, her whole body looked like a reflection in a broken mirror. She dashed towards one assailant and slashed at his face with inhuman speed. At the same time, she raised the pistol in her left hand and a bolt of lightning lanced from the unloaded barrel into the chest of another of the sailors.

There were three of them left, including the one in charge. I'd regained my wits enough to take a shot at him, but it went wide. Jennifer stood still, but she practically buzzed with energy.

I was sure they were going to run; it'd be foolish to stay. For a moment to two lackeys looked back, but the captain just snarled at them—who did they work for who was my terrifying than Jen? The captain ducked for cover to load his rifle, and the last two rushed Jennifer with their long knives and reckless abandon. She waited till the last moment before parrying the first stabbing thrust and delivering a deadly riposte to the man's heart. The second managed to get to her while she was pulling her blade out and slashed at her midsection. The knife stopped dead in the shield, the manifested glass fissuring under the force.

"Ha! See this, Charlotte!? I wasn't sure it would stop a

blade!" Jennifer yelled across the warehouse, almost gleefully unaware of the carnage around us. She looked like she was waiting for me to respond and when I didn't, she proceeded to punch the man in the face with the hand guard of her sword. He fell so hard it was as if he'd been kicked by a horse.

Another crack rang out, and Jennifer doubled over and cried out in pain. The shot from the captain's rifle had evidently found its mark on the shattered section of shield. Arcane glass danced off the floor before evaporating, and Jen pulled a bloody hand from her gut.

"Wasn't expecting that," she said, slightly bewildered. Not to let the momentary success go to her opponent's head, she leaned into a four-point stance and drove forward with preternatural power and cleared the 10-yard distance in two strides. She hit the man mid pounce and barrelled him into the ground. When she stood, she left the blade of her sword impaling him to the ground.

Chapter 11

In the maelstrom of dust and powder smoke around me, I could hear the dying gasps of those who weren't killed outright by shot or sword. The ferrous smell of blood mingled with the fouler, more acrid stench of fresh death. I moved my hands mechanically to make the pistol safe and slid it into the holster without conscious thought. As the world settled, my mind eased out of its state of hypervigilance, and the reality of the situation sank in.

Maybe the tincture-induced block in my mind that kept me focussed on the moment had given way, or maybe the moment itself had just become too fucked up to ignore. I stumbled over to my stoic mentor in disbelief of what had just happened—of what I'd done.

"Fuck. Jen. What the fuck was that!?"

"Language, Charlotte," Jennifer said, punctuating the sentence with a sickening squelch as she retrieved her sword from its temporary sheath.

"Fuck my language!" I snapped back at her, filled with contemptuous fury—if ever there was a time for swearing, it was then. "Were you planning on telling me at any point that your plan was 'shoot first, don't leave anyone alive to question'?"

"Plans evolve and change over time," she said, far too casually for my liking. I swear I almost slapped her. "I gave you every opportunity to leave—if you don't like the way I operate—"

"What I don't like is being kept in the dark. Trust goes both ways, Jennifer." That was enough to give her pause.

The flickering torch light made her eyes shimmer, like two little drops of gold set into white marble. The lingering magic she was under made it too hard to tell, but for a moment, I thought she was fighting back tears. "I trust you with my life, Charlotte."

"What good would that be if we'd both been killed?"

"Now, I really do think you're overreacting. I had everything under—Ah!" Jennifer doubled over and grabbed her abdomen—her hand came away bloody.

"Shit," I said and ran over to her, concern taking over from my anger. "How is it? Did you bring a healing draught?" Wounds of varying degrees were quite treatable with the right Alchemical mixture, but the potions usually took a lot out of you.

"No, didn't expect to need one. I'll be fine, the concoction I took should help enough."

I tried to meet her gaze, but her eyes moved too quick for me to keep up. "You're still vibrating, what is that?" Her skin pulsed with energy at my touch, like a beating heart of Arcane origin. Jen smiled warmly and pushed her cheek against my palm, as if the small act peeled back her mask.

"A mix of things," she answered a moment later. "I'll show you the formula when we get back to the shop, but you won't believe it when you see it. It'll wear off soon, and I'll feel like a tonne of bricks just landed on me. Let's check these crates, maybe find a manifest." She took a few steps and stumbled to her knees.

"Jen?"

"I'll be fine," she said, her voice unsteady. She spat a mouthful of blood on the floor. "Just give me a moment."

There wasn't anything I could do to help her, so I worked my way around the unloaded goods as quick as I could—the sooner we got what we needed, the sooner I could get Jen back to the shop. I tried my best to avoid looking at the bodies. There were some normal trade goods—spices, silks, that sort of thing—likely those were used as cover for anything illicit. Anything illicit, such as more opium than I had ever seen in my life. Almost a tonne, I figured. After that, Naphtha in large quantities, fire salts from northern Africa and a barrel of pickled organs I didn't recognise. The ingredients for transmuting Black Ember, perhaps?

As strange as all those things were, the strangest was a large crate that had been abandoned right by the ship. Unlike the others, it had reinforcing iron bands, and a huge padlock. Bore holes had been cut into the lid of the box and it smelt of something acrid and vile. "What the hell?"

"Charlotte, don't take another step," Jennifer stood and stepped up behind me—the floorboards under the crate creaked. "There's something alive in there."

The box rattled ferociously; a deep grumbling roar from whatever was inside it shook me to my core. "Jennifer?" I stepped back, all too aware of every single minute sound I was making.

"Get behind me," she put an arm out and pushed me backwards. The crate rocked again, the iron bars warped, and the lock strained against the lid. The creature within snarled and hissed.

"Jen!?" fear boiled up in me and I moved further back.

"Go!" Jennifer ordered, but before I could start running, the crate exploded outwards and sent huge shards of wood and metal our way. I threw my arms up and the shrapnel left a cobweb of shimmering cracks in my shield.

A scaled beast shook the remains of the broken crate from its long snaking back, and unfurled a pair of leathery, bat-like wings. It was the sort of creature you heard about in fairy tales and horror stories, the sort of thing that had been driven to extinction by order of Crown and Church. An exotic beast that prowled lands where no human dared to tread—probably Australia—and someone was stupid enough to bring it to London.

"Is that a fucking dragon!?" I yelled, and the creature shrieked back at me. It whipped out a long, barbed tail and reared up with wings spread wide. The yellowy brown scales shimmered in glow of the torches and gas lamps, contrasted by its pale, ivory underbelly. Its teeth were as sharp as spears, and its face was crowned by bony horns protruding through its skin.

"No, just a wyvern, no fore legs," Jen said, so nonchalant she might have been correcting a math problem. She loaded her pistol and stepped forward with head held high. "Watch that tail, the barbs are venomous."

"You are not going to fight that thing. Are you insane?" There had to be something I could do, anything to stop her. We'd both done so much already, but somehow Jennifer stood proud, spreading her arms wide. She was getting the Wyvern's attention; she was protecting me.

"Just stay behind me, keep your eyes open," she was looking around frantically. "Aha, yes, there! In the captain's coat, there's a paper in the breast pocket. I'd wager that's the manifest." The beast snapped forward—Jennifer flinched and then winced in pain. "Charlotte, it's time for you to go," she said.

"I can help," I said, but the fear in my voice betrayed me. A rumble of thunder and flash of lightning distracted the Wyvern, and I took my chance to get close to Jennifer. "You can't do this alone." She grabbed my wrist and something sharp scratched my skin. I looked, expecting to see her nails digging into me, but there was… nothing? She was just holding my wrist.

"You can help Charlotte; it is incredibly important that you grab that manifest and get back to the shop where it's safe." Jennifer was speaking very plainly. She was right, of course, that was incredibly important. A fog rolled into my mind, blurring my thoughts—we were in danger, I needed to fight—but the manifest, Jennifer said that was incredibly important. "Charlotte, I will meet you back at the shop, I promise. Now go!"

"Yes Charlotte. Go," a new voice echoed. Standing on the ship was a tall man in a gentleman's suit and hat. He had a cane topped with a crystal orb, and the left sleeve of his jacket was split up to the elbow to reveal the unmistakable Mage's Brand. Even from where I stood, a good fifteen or twenty yards, I could make out the distinguished features of his face, a pointed black beard with a touch of silver grey, fierce bushy eyebrows, and high cheekbones so sharp they could cut steel.

"Fuck," Jennifer and I said in unison.

The mage raised his cane, and with it he drew out an arcane sigil. His voice undulated with deep forbidden tones, and I felt a rush of energy flow past me where it seemed to coalesce around the crystalline focus. A wave of invisible force lifted me off my feet and threw me into the nearest wall. I landed with a hard crash and struggled to catch my breath. Forget the subtle flexibility of Worker's Cant, or the Arcane bastardisation of Alchemy—that was real magic, a level of control of the Aether that only the most powerful, most skilled mags could perform. It hurt like a bitch.

Jennifer's voice echoed in my ears, but when I looked at her, she wasn't talking. *I will meet you back at the shop, I promise.* The words invaded my thoughts, echoing unnaturally—and I didn't question them.

The world span around me, as if half my brain was ready to fight, while the other demanded I run, just like she'd told me to. There was a piercing shriek and I turned quick enough to see the Wyvern leap into flight towards Jennifer.

I had to move, I had to act, I had to do something—anything. Jennifer's command won the war in my head, and I sprinted to the corpse of the ship's captain. There was a folded wad of paper in his pocket, and I stuffed it inside my coat. As I got back to my feet, I saw the flash of Jen's pistol going off into the face of the airborne lizard.

"No!" I yelled as the beast, still very much alive but dripping scarlet blood, crashed into Jennifer. It pinned her down and her shield cracked under repeated strikes from the thing's barbed tail. The side of my mind that wanted to fight took over, and I drew my firearm and pulled the trigger. It didn't matter that I'd forgotten to load the damn thing, because the small bolt of lightning was enough to throw the creature off balance so that Jennifer could drive her blade into its soft underbelly.

Reality started to come apart—my addled brain struggled to keep up with everything that happened. My heart roared in my chest, like an overheated steam engine ready to burst. I wanted to scream. I wanted everything to just stop.

The last thing I remembered was Jennifer's voice—and it really was her voice—cutting through the haze. "Charlotte, please! Go!" I spared one glance back at her, tears ran down her face and there was fear in her eyes.

Without another thought, I ran.

October 10th, 1834

A Promise Made in Vain

Chapter 12

The next day, I awoke in the spare bedroom of The Potent Solution. I was still dressed in the clothes I wore the night before, and I felt like a reanimated corpse that hadn't actually had the luxury of animation. What the hell had happened? I could scarcely remember anything in real detail after Jen and I broke into the warehouse. Did I get shot? I was pretty certain I got shot. There was a dragon—no, not a dragon, a wyvern—or was that a dream? I rubbed the sleep from my eyes and sat up in a haze.

One of the first things I was taught after becoming an apprentice alchemist was that recording the side effects of new or unfamiliar formulae was of the utmost importance. The morning after effect, in particular, is an oft-referenced characteristic of any well studied alchemical product. One of the few habits Jennifer successfully drilled into me in the early days of my apprenticeship was waking up and immediately writing down how crap I felt after a day of potion making.

I couldn't find my notebook, which should have been on the bedside table where I normally left it. It wasn't until I fully comprehended that I was still wearing my coat that I thought to check the pockets and found the little blue gift sequestered away into the inside left breast. The mediocre mattress groaned as I flopped back onto it, and I scribbled the symptoms of my alchemical hangover into the book.

High pitched, intermittent tinnitus in left ear. Common side effect of Quinine, source – Stimulant, formula unknown, other ingredients – sulphur, antimony, coca leaves, aqua vitae. Cold sweats, hot flashes, shivers, source – shield mixture according to Jennifer's advice, formula unknown, all ingredients unknown. Migraine headache with aura, Aqua Vitae? Usual side effect not severe, complication with Coca? Or instead from shield mixture?

<s>Neck pain,</s> Whiplash—*did I get shot in the face?*

Even thinking about why my head hurt so much made the pain even more unbearable. I checked the time on my pocket watch, saw that it was already past noon—and against every fibre of my being—I pulled myself out of the pile of blankets and pillows. Where was Jennifer? She normally would have checked on me—something was wrong. Her words echoed in my mind with unnatural longevity—*I will meet you back at the shop, I promise.* That was right, she wouldn't be back. I'd just have to wait. Why did I think that? Something was clearly wrong, wasn't it?

The spare room had a closet that over time had filled up with clothes I'd left at the shop—it was handy to have spares, in case of spillages in the lab. The clothes I still had on were muddy, damp, and starting to take on a musty, sweaty smell. I stripped off and dropped my soiled clothes into the makeshift wash pile in the corner of the room and caught a sight of myself in the long mirror beside the closet. Honestly, I was surprised I was still alive.

For starters, I had a black eye the size of a saucer over my left eye—I definitely got shot in the face. Three other bruises stuck out like targets to show where else the shield potion had stopped lethal gunshot wounds. One spread from my shoulder joint over my right breast to the nipple, another across my midsection, and the last on my knee which looked a little like a rabbit's footprint. I wondered if that would bring any good luck.

I wracked my brain to try to remember what happened, why I'd been shot, or where Jennifer was. I needed to go look for her, something wasn't... The migraine flared in response, only abating when I turned my attention elsewhere. I checked myself over for any other wounds, then pulled on a loose-fitting shirt and pair of trousers that looked clean enough and headed downstairs.

I was in no condition to greet customers, so I made the executive decision to leave the shop sign in the closed position. The shop floor was filled with a gloomy, dull light coming from outside. The storm had abated evidently, but the grey cloud remained implacable above the streets of London. The front door was locked, and Jennifer's coat and satchel were nowhere to be found. Jennifer was in trouble, she was in trouble, and she needed me and—the pain flared, as if the light from outside had physically pushed me back away from the door—*I will meet you back at the shop, I promise.* Was I hearing Jennifer's words, or remembering them?

I tried to put my mind at ease by fixing myself a late breakfast and a strong cup of Darjeeling tea, which helped a small amount. It should have been clear to me that something was wrong—I should have been reacting in some way to what had happened—we'd fought a wyvern and shot up a warehouse full of people I hoped were criminals. Jen stayed behind. She needed me to do something—I should have felt something, any emotion other than placid patience. But there was nothing—no panic, no anxiety, no fear. Nothing was wrong, everything would be fine if I just stayed put.

I screamed—but I didn't. Something was wrong—but I couldn't think that—if something was wrong, I would have to leave. I couldn't leave. The pain was unbearable, but I needed the pain—the pain reminded me that nothing was wrong…

Jennifer was a brilliant Alchemist; but even she couldn't have predicted that my peculiar mind would respond so chaotically to the concoction of potions she'd given to me. As I struggled to make sense of what was happening—all the while going about the day like it was any normal day—an intrusive occupant in my mind made sure I couldn't. *I will meet you back at the shop, I promise.* Was there any use fighting it?

The tea at least helped with the hot and cold flashes, so I re-boiled the left-over water and made myself a second cup before heading back upstairs. In one of my classic scattered states of mind, I soon found myself standing in Jennifer's office carrying not just my tea, but also a stack of books that needed to be put away, and a few letters that had been delivered that morning. To top it all off, all of those things—even the tea—were promptly forgotten, when I noticed Jen had left a few open books on her desk.

Jennifer's desk chair was one of the only comfortable pieces of furniture she owned. A birthday gift from my father and me; I'd helped my old man make it after one too many days of hearing Jen complain about her sore buttocks. It was mahogany, and had a big, cushioned seat and back, made from red velvet and duck feathers. I carefully sat down, wincing a little as I did, and looked over at what Jen had been reading. A casebook took up the centre position of the pile, Jen had copied down her notes from the scene of Timothy Waters' death. An older book, which appeared to be full of Jennifer's handwriting, was open on notes about Black Ember dated five or six years earlier. The notes were unfortunately unhelpful. Two tomes with similar bindings turned out to be consecutive issues of the Annual Alchemical Journal, dated 1832 and 1833. The articles Jennifer was reading were on "The Advantages of Intravenous Injection of Alchemical Potions, Tinctures, Decoctions and Concoctions by J. Morton" and "A Review of Surrogate Reagents and their Side-Effects by E. Elric and G. Haute-Bellegarde."

Jennifer had mentioned surrogate reagents in the cab ride, something about averting troublesome side-effects—perhaps she wasn't as successful as she hoped, which would explain why I felt so strange. I could ask Jennifer about the manuscript when she got back, which I hoped would be soon. Her voice had grown distant in my mind, but the words still repeated to reassure me that waiting was the right idea—*I will meet you back at the shop, I promise.*

The last of the books was a battered, leather bound pile of yellow pages covered in stains, which was dangerously close to no longer being a book at all. I delicately moved the fragile old thing in front of me—Jennifer's personal formula book. It was closed, most likely a vain attempt to protect it from spilt tea. The leather cover was faded at the edges from years of use but was once a charcoal black. Cut into the centre was the squared circle, the alchemist symbol denoting The Philosopher's Stone.

The symbol appeared again on the first page, drawn in black ink by Jennifer's hand. This iteration was detailed however, with notations and labels. Jennifer practiced a newer branch of Alchemy called Universalism, which attempted to find a unifying theory between the many schools of thought and alchemical traditions. To a Universalist, The Philosopher's Stone was less a tangible, empirical substance that could be synthesised by study and experimentation, but more a state of mind and full understanding of the bridge between Mundane and Arcane. It wasn't the only view, however, and alchemists were known to fiercely disagree with each other on the subject.

I recalled a time Jennifer had invited me to a lecture held at The Royal Society in Somerset House, ostensibly on the topic of Iridium and its Arcane properties. Half an hour into the talk, however, the gentleman speaking made the apparently audacious remark that the insolubility of iridium in Aqua Regia meant it could be an inert, primordial form of the noble metals. The comment was immediately challenged by a Swedish alchemist as an atrocious dereliction of centuries of research, sparking a debate that went on until dinner was served three hours later. To make things even more ridiculous, when the organisers attempted to seat the speaker and his challenger separately, it was made apparent they were in fact man and wife. Needless to say, Jennifer and I left before dessert.

Within her formula book, Jennifer had annotated the Squared Circle to highlight different connected properties. The inner circle represented the self, conceptualised as Mind, Body and Spirit. Surrounding this was a square, which had come to be understood as representing the Arcane. The four points of the square denote Earth, Wind, Air and Fire, the fundamental elements of magic. The outer triangle can be interpreted as the boundary between the Arcane and Mundane achieved by unity of the self. Its points represent Mercury, Sulphur, and Salt, which relate to the Mind, Body and Soul, respectively. Beyond all that, the final out circle represents the infinite limits of the Arcane and the Mundane.

I turned the page to a list of contents that had been slowly added to over the years and groaned when I remembered it was all written in codes and ciphers. Alchemists are a petty bunch, truth be told. Theft of research is a real problem, and with the exception of published works, most alchemists choose to record their studies in a form not easily read. Jennifer's particular encryption was an annoying combination of a Vigenère cipher that required a key word to solve, and a fake alphabet that required a substitution chart to change the decoded words into legible English.

I'd got pretty good at finding words and phrases that I recognised on sight from Jennifer's writings, but studying the formulae I was interested in was going to be a much more involved task than I had the energy for. I struggled through the contents page on memory and was able to track down what I was sure enough were the correct pages for the Stimulant and Shield Potion, but I just couldn't concentrate enough.

Nearly two hours had passed since I had awoken, and Jennifer still hadn't returned, which was weird, because she promised she would. What made matters worse, I thought, was that despite the hot flashes and headache had faded, the incessant tinnitus was getting worse.

I leaned back in the chair and grumbled as the ringing got louder and louder, and more and more insistent and repetitive. The ringing then changed to a banging sound, which is when I realised that it wasn't the tinnitus at all, but rather someone at the door. I wondered who would have the audacity to knock while the shop was obviously closed, and then it hit me like a charging thoroughbred. "Elly… bugger!"

Chapter 13

I sincerely considered ignoring the knocking at the door, even more so when I saw my reflection again. A vain part of me that I didn't even know existed was horrified by the idea of Elly seeing me in my current state. But another part was even more horrified by the idea of standing her up—I owed her better than that. Besides, after everything we'd been through, she'd probably seen worse—I wasn't even drunk.

Elly stepped into the shop all smiles—she hadn't seen my face yet—wearing a patterned yellow dress that showed off her collarbones. The sleeves were plumped around the elbows, an ornate brass buckle fixed a belt around her waist, and the skirt was decorated with silk trim and satin bows.

When my eyes finally made it up to hers from their downcast start, I managed to mumble out, "You look wonderful," before the smile broke from Elly's face.

"Well, you look like shit," she said, deadpanned. Without a moment's hesitation, Elly stepped up to me and—standing on tiptoes for a good view—ran her fingers along my black eye. I grimaced but didn't pull away—part of me even enjoyed being so close. She let out a soft gasp of amazement as she tested the bone around my eye. "How on earth did you manage this without any breaks in your supraorbital?

"That is a long story," I said. Elly dropped back onto her heels and frowned. Determined to change the subject, I tried to laugh it off. "Am I to take the impromptu examination to mean it's Dr Chynoweth these days?" Elly had been studying medicine while I worked unsuccessfully toward my bachelor's.

"That's right," she said (I slipped in a quick, "Congratulations."). "I'm still looking for work, or an office to set up my own practice, but father has been keeping me busy." Elly's old man, Mr Chynoweth, was always looking for new projects and exciting endeavours. He'd made his fortune on copper in Cornwall and moved to London to expand his business—that was how Elly and I came to meet.

"How is your old man?" I asked, awkwardly.

Elly sighed. "A little too glad to have me back, and a little too slow on the uptake around certain… changes." She chewed her lip in the way she always had when there was a lot on her mind. Before I could decide how to comfort her, Elly clicked her tongue and said, "but I'm not here to talk about my Da', Charlotte." She looked at me with those big, gemstone eyes, and my breath caught in my throat.

I hadn't realised how much I was aching to hold her in my arms until Elly pressed her body against mine. Elly's hands crossed against my back, and she sighed longingly, with her head on my chest. On any other day of my life, I would have stayed there forever, but she just happened to be perfectly proportioned to cause an altogether different kind of aching.

"Ow, ow, ow," I said, pulling away a moment too late. A wave of pain emanated from the bruises on my stomach and breast, and they kept on throbbing even after I broke contact. Elly gave me a concerned look, and I tried to reassure her. "It's nothing, really, you should see the other guy."

Hand on hip and eyebrow raised, Elly said, "I thought you were an alchemist these days, not a boxer?" Then she shrugged and started to look around the shop. For a moment, I was mesmerised by the way she moved—Elly had taken as naturally to femininity as a fish to water. I had always been more like a cat, able to swim, but only begrudgingly. She stopped beside a display of hair growth ointments, topical shaving soaps, and a variety of other herbal remedies of the same sort.

I came along beside her and leant back on a display table opposite the shelves she was looking at. "If you want my honest opinion, none of that works. We keep the real magic upstairs." It was only when I saw the look on Elly's face that I realised how stupid that sounded.

"So," she said, expectantly, after the blush had faded from my cheeks.

I narrowed my eyes, confused. "So…?"

Elly deflated in an instant, rolling her eyes and sagging her shoulders. "You've forgotten, haven't you? Of course you have, you're hardly dressed for a nice lunch," she said, and if that didn't sting enough, she added, "I don't know why I expected any different."

Of all the people in the world, Elly probably understood better than anyone how my mind worked. She'd had a front-row seat for most of our childhood of my inattentive dazes, bursts of hyper vigilant focus, and desperate need to seek out new information. When we were in Cambridge together, she was one of the few people who could pull me out of my month-long funks and refusal to engage with my studies. All that experience gave her the precise knowledge of where to plunge a knife into my heart—and truth be told, I probably deserved it after everything I put her through.

My heart caught in my throat, which made it all the more difficult to choke down the anguish and tears. "I didn't forget. I just got a little side-tracked." Elly turned away from me, arms folded across her chest. "Please, look, it's all dreadfully complicated—I was working on a case with Jennifer, and—" my voice trailed off, and the echo in my mind returned. *I will meet you back at the shop, I promise.*

Elly touched my shoulder and made me jump—I didn't notice her closing the gap between us. "Is everything all right?"

"I—I don't know," I mumbled. My mind had become a distorted mess again, like someone had upended the contents of a hundred filing cabinets inside my head. "There's nothing I want more than to go have lunch with you, but I can't leave until Jennifer gets back." The words I was saying didn't make any sense, but I believed them all the same. "She promised that she would meet me back here."

I will meet you back at the shop, I promise.

Eloise regarded me with a medic's trained eye, looking for any obvious signs behind my distress. "Where is she, Charlotte? Did she say where she was going or when she'd be here?"

I wracked my brain, a faint aura crept into my vision,

accompanied by a dull ache. "I don't remember. That's weird, right? We were at a warehouse, I got shot—"

"You got shot!?" Elly exclaimed.

I waved her away from me. "It's nothing, magic shield—that doesn't make sense, I know—but Jennifer…" *I will meet you back at the shop, I promise.*

There was an insistent knocking at the door—I looked up, desperate to see that it was Jen—but it was the broad, uniformed form of Inspector Baker that I saw through the pane of glass. I waved him in—then, realising I'd locked the door again, opened it for him.

Baker removed his top hat and fussed with his hair. "Miss Price," he started, in an urgent tone, before he spotted Elly, "my apologies, I didn't expect you to have company." It was then that he looked me up and down, realising the state I was in, and said, "Pardon me, Charlotte, but you look like you've been kicked by a horse."

"It's a long story," I said, biting back a grimace of pain. "To what do we owe the pleasure?"

"There's been another fire, ma'am. I was hoping that you and Ms Morton might take a look," Baker explained. He was uneasy—which was jarring for a man of his size—and kept fidgeting with the rim of his top hat.

"Another fire? Where?" I asked. A second blaze like the one caused by Timothy Waters, so soon after the first, would have been downright bizarre. I tried to think of what Jennifer would say—*I will meet you back at the shop, I promise.*

Baker cleared his throat—had my mind drifted for so long? "On the Dogs, ma'am. A warehouse, by the looks of things." My heart stopped—it couldn't be. "There's another body, too." If it was possible for a heart to stop twice, mine would have done just that.

The migraine aura burned through my vision with a vengeance. An agonising surge of pain hit me like an ice pick being driven through my skull. Baker was wrong. He had to be. It can't have been there. Like so many alchemists before me trying to square the circle, I couldn't make sense of what the inspector was telling me. Jennifer promised she would meet me back at the shop, and Jennifer was last at the warehouse—so that warehouse couldn't be the one Bake was talking about. Because if it was… and if the body… *I will meet you back at the shop, I promise.*

The world span around me. Baker and Elly both reached out to help steady me on my feet, but I pulled away reflexively, as though they were both too hot to touch. In between bouts of confusion and agony—still addled by the cocktail of alchemical side effects my brain was swimming in—I finally managed to struggle out the question on the tip of my tongue. "The fire. Stewart Street?"

"How did you…?" Baker had started to say, before I hit the floor—hard.

Elly's voice came from a million miles away. "Charlotte, you alright love?"

What happened that night? It was like trying to see through broken glass. All the pieces were there, but too jumbled to make sense. Jennifer asked me to leave—why did she ask me to leave?—why did I bloody listen to her? A shard of memory was buried deep in my mind, something that Jennifer needed me to take with me—what was it? She was weeping when I left. I battled against the pain and the mind fog, trying to find the fragment that had got lost.

I will meet you back at the shop, I promise.
I will meet you back at the shop, I promise.
I will meet you back at the shop, I promise.

Chapter 14

The dread consumed me. I collapsed to the ground and my head felt as though it was being cleaved in half. The echoes of Jennifer's voice embedded deep into my mind by her suggestion potion, screamed inside my thoughts in defiance of the words the Inspector had spoken. As the truth, the real truth, dawned upon me, I was sure my heart had been torn from my chest. Deep in the pit of my own mind the unconscious fears and anxieties I buried so easily manifested twisted visions of what Jennifer's mangled corpse might look like. All the pain and frustration of the past two days clawed their way back to me, and it felt all too easy to stay in that dark, depressing place in my mind.

But I knew better than to underestimate Jennifer Morton. Don't ask me how, but I knew she wasn't dead. Jen would never be so gauche as to go out in a warehouse fire in the arse end of London. She was alive, I had to believe that—I willed myself to believe it—because if I didn't…

The grip that Jennifer's promise had on my mind was finally broken, and her voice no longer intruded its way into my thoughts. It was then, finally, that recalled the sharp scratch on my wrist, and the perfume smell that followed. Just as Bryce had believed Jennifer enough that his own mind manifested pain when he lied, I'd driven myself almost mad believing that she'd come back to the shop.

The weight of what she'd done took much longer to hit me than the few lucid seconds I had on the floor, but it did give me one more reason to find her alive—so I could slap her in the face.

Elly was sitting beside me on the floor, cross-legged under a pile of fabrics. Peeking out from my arms and tucked knees, I said, "The floor's terribly dirty. You'll ruin your dress."

"I'd say the same about your trousers, but they don't look

to be in the best condition." She had a cute half-smile on her face, and her hair dangled down over her shoulders as she cocked her head at me. "How was the pit?"

"Shit. As always." I kicked my legs out straight and ran my hands through my hair. My breath was short, but at the very least my head had started to clear. The floor was not comfortable, but as I was already there I leaned back and held myself up on my palms. "Right, did I introduce you two yet?"

Baker and Elly shook their heads. His posture indicated he was quite uncomfortable by my choice to stay seated, and she was stifling a giggle. They seemed almost like polar opposites—big, stocky, and graceless Baker, and small, lithe, and plush Elly. And me, of course, smack bang in the middle.

"Silly me. Inspector Anthony Baker, Metropolitan Police, Stepney Branch. Dr Eloise Chynoweth, Bachelors from Cambridge, childhood friend."

"Pleasure, sorry, no you," they both said at the same time.

"Great, pleasantries done. Inspector, I apologise for my moment of discomposure."

"It's quite all right. Charlotte, has something happened to Jen?" Her very name was a knife to my heart. I had to look away to blink away the tears I didn't want Elly to see.

"We," the words stumbled from my mouth, "We were there, Inspector, Stewart Street."

Baker stepped back, aghast at my statement. His eyes narrowed, his mouth gawped and pursed, his head tilted, and the inner corners of his brows turned upwards. Each expression a question, the answers all the same.

I lamented the thought of standing—no one ever tells you that those sore knees your nan has first greet you in your twenties—but it was time to take things more seriously. Elly held out a hand and yelped as I pulled her up with a little more force than she was expecting for a dainty ascent to her feet. I straightened myself out as much as I could, and turned to Baker. "Jennifer and I learned that the Black Ember we found with Waters was being bought in through a warehouse on the Dogs, an operation run by a man named Hawkins."

"Hawkins? We haven't seen hide nor hair of him for six months at least," Baker said, concerned. "Blast her, always running into danger without a backup plan."

"You can say that again. There was trouble, a lot of trouble," I said. I began to pace, an unseen force driving my body into motion to keep my mind steady. "Suffice it to say Jennifer told me to leave, and she didn't come back."

"You can fill me in on the way there, then. There's a cab outside, we best not keep it waiting any longer," Baker said. I nodded, then turned to Elly. The inspector cleared his throat, "I'll give you two a moment," he said to me, before bowing his head to Elly with an accompanying "Ma'am." With a swish of his swallowtail coat, he exited out the front door.

"So," Elly said.

"So," I repeated.

"I'm sorry, about what I said earlier, it was unnecessarily harsh of me." She put a gentle hand on my elbow and gave me a warm, sympathetic smile. I don't know what I'd done to deserve her, but she always seemed to know when I needed a rock to steady my heart. Despite all the differences, Elly was still… Elly, and that gave me hope.

"I promise I'll explain everything, but every minute Jen's missing—" I said, not really knowing what might happen.

"I know. I'll see you soon," she said, and on a day when I thought nothing could ever surprise me again, she kissed me on the cheek. It ended almost as soon as it began, but my skin buzzed as she walked away for a moment that stretched out into eternity. I held my fingers to my face. What I would have done for more than just a kiss, for that sensation to last forever—like a lingering essence of sorts, which happened to be exactly what I needed to find Jennifer.

Baker practically jumped out of his skin when I leaned out the door, yelling that I needed five more minutes, and I was back inside before he could object. It just so happened that I had the perfect formula for investigating the warehouse. Just as my skin longed to hold on to any trace of Elly's touch, so too does the Mundane world grasp at the lingering traces of

Arcane forces. If more magic was at play on Stewart Street, as it was in Stepney, then it would have left some form of imprint.

Those imprints would be all but imperceptible without the right tool, and two or three months earlier I'd developed one of those tools. Jennifer had figured this would be possible for some time and assigned the problem to me as a research project—it was pure bliss, I spent four weeks in the lab, and didn't have to serve a single customer—and I'd proven her theory quite successfully. All it would take was some powdered silver, rock salt, half a cup of aqua regia, the optical nerve of a tawny owl, and some energy.

Alchemy, essentially, is all about symbolic transmutation. You take the properties of one thing, mix it with some reactive materials, and transform it into something else. Of course, it's never quite that simple, and most novice alchemists either blow themselves up in their first attempt or spend at least six months perfecting a recipe for the Purest Green.

I was pressed for time, so I wouldn't be able to do the kind of slow, five stages of transformation bullshit that proponents of more classical alchemy advocated for in every formula. No, this recipe was quick, dirty, and hard to fuck up. The salt is an alchemical base—along with Mercury and Sulphur, it is the core of all alchemical formulae—it represents the mortal body. Silver is magically inert in its pure form, which makes it the ideal carrier for any Arcane energies you wish to impart. Aqua Regia is an acid that dissolves noble metals— now, if you know anything about chemistry, you probably know that dissolving silver in a poorly ventilated lab is a bad idea. Luckily, Alchemy isn't—quite—chemistry, if things go right, the normal rules don't apply.

Finally, was the optical nerve. This is where the transmutation part of the whole formula comes in. All magic relies in some part on symbology—the cultural meanings of symbols, reagents, and language all shape the Arcane. As mages use symbols and language to manipulate the Arcane with their minds, Alchemy does the same through physical transformation of symbolically resonant substances. The very essence of the ingredients woven into the Arcane by millennia of human understanding—such as an owl's ability to see beyond human perception—becomes a tangible, magical effect.

I bashed together the salt, silver and dried nerve fibres with a pestle and mortar, before pouring the powder into a boiling flask that I'd filled with Aqua Regia. The mixture bubbled slowly until I put it over a spirit burner to speed up the reaction. This is where things got difficult. If I didn't correctly channel and manifest the Arcane energies, regular old chemistry would take over and I'd die from inhaling poisonous nitric gases. But if I put in too much energy I could die from the ensuing explosion. If I had time, I would have used the worktable in the lab, which is specifically designed for slowly collecting and attuning magic, but without that luxury I'd have to resort to cruder methods.

As the mixture started to bubble more furiously, I fished out a flawed, brittle blue gem about the size of a grape from a jar on a nearby shelf. I weighed it in my hand, figured it was just right, then held it above the flask and crushed it. There was an instant coldness in my hand, like I'd stuck it under the ice on the Thames in winter. Although I couldn't see it, the energy stored in the crystal was collecting in the boiling flask. To my satisfaction and relief, the mixture stopped bubbling away and turned a kind of yellow ochre in colour. I extinguished the burner and transferred the newly made potion into a small vial fitted with a pipette in the stopper.

I held the mixture up to the light from the window, and said quietly to myself, "I'm coming Jen, and I've got my eyes open."

Chapter 15

Whatever lingering Alchemical effects I'd experienced throughout the morning had finally faded. As the picture of what had happened resolved in my mind, so too did the ramifications. I'd killed people—and despite all of Jennifer's moralising about self-defence, it didn't feel right. I kept to the facts as I filled Baker in on the key details of the night—after he'd admonished me for running off to the lab, "just like Jennifer would"—and I didn't linger on my emotional response. All things considered; his reaction was much more subdued than I expected. Baker was a good listener, patient and attentive. I could see why Jennifer liked him. He seemed almost used to the idea of Jennifer running off on some vigilante spree, I suppose because they usually deliver results.

When the cab pulled up to the north end of the street, the last wisps of smoke were rising above the rooftops. I stood in stony silence at the end of the muddy road—at the same time, flashes from the night before were juxtaposed. Incessant echoes of the conversation I had with Jennifer invaded my mind, interposed with the din of the surrounding industry. I looked for the tracks that lead to the warehouse, but they'd been covered by the traffic of the morning.

A trot, the driver was in a rush.

The brick and sheet metal construction of the warehouse meant that it escaped the blaze mostly intact. Black scorch marks burned through from the gaps in the door frames and between the joins of the steel sheets. The smell of ash and scorched metal overpowered the stench of the river, but it was different enough from the putrid smell of death that lingered at the tenement in Stepney.

Perfect time for us to sneak in unnoticed.

Something was off about the whole situation. Timothy

Waters didn't burn down his place of slumber. Could this have been the same kind of magic? Was it even magic at all? Baker was keeping his distance from me but watched intently, just like before. If I knew the way Jennifer worked, and I do, she'd told him one too many times not to interfere with her investigations.

There wasn't much more I could have learned from the outside of the warehouse, but I was apprehensive about going inside. Somewhere in the back of my mind, the dark pit of my imagination was conjuring new, horrific ways for me to find my missing mentor.

Just tell me what you need me to do.

The rush I felt when I headed to the lab was beginning to fade, and I was sinking into an inattentive and almost listless mood. Despite the complete normalcy of such a mood, I couldn't help but remember the near supernatural focus of the night before and lament the closing fog in my mind. The ingredients of Jennifer's stimulant started to rattle off in my mind when I felt a hand on my shoulder.

"No time for daydreaming, Ms Charlotte. You ready to go in?" the Inspector asked me, making me realise I'd been staring at the scorch marks around the warehouse entrance. I nodded, and with a wave of his hand, a pair of uniformed officers pulled open the damaged doors.

Inside was carnage. My first instinct was that someone had set off a bomb. The racks and shelves that were stacked with imported goods the previous night had been violently thrown into the walls. Most of the wooden floorboards had caught ablaze, some burning away completely, revealing the concrete foundation below them. Barrels, crates, and sacks had all been blasted apart by the force of the blast, and the remnants of their contents that didn't burn were still scattered among the corners of the building.

The blast was so powerful that it even blew a hole in the roof that I hadn't noticed from the outside. The roof timbers were cracked and warped from the heat, and the sheet steel looked like it had been torn apart.

At the epicentre of the destruction was a lone, blackened

figure. Like Timothy Waters, the body had seemingly burned from the inside out, but that was where the similarities ended. I could tell from the doorway that the body was that of a woman of middling height and frame. She was on her knees, with her legs in an open posture and her back was arched to an almost inhuman degree. As I got closer, I could make out her face, and the expression was more haunting than the painful screams of Timothy Waters. The blackened, charred skin reached up to her mid neck, leaving most of her face red, blistered and burned. Her mouth and eyes were open, not with pain, but with rage. With her arms outstretched, it was like she was letting out some eternal battle cry, or the roar of a wild animal.

I had but one comfort, looking upon the woman's ruined corpse: It wasn't Jennifer.

I may have misjudged how ready you were for all this.

I took out the notebook that I had almost forgotten even existed and started to scribble down my observations. One thing was clear to me as soon as I started to put my thoughts onto the paper. Unlike the fire in Stepney, this had been no accident. Timothy Waters had fought to internalise his magic—the excess energy from his Black Ember high that Bryce had explained—so as to protect others from harm. Whoever this woman was, she'd let it go. Perhaps she thought she could control it—taper down or redirect the energy—or maybe she was an unwilling pawn?

What I couldn't tell from the scene as I looked around, is where Jennifer had gone. If she'd escaped before the blaze, then why didn't she return to the Solution? If she'd died in the fire, where was her body? In fact, none of the bodies of the sailors and dock workers we had fought with were anywhere to be seen. Someone had removed them.

I was about to head over to Baker and explain to him my findings, when I suddenly remembered the potion that I'd so hastily run off to make. I took the little vial out from my pocket. The liquid inside was still the same shade of yellow, but it had developed a little sediment that needed a good shake to redissolve. The mixture had a fairly neutral scent when I opened it up, and it flowed into the small dropper with ease.

With my head held back, I opened one eye as much as I could, and braced myself while holding the dropped above it. I squeeze the little bulb on the dropped slowly and watched as the slightly out of focus droplet formed above my pupil. The potion stung like a bitch when it hit me my eye, and I could feel it creeping through my sinuses and into my bloodstream. It was like sniffing a strong acidic solution, bathing my eyes in alcohol, and blaring a foghorn in my ears all at once. I swore like a sailor as I dropped the bottle in the ground and grabbed my head, squeezing my eyes shut as tight as I could.

The burning sensation slowly faded, and my senses came back to me—and boy, did they come back. I could hear the officers at the end of the street talking, and the cawing of birds across the river. The smell of ash and blood filled my nose, along with the strong smell of the sea blown in across the water. Despite the barrage of information, I wasn't over-whelmed. I could pick out and focus on each individual sensation, isolating myself from the rest.

The biggest change, however, was in my eyesight. Every detail became more defined, down to the minutest of cracks and specks. I looked at my hand and could see the individual hair follicles in my skin as if under a microscope. Around the room, what had been a deathly stillness of ash and wreckage seemed to come to life. Tiny embers still smouldered in the corners of the room, sending up little wisps of ash. There was a subtle asymmetry in the way the blast had thrown things around and there were traces of movement, now visible in the tiny disturbances of ash and dust around the floor.

The most dramatic effect of my improved eyesight became apparent as I focussed on different parts of the room. Trails and motes of soft light, of varying colours, filled the room. The remnant energies and auras of the Arcane, still lingering in the Mundane world, filled the warehouse like nothing I'd seen before. Like a thousand dancing fireflies, drifting in and out of the light, each one with a story of a spell or enchantment.

The trouble, of course, was now I didn't know what to

start with. I had an entirely new source of information, but hell, if I knew how to interpret it properly, or even write it down in a way I could understand later. In all my tests and experiments with this particular formula, I'd never used it somewhere with so much Arcane residue.

My mind was filling up with malformed and unfinished thoughts, things like "Maybe I should go look at—" "I wonder if the… is still there—" "What happened to—" and "Why can't I just…." Frustrated with my inner monologue, I started to voice my thoughts to try to force something concrete to form.

"Right, let's start from the beginning," I said, quietly so Baker wouldn't hear. "We came in here," the side room and the doorway that lead to it were blocked off by a fallen rack of shelves. That was where Jennifer had put the first of the guards to sleep with the injector on her wrist. I could just about see into the room, and as I expected, there was nobody present.

"The fighting started over here." The area we first took cover was close to the epicentre of the explosion, and as such nothing much was left there. Looking over that spot is when I noticed a few small motes of light following me, residues of the shield potion, I realised, when the motes gathered around the parts of my body that I'd taken bullets.

"Jen came from up there," I muttered as I inspected the roof timbers. It took a moment to find it, but when I found the right spot, there was a snaking trail of wispy light descending from the ceiling and then darting about the room. The residue from Jennifer's speed potion took on a light blue colour, and it seemed to vibrate in the air. Following the trail of light was just what I needed, and it let me piece together Jennifer's movements.

"Charlotte don't take another step. There's something alive in there."

The loading dock was far enough from the explosion that it had escaped mostly unaffected. There was blood here, some of the patches followed Jen's trail of lights, others where the body of the ship Captain had been, and more where I suspected the wyvern had finally died. It was getting hard to trace the sequence of events now. After I'd left it was evident that Jennifer and the mysterious mage had fought intensely. Arcane residue darted across my vision like a meteor shower all around me, and I had no hope of discerning what spells might had been cast,

Jennifer's trail ended abruptly, still among the many dancing lights on the loading dock. Had she been killed? There was no more blood, but magic could kill without a wound. No, I realised, she hadn't been killed. I'd been focussing so much on the auras that I'd neglected to look at the evidence of movement left about the loading platform. This was even more difficult to decipher than the lights, so many footprints and drag marks laid over each other.

Slowly, I managed to tease apart some more of Jen's movements. She'd kept going after the potion's effects had worn off. I couldn't work out if she'd won the fight, but I did think she'd got away. But where?

I was looking out across the Thames from the loading dock, and I could see the opposite bank, lined with yet more warehouses and jetties. There was something missing, something big that I just couldn't put my finger on. Jennifer must have had a way out.

"You can help Charlotte, by grabbing that manifest and leaving."
The manifest. Of course! I'd been so focussed on the warehouse that I'd failed to notice that the bloody ship was gone. I took the crumpled piece of paper in my pocket, which I should note I failed to show the Inspector.

"Let's have a look at this," I said, talking out loud again. "'Report and Manifest of the cargo laden from Shanghai', bloody hell. Blah blah 'aboard the vessel Hyacinth', blah blah 'Captain Papadopoulos' blah blah 'bound for London'." Holy shit, I thought, Jennifer was right about this being the evidence we needed, and I was a fool for not actually reading it.

Reading the list of cargo gave me a suspicion. I remembered going over the various crates and things the night before, and the manifest confirmed the large quantity of Naphtha that had been bought in. Naphtha was a liquid fuel, often confused with white spirits and such, and it was the last piece of the puzzle I needed to work out what had happened, at least to some degree.

Inspector Baker was waiting by the entrance to the warehouse and greeted me with a knowing smile. "If I didn't know any better, I'd have said it was Jennifer working that scene. Are you sure she never took you out on a case before?"

I shook my head. "No, she'd taught me some things over time, but it's much the same as researching a formula," I said, not entirely confident in the statement.

"As you say, ma'am. Now, what's the verdict?" he asked.

"Arson, that I'm sure of. Unlike our previous victim, this fire was deliberate." Baker and I walked together towards the corpse at the centre of it all. "Our source from last night told us that Black Ember, the drug that does… this," I said, gesturing at the women, "is a kind of magical substance that enhances a mage's abilities. Essentially letting them cast bigger spells."

"I see, but why would this poor soul do that to 'erself? Why here?" he tugged at his beard, and I noticed he was very obviously avoiding looking at the woman. She was dead, I thought, naked or not.

"A cover up, I think, or some kind of distraction? Look at this," I said, handing the manifest over to the Inspector. "I found this last night on the body of that ship's captain, only there's no ship here anymore, and none of the cargo we saw unloaded is here."

"This is quite the list of imports, but how do you know it's not here?"

"Well, let's assume the explosion and fire were solely the work of our mage friend here. If the cargo had been left, the Naphtha would have been caught in the explosion. There was enough of the stuff on that ship to level this building, and the ones next to it. No, the cargo was removed, along with the bodies of the sailors, Captain and dock workers we fought."

"And Jennifer?" he asked, pensively.

"As far as I can tell, she wasn't here when the place exploded. My gut tells me she stowed away on the ship, but god knows what happened after that to stop her coming home." I expected Baker to ask another question, but he was silent and thoughtful, so I just kept going. "Right, so there's a fight, it's clear that whatever operation here isn't going to stay secret anymore, and those running it can't risk your lot coming about, finding a bunch of bodies, and confiscating enough opium to knock out a herd of elephants."

Baker was nodding along, "So they reload the cargo to drop it off somewhere else, move the bodies, and send this young lady to…?"

"Clean up. Maybe it went wrong, she lost control of the spell and the Black Ember, or this was the intended effect."

"This is getting more and more complicated by the minute. I'm still not sure why they'd use a mage," he said.

"Neither. They had the fuel; they could have set the fire themselves. They wanted us to find this body." I got down on my knees in front of the woman's burned remains, trying to imagine what would lead someone to do this. I looked into her eyes, or what was left of them. "Who were you?" I asked quietly, and then something caught my eye.

I'd been ignoring the woman since I applied the eye drops, knowing all too well that the Arcane residue from the spell she cast would have drowned out everything else if I focussed on it. But, as I let myself see it, my vision filling with angry red orbs of agitated light, another set of lights resolved along with them. They were dim, taking on a violet shade, and sat perfectly still on the woman's neck. No, I realised, not on her neck, in the skin. There was just enough uncharred skin that I could just about make out the source: a tattoo.

Chapter 16

"Rosehouse? You mentioned him earlier. Why do I know that name?" Baker asked me. We'd stepped outside the warehouse, and I'd explained about Bryce's tattoos.

"His father is a Viscount, Kidderminster or something. He was involved in a drug scandal sometime last year."

"Right, must be that. You think he'll have more to say?" Smog rolled in over the river from the manufactories on the south bank, and I was too preoccupied with watching the sky to respond to the Inspector's question. "Miss Charlotte?"

"What? Sorry, right, Bryce. I don't know, but he's the only person I know with those tattoos. I just have to find him." I didn't look at Baker as I spoke. Something had been gnawing at me in my subconscious and I was only starting to notice the rawness of my mood.

"You don't have to do that; my boys will find him."

"No," I said, much too fast and much too forcefully. "Sorry. It's fine, I can do this. Jen—" the rawness intensified, "Jen will have the information I need." I wouldn't need the information if Jennifer had told me anything before running off the other night. I wouldn't need to be tracking her down if she'd taken a moment to think about what she was doing. If she hadn't…

There was a red welt on my wrist where Jennifer had dosed me with the suggestion potion, which had started to itch. With that came a rush of furious grief as my heart sank into the bubbling pit of my stomach. I couldn't understand how she could do something like that to me—all that pain, confusion, and anger. Even if it might have saved my life, even if she thought she had no other choice. Despite my best efforts to hold myself together, the tears broke free, I buckled at the waist, and I cried.

"Miss Charlotte?" Baker said, uncomfortable with my

public display of emotion. He put out a hand, but obviously had no idea how to console someone.

"She drugged me," I said between sobs. "Why would she do that?"

"I… don't know, miss. Jennifer always had her ways; I didn't always approve." He finally decided what to do with his hand and put it on my shoulder. "This isn't the first time she's done something stupid and disappeared, and I doubt it will be the last."

Baker had a strong, stoic face, but it wasn't enough to hide the pain in his sable eyes. I remembered the restrained joy he'd shown days ago. "How do you do it?" I asked, straining to keep my words steady. "How do you cope with all the rage and pain, and still feel this crushing dread that you'll never see her again?"

For the first time, I saw the man behind Inspector Baker—the one he'd kept hidden under his jovial smile. A man who carried a wound in his heart that hadn't fully healed. "Aye, that there is the crux of it, Charlotte." Just Charlotte, that time—no Miss Charlotte or Miss Price. "I couldn't cope with it. That is why Jennifer and I are—what we are." Baker was no longer talking to me as an inspector of London's Metropolitan Police, the blue of his swallowtail coat symbolic of his grief.

The moment hung in the air as Baker searched the world around us for the words he needed to say. When he finally spoke, it wasn't out of sadness. "When you love Jennifer, it's like loving a thunderstorm. She comes crashing into your life, and you can't help but be in absolute awe of everything she is. You marvel at every move she makes, every deduction you couldn't hope to make—she's like a bolt of lightning peeling away the darkness of the night. Then one day, the lightning strikes you—right in the heart—and you tell yourself, 'Oh, what are the odds of lightning striking twice in the same place?' Have you ever looked up at St Paul's during a thunderstorm? Turns out, the more lightning strikes the same place, the more likely it is that it'll strike there again. Eventually you realise that the safest thing to do for yourself and the lightning rod in your heart is to seek cover and admire the storm from afar."

There wasn't anything I could say that would do Baker any justice. I imagined all the times Jen had come crashing into my life, and how awed I'd always been. When the silence had dragged on a little too long, I finally spoke again. "Do you think we can find her, Anthony?"

Baker straightened up at the sound of his name, as though it was a trigger that set in motion his training as an officer. "Look, all that matters right now is you're here and safe. Now, if you are anywhere near as brilliant as Jen has said you are, then I have not a single doubt that we can find her."

Brilliant. The word hit dully against my ears. I wasn't brilliant, not alone, not without her. Where would I be if not for her? If I was brilliant, it was because I reflected a little bit of her shine back into the world—what was I if she was gone? What was a storm without the thunder and lightning? Just rain and wind and cloud.

The inspector lifted up my chin with a big, meaty finger, his jovial manner back in place. "We can do this. You get yourself home and rest before you do anything else, you hear me? My boys and I will see if we can find the ship that was here, it must have docked somewhere. The Hyacinth you said. Out of Shanghai?"

I nodded and left Baker to wrap up the scene with his officers. My brain was totally shot, I'd needed every shred of willpower to keep my eyes on the task at hand, and now I needed to switch off. I walked from Stewart Street up to Poplar in the hopes of finding a Hansom. The grey clouds that were hanging above the city were starting to darken, and I hadn't bought an umbrella.

Luck was on my side, and the first drops of rain started to patter on the roof of the two-wheeler cab just after I got in. I let go of the stress I'd been holding in once we set off, and just watched the buildings and streets go by. It was like sitting three feet back in my mind, aware of the world as it turned around me, but not processing anything.

I should have gone home, actually home I mean, and not to the Solution. But, when the cab finally rolled to a halt and I came out of my daze, that's where I found myself. I didn't have the energy to correct my mistake, so I simply paid the cabbie and stepped up to the empty shop. Maybe all this running around would have been for nought, and Jennifer would be there, drinking a cup of tea and wondering where I'd been all day. I could hope, I suppose.

The side effects from the eye drops were beginning to settle in, blocking my sinuses like a bad cold. It would last a few hours, at most, a small mercy for my arrogance in rushing the transmutation. What I would have given for night cap, decent blankets, and someone to warm them with me.

Baker's voice rattled around in my head, telling me to rest, but every inch of the shop reminded me of Jen and that she wasn't there. I went to the study and scoured the bookshelves for case files and dossiers. There should be something about Bryce that I can use, some knowledge Jennifer had that helped her find the mage. There were hundreds of notebooks and folders crammed full of writings, newspaper clippings and pages torn from who knows where. I must have spent an hour or more pulling things from the shelves, only to be disappointed with their contents. Even after finding the relevant section on the shelves, the fog in my mind was so thick that I couldn't make heads or tails of the organisation.

What would I even do if I found him? I doubted he'd be willing to get a drink again. Jen would have known what to do.

I was achingly hungry by the time my mind gave up on the search and allowed other thoughts to come forward. I found some food in the kitchen downstairs, and a half-full bottle of gin that I polished off as I ate.

When I finally fell asleep, my thoughts were of the young woman in the warehouse—why burn down the warehouse? Making it seem like the evidence had been destroyed was the obvious reason, but there were plenty of ways to do that without leaving a corpse behind. Who was she working for, and why did she sacrifice herself for them?

October 11th, 1834

Home

Chapter 17

MAGIC to blame for DOGS FIRE – The London Chronicle
Explosion of ARCANE Origin – The Examiner
Radical Mage Destroys
Warehouse. ARE WE SAFE? – The Sun

"How did they even find out?" I asked Elly, who had come around early the next morning with a stack of the morning's papers. I'd almost swooned when she arrived wearing a pale blue day dress—with a deep and broad neckline that showed off the gentle slope of her shoulders—but I managed to get a hold of myself before she noticed. I, of course, looked as much of a mess as I had the day before—though thankfully the bruises were healing unnaturally quickly—but Elly didn't seem to mind.

We sat around the small kitchen table in the back of the shop with a steaming pot of tea that Elly poured into some questionably clean cups. She shrugged at my question, and said, "My bet, someone in the Met told them. A constable looking for a quick penny, maybe. Sugar?"

"Yes, please." I skimmed through the article in The Sun, which was certainly the most sensationalist of the lot. "Listen to this, 'What luck it was, that no one else was present during this *blatant act of violence*. How can our city stand by when the so-called London University, if it can even be called such an institution, is educating the branded in refined use of their devilish powers? When one individual, a vagrant woman of no standing this paper understands, can wield such strength as to warp solid steel? When will our leaders stand up to this *insidious, growing menace?*', emphasis is my own." I dropped the paper on the table in a gesture of disbelief and took a sip of the piping hot tea. "Absolutely absurd."

"Maybe you should put out a statement—my Da' has a

friend at The Times he could reach out to. Set the record straight," Elly suggested. She'd also bought some iced buns with the papers and daintily pulled one apart with her fingertips.

I took one of the buns and stuffed half of it in my mouth, hardly stopping to chew before speaking. "To say what? That there's a magical drug on the streets, which could make any mage who takes it violently explode. But it's not all bad, some of them won't explode, they'll just die horrifically as they try to stop an endless stream of magic pouring forth from the Arcane." My tone was the peak of British sarcasm.

"A fair point. Then what are you going to do?" she asked. Her little nibbles of food were quite adorable and matched by equally adorable sips of tea. She must have caught me smiling, because she narrowed her eyes at me suddenly over the rim of her teacup.

"Keep my eyes open, look for the truth." Jennifer's words had been echoing in my mind all morning. It felt good to speak to them aloud. "The papers, the Black Ember, the warehouse. There's something connecting them together, and I need to find it. Hopefully find Jennifer along the way."

I was feeling quite jittery that morning, with an inexorable need to keep my hands busy. The edge of the teacup had a satisfying little chip along the rim, which I repeatedly ran my fingers across. Of course, once I took a sip of the tea and put it down in a different place, my hands unconsciously found the next thing. The newspaper pages provided a pleasurably audible ffffflip if I ran my fingers through them, but that seemed to bother Elly after a few times.

I settled on twirling a pencil between my fingers, a trick I'd got quite competent at, and with my hands occupied, my mind started to work. If I wanted to find Jennifer, then the first thing I needed to do was find Bryce. Any doubt that he'd been hiding more of what he knew vanished the moment I found the tattoo at the warehouse—mages were rare enough, and mages with Arcane tattoo ink? I certainly couldn't trust him, however, and I'd need to take precautions if things went sideways. Jen's shielding potion stopped bullets and blades; might it stop a fireball?

"Charlotte, you're doodling on the Chronicle," Elly said to get my attention. The sketch was of a stick person defiantly deflecting a fire ball with their hand. I snickered and went to reach for a teacup that was no longer there; only then did I finally realise how deep in thought I'd been. The pastries were all gone, and Elly had already cleared the table of everything but the neatly stacked newspapers. "Are you going to drop in on your father today?" she asked.

Father… "Fuck!" I exclaimed.

"What, what's the matter?" Elly asked, but I was already scrambling toward the stairs.

"Fuck, fuck, fuck." I reached the door to the lab just as Elly got to the top of the stairs. "Forgot the fucking—how could I be so stupid!?"

"Charlotte, you're not making any sense." She grabbed my shoulder, and my brain ricocheted to a halt. "Take a breath. What's going on?"

I did what she said and got to my senses. "Father. He has not been well, he never really recovered from the pneumonia. He needs a special decoction to keep him going. I was supposed to make it the other day, but all this shit happened and…" I grumbled and punched the door frame. "What am I supposed to do? Jen could be in all sorts of trouble, but father he… he hasn't missed a day without his medicine in over a year—I don't know what could happen. He better not be working."

"Look, I can tell you're worried, but nothing will get done about it if you stand there complaining," she said patronisingly. "What needs to be done? Let me help you."

I shook my head. "Elly. No, I need to—"

"No, you don't."

"You don't know what I was going to say."

She leaned back and put a hand on her hip. "No? 'I need to do this on my own.' That cover it?" Was I really that predictable?

"Fine, maybe you do know. But I still can't ask you to help, I can't put that on you."

"You're not asking me, that's the problem." She cocked an

eyebrow at me. She was right, and I hated it—I balled up my hands and walked down the hallway to look out the window. Elly had always been too smart for my own good, but now she was adorable while doing it—how is that fair? "If you didn't need to tend to you father, what would you be doing?"

I let out an exasperated sigh. "Jen's got dossiers on all her contacts and leads. Bryce will be in one of them, and hopefully I'll be able to work out where he's likely to be. I tried last night, but…"

Elly smiled and said, "Well, I can do that for you."

"What?" I said, flabbergasted.

Entirely, bafflingly serious, she actually said to me that scouring through logbooks and files, "Sounds like fun."

"What part of that sounds fun?!"

"Digging through books, cross-referencing sources, finding patterns in information, reading about the salacious lives of the city's prominent figures."

The look I gave her was one of suspicion and contempt. "You and I have a very different idea about what's fun."

She winked at me. "I know what you find fun, Charlotte. Besides, there's probably a dossier about you in here somewhere. This the office?" She opened the door to Jen's office, and I ran to catch her.

"Don't you dare!" I snapped.

"Finish your dad's medicine quick enough and I won't have time." Fuck, she knew exactly how to ruffle my feathers. Elly took one look at the state of the room and scoffed, "Blimey, how do either of you get anything done?"

"It's organised, just messy. We know where everything is," I said defensively. I then took a look around myself, and corrected, "Where most things are."

I showed Elly where the dossiers were in a playful huff and then straightened myself up and headed to the lab. I was more annoyed with myself than I was with her. I'd been foolish and forgetful. I should have sent word; I should have made Father's medicine when I had the time—if I cared more, I might have remembered. But that wasn't fair on myself; I didn't forget out of malice or spite, I just simply… forgot, almost as if the things and people in my life vanish from reality the moment I lose focus on them.

I started gathering up the ingredients and apparatus I needed. Father's ill-health was what forced my early departure from my studies in Cambridge—that and my failure to meet my professors' exacting standards. In my desperation to treat his symptoms, I stumbled upon my first alchemical creation.

I was working on a simple poultice, an old wives' tale type of thing that I'd read about in a book. Entirely non-magical, you should understand. Two things happened by accident that changed my life. First, a trace amount of mercury was left inside a bottle I was using to mix some ingredients. Second, the flowers I purchased to extract nectar from happened to have been picked from a fairy ring. I had actually given up on the particular recipe and overnight, the small amount of magical energy from the flowers transmuted the mixture.

When I discovered the transmuted decoction the next morning, it was emanating a soft pale light, and I did one of the stupidest things I've done in my entire life. I gave it to my sick father. Now, being what I could only describe as a "complete fucking idiot," I was unaware of the fact that magic always came with a cost. The decoction worked, my father was essentially cured of his ailments, it was a miracle, it even got in the paper. But my hubris was punished—I knew next to nothing about magic back then, and the formula I'd created was raw, chaotic, and flawed. I had no idea that as the magical effects wore off, that there would be side-effects. I watched in horror as my father fell into a coma.

If it hadn't been for that newspaper article, he'd have died. But, to my luck, Jennifer happened to read The Times that day and knew exactly what was going to happen. Jen saved my dear father and saw in me a potential that no one else had before. She showed me how to refine the decoction, and make the side effects more than manageable. She gave my father his life back, and she gave me a new one.

As I worked through the steps to brew Father's medicine in

the lab, which I could practically do blindfolded, my thoughts lingered on just how much I owed Jennifer. Despite all her flaws, she'd saved me—I had to do the same for her.

Chapter 18

Elly was happy to keep working through the dossiers into the early afternoon, so I departed from the otherwise eerily quiet Solution at around one O'clock to head home to see Father.

It was a dim and miserable day, though the humidity and storms had thankfully given way to a more normal on and off drizzle. I tried to find a Hansom Cab to get me to Camden, but it seemed everyone in the city had the same plan that afternoon. It wasn't that far a walk—forty-five minutes normally, but I could do it in thirty at a push—and a stroll past Regent's Park would help clear my head. As much as I'd stressed, Father was responsible enough to take it easy when his medicine was running low—and I could use the time to work out what I'd say to Bryce.

Maybe it was my working-class upbringing talking, but I wasn't all that sure Mr Rosehouse would respond to an appeal to his conscience. He came across to me as quite self-involved—but maybe there was a way to get through to him without Jennifer's extreme methods. He knew the danger Black Ember posed first-hand—could he stand by idly while it spread through the city? Or perhaps I could get some dirt on him—a jilted ex-lover or gambling problem?

I'd always had a curious relationship with the passage of time, and before I knew it I was rounding a corner off Camden High Street not far from the canal, onto the little street I'd grown up on. The houses here were starting to show their age, but not much had changed in all the time my father and I had lived there. The road was cobbled and narrow, and the homes all built in a rather plain style with ruddy brown brickwork. I waved to a few familiar faces as I strolled by—my gaze lingered on the two women around my age, smoking cigarillos outside Mrs Sorrel's brothel. About the only thing that had substantially changed was the home that my father and I lived in, which had a refurbished shop front fitted a year or two back.

Father was a damn good cabinet maker and carpenter—one of the best in the city, if you ask me, but I'm biased a little. In fact, his craftmanship was the reason Elly and I became friends as children from very different parts of society. Mr Chynoweth had come into some considerable wealth mining copper in Cornwall and moved to London to explore new business opportunities. My old man's work preceded him, and the two came into a business agreement to furnish Mr Chynoweth's new home. Years later, they were still as fast of friends as Elly and me, and Mr Chynoweth gladly financed a new shopfront in Camden for my father.

When Father built the new shopfront, I'd complained that it looked exactly like the old one, only it didn't look old anymore. The cream-coloured paint on the woodwork was fresh and glossy, the glass in the windows clean, and the sign no longer worn and faded. "A Wright's Price," father had called it, as fathers tend to do.

As I reached the front door, my gut turned—the shop was open, and I could hear the sounds of a hammer and chisel from the street. He was working. He knew he wasn't supposed to work if his medicine ran out. I'd told him that a hundred times. I pushed open the door and walked through the shop floor, which was filled with a myriad of finely crafted furniture, chairs and tables, doors, and doorframes, armoires, and chests of drawers. The smell of wood shavings filled the air—mahogany, if my nose could be trusted—along with the tantalising scent of fresh bread coming from a baker's loaf on the front desk.

My entrance evidently wasn't as quiet as I thought, because the sounds of a hammer and chisel coming from the workshop were interrupted by a bellowing, "Hello, hello, hello, helloooooo." I wandered out to the yard in the back, and found the old man was hunched over a length of wood, carefully carving away to bring his imagination to life. "Charlotte? Where the bloody 'ell 'ave you been?"

I sat down on a stool across from him. "Working," I

answered, my tone sharp, "which you shouldn't be doing. How many times have I told you it's not safe to work if your decoction wears off?"

"How many times have I told you to let me know if you're coming home or not?" There was an anxious pause before we grinned at each other, and a moment later he'd dropped his tools and scooped me up in a bear hug. "I was worried about you." He was a little gaunt, but as strong as ever.

"Hello, father," I said, burying my face in his shoulder. I wanted to stay there forever, but I knew my frayed emotions would break free if I did. "I'm sorry. I'm so sorry. I know, I didn't write. I should have. It's been hectic these past few days." I swallowed my guilt and sadness away, and stepped back from the embrace.

He smiled and scratched the back of his head. "I'm sorry, too. I know I'm not meant to work today, but I got a commission, a big one. Professor Cummings ordered a new armoire for his office."

"I'm sure the Professor can wait an extra day or two for a wardrobe, Father. Your health is more important," I said. It always felt strange telling him this, as if I was parenting a parent. "Speaking of which, I have your medicine," I presented the bottle of pale liquid to him, which he gladly accepted and put into the pocket of his leather apron.

"Right you are, my girl. I assume then that you spoke with—" he said her old name, and despite only knowing her as Elly for a few days, it was jarring and wrong.

"Elly, Dad," I interjected.

Puzzlement flashed across his face for a moment, and then realisation, "Yes, Elly, damn it. Bad enough with names, then folks change 'em. Don't she look a picture, though, reminded me of your mother a little."

"Ew."

"Not like that, you rascal," he said, before letting out a joyous chuckle. "She's pretty is all. You, on the other hand, look like you've been fighting. Matthew Burton giving you grief again?"

"I haven't spoken to Matthew Burton in ten years, Dad.

Not since I broke his arm. No, this is…" I didn't know how much to tell him. He shouldn't have to worry about me getting into firefights and going toe-to-toe with wizards. "Just a scuffle, an idiot at the pub," I explained. I tried to hide the lie and my feelings, but something in my expression gave me away.

"Charlotte, dear, is everything alright?" he said, and placed a big hand on my shoulder. I looked away from his gaze, trying to hold myself together.

"It's fine, it's nothing really," I answered, in perhaps the most unconvincing way possible.

He took on a sterner tone. "Charlotte Elizabeth Price, I let you get away with a lot of nonsense and peculiar tendencies in your life, but lying ain't one of them. You disappear with no word for days and come back home bruised and battered. I deserve to know what happened and who's responsible."

I cracked like ice on the Thames at the end of winter. Slowly at first, a tear, a sniffle, and then it all came. Guilt, shame, fear, anger, rage, helplessness. Just barely stopping myself from sobbing, I blurted out as much as I could. "Jennifer's gone, missing, kidnapped, dead, I don't know. There was a fire, a mage, a dead man and a fight, and Jen told me to run. She made me run, and when I tried to find her again, she was gone! I don't know what to do. I can barely hold myself together, and the one person who knows how to help me overcome my *peculiar tendencies* is the person who fucking disappeared."

"Charlotte," my father said, trying to comfort me, but all it did was divert my attention into an unpleasant part of my mind.

"And you!" I snapped, pointing at his chest, "You have the damn audacity to lecture me on my behaviour when you can't do the only bloody thing I ask of you and take one day off work so you don't hurt yourself!" I buried my head in my arms on the worktable, unable to look him in the eye.

"Feel better, now? Hmm, does telling me off solve your troubles, girl?" The anger and hurt in his voice was like a knife to the heart. He paused, thinking carefully about what he wanted to say. "I work because it gives me purpose. You worry about my health because you had to watch when I was dying, but I was the one withering away. I was the one who could do nothing but watch you fall into despair and obsession. You gave me a new lease, you and Ms Morton, but that don't mean you get to tell me how to use it."

We didn't talk about when he was sick much, or rather, I never wanted to. I had sunk into despair back then, almost fully given over to the cruel monster in my unconscious, desperate to find a way out. Had I really been so self-absorbed that I never considered how my father felt through it all? Was I such a wretch?

I turned my head out from my arms. "I'm sorry."

"I can't cut oak with sorry, Charlotte."

I was speechless.

"Maybe you're right, and Ms Jennifer is the only person who's ever got you to work. Or maybe she just gave you the tools, and the knowhow to do it yourself."

"I can't, it's too much."

"Bullshit, pull yourself together. Don't think I don't see what's going on. It's hard, and you think it's better to just not try," he barked. I'd heard that a hundred times before and believed it most of my life.

"No," I said.

"No?"

"I want to try. I've always wanted to try. But I don't know where to start, I don't know how to carry on and I don't know how to finish. Every step that should be easy feels like a marathon."

"Listen to me, daughter of mine. That voice inside you, the one that tells you that you can't do these things. It's lying—because you done them all before. You taught yourself enough about science for Mr Chynoweth to pay your way to Cambridge, you got nine-tenths the way to saving my life when everyone else had given up, and you made yourself a fine young woman without a mother here to guide you."

"I didn't do those things on purpose."

"You did it though, and you can do it again."

In a weird, roundabout way, I finally started to see what

he was trying to do. I let the words sit with me, poked them, and worked them with my mind like a baker working some dough. The first thing I had to do, the thing Jennifer was always so good at, was convince myself I could do it. "Thanks, Dad."

Chapter 19

Shortly after our talk, I made my excuses to get back to the shop—and explained I'd be staying there till I found Jen—then got a cab back to Carnaby. I didn't so much have a renewed sense of determination or vigour, but Father's advice would be enough to carry me through the rest of the day, at least. When I arrived back at the Solution, I was greeted by a smug and confident Elly.

"You found him?" I asked, taking off my coat and ditching it on the office couch.

Elly was sat at the desk, sipping a mug of tea. "I found him." The words gave me a rush of excitement and I practically leapt across the room to give Elly a hug.

"Where is he?" I asked excitedly and stepped back to let her breathe again.

Elly sat back down in the chair and leaned back to strike a nonchalant pose. "Jennifer pinned down a few of his haunts. The King's Head, which you two visited, and I figured wouldn't work a second time. A few cafes and parks, but none that he visited with any regularity," she explained.

"I'm waiting for the good news here," I interrupted.

"But there is one place he visits almost every week. A private member's club, very exclusive by the sounds of it, based on Pall Mall," she said. She held out a clipping from a newspaper for me to see. It was a non-descript advertisement for a private member's club.

"Sounds, normal? For a member of the upper class, I mean," I said, taking a closer look at the clipping. "The 1735 Club? Could they be anymore generic?"

"Those gentlemen's clubs are rarely what they present themselves to be. I hated them. You go to chat about ethics or art and half the people there are looking for harlots and the rest are dull morons and politicians."

"Those sound like the same three groups of people," I said, garnering a small chuckle. "This advert isn't making a very good job of things, is it? 'The 1735 Club, no 97 Pall Mall, London. Paintings, quiet conversation, and guaranteed privacy for like-minded practitioners. Mondays, 10 AM–3 PM. For mark of entry, contact Janet Horne.'"

"What could they possibly mean by 'mark of entry'? Some kind of invitation?" Elly asked. "Odd that there aren't any more details."

"It's downright bizarre, honestly. Practitioners is a very strange word to use. Why would anyone want to attend after reading this?" I sat down in the armchair and looked again at the strange advertisement. What exactly was the 1735 Club a club for that would make Bryce Rosehouse attend it so frequently? Was there something in the advert that I'd missed, that Jennifer had missed? The moment of pause gave the rest of my senses a chance to catch up, and something was off about the office. It was tidier. "Hang on, did you clean while I was out?"

"I don't know what you mean." She definitely did. Several shelves had been restacked so that the books all stood up, all the dirty crockery and laundry had been removed, and even Jennifer's desk was looking a little more organised.

"You can't just clean someone else's office, Elly."

She turned a little pink in the cheeks and crossed her arms in the chair, which I noticed was much too big for her. "Well, someone had to. I couldn't focus with all the mess, so I just put the more distracting things away properly."

I lounged back and gave Elly a suspicious glance. "And here I thought you couldn't get any stranger." Her eyes met mine and I softened, feeling a warmth within me that washed away my anxiety. Had she always had that effect on me? My memories of university were such a blur, that I could hardly remember how she used to make me feel.

"What are you thinking about?" she asked me. "I know that look."

"What look? I don't have a look."

"You have many looks. This one is something like 'I bet their lips taste nice,' or 'I have indigestion,' they are quite similar." I imagine I turned a shade of fuchsia at the remark, and Elly burst into a fit of giggles.

I stammered a few half sentences, before my mind finally caught up with my mouth. "I'm not sure I like this new brazen attitude you've developed."

She flicked her hair back and scoffed, "oh? Are you going to tell me how it's uncouth for a lady?"

"Bugger that. Be whatever kind of lady you wish."

"Well good, because I'm going to be brazened, and you're going to love it." She sat back in the chair, looking very sure of herself.

I chuckled softly, then sat forward and remembered the newspaper clipping. I read the strange words again, and a thought popped into my head. "What if it's not a gentleman's club, per se?"

"How do you mean?"

"What if this 1735 Club is just posing as a stuffy private members group and is actually something else entirely? Something only those in the know would recognise." The thought wasn't quite fully formed, but in the back of my mind, a thread was being spun. "What happened in 1735?" I asked, somewhat abruptly.

Almost without hesitation, Elly responded, "The world's first successful appendectomy."

"Right. That's interesting. What happened in 1735 that normal people would care about?"

Elly gasped, "You wound me."

"You're a doctor, you'll manage." A second after I spoke a ball of paper flew across the room at my head. Quick on my reflexes, I caught the projectile out of the air and held it up triumphantly. I lounged back with a smirk on my face, and said, "Perhaps I should have had my suspicions about you, Elly, you always did throw like a girl."

"Now who's being brazen?" Elly rolled her eyes, but she couldn't hide the dimples when she smiled. She huffed a moment later, and said, "Anyway, this Mr Rosehouse is hardly normal people, is he. His father is a Viscount after all."

"You're right there, and he's a mage." I wracked my brain, trying to remember anything that might decipher the meaning behind the advertisement. Had Bryce said anything that could tip me off? "Mark of entry. Janet Horne. 1735."

Don't rat me out to the witchfinder general…

Like a bolt of lightning, it hit me. "Elly, third shelf on the bookcase to your left, there are record books of public executions. Get me 1720 to 1730, will you?" I asked, jumping into motion toward a different bookshelf on the other side of the room.

"Not that I have any idea where you're going, but wouldn't you need 1730 to 1740?"

I found the book I was looking for a vaulted over the back of the couch so I could lay it on the coffee table. "No, no, 1735 is the date of something else, but it's related." Elly held up a book for me to see. "That's the one, bring it here." I opened the book of executions and began scouring the index for the name Janet Horne. "1727, Janet Horne and her daughter were sentenced to death for the practice of witchcraft, the daughter escaped but Janet Horne was put to death," I turned a few more pages in the other book and continued, "which would make her the last person executed as a witch on British soil, because eight years later Parliament passed the Witchcraft Act of 1735, ending the witch hunts in this country."

"It's a private mage's club?" Elly asked.

"An illegal private mage's club. The very same act that ended the death penalty, outlaws the political organisation of mages, among a dozen other restrictions on rights to work, vote, inherit property. It stopped the killings, but it didn't exactly make life easy." I sat back, all too proud of myself for cracking the problem, with an enormous grin on my face. For the first time since Jennifer had disappeared, I felt as if I might have had a shot at finding her. All I would need to do next was infiltrate a secret society of mages. Simple enough.

Elly sat in the chair opposite me and leant forward to read from the books. "I'm still a little confused, if this Janet

Horne lady has been dead over a hundred years, how would you get a mark of entry?"

I sat forward again, still beaming at my momentary brilliance. "You would have to be born with it. The mark of entry is the brand. No brand, not a mage, sorry you can't come in."

"You don't need to get in though, do you? You could just wait for him to arrive and stop him," Elly said.

"Sure, but what's to stop him from getting past me and going inside? No, if I get in, there's less places for him to run—plus I can watch and see who he speaks to, what they talk about. Heck, the other mages there might know something he doesn't, this could be a gold mine of information. There has to be a way…"

Realisation dawned on Elly's face. She bit her lip and looked off to the side, deep in thought. I knew not to interrupt her in moments like this, so instead I waited patiently and simply admired the view. "You could fake it, the brand, I mean."

"I was hoping you would say that. Has anyone ever told you how pretty you are when you're thinking?"

She turned a deep shade of crimson and cried "No!" in perhaps the most adorable moment of defiance I had ever seen.

"It's true," I said, enjoying her blushes far too much for my own good.

"Stop it!"

I knew better than to embarrass someone too much, so I quickly changed the subject. "How would we fake it? I could brew up a potion or something that might mimic the effect."

Elly chuckled and collected herself. "I don't know anything about alchemy, but I would advise against trying to turn your forearm into scar tissue." She got up and fetched a bag of her belongings that she'd bought with her that morning. From within, she produced a few small tins. "A bit of rouge, soot powder, and a careful application of a lip pomade could make a convincing replica."

"That could definitely work, assuming it doesn't rain or smear under my sleeves. Then there's the question of what to say to Bryce when I get in." I started to pace the office, my brain picking up a little more steam. "He seemed like a nice enough guy, to be honest, caught up in the wrong things and too gruff for his own good. Maybe I just tell him the truth?"

"Aristocrats rarely enjoy the truth," Elly interjected.

I shook my head and absentmindedly stepped up onto the coffee table, across and down again during my pacing. "He didn't seem like your average toff to me. Jen said he'd been disgraced in some way, and I get the feeling he has no fond thoughts for his station. Plus, this secret club means he's in some pretty deep shit, maybe I could leverage that somehow?"

I picked up one of Jennifer's canes and started twirling it, not too flashy as to risk dropping it, however. Elly was watching in amusement, anticipating the moment my fidgets would grow bigger than their britches, having seen it happen many times in our childhoods.

"Then there's the question of protection." I flipped the cane and caught it in a raised hand to guard against an invisible foe. "Jennifer has a shielding potion. If she had some extra doses, or hell, if I could brew it from the formula, that might work. No idea if it would stop Arcane fire, suppose I could test that with a little Greek fire, or the discharge from the duelling pistols. Though, Arcane lightning isn't exactly the same thing." I flipped the cane again, only this time it spun a half turn too much and bounced off my palm to the floor.

Elly tried to stifle a giggle, but it burst out once I turned to give her a stern look. "Still as clumsy as ever," she chided.

"I'll have you know I've become much less clumsy than when we were children," I said before my mind skipped, "Oh god! Father thought I'd been spending time with Matthew Burton again."

"Matthew Burton, the one you used to," she slapped her palm with a backhand, "with and you'd both show up with fresh bruises?" I responded with an affirmative half-moan, and Elly followed up with, "Didn't you break his arm?"

"Yes, but it was an accident," I said with tongue in cheek—it was entirely Matt's fault; he lied when he said he could tie a ring-hitch knot. "Anyway, assuming I can sort out the shield potion, I should be fairly safe if things go sideways with Bryce." My father had once likened having a conversation with me in one of my more manic headspaces, to trying to have a conversation with a racket ball.

"Seems like you have things worked out then," Elly said, crossing the room to stand by the couch where I had been twirling the cane. "Just take your time and think, don't rush into things."

"I like rushing, and I don't like thinking," I responded with a sulk.

She put a hand on mine and squeezed. She looked up at me, smiled warmly and said, "Some things are best done slowly, Charlotte." My brain skidded to a halt, caught up in a knot of emotions. Suddenly, all the casual flirtation felt much more real, and it jarred against two decades of memories where I'd seen Elly, ironically, as a brother. Had I just been fooling myself with playful banter, or did I really want something more? Something that hadn't seemed possible before she tumbled back into my life in a pretty blue day dress. Perhaps I'd always wanted more, and kept the feelings hidden from even myself in an act of self-preservation. I stood there, holding her hand and looking deep into her big blue eyes, resisting the urge to kiss her. I almost did, until the little monster in my head reminded me that Jennifer was still missing.

I flopped down into the couch, looked up at Elly and said, "Thank you, by the way, I don't know what I would have done if you hadn't showed up the other day. Probably blundered into some inescapable danger."

"Let's just stick with escapable dangers, alright?" she replied before perching herself next to my feet. "Hungry?"

"Famished!"

Chapter 20

We settled down at the coffeehouse across the road from The Potent Solution, with a stack of pastries and cured meats to keep us company. Not one to focus on a single task at a time, I bought along Jennifer's battered old formula book so I could go about decrypting the recipe for the shield potion. Elly browsed the classifieds in the paper in search of work befitting her training, and we enjoyed some of the best coffee in the city.

"Can you make it?" Elly asked as the coffee began to run dry. I was most of the way through deciphering the diagrammatic formula, which showed the precise arrangement of lab equipment that allowed for the transmutation to take place, and I was honestly baffled.

"I don't know yet, maybe?" I answered, sitting back from the book to rest my eyes for a moment. "This is the most complex arrangement I've ever worked on. Jennifer must have been mad to even try this."

"You really look up to her, don't you?" She tilted her head and smiled softly at me.

The question gave me pause; three days before, I'd have answered immediately, but my faith had been shaken. "Jennifer is… complicated. Utterly brilliant, charming, beautiful. But I can't help but wonder if, all this time, she's only been showing me the parts of herself she wanted me to see."

"You can't blame her for that though. Everyone hides things. I should know," Elly said, and she was right. But that didn't make me anymore comfortable with what Jennifer had done.

"I supposed right now I just don't understand her as well as I thought. Much like this formula." I stared again at the geometric diagram, a collection of intersecting shapes which denoted the steps necessary for producing the alchemical transmutation. In a complex formula, the specific arrangement of lab equipment can be just as important as the processes used, allowing for the correct flow of magical energies. "How about you, any luck on the job front?"

"Unless I want to be nurse or a veterinarian, unfortunately no," she said, looking back the newspaper with disdain. "I'm a doctor, not a horse breaker."

"Why not set up your own practice? Surely your father needs a new investment opportunity." I asked.

Elly rolled her eyes. "Father would invest in a rabbit farm if you told him they shit gold. I could ask him for help, yes, but I want to do this on my own merit."

"That's admirable, maybe more so if he didn't pay for your education already."

"Oh pish-posh. Let me have this one."

I relented and went back to finishing my decryption— why Jen tried so hard to protect her work I have no idea; it was absurdly paranoid. Elly was collecting up the dishes and mugs for the young man in charge of serving us to collect. I was almost ready to give up and head back to the shop when I made a startling discovery. "By Jove! I think I have it."

Elly perked up at my exclamation. "Oh? You can make it?"

"I'm a lot more certain than the last time you asked me. I was confounded by the final ingredient here, it's a symbol I haven't seen before," I explained. I showed Elly the page I was decrypting and gestured to a little drawing of a head. It had big, pointed ears and sharp teeth, and looked not at all human.

Elly giggled at the sketch. "Are you sure Jennifer isn't just playing tricks on you?"

"Not at all, this is the core ingredient. The notation just says 'goblin', though."

"As in the little creatures from fairy tales?"

"That's what I thought at first, but the recipe talks about grinding it into a powder and heating it with Sal Almanac and Charcoal. So, I realised, it's not talking about some dried guts from a goblin, which would be impossible to get hold of at short notice, but some kind of ore. This symbol here—" I was saying before Elly interrupted me.

"Goblin guts? From actual goblins? You can get those?" she asked.

"Not at short notice, no, I just said that. But look, this part here is talking about calcination, which is a similar enough process to smelting when you work with ores."

"But if it wasn't short notice, you could get goblin guts?"

"Why are you so obsessed with goblin guts?" I asked, finally catching up with the conversation.

"Because as far as I know, goblins aren't real?" she said quizzically.

I stared at her intently for a moment, and then said, "I'm trying to work out how to brew a magic potion that creates an immaterial, regenerating shield of Arcane glass, and you're telling me you don't believe in goblins?"

"Well," she said, sitting up straight, "when you put it like that. An ore, then?"

"Yes, an ore. The German word for goblin is 'kobold', they use it for little mining sprites that cause all sorts of annoyances. It's also the name for an impurity found in local sources of copper and nickel, kobold ore. Of course, we now call it by a different name," I explained.

"Which is?"

I grinned triumphantly. "Cobalt."

"Oh. Oh, I see! Brilliant Charlotte, just brilliant!" She clasped a hand over mine and grinned at me. "I knew you could do it."

My cheeks turned very hot, and I pulled my hand away and started packing up the books and papers I had to try and escape from the embarrassment. "Come on, let's get back to the shop, decrypting this formula is only the first step."

***

It was late in the evening by the time I'd collected together all the ingredients and equipment I needed to brew Jennifer's potion, and the better part of my instincts knew not to start till morning. I wouldn't want to fall asleep while heating the kobold ore and die from arsenic poisoning, after all. Elly had stayed and kept me company, though I suspect it was partly an excuse to continue cleaning Jennifer's office. I protested, but in truth I needed her there. My emotions were frayed, and her grounding influence on me was about the only reason I hadn't broken down into tears at the coffeehouse.

"It's getting late, father will be wondering where I am," she said as the little clock in the office chimed an eighth time.

"Too late to send a note, I suppose." I sat on the arm of the sofa and stared at the clock, its hands ticking away.

"I really should be going," she said, but there was a note of doubt in her voice. She came to stand beside me and took one of my hands.

"Please don't." She was short enough that our eyes were near enough level where I sat, but I couldn't bring myself to look.

"I'm sorry, sweetheart," she said, "My Da' is a bit less forgiving than yours on not coming home at night. He'd have the whole metropolitan police force out before sunrise to find me."

She paused and stroked the back of my hand, so gently that it tickled just a little. The sweet vanilla in her perfume filled my nostrils and drew me closer to her. Our eyes met, and in an instant, I was lost in them again. My heart ached and roared; I wanted her more with every second that passed. Her breaths were short, her gaze darted between my eyes and my lips. I brushed away the hair that had fallen across her face and expected her to pull away. Instead, she pressed her cheek into my hand and nodded softly.

I kissed her, and the world melted away. There was no Black Ember, no secret society of mages, no looming unknown threats. Just us. I pulled her close and the warmth of her body against mine was like the summer sun, and all I'd known before was ice and snow. For what felt like a myriad in moments, she kissed me back, and I prayed for a myriad more. "Stay," I said as she pulled away, every inch a mile.

"I can't…" She trailed off, bit her lip, and looked away. In all the words, in every language, I knew there was nothing I could say to change her mind.

I let go of her hand, took a moment to collect myself,

and stood up. "I'll see you out."

"Charlotte, I…" she began to say, but I held a hand up to stop her.

"Let's not say anything to spoil the good day we had. I'll be fine, promise." I was lying, of course. I wasn't fine to begin with and I certainly wouldn't get any better. I suspected she knew that.

We lingered by the door, neither of us willing to say goodbye just yet. I wanted nothing more than to kiss her again and taste her sweet lips one more time. She smiled and said, softly, "There's that look again. I'll try to stop by tomorrow." With that, she left, and I went to bed.

October 12th, 1834

A Study in Shielding

Chapter 21

Alchemy is maybe the most dangerous game of trial and error you can play. There is a fine line between certain death from the rules of Mundane chemistry, and certain death from the unpredictable nature of the Arcane. What seems like a stable transmutation one minute may in the next release a cloud of toxic fumes, or an explosion of magical energy. With that in mind, I found myself standing at the threshold of the laboratory, geared up in a heavy, durable apron, protective goggles, gloves, and face covering, ready to brute force the most complicated potion I'd ever made.

I was an idiot. A genius, but also an idiot. This is what I was good at, though—all the self-doubt in the world couldn't stop me—potions were my thing, and I was going to succeed even if it killed me.

Wait, scratch that, I wasn't going to let this kill me.

Now, some things in life deserve all the time you can give them—potion making is one, sex is another—and I can't help but admit that I felt a certain passion for what I was about to do. I wandered the stacked shelves slowly, taking in the pungent odours and picking out the perfect samples of gold, silver, and iron. The boiling flasks were cleaned and lovingly dried, before I set them out in their precise little alcoves laid into the surface of the worktable. When I ran my hands along the corners of unfinished oak, it was with the gentle caress of a long-lost lover—as if the tips of my fingers could say, "I'm here now, let's take this slow."

I carefully placed the metals into their beakers and slowly added the exact measures of acidic solutions to dissolve them.

To the silver and gold, I used Aqua Regia. The colourless liquid turned a deep saffron colour on contact with the noble metals, draining away the lustre from the precious tablets almost immediately. With a little bit of heat, liquid began to bubble and hiss. Layer by the layer, the silver and gold were stripped away and a dark orange gas billowed out of the flasks like fog rolling into a valley.

The iron was likewise dissolved in a concentrated solution of Aqua Fortis. You would have been forgiven to think to flask contained only water, until it met the iron and ate away at it, piece-by-piece, like a rodent tearing away crumbs from a piece of bread. The solution foamed and bubbled, rising and falling in a mesmerising loop—as though it was breathing.

I watched the reactions intently, only stepping in when necessary to agitate the liquids or adjust the heat from the spirit burners. There was a low hum throughout the lab, right on the edge of my perception, that tickled at the hairs on my arms. Magic, coursing along lines of focus and into the carved design of the worktable. There it was channelled into the reactions, bridging the gap between the Mundane and the Arcane. Over time, all that was left were three flasks of filled with off-colour solutions—and no trace of the metals within. Each solution served a purpose in the final product: iron for strength, gold for longevity, silver for potency.

Pounding the blueish-grey cobalt ore into submission—by which I mean a very fine powder—proved to be a difficult but deeply rewarding task. It had been a stressful few days, and I revelled in unleashing all that pent up anger and frustration with a heavy stone mortar and pestle.

My heart raced in my chest—one part exhilaration, one part exertion—as I approached to formulas climax. The magical energy in the room was palpable, like a breath that catches in your throat. Now was not the time for tenderness, but to press on with full force and draw out the Arcane nature.

Calcination is the process of heating a substance to just below its melting point for an extended period of time—it is important to keep it right on the edge of that phase change— to purify it and allow it to mingle with Arcane energies. Teetering on the edge of violent eruption and a pitiful fizzle, the cobalt solution thickened into a slick, clear blue syrup that was ice cold to the touch—in spite of the roaring burner beneath the flask—and sent a shudder down my spine. This was the purest form of the liquid glass created by the potion, but it would take care to prolong the effusive transmutation; a fixation developed with Sal Almanac and charcoal was enough to make the magic last.

The long, slow resolution came when the rainbow of metallic solutions was combined in a curved, elegant glass alembic, with a heaped tablespoon of powdered sulphur, and brought to a gentle boil. A necessary period of recuperation, as the potion slowly distilled through the tapering glass tube, drop by drop. When all was said and done, I let out a soft, satisfied sigh, and decanted the pale blue potion into the chambers of five heavy syringes.

A whole day had passed me by, and I could hear Jennifer's voice in my head echoing a lecture about pacing myself, ("A tired alchemist is a dead alchemist, Charlotte," she always liked to say.) But she wasn't there, and I could hardly knock myself for having a good time.

***

Later that evening, in what was turning out to be a strangely regular occurrence, I once again found Elly at the door. Only this time, quite unexpectedly, she was drunk.

"I said I would be back," she said, swaying a little and with a dopey smile on her face. "You smell funny."

I sniffed my clothes. "It's the Sal Almanac, I'll change once we get upstairs. How much have you had to drink?"

"Well, I had one glass of wine, and then father decided to reminisce on the old days, if you know what I mean, and that made me sad, so I had—" she counted on her fingers before stating "more wine!" and then she started giggling.

"Well, I haven't had any wine, so you might have to dial it down just a smidge. How did you get here?"

She giggled again and pushed an invisible pair of glasses up her nose. "They have these marvellous things called Hansom

Cabs."

In my head, I updated my assessment of the situation—Elly wasn't drunk; she was pissed, sloshed, rat-arsed, totalled, bladdered, lashed—you get the idea. She needed a lie down, and probably a bucket within arm's reach. "Right, of course. Let's get you upstairs." I led her up to the office and sat her down on the couch. After fetching a bucket and a few blankets, I settled next to her. Elly, almost instinctively, snuggled up next to me. I shrugged and put my arm around her, content as long as she was comfortable. "Sorry about your father."

"Is not your fault, he's just… Old dog, new tricks, you know?" The Cornwall was coming out much stronger in her accent, which was quite amusing. In Cambridge she'd adopted a fairly haughty tone to try to fit in with the other gowns in her class, and I was impressed that she never slipped from that note of lyrical silver she'd added after I left.

I tried my best to reassure her, but honestly, I had no idea what I was doing. "He'll get there."

Elly grabbed at bundles of my shirt and started to sniffle. "He just doesn't understand, he can't understand." There was a rawness in her words, as though she'd held them back so long that they'd chafed in her throat. "No one can. I feel like a prisoner in my own body, and no matter what I do, I can't make people see the real me."

I brushed a lock of hair from her face and traced a finger along her shoulder. "I see you."

"No, you see a version of me." She sat up straight and looked down at her body—I followed her gaze over her chest, her hips, and her hands. "I am fake—a fraud. None of it is real, it's not even skin deep."

"Hey. You're real to me."

There was a pained look in her eyes, all knotted up in the crease between her brows, that I hadn't seen on her since she arrived back in London. I recognised it immediately, because that was how she always used to look, when she thought no one could see her. All those years she'd been suffering, and I didn't see it for what it was.

I wiped away a tear from her cheek. She nuzzled against the palm of my hand. "You're the most wonderful, radiant person I know. I wish I could help you see that."

Elly scoffed and turned away from me. "You'd need a miracle for that…" Then, curiously, she trailed off and looked around the stacks and bundles of books all around the office. In her own, admittedly alcohol induced way, she realised something. When Elly turned back to me, she swallowed her heart back into its rightful place, and asked, "Your Alchemy, it's like magic, right?"

"Something like that, yes," I said, trying to hold back a sly smile. "Why do you ask?"

She looked suddenly unsure of herself, like a student slowly lowering their hand upon realising their question was indeed a little stupid. "I feel like I'm putting on a costume every day, just to try and make people see me for who I am." Her voice quavered. "But, what if… what if there was a potion that could help me?"

I sucked my teeth and got up from the couch. "Fuck." My already overworked mind found its third—maybe fourth or fifth—wind. I paced around the room, double snapping my fingers—that's snapping with both the ring and middle finger on one hand, the only thing I learned to do in my first six months in Cambridge. My mouth of was making sounds, but it wasn't exactly conversation. "It'd be complicated… I suppose I could—no that wouldn't—too chaotic, too ephemeral… but father's medicine…"

"Look, Charlotte, if it can't be done, it's fine. I'm fine. Don't worry about it," she muttered.

I stopped in the middle of a thought, and gave Elly my best, *don't underestimate me*, look, then asked, "I'm sorry, did I say I couldn't do it?" A new fire was kindling inside me, I could do it, at least I thought I could. It'd take some real work, real innovation, but I was running off the high of cracking a four-stage transmutation in less than a day, I was good at this. "You deserve to be happy, if I can help, I will."

"But, no, you have to find Jennifer, don't waste time on

me," she pleaded.

I flopped back onto the couch and put an arm around her shoulder. "Time spent helping you will never be a waste."

It didn't take long for Elly to finally succumb to sleep, snuggled in my arms. She didn't even throw up, which was impressive. We stayed like that till morning, warm, safe, and together.

October 13th, 1834

The 1735 Club

Chapter 22

I awoke stiff and aching. Sleeping on the couch had not done anything good for my back. As the last memories of the night's dreams drifted from my mind, replaced by the flood of reality, I groggily pulled myself upwards and stretched. A short moment of panic overcame me, as I realised that Elly was no longer lying next to me. I was reassured, however, by the smell of bacon and coffee, and Elly came into the office with a breakfast tray.

"Good morning," I said, "did you sleep well?"

"'Bout as well as I could have given the circumstances," she said, having fully dropped back into her native Cornish accent. It was still higher and more lilting than I remembered, but it made me grin all the same. Elly had a sense of calm about her that eased my nerves. We hadn't spoken about the kiss, and I was wholly unprepared for her staying the night.

"You're cute when you speak west country," I said, dodging the elephant in the room. Elly put the tray down on the coffee table and sat across from me, and as I squirmed upright, I realised she was wearing just her underclothes. Her petticoat was muslin, and fairly plain, with a little structure around the skirt. Of course, I was still wearing the clothes I slept in, but the heavy linen shirt provided enough modesty in the morning chill.

I reached over to grab a rasher of bacon from the plate, but Elly slapped my hand away and pointed to the fork. "Don't be a bloody animal."

I was taken aback. "It's only bacon, we're hardly having breakfast with the King of France," I said with a mock sense of indignation, but Elly seemed to pick up on it and laughed.

"Just use a fork," she said through her soft giggle.

Elly finished eating before me and collected her bag while I was finishing up. "Right, give me your arm," she said, laying out an array of make-up products I couldn't begin to name. She started to paint in the space on my forearm where my fake brand would be with a pinkish powder. Her fingers were soft, and her every touch tantalising. Questions gnawed at my mind as she worked, but I struggled to find the right words. When I finally resolved to break the silence, she beat me to it. "About last night."

"Yes, about that."

"I was wine drunk, Charlotte, and mad at my Da'. I don't even really remember what I was saying." She was biting her lip again as she worked a more vermillion coloured shade into my skin. I braced myself for her to say the worst; that she regretted staying, that I stepped over the line when I kissed her, that maybe we'd got too close, too fast. I was so ready for her so say the words and for my stomach to drop, but once again she took me completely by surprise. "Thank you, for taking care of me. For listening."

"Oh," I said, my mind still reeling itself back in. "You're very welcome."

"I know I've already asked a lot of you, but there's something else," she said, now choosing between a few lip pomades. "About me staying, for a bit. I can tell you're in need of company, and I love my Da' and he loves me dearly, but… It's just all so new for him, I sprung it on him when I got back in Town, and I think I need to give him some space." She settled on a crimson colour to emphasise my veins.

My heart must have started to do somersaults, but I did my best to keep my composure. "Absolutely, whatever you need."

"And you, if there's anything I can help you with, just ask." She smiled, and then inspected her work. "There, all done, as best as I can do without a reference."

"It's remarkable," I said, quite taken by the likeness to the brands I'd seen up close the past few days. I finished off the last rasher of bacon, and a thought popped into my head. "I could use your assistance with something else this morning, actually." She perked up at the suggestion. "The potions I made yesterday need testing. I need you to inject one of those glowing vials of mystery goo into your arm and let me shoot guns at you," I stated with a sardonic smile.

Elly was not amused, "You are awfully flippant this morning, given the circumstances." She'd begun to work her voice back into her usual accent, but the odd word still slipped through with a west country twang. She looked at me solemnly and said, "Are you alright?"

I sighed a looked back at her, suddenly feeling sullen, "What does it matter if I am or not? You're right, Jennifer is out there—if I'd been the one to go missing, she would stop at nothing to find me. I can't let her down, she's given me more than I could have dreamed of, and now she needs me. And I'm sorry, but I'm trying my hardest to stay calm and making jokes helps me cope."

She looked at me apologetically and said, "As long as we're both clear that you were joking." I looked at her with a face that said I was definitely not joking. "Why do you need me to inject the mystery goo and shoot me!?" she exclaimed, full west country.

"Because the side effects of the shield potion include several hours of complete loss of body temperature control, and I can't sneak into a secret society with a fever," I explained. Then, with my best puppy dog eyes, I said, "Don't you want to help me find Jennifer?"

Elly pouted. "I hate that you are making sense right now. Aren't I going to end up all bruised like you did?"

"I'll use a small charge of gunpowder and aim somewhere that people won't see, promise," I answered, trying to put on a more serious front. Elly pouted more, but eventually agreed.

***

An hour later, we were back in the office. Elly was nursing a red welt on her ribcage, and a white electrical tree scar on her back. I was sitting beside her with a letter opener, several blankets, and a bucket of water I'd laced with a handful Arcane cooling crystals. Watching my pocket watch, every minute I tapped Elly's shoulder with the letter opener to test the shield.

"Fifty-eight minutes," I said when the shield finally faded, and Elly yelped at the point of the blade. She started sweating, and I lifted her feet into the cold water. "A perfect test, Dr Chynoweth, much appreciated."

"I. Hate. You," she grimaced. She started to shiver and pulled her feet out of the water, then dived under the blankets. "You owe me, big time."

"Anything you want," I checked the time, "But, I need to get going if I'm to catch our stray mage. Are you going to be alright?" She nodded, then surreptitiously looked around the office. "Are you going to clean more as soon as I leave?"

"What? No," the sarcastic pile of blankets responded. "Maybe a little."

"So predictable," I jested.

I washed my face and set about deciding what to wear from the assorted clothes that had migrated from Father's house to the shop. I tried to follow Jennifer's example, opting for a high-collared shirt, black waistcoat, and a long skirt. I grimaced at the corset I resigned myself to wearing. Upper-class society had decided that pencil-thin waists was the done thing, much to my distaste—what happened to a simple stay to keep your chest supported? I fussed far too long to find a happy medium that didn't exist between supporting my breasts and crushing my lungs.

It was when I was tying up my hair in the mirror and had the annoying realisation that, despite how uncomfortable I was, I looked damn good. My boots and long coat completed the ensemble, making me look almost competent. I collected up the supplies I needed, including a dose of the shield potion and my pistol, both of which I hoped I wouldn't need. With nothing left to procrastinate with, I bid farewell to Elly and headed out.

On the streets outside, the market was already alive, Mr Long's butcher shop was busy, and the Bakery owned by Mx Penrose had filled the street with the smell of fresh bread and pies. I waved down a passing cab and told the driver to take me to Pall Mall as I got in.

The cab ride was uneventful, and I was dropped off at

the east end of the long street. I looked out over what was to become Trafalgar Square, currently a construction site— along one side was the skeleton of the new National Gallery, workmen slaving away at the building like ants. It would be a few years till the gallery was completed yet, but it already struck an impressive form.

I looked down the old street, the buildings on either side dignified and grand. Much like the rest of London, the street was a mix of architectural styles, a cultural convalescence of different time periods and aesthetics locked into the stonework of architects over the centuries. Elizabethan and Jacobian buildings stood side by side with the newer neoclassical and baroque terraces.

It was around nine when I arrived, and the meeting wasn't due to start till ten, so I decided to find somewhere inconspicuous to wait. There was a small tea house nearby that I'd intended to visit for some time. A little sign hung off a bracket reading *Madame Siddiqui's Comfort,* with a picture of a teacup and saucer over a jasmine flower.

The smell of warm vanilla, cinnamon and orange peel washed over me as I entered. Several people were already sitting at tables, drinking in the sweet chai tea, and letting the steam fill their nostrils. An Indian woman in her late 50s came flowing out of a back room, wearing a sari of red and gold gracefully draped and wrapped around her body. When she spoke, her voice was calm and song-like, "My dear, welcome to my place of comfort, I am Madame Siddiqui. How may I be of service?" She put her hands together and bowed ever so slightly.

I bowed my head slightly in return, unsure of the etiquette. "Tea would be wonderful. I'm waiting for a friend; may I sit by the window?"

"Of course, my dear, I'll bring you a fresh pot. This is the finest chai you will ever taste, please take a seat," she gestured to one of the window side tables and took the teapot into the back room. Every movement she made was like water flowing, graceful and elegant.

I looked out the window and counted down buildings till

I found No. 97, where the 1735 Club was located. This was a new building with a white stone façade. The windows were tall and thin, with triangular pediments over the top supported by simple columns. There was a certain elegance to the building, which belied the hidden secrets within. How did a group of mages, traditionally disenfranchised as they were, afford to host their gatherings in such a place? Mr Rosehouse, perhaps?

Madame Siddiqui came back carrying a pot of tea, and a teacup and saucer on a tray. She placed them down on the table and hummed a soft, lilting tune while tapping a pair of beads together in her hand. Steam rose from the pot, and the soft refrain of Worker's Cant came to an end. "I suggest you wait a moment before drinking, just enjoy the smell while it cools slightly. Can I interest you in any pastries or sandwiches?"

"Just the tea for now is perfect, thank you very much," I smiled and took in a deep inhale through my nose of the sweet-smelling tea. "It does smell amazing."

"Do let me know if you need anything else, dear," and she was away again, drifting through the teahouse to attend to the other patrons.

I just sat for a while, enjoying the tea, and watching the people pass by outside. A young man walking with a shy girl. An old couple going into the bookshop at No. 59. A slender woman, walking alone in a black mourning dress, stopped across the road and for a moment I could have sworn she had looked directly at me. When I looked again, however, she was gone.

Soon, my mind started to ache against the dull monotony of people watching. I caught myself absentmindedly rapping my fingers on the table and realised I needed something to do while I waited. I took out my notebook and started sketching formula diagrams, before devolving into absentminded doodles. How did Jen handle all this time on an investigation where nothing happened? What would she be doing? Probably hatch some brilliant plan that she wouldn't tell me about. I'd just have to do my best, and hope she'd approve when I found her.

It was only when I went to drink again from the teacup and found it empty, that I looked back towards No. 97 and saw the ragged form of Bryce Rosehouse coming up the street. "Found you," I said, quietly.

Chapter 23

Bryce hurried down the Mall, his hands buried in the pockets of his frock coat and his eyes turned to the ground. He walked up the steps to No. 97 and rapped the brass knocker on the large black door several times. He was greeted by an older man, pale skinned, and maybe in his mid-fifties. The pair exchanged some words, the older man attempted to put a hand on Bryce's arm, but he rejected the gesture. More words were said, and they went inside the building.

The door of the café opened and the young woman in the mourning dress entered. She wore a lace veil, and her dress had a slender fit not often seen in the fashion of the day. She was unlike any woman in mourning I'd ever seen. Her demeanour was fierce and stoic, and a little bit terrifying. I watched her for a moment, lost in her presence. She moved like a circus performer or dancer; deliberate, graceful steps, standing tall and confident. Even when she sat, she was tense, and I was reminded of a coiled viper. The hairs on the back of my neck stood up, as if in anticipation.

Focus, I thought to myself in Jennifer's voice, a simple attempt to snap me back to reality. It didn't have quite the same effect, but I managed to regain my composure and push the woman to the back of my mind. I gathered my things and left some money on the table for Madame Siddiqui, then left the café.

I crossed the street, dodged a carriage that pulled out of an alleyway and nearly ran me down and hopped up the steps of No. 97. The knocker was heavy and made a dull thud on the door. Within moments, the door swung inwards and the old man I had seen from across the street was now in front of me. Up close, I could see his liver-spotted skin and wide face. "Can I help you, madam?" he said in a low, cracking voice.

I ignored the panic in my chest, and confidently said, "yes,

I'm here to see Janet Horne." I wasn't wholly sure on the correct protocol of infiltrating a secret society, but I hedged my bets, nonetheless. The old man regarded me intently, sweeping his cataracted eyes over my whole person.

"I'm afraid that you have the wrong establishment, madam." He made to close the door, but I put my hand out to stop him. "Madam?"

"Please, sir, the advertisement mentioned a mark of entry." I pulled up my sleeve to reveal the forgery Elly had expertly applied to my skin. "There is a meeting, correct?"

The man nodded and stepped aside. "Most of the other guests have already arrived, please do try not to disturb anyone until the speeches have ended." He made to take my coat, but I refused, not wanting to reveal the pistol slung under my arm.

"Speeches?" I asked.

"Of course, madam, this way."

Inside was brightly lit by a window at the other end of the corridor. The walls were painted white and intricate plaster mouldings decorated the corners where they met the floor and roof. The floor itself was varnished wood, and my boots made an audible *thud thud* as I walked. When the door closed behind me, a curious sensation filled my ears, a feeling as if the air in my ears was sucked out. It was oppressive, like being underwater, and I soon noticed that I could hear nothing but the sound of my boots.

I tried to speak. "Excuse me, sir?" I could hear my voice, but it sounded different, like there was cotton wool in my ears. The door man didn't respond. I couldn't hear his shoes on the floor. What sort of magic could do this?

I had a thought, and placed a hand on his shoulder. "Excuse me?" I said again.

This time the butler turned. "Madam, privacy is of utmost import this morning, please do not speak with anyone who does not wish to be spoken with." His voice was muffled and sounded deeper, more resonant; I was hearing it inside my head. Putting aside the fascination of the magic at work, I was instead relieved that I could seemingly speak with Bryce without worry of any eavesdropping.

I was led into an expansive room, which turned out to be a gallery of sorts. Bryce had said he loved galleries. Art hung around the room in a wide variety of styles. The roof was decorated with murals featuring portraits of people I wagered were members of the same family. Chairs had been arranged in rows, facing a small table, next to which a middle-aged woman was animatedly talking. At least, I think she was talking, but I couldn't hear anything.

All kinds of faces looked back to her, people from all walks of life from labourers to bankers, about thirty in total. There was even a vicar. They all had one thing in common: a rolled-up sleeve that showed the mark on their flesh. Some were ragged and tired, while others seemed almost content. This was the 1735 club? It was nothing like the upper-class members' clubs it posed as, but the ragtag group also didn't look like a secret cabal. They were just people, bought together by strife.

I sat down in the back of the rows of seats and tried to find Bryce. Before I could, however, someone sitting a few chairs down from me waved to get my attention. I looked at him, puzzled. He was young, maybe just turned twenty, had dark skin and wore the clothes of a factory worker. He held a wire cable of sorts and gestured to the floor where the same cable ran by my feet. I picked it up, and in that very moment, sound rushed backed to my ears.

"Right, that's the minutes of the last meeting dealt with. Thank you Daniel," the woman at the front was saying. She had a thick Irish accent and spoke with a fiery passion that matched her larger-than-life gesticulations. "I see we have some new faces in the room. Allow me to be the first to welcome you to the 1735, and remind you that secrecy is of the utmost importance." I tried to look as inconspicuous as I could as a few people looked around to find the newcomers. "My name is Margaret Brady, I'm the current president of our organisation. Let's move on with the agenda, and if you have any questions, you can find me when tea is served. Item one is the leafleting campaign. Georgia?"

An ample-bodied young woman with auburn hair stood up and took the end of the cable from Ms Brady. She spoke with a refined accent—not quite aristocratic, but definitely middle-class. "Thank you, Madam President. As some of you will know, we have been looking to produce some leaflets detailing the proposed reforms to the WA 1735—" that's the Witchcraft Act, it wouldn't be a political meeting without at least one acronym, "—to drum up some public support. I'm pleased to announce that we've found a printing house willing to produce them, however, due to the nature of our organisation, the price is…"

"How much, Georgia?" It was Bryce's voice, but I still couldn't see where he was sitting.

"Mr Rosehouse, it's out of our budget. They say it'll cost them extra to make sure it can't be traced back to us," the woman explained, and a murmur of indistinguishable voices filled my eyes.

The cable shook in my hands, and the voices died down. "Everyone please," said Mrs Brady, "try not to speak over each other."

Bryce spoke again. "If it's simply a matter of funding, it can be dealt with. We can discuss it later." Was Bryce bank rolling this whole society? I'd figured he was rich, but that seemed like a huge risk—maybe I didn't know him as well as I thought.

"Thank you, Mr Rosehouse. That will be all from me, then, Madame President," Georgia said, before retaking her seat.

Mrs Brady stood back up and checked a sheet of paper on the desk. "Item two, and I would like to ask everyone to please keep their heads. The matter of Timothy Waters and the incident at the warehouse on the Dogs." There was a clamour of noise, followed by a vigorous shaking of the cable. "Everyone, please. Now I know you're all worried about the papers, but we've been here before," Mrs Brady said. "The press will always print whatever tripe they want, but we know they are just trying to stoke up fear. They know we're winning; they know that public opinion is moving in our favour, and they're the ones that are scared. They fear us because they don't understand us, because they choose not to understand us. We cannot give in to their narrative of fear."

"Is any of it true? They say the warehouse was arson by magic!" a man interjected, his voice low and strained.

"We don't know how much of it is true. I have it on good authority that Mr Waters died of a drug overdose—as for the fire on the Dogs, it's probably just a scare story devised by our opponents." The president took on a placating tone, and a murmur rippled through the cable. "Please, be patient. Before long the government will bring forth the debate on the WA. I have faith that we'll gain our freedoms; to live up to our potential, use our talents openly and unrestricted, to choose our own destinies." Mrs Brady was curiously optimistic; did she have friends in government? Bryce's father was a member of the House of Lords—perhaps he was involved with the 1735 as well—that might explain why and how Bryce funded the society.

Another voice, of indistinct sex and a soft timbre, spoke up. "How can we trust Parliament? What if they push their own amendments that make things worse? What about the rumours from south of the river?" Finally, someone talking sense. When had the Lords and the Commons done anything that didn't help themselves?

"The rumours are just that, rumours. There's no evidence to back them up." Mrs Brady was holding her hands up to try to calm the room. I made a mental note—if there was any weight to those rumours, it'd be a good idea to try to find out what they were.

"But Billy Parker said..." the voice said. They sounded as if they were holding back tears.

"Tabitha, please, we all miss Billy, but you need to come to terms with the fact he's not here anymore," Mrs Brady said, cutting them off—curiouser and curiouser—who was Billy Parker? Just how much had Jennifer and I missed about the goings on in the mage community? "Let's take a break everyone, we'll resume in fifteen minutes. Have patience and faith wherever you choose to place it. There's tea and cakes at the back of the room." She dropped the end of the cable and began speaking to someone near her, the conversation muted.

The young man sitting near me scooted up to my side and held out his hand expectantly. It took me a second to catch on, but I placed my hand is his and he smiled. "Pleasure, first time?" His voice was higher in pitch than I expected, even when it was filtered by my own internal resonance.

"Oh, yes, I saw the advert. Took me a while to work it out, though," I replied, trying to be inconspicuous. "Sorry, what's up with the—" I gestured to our hands.

He squeezed my hand affectionately, his skin calloused by hard work. "Not the foggiest, on the technical details—supposed to keep us secret, make sure no one is listening in. I can barely manage a verse of Cant, though, this is something else. Proper magic."

"You don't think Cant is proper magic?" I asked, intrigued enough that I forgot why I was even there.

"Well," he said, taken aback slightly, "it's like grammar and spelling, right? There's the King's English and the proper way to say things, and then there's folks like us." He grinned at his analogy.

"Quite right, I suppose," I said, amused at the thought. "Charlotte, by the way. I'd shake your hand, but…"

He laughed, though it was more of a childish giggle, really. "As you say. Name's Caspar, Caspar Smith."

"Pleasure." I looked around the room, and in the corner of my eye I spotted a familiar mass of shaggy black hair. "Sorry, I need to. Sorry." Caspar looked at me puzzled, but I let go of his hand before he could say anything else.

Bryce Rosehouse was standing apart from the rest of the group, admiring a painting that hung on the wall. It depicted a ship at sea, caught in a storm that threatened to capsize it. I stepped up beside him nonchalantly and touched my hand against his. "When you said we'd go to a gallery, this isn't what I was thinking."

"Who—" he said, turning on his heel. I saw him mouth the words "…are you? You!" before he grabbed my hand with some force, and his voice came back into my head. "What are you doing here? How did you find me?" he asked, speaking with the tone that incredulous, angry drunks use. After a pause, he added, "Were you followed?"

"It's complicated, I need to talk to you. It's about Jennifer and the fires," I said. "I wasn't followed, I came alone."

"How dare you come here, how did you even get in?" he said, lifting my arm to inspect the brand on my skin. "You didn't…"

I looked around hesitantly and pulled Bryce further from the group. "I'm not. It's rouge and lip pomade." He made a disgusted look, and I felt awful for it. "I'm sorry, it was the only place I knew I'd find you, and it's dreadfully important."

"I can't believe you. First you kidnap me, and now you're sneaking into a private meeting. Do you have any idea the danger you could be putting these people in—what would happen if the police got wind of what we're doing here?" He looked around nervously.

"No, I…" I stammered, searching for justification for my actions.

"Of course, you don't. You should leave, Miss Price." There was a firmness in his words, but he didn't let go of my hand.

I waited a moment, then my eyes dropped to the floor. "I've been an awful judge of character, haven't I? All of this," I gestured around the room, "is it your doing? That's very admirable."

"Not all of it, Mrs Brady has been running the club for years, I just signed a few cheques."

"It's more than that, I suspect. I know what it's like to want to make amends for mistakes you've made," I said. I squeezed Bryce's hand to make him look at me. "Please, I need your help. The warehouse on the Dogs, it's the one you told us about, we were there…"

His eyes went wide. "You what? I had a suspicion you were involved, but… You shouldn't be here; if Hawkins knows you're involved… Do you have any idea who you are dealing with here?."

"I know full well who I'm dealing with. I'm not an amateur," I responded, putting on an air of confidence I absolutely did not deserve. Truth is, I hadn't a clue what sort of man

Hawkins was, and I needed Bryce to fill me in. "Look, Jennifer's gone missing; she never came home from the warehouse, and when I went back it'd already been burned down."

"The papers are saying a mage caused it. I'm sure Hawkins burned it himself to cover his tracks and fed them the story," he said dismissively.

"Only half right," I said confidently. "I think it was burned down deliberately—with Black Ember. The mage that did it, her body was still there—she had a tattoo, just like yours."

Bryce's jaw dropped, and he struggled to form words in his state of shock. He was just starting to say, "What do you mean?" When I looked past him and for a brief moment, I was convinced I'd seen a ghost. The woman in the mourning dress was standing in the doorway to the gallery. Only she'd removed her skirt to reveal slender black trousers, laced up the outside leg with red ribbon, and a pair of knives sheathed on each thigh.

"Bryce," I said, wide eyed. "Remember when I said I wasn't followed."

His face turned from shock to fear. He turned, and we both watched in horror as the veiled assassin pulled a black pellet from a pouch on her belt and lit its fuse. "What have you done?" Bryce whimpered.

Chapter 24

I didn't hear the explosion, but I felt it throw me and Bryce across the room. The wooden panels on the walls and floor splintered with the force, and the windows shattered out into the street. The spell muffling sound in the gallery protected my ears from the explosion—quite the unintended benefit. My backside ached where I'd hit the floor, but as far as I could tell, I was unharmed. I quickly regained my composure and scrambled across the floor to where Bryce had landed.

"This isn't good, we have to leave," I said. Chaos had erupted in the gallery, chairs had been thrown wide by the blast, and the gathered members of the 1735 Club were scattered. No one moved to engage the assailant, with those who could move freely made to help those who couldn't.

"Obviously!" Bryce barked as we helped each other up. He was surprisingly light and nimble on his feet, in contrast to his earlier apparent oafishness. In a flash of movement, he pushed me aside and caught one of the small explosives in mid-air, and in a perfect cricket pitch, he hurled it back. The bomb exploded before it reached our attacker, and she stalked toward us through the smoke.

I raised my pistol and hesitated—that proved to be a mistake. The woman darted towards me, causing me to flinch and fire a shot wide. She stepped inside my guard and lunged with her blade. I managed to dodge out of the way, but she was so fast that when she stepped in again, I was sure she would find her mark. Before the blade made purchase, however, she was sent hard to the ground by a burst of searing hot flame.

To my right, Bryce's arms were wreathed in fire. It lanced around his wrists and hands like a living serpent. The dragon tattoo on his left arm glowed orange as he uttered the words of power for another spell.

I took the opportunity to put some distance between myself and our assailant. Ducking behind a couch, I reached into my satchel and pulled out the heavy steel syringe filled with the milky blue shield potion. I pushed the cold needle into my arm, injected the formula, and gasped as the magic worked its way through my body. The soft mist settled over me, forming into a sheen of protective Arcane glass. I couldn't dodge this woman, but I could take a hit and use the chance to get back at her.

The couch exploded. Another percussive blast just a few feet behind me destroyed my hiding place. However, the shield did its job. Not only was I unharmed, but I was also unmoved. I stood up and the crystalline matrix reformed around my body. Bryce gave me a look of surprise, and the assassin gave me one of disdain. She rolled her shoulders and pointed the knife at me. As swift as I could, I reached into my bullet pouch and pushed the new round into the muzzle of my pistol, but she was on me before I could get it down with the ramrod.

The blade cut across my face and I was pushed off balance, and my vision turned into a kaleidoscope of colours. I felt a blow against my side, then my right leg. The shield held, able to sustain multiple blows to different locations without breaking. I ducked to the side and finished loading the cartridge. I bought my pistol to bear as my vision returned fully and fired at point blank range. She went down on one knee, turning to get a good angle on me, and my shot took her in the shoulder. She buckled, and I ran.

Bryce had separated himself from the fight and made for another door, darting past the other members of the 1735 Club as they fled through the main entrance. "Oh no you don't!" I said, but of course no one could hear it. The woman was lying in a pool of blood, and I ran after Bryce. I caught up to him and grabbed his arm. "Where do you think you're going? You're coming with me!" I said.

"No chance! You've already proven you are in way too deep—Hawkins clearly knows who you are, and he won't stop till you're dead—I'll get by on my own." There was a fire in his eyes.

I was not ready to play this game with him; I pushed my

pistol into his gut and met his gaze. "No, you are coming back to the Solution with me, and you are going to help me find Jennifer." I stared him down and for a few moments. It felt like we were looking into each other's souls. He was as scared as I was, but there was anger in his eyes. He broke first and looked at the floor.

"Fine, but… blast! We need to go now!" He let go of my hand and turned for the small side door. I followed, but the assassin, covered in blood from the wound on her shoulder, stalked towards us.

Bryce had the door open, and it led into another white hallway. We ran down it, passing doors and passageways which could have been an escape route. I tried to shout, "Where are we going!?" but to no avail. All I could hear was the click-clack of my boots on the wooden floor, and my heavy breathing. Bryce turned a corner, and I began to feel like we were in a labyrinth, not a building on Pall Mall. As I wheeled around, I spared a glance behind us. The assassin was still coming. She snarled and bared her teeth, like a wolf on the hunt.

Bryce must have known where he was going, and after turning two more corners, I found him fiddling with a lock. "Let me," I said—much less a request than a demand—as I shoved him aside and reloaded my pistol. I put the barrel up to the lock and fired. The latch shattered, and the door swung free on its hinges.

Stepping outside was like being hit by a wall of sound. We emerged into an alleyway behind the building, sounds from the street flooding into me like a lake bursting a dam. I doubled over, clasping my ears and tried to rub them to move the air bubble trapped inside. Bryce stepped out and patted my back. "You'll be fine, let's go!" His voice was back to normal, no longer attenuated by my own internal resonance.

I stood up and, with my ears still ringing, tried to get my bearings. The Mall ran east to west, and we needed to head east. "Come on!" I yelled to Bryce. "We get out to the street, take Waterloo Place, then Regent Street and we'll be a stone's throw from Carnaby and The Potent Solution."

"Lead the way," he said and gestured for me to move. The alley way was muddy and refuse and waste lined the walls, making it hard to pick up any speed. Rich or poor, these places are all the same. "Charlotte, she's coming," Bryce said, and I turned back to see our pursuer leaving the building.

She doubled over, much like I did, at the sudden regaining of her hearing but recovered quickly and began to chase us again. "Shit, come on," I shouted.

We ran down the long alley behind the Mall and burst out into Waterloo Place. People around us looked stunned. One woman screamed when she saw my firearm. I holstered it and made my way north along the road, with Bryce close behind me. We had to dodge through the crowds and street traffic, and for a moment, I thought that would give us some cover to escape. Then Bryce caught his foot on the pavement, and went down to the ground, hard.

"Shit, Bryce, you better be conscious," I said. He groaned as tried to lift him, and his eyes rolled back into his head, briefly. Then, as I was on my knees next to his limp body, our pursuer found us. I thought I heard a guttural word of power being spoken, and a moment later, she backhanded me and sent me flying. She was so strong, so fast. Blood ran down the length of her arm, but it didn't seem to bother her at all.

I scrambled to my feet and pulled out my pistol in time to catch her standing over Bryce. "Hey, he's mine," I said, breathing heavily and levelling the firearm at her. Every inch of me ached, and if I survived this, I knew I'd be sore as hell in the morning. She stepped over Bryce and stalked toward me, and this time I didn't hesitate. The firing crystals of the unloaded pistol crashed together, unleashing a thunderclap that echoed down the street, and a lance of Arcane electricity that struck the assassin. But she kept coming, nonetheless. "Shit."

She slashed at my face, and my ankle turned under me as I stumbled beneath the blade. I felt a blow to my back as her knife struck the shield and bounced off. I used the momentum to roll away, coat flapping, and stood back up.

I was almost done. My legs were sore from running, and

I was completely out of breath. I levelled the pistol, but she batted it away and slashed at my face again. The shield broke, and as the crystalline structure reformed, she quickly darted the blade into the gap and cut into my cheek.

"This has been fun, whelp, but now it's time to pay for what you've done," she said to me in an upper-class accent—when did ladies start training to be hired killers?

"Oh," I panted, "so it's revenge? Bit excessive, don't you think?" Now was not the time for jokes, but I needed to buy time to find a way out.

She lunged, aiming the knife at my chest, but I managed to whip the butt of my pistol into her forearm and deflect the blow away from my vitals. The knife found purchase on my shield, and I looked down to see the lattice reconnecting around my lower abdomen. One of her long gloves had come loose in the fight, and for a second, I caught sight of the distinctive brand on her arm.

The assassin broke the knife free and then drove into my gut. The shield shattered around the blade—immaterial glass cascaded onto the floor, covered in my blood. The pain was hot, sharp, and sudden, and my shirt turned wet in seconds. I let out a weak, pathetic gasp for air and stumbled back from her. She stalked forwards slowly—she was taunting me, like a cat playing with its food—then my heel caught on a cobblestone. The assassin stood over me, silhouetted by the late morning sun, like a vengeful angel; covered in blood, with a face of pure malice. The pain was unbearable—worse than anything I'd ever experienced—but I was pretty sure it wouldn't last much longer. "Did you really think you could interfere with our business and live to talk about it?" she gloated.

Suddenly, the air turned blisteringly hot, and archaic, otherworldly words of power echoed from behind the assassin. She burst into flame as a dragon made of pure elemental fire erupted from the ground beneath her. I still remember her screams as she died, blood curdling and ethereal.

As the fire died, and my vision began to fade, Bryce was standing over me. "Charlotte? Oh, shit, that's bad," he said, but he sounded like he was a hundred miles away.

I heard others talking, gasps of terror and the sounds of people fleeing. "Heathen! Wizard!? Mage!"

"Charlotte, you're going to bleed out, damn I need to do something. Charlotte, can you hear me?" Bryce said with what sounded like worry. I nodded weakly. "I need to cauterise the wound. I can't move you like this. This is going to hurt." There was a quiet click, and almost inaudibly, he whispered an impish word of power. There was a searing pain on my side, and he burned my wound shut. Then I fainted.

Chapter 25

My left side felt like it was on fire, which I suppose it had been. Not only that, but there was also a deeper pain, something throbbing and pulsing inside my abdomen. My head was swimming, and as I drew myself back to consciousness, I realised I was in Jennifer's office, sat in one of the mismatched armchairs.

I tried to sit up, and pain shot through me. "Argh, god dammit!" I exclaimed, then a thud came from the hallway and a few moments later Bryce appeared at the door. He had ditched his waistcoat and wore a white shirt. At least it was white before it was covered in blood.

"Oh God, Charlotte, don't try to move," he came up and pushed a cold towel into my side.

"Fuck. Shit, fucking, bollocks that hurts!"

"Just hold still, we'll, ummmm, get a doctor, or oh god," he stammered and began pacing the room. Trying to keep my eyes on him just made my pain worse.

"Stop, stop moving, just stand still will you," I tried to weakly grab at him. "My, my stomach. Something, throbbing really deep."

"I… I had to… I had to seal your wound. But…" He wasn't making complete sentences and he wouldn't stop pacing, and somehow that was more frustrating than dying.

I strained, "Bryce!" I exhaled deeply and then had trouble catching my breath again through the pain. "Bugger, I think. I think I'm bleeding internally. Where's Elly? She should. Be here."

"The shop was empty. There's no one else here," he said. I tried to think where Elly would have gone, and why it had to be now she wasn't around. "W-w-w-w-what do we do? Why am I even here, why did I have to follow you? Why did you follow me? Oh fuck, the club…"

My head was swimming. I knew I had to act, treat the

wound in some way before death took me. The thoughts ran through my head, spinning round and round, and Bryce's stammering and pacing were doing nothing to help my focus. There was a healing draught that would work, but it wasn't meant for internal wounds, and I was in no shape to make it. I needed to tell Bryce, get him to take me to the lab. I just needed to say the words. Why was it getting so difficult to talk?

"B–Bryce," I said softly. "Need to go to the lab."

"What, no you can't move," he said obstinately.

"Bryce, take me to the lab, or I'll die."

He hesitated, but I looked him dead in the eyes and he sighed before coming towards me. "This is going to hurt," he took my arm and tucked his shoulder into me and pulled me up to carry me. I grunted in pain but did my best not to scream. Moving to the lab was one of the most prolonged painful experiences I had ever had. I felt like my guts were going to burst out of my side.

Bryce put me down in the chair next to Jennifer's Alchemy table. The afternoon sun was coming through the window told me I had been out for a few hours. "Right, we need, to make, a healing…. Draught," I said through heavy breaths.

"A what?" Bryce responded.

"It's a potion, for treating wounds, it accelerates healing." I gestured at the equipment on the table. "Don't worry, I'm good at those." My vision went black and a few moments later I felt Bryce's warm hand tapping me on the cheek.

"Charlotte, you can't make a potion in your current state," he looked like a scared puppy.

I smiled and let out a sardonic laugh. "I'm not going to make it. You are," I stated, clearly delirious.

I was lying with my head back and my eyes closed, but I imagined Bryce's face must have been as horrified as his reply. "What? Me? I can't do alchemy. How do you expect me to make it? I've never even seen any of this equipment!"

"Will you. Calm down. I'm going. To tell you. What to do." I paused for a moment and took a deep inhale and exhale. Pulling myself up in the chair, wincing at the pain,

I looked over the lab table. "Don't worry, this will be really simple. All we need to do is make a paste of turmeric, garlic, and lemongrass, then add that to a solution of salt and aqua vitae. Heat the whole thing over a gentle flame till it thickens. The magic will do the rest."

"Oh, well, that sounds very easy. How come everyone doesn't do that?" he said, puzzled.

"Because you need to do everything in a precise order, the equipment needs to be laid out perfectly, and then you need a source of magic. Timing and geometry are just as important in alchemy as ingredients. You have to be precise, it's how you go from a smelly paste to transmuting the—" I paused to breathe, and my side began to throb even harder. "It's how you draw out the magic."

"Right, that makes no sense, no matter," Bryce said unconvincingly. "Where do we start?" His hands were shaking at this point, and I realised that I was about to put my life in them, the same hands he had nearly tried to kill me with a few days prior.

"Step one, get the ingredients and measure them out," I said, and rattled off the list of reagents and their quantities from memory. "You need the pestle and mortar, the granite one, not the marble. The lab table has divots, put it in the central one," I instructed.

"Why the central—" he began to say, but as he leant over the table a sense of realisation formed on his face. "Oh, there's ley lines here, I can feel the energy flowing through them."

"Can you marvel at Arcane phenomena when I'm not dying? Take the herbs and spices and pound them into a paste. One at a time in the order you collected them. Grind each till they are smooth before adding the next," he did as I said, and I focussed on the rhythmic thumbing of the mortar to help me stay conscious.

The world was starting to get fuzzy, the edges of my perception drifting into the unknowable. Even the pain began to numb, as if it was filtered out, no longer useful information. Two emotions jostled for prominence in my mind, fear of imminent death, and frustration that I was putting my fate in someone else's hands. The hands of a man who had no idea what he was doing.

"Charlotte? What do I do now?" Bryce was saying, and I snapped back to reality again.

"Put the spirit burner in the North slot on the table," I said wearily, and clicked my fingers to the correct position when Bryce looked puzzled at the table. I hadn't expected how tired dying would make you. I felt like I could sleep for a week. Or eternity if things went poorly. "Get a boiling flask. No, a smaller one, add the salt and Aqua Vitea. Be careful, that's a high proof spirit, don't spill it."

Bryce diligently followed my instructions, a before long a rather sedate reaction bubbled to life in the flask. "It's boiling, what comes next?"

"Add the paste, then it needs—" The world swam around me, and my vision blurred. The throbbing pain intensified to the point where every beat of my heart was like being crushed in a vise.

A distorted shape moved in my field of vision and kneeled in front of me. Bryce's face came into focus, full of panic. He mopped the sweat from my brow with the cuff of his shirt. "Stay with me, Miss Price. What does the potion need?"

"M—Ma—" Another wave of dizziness and confusion washed over me. I knew what I needed to say, but the word wouldn't come. Bryce moved his hand from my forehead and pressed his fingers against my neck, feeling for my pulse, and I caught a flash of the scarred skin amongst the ink on his forearm. My arms were as heavy as tree trunks, but I managed to grab his wrist and jab a clumsy finger into the sword-shaped birthmark.

"Magic?" Bryce asked. I nodded, and he got up and walked back to the table. "What kind of magic?"

At last, I managed to take a full breath, and my senses pulled back into full focus. "Just raw Arcane," I said, still gasping for air. "It won't need much, enough to speed the reaction up."

Bryce nodded and concentrated on drawing forth a bead of golden light in his palm, muttering a verse of Cant as he did. It usually took hours for those draughts to collect enough ambient magic for the reaction to start, and Bryce had got it going in seconds—maybe having a mage around more often would be useful.

Watching the milky liquid slowly start to thicken and change was painfully slow, almost as painful as the wound doing its best to kill me. All told, creating the potion took nearly forty minutes, and Bryce would not sit still when he couldn't do anything. I had to send him to get some water from the kitchen just so I didn't have to listen to his boots rapping on the floor any longer.

I'd be lying if I said I didn't think about my impending death as I sat alone in the lab. Would it hurt in the end? It was hurting a lot right now. I wasn't a religious person, but I couldn't help wondering about "after." In a world where a man with a marked wrist can tear asunder a building, or part the sea, one doesn't really see the need for gods and afterlives. I thought about Jennifer, was she still alive? What would she do if I were the one who went missing?

"Is it done?" Bryce said when the last bubble popped and the potion settled. He held it up to the light, and it gleamed, slightly pearlescent.

"It looks perfect. Now, because of your frankly brilliant idea of cauterising my wound, we are going to have to get creative. The draught needs to be applied directly, otherwise it won't heal fully." I grunted and pulled myself to my feet.

"Where do you think you're going?" Bryce said, reaching out to me.

I walked to the closet. "We need a syringe, and I'm not letting your filthy hands touch them." I was limping hard and had to grab the doorframe of the closet to stop myself from falling over. The rest had done me well, though. I was still in a lot of pain, but I felt more able to move.

"A syringe? You're going to inject this? Is that safe?"

"Didn't they teach you in Lord school not to ask so many questions? Christ on a bicycle, you are tiring. Trust me, I know what I'm doing!" I did not know what I was doing, but Bryce did not need to know that. I pulled one of the stain-less-steel syringes from a bath of sterilising liquid and dried it off, then hobbled back to the worktable. I leaned on the edge of the table and put the syringe down. "Come here. I need you to get these clothes off."

This was apparently the most shocking thing I had said to Bryce all day, as he went beet red and froze. "I beg your pardon?"

"Just come help me take this off, I need to see the wound," I was already unbuttoning my ruined waistcoat. It was coated in blood and there was a hole in it where I had been stabbed. Bryce came to his senses and stepped over to help me take it off my shoulders and I started untying the laces of my shirt. "Ah that hurts. You'll need to lift it off me, and then cut the laces on the corset."

"Miss Price I couldn't possibly. This is too far. I've helped you make your potion, but I cannot undress you."

"Now is not the time to develop a sense of prudishness, Bryce. I'm dying, and you are worried about your damn dignity!?" I snapped at him. He stood aghast, a look that was becoming very familiar on him. Then, reluctantly, he helped. First lifting off the shirt, and then taking a small blade up the back of the corset to cut the laces in one go. I doubled over in pain as the pressure of the undergarment released.

With my abdomen exposed, I could finally look at the damage. Black, blistered skin covered a four-inch-long, one-inch-wide patch of skin. Blood had dried onto my sides and down into my trousers. The skin around the burn was a deep ruddy purple, where the blood had been pooling inside my torso.

"Give me the potion," I said to Bryce, and he handed me the flask. I filled the syringe with the white fluid and then tenderly touched my burned skin. Strangely, to me at least, it didn't hurt to touch. I felt the wound, trying to find where the knife had gone in. I slowly pushed the needle in and gasped when it hit the flesh that hadn't been cremated. I braced myself, as best I could, and depressed the plunger.

Coldness flooded my body. I breathed in sharply, and said, "Oh boy, ah yeah, that's working." I could feel the flesh on my side tightening and stitching back together. I dropped to my knees and grabbed my abdomen. I was shivering and holding back the urge to convulse as my body healed much faster than it should.

Once the sensation of my body stitching itself back together faded, I looked up and Bryce was watching me intently. "Getting a good view there?" I said, as a wry smile curled across my lips.

Bryce turned red again and looked away. "I was just making sure you were alright," he said, clearly embarrassed.

I checked my side, and the burned skin peeled away with ease, revealing a supple pinkness underneath that was tender to the touch. The bruising was gone, and the only evidence I had even been wounded was a small white scar, and the dried blood, of course.

I stood up and Bryce turned back to me. He looked quite relieved and let out a long sigh, as if he'd been holding his breath for the last two hours. "I'm glad you are alright," he said. Then he covered his eyes again. "But you should put a shirt back on."

I looked down at my bare chest and laughed. Oh, it felt good to laugh, and it felt good to not be dying. "Yeah, yeah. God, you act like you've never seen breasts before," I said, mockingly. "Oh, and one more thing, I'm probably going to pass out again in a minute or so, side effect of the potion." I was about to head to the spare bedroom when a ruckus came up the stairs.

"Charlotte!?" Elly called, "Charlotte, what's going on? There's blood...." She opened the door to the lab, saw me, bloody and shirtless, and then looked at the embarrassed Bryce behind me. "Oh," she said, and then I passed out again.

Chapter 26

Elly was tending to the bloody wound on Bryce's head when I awoke. It was bad by the looks of things, and I felt awful for having not noticed it. Despite his demeanour, he must have been pushing through the pain with some serious will-power to help me. My face was sore, and I realised the cut on my cheek had been stitched closed. The stitches would fall out in an hour or so if the healing draught had enough power left after saving my life.

"Thank you, Doctor," Bryce said as Elly finished his stitches.

"She likes to be called Elly," I said from the couch, alerting them both to my renewed state of consciousness. I'd been dressed in a shirt, and a blanket was put over me. Of course, such was the side-effect of the shield potion that I suddenly became feverish and kicked the blanket off.

"Don't you start, missy. You are damn lucky to be alive. Do you know that?" Elly said sternly. "I go out for an hour and come back to find blood everywhere."

The opportunity was too good to pass up. "And after you did so well at cleaning the place up," I said sarcastically.

"I will stab you again," Elly responded, with not a hint of sarcasm. She came over and sat on the coffee table. I moved to sit up, but she pushed me back down and started checking the remnants of my wounds. "Stay still."

"This is Bryce, by the way," I said, trying to deflect some of Elly's ire.

"We've been acquainted. He kindly filled me in on your escapades. Apparently, it was quite the daring rescue—a dashing hero saving a damsel in distress, the way he tells it." I scowled at the very notion that I could ever be considered a damsel, no matter the distress I was in. As for Bryce being dashing? I'd have laughed at the idea, but there was a sudden pain in my chest where Elly prodded me. "You've broken a rib."

"I don't think getting stabbed and apparently breaking a rib counts as an escapade." I pushed Elly's hands away more defiantly and sat myself up, suddenly shivering again. "Thank you, doc, I'll be fine." Bryce cleared his throat. "And thank you, Mr Rosehouse, for not cocking up an entry level potion."

He scoffed, "You have some nerve…"

"Fine," I interrupted him, "I mean it, really, thank you, both of you." I buried my head in my hands and rubbed the sleep from my eyes with a groan. "That was a fucking disaster. I should have realised I was being followed." Jennifer would have realised. "She was really going to kill me… and for what? There's got to be more to it than revenge for some drug runners." Bryce was right, I was in too deep. "Fuck."

Bryce rolled his eyes. "I just hope no one else got hurt. You really didn't think that those people didn't want to be found."

I could have thrown something across the room, but I kept a lid on my temper. "I… don't know what to say. I'm sorry."

"Yes, well, there's other things to worry about right now. In the gallery, you mentioned the fire on Stewart Street. You said the mage had a tattoo," Bryce said. He was on edge and nervously pacing the room.

"That's right," I responded, desperately trying to unjumble my brain after nearly dying. "I couldn't make out the design. She was too badly burnt, but the ink was unmistakable. What is it, anyway? Some kind of focus or channelling substance? Or is it a mnemonic compound that helps form the words of power?" Bryce was apparently quite annoyed at my changing the subject and scowled at me.

"That is not relevant to the matter at hand. What else do you know?" he pressed. There was something different about him, compared to when he sat in this office several nights earlier. He wasn't drunk, that was for sure, but there was an air of composure about him, despite the nerves. It suited him, actually.

"The tattoo was on the back of her neck, that's all I can say for certain. She was young, medium build, fierce looking—but she was pretty badly burned."

A forlorn look came over him. He stopped pacing by the window overlooking the street and put a hand up to the glass. "Monica Talison."

"Who was Monica?" Elly asked before I could.

"We were students together at London University. We were among eight others in the inaugural class on the new Bachelors in Arcane Studies," he responded. "A few of us devised the tattoos as a way to, how do I put this delicately? Cheat on our exams."

I looked at him curiously. "Why would one of your former classmates be doing dirty work for Hawkins?"

"I'm as confused as you are—the last I heard; all my former classmates had gone missing." He clenched his fist, but there was no anger in his face.

Elly looked at Bryce and said, "Missing? Missing how?"

Bryce turned, his fingers tracing the ink etched into his skin. "They never returned for the autumn semester. I was expelled in the spring—when I was caught dealing the Ember—and I'd lost touch with most of them. By September they had all vanished. No investigation, no calls for information—nobody cared about half a dozen missing mages."

"Except now one of them has reappeared, and she damn near blew up a building," I said before pausing and looking at Bryce. "Well, I suppose two. That assassin was a mage as well. I saw her brand before she stabbed me—she another of your former friends?"

Bryce looked surprised that I'd made the connection, then nodded. "Bethany Henderson. I didn't realise until after that fight and saw what was left of her face under the veil."

"Were any of them in the 1735 Club?" I asked. Bryce looked away from me, clearly not interested in talking, but his expression gave me all the information I needed. "Let me guess, Billy Parker? The one that disappeared. Or died? What the hell, Bryce? What else aren't you saying?"

"I don't know," he said.

"You don't know!?" He shook his head. Fucking typical. This was all getting far too convenient to be a coincidence.

Missing mages showing up, a member of the 1735 Club disappearing, the Black Ember, and Bryce right in the middle of it all. "You are so full of shit, Bryce, people must think you're Father Thames. Start talking."

He looked flustered, and almost ready to run. I suspect he would have done if Elly hadn't reassured him. "Mr Rosehouse, we really need your assistance. Charlotte's attitude aside." I glared at her. My attitude? My attitude was entirely justified.

"Start with Billy Parker," I said, trying to calm my voice.

Bryce ran his hand through his hair, which had turned into a greasy, sweaty mess. "Billy was the one who introduced me to the 1735. He was a good kid, but a bit of a radical. He helped me get sober and thought the club would be a positive environment."

"What happened to him, Bryce?" Elly asked. Her voice was like sweet honey and soothed even my frayed temper.

"I genuinely don't know," he said, apologetic. "He stopped showing up to meetings. He was reported dead sometime later. Drowned, in the Thames. But the body… The body was too far gone to identify properly." Bryce finally stopped pacing for good and sat down. "For a time, no one in the 1735 believed it, but one by one, we all gave up on Billy."

"This was before the rest of the class went missing then, right? None of them were reported dead?" I asked. Bryce shook his head. "Billy wanted to help you back on the straight and narrow, so I suppose he wasn't partaking in your extracurricular activities?" He shook his head again. "What about the rest of the class, what do you know about them?"

"Not much, I'm afraid. I was the oldest by five or so years—they were all fresh out of college. Monica and Bethany were the only women, there was one ambiguous individual, and the rest were men," Bryce explained. "All from fairly well-off families, as you'd imagine."

The cogs in my brain kicked up a gear, the thread of the mystery starting to unspool. "Right, so, you get expelled for dealing in Ember—but you weren't the only one taking it?"

"I sold to all of them, in varying amounts."

I nodded as Bryce spoke, then said, "So when you go clean and join a secret mage liberation group, you classmates need a new source—and they find Hawkins?"

"I suppose they must have done."

"Now, Billy Parker disappears, presumed dead. What if he found out they were still partaking—found out where they were getting the drugs from?"

"He would have told me if there was still Ember at the University," Bryce said, grimacing with frustration.

"Not if the others got to him first, not if Hawkins did." I started to pace the room myself. "Billy dies, then the rest of the class all disappear without a trace. They could all be working for Hawkins now. The question is why."

Elly chimed in, "if they're all hooked on the Ember, isn't that reason enough?"

"Maybe," I responded. "But the timing is too coincidental—in the meeting, people were talking about amendments to the Witchcraft Act—movement towards some actual positive progress. At the same time, increasing supplies of Black Ember start coming into the city. Some of which leads to the untimely demise of Timothy Waters in Stepney. Hawkins isn't just selling drugs; he's using mages to sow discord among the public." I paused my stream of consciousness to catch up with what I had said. The connections were tantalisingly close, I just needed to grab them. "Timothy Waters, Stewart Street, the Black Ember, Billy Parker, the Witchcraft Act; it's all connected."

There was a pregnant pause. No one seemed to want to break the silence.

"So," Elly said after a few moments, "If we can find the rest of Bryce's old classmates, we might find the source of this drug, and where Jennifer might be?"

"Precisely what I was thinking. Bryce, who might know the most about your classmates? Who could help lead us in the right direction?" I asked.

"Professor Carrington, I'd suspect, he was our principal instructor." Bryce was a million miles away; I was surprised he hadn't gone completely monosyllabic. I scrunched up a ball of paper and threw it at him, which seemed to snap him back into the room with us. "Excuse you."

Elly laughed, and both Bryce and I shot her with piercing looks. "What, usually Charlotte's the one off with the fairies. It's funny to see her get a taste of her own medicine."

"Irrelevant," I said. "Bryce, this Professor, do you think he could help us? We might know some things he doesn't, and vice versa."

"Potentially. I haven't spoken with him in quite some time. He's friends with my father, and neither of them are particularly fond of me since my expulsion," he pondered. "I can reach out."

I nodded. "It's something, at least. I need to track down Inspector Baker and see if he has found any leads on the *Hyacinth*." Something else gnawed at my thoughts, something I'd forgotten in the jumble of information we'd uncovered. The only problem was that I didn't have the foggiest of what it was. I put the thought aside and got to my feet. "Right, it seems like we have our next steps planned. Let us know as soon as you hear from the Professor, Bryce."

"I will, but I'm still not certain if I should trust you, Charlotte Price," Bryce said.

"Likewise," I responded.

Elly, not to be left out, chimed in, and said, "Well, I think you are both a little ungrateful to each other, and for what it's worth, I trust you both." I cocked my head at her quizzically, but she just smiled in return. "Mr Rosehouse, it's been a pleasure, but Charlotte needs to rest now, and you should too, with that concussion."

"Quite right, I'll be on my way. I will relay anything I learn from the Professor post haste. Doctor, Ms Price," Bryce bowed, and made his way out the shop. I waited for the doorbell and turned to Elly with a wry smile.

"Now, Doctor, you have me all alone and bed stricken. Whatever shall you do?" I said with a faux swoon.

"Provide you with professional medical care and ensure you don't overexert yourself. Oh, and this," she jabbed me in the ribs, and I yelped in pain. "That is for scaring me and for shooting me this morning."

"Ow, what happened to do no harm!?" I cried. But alas, Elly ignored me and went to make tea. While she was downstairs, I scribbled down a missive to send to the Inspector, inquiring on any updates from his investigation.

October 14th, 1834

Industrial Revelations

Chapter 27

The next morning, the papers had once again leapt at the opportunity to twist the events of the previous day, with The Chronicle running "MAGICAL VIOLENCE in PICADILLY," and The Sun printing "New Calls for CLAMP DOWN on ARCANE ARSONISTS." The former ran a nonsense version of events of my confrontation with the assassin that painted Bryce as a mad pyromancer, while the latter worryingly suggested movement in government to enforce tougher controls on the use of magic. Despite the efforts of the 1735 Club, it seemed that perhaps the reforms they'd hoped for were no longer as certain.

I peered over my broadsheet as the cab rolled to a halt outside my destination and looked around for anyone suspicious. I wasn't about to let my brush with death put a stop to my search for Jennifer, but there was no harm in being a little more careful. The sky over the Stepney police station was dappled with soft grey cloud, black smoke, and the odd fleeting patch of blue. There'd been a drizzle again overnight, but the worst of the stormy weather had finally passed.

Elly had accompanied me, having decided she needed to keep a closer eye on me. She hopped out of the cab before me and looked up and down the street. Instead of the elegant day dresses she'd worn the days before, today she was wearing a much more practical pair of tweed trousers and a matching jacket. It was an adorable look, in a utilitarian kind of way.

A portly man in a blue swallowtail coat, black trousers and top hat stood outside the slender three storey building. "LONDON METROPOLITAN POLICE" was emblazoned above the entrance, but it was otherwise plain in construction and decoration.

I paid the cabby and stepped out, slinging my satchel bag over my shoulder. My boots splashed in the small puddles, and

I fumbled to button up my coat as I approached the officer on guard. I looked a wreck again, and the officer gave me a ghastly frown upon seeing the dark purple bruise on my cheek where yesterday I'd been cut. I was right that the stitches had fallen out, but the healing draught did nothing to prevent the bruising.

"Can I help you, uh, ladies?" the officer said with a deep cockney accent.

"Yes, we're here to see Inspector Baker on request, is he available?" I'd managed to get my letter to Baker in the evening post, and by the morning he'd written back, asking me to come down to the station post-haste.

"He arrived but moments ago, ma'am, shall I alert him of your, uh, arrival?" the man explained. The officer's nervousness gave him away as a rookie. No doubt he'd been made to stand out here as some sort of hazing ritual from his colleagues.

"No need, he should be expecting us. Good day to you, sir," I replied. Elly and I walked up the steps to the station together, and I held open the heavy oak door for her. Who said chivalry was solely the province of men? The sound of the street was replaced by the sounds of people talking and working—the smell of factory smoke largely replaced with the smell of pipe smoke and sweat.

To my left, there were benches and tables where a dozen or so off-duty officers sat, eating, and joking with one another—the blue of their uniforms stark against the drab, earthy interior—. To the right, a group of people were waiting in some chairs, while a uniformed woman took their names and answered their queries. I asked the officer sitting at the reception desk where I might find Inspector Baker and was taken to a small office in the back on the building.

I knocked on the door and waited patiently. After a few long moments the door opened and a bedraggled and damp looking Anthony Baker stood before me. "Miss Price, and Dr Chynoweth, wasn't it?" he said, a note of surprise in his voice.

"That's right, but you can call me Elly," the good doctor responded. "I thought the two of you might need an expert eye if any other bodies turn up."

"Right you are. Thank you for coming so quickly, Charlotte. I regret I missed the evening delivery yesterday, but I see you got my letter anyway."

He stood aside, revealing what counted as an Inspector's office in the Metropolitan Police. A simple desk stood in the centre of the room, accompanied by a chair just as simple. A bookshelf lined one wall, filled with neatly organised ledgers. In one corner there was a coat stand, adorned with Baker's blue swallowtail. The room was lit by a window, but several candelabras lay about the surfaces.

"Thank you, Inspector. Your letter said you had some new information on Jennifer's disappearance," I said as I walked in and stood beside the desk. Inspector Baker, ever the gentleman, pulled a chair from behind the door and offered it to Elly, before sitting himself. I stayed standing.

"That I do, Miss Price. After our encounter the other day I had the boys round up a few of Hawkins' known associates. Petty thieves and drug runners mostly," he began to explain, pausing to drink from a steaming mug of tea. "Mm, that's good, just what I needed. Can I get you some?"

"No, no, I'm quite alright. Please continue."

"I'm fine as well," Elly said in a deadpan deliver, while glaring at me. I averted my eyes, lest my soul be burned away.

"Well, they were all very adamant they knew nothing about the Black Ember, and I'm of a mind to believe them," he leaned in conspiratorially, "We tried a few surreptitious operations you see, trying to buy some of the stuff, but no one knew what we were talking about."

"The Ember isn't being sold?" I said, puzzled.

"No, I reckon Hawkins is stockpiling the stuff—waiting for the opportune moment. Now I know what you're thinking. If no one's selling, then where did Timothy Waters get his?"

"A different supplier?" I answered, knowing I was wrong.

"Maybe, or maybe he stole it, I thought. So, I went to Waters' last place of employment, remembering the seal that was on his little pouch. The same seal, I realised, as was on the sign at the warehouse on Stewart Street," he explained.

Baker's face lit up very proud of his deduction.

"Sparrow and Son's? I think it was," I said, leaning in, my interest piqued.

"The very same. Imagine my surprise, then, when I arrive at the Millwall docks and question the harbour master, that he explained to me that Sparrow and Son's doesn't exist. No ships, no contracts, no employees. Just a name and a seal."

"A strawman company," Elly said, realising where Baker's deduction was going. "One of father's competitors set up a dummy operation some time back, posing as a smelting corporation, but in actuality, they were just buying up cheap ore and selling it on."

"So, if we could find out where Waters got his supply, we could find out who really owns Sparrow and Son's, then we find Hawkins and Jennifer?" I asked.

"Precisely, Ms Price, and this is where my true master stroke comes in. If the trading company didn't officially exist, then neither did your missing ship," Baker stated. He rested his elbows on his desk and paused for dramatic effect. "We were no longer looking for a trading vessel called the Hyacinth, then. I spoke again to the harbourmaster at Millwall, and the one at London Docks, enquiring after any and all late arriving ships on the night of the Stewart Street fire."

I leaned in again and interjected, "The manifest they provided would have been fake, but most likely they would just lie about the goods, not the locations, to add a sense of legitimacy. Were any of these ships out of Shanghai?"

"Just one. Millwall docks, it should still be there." He had an inviting smile on his face that said, *and if you wanted to come along* without him even saying another word.

"Then we should leave immediately. If they are planning on moving the ship, they could do it at any time," I turned and picked up my coat from the stand and began buttoning it. Wordlessly, Inspector Baker also rose and moved to don his long blue coat. A flash of metal on the inside of his coat caught my attention. A flintlock pistol. Curious, as officers of the law didn't normally carry firearms.

The police cab we took to Millwall Docks was a heavy four-wheeler, drawn by a jet-black horse. The journey from Stepney was short enough, but we had to stop a few times in the morning traffic. The Isle of Dogs buzzed with activity, with boats and ships of all sizes filling the moorings of the West India Docks. When at last we rolled to a stop at the north-west corner of Millwall and stepped out onto the wharf, I could hardly keep my head on straight.

There were dock workers moving crates, barrels, and sacks on and off of ships of all sizes. Carts were loaded up and sent off to their next destinations, and rowdy sailors disembarked from vessels that had arrived that morning. Every other minute a bell would sound, signalling the coming or going of more vessels, and above it all was the constant mewing of seagulls.

Baker led the way, and Elly and I followed. We were given a wide berth, which came as no surprise. About halfway along the wharf, Baker flagged down a man in a dock master's uniform. "Good day sir, Inspector Baker, London Metropolitan Police, this is Charlotte Price and Dr Chynoweth, my associates."

The dock master was a stout man, with salt and pepper mutton chops. He looked at Baker with disdain, and me with disregard. Elly he ignored entirely. "Inspector, eh? What does Peel's Bloody Gang want with my docks today, huh? Come to arrest more of my workers for enjoying their evenings?" His voice was shrill and raspy, and he spoke with an almost permanent sneer.

The Inspector ignored the insinuations of misdeeds and pressed the dock master, "We're enquiring after a ship that arrived late some nights past, inbound from Shanghai. I confirmed with the dock master on duty just yesterday that it was here."

His sneer deepened, "What my colleague may or may not have confirmed is not my concern. I'm unaware of such a ship."

"Well, then you wouldn't mind us checking your records of arrivals. Just to make sure everything is in order, of course," I said pointedly.

He made a mono-syllabic sound and wiped his brow again. "I'm not sure I could, Miss Price, was it? There's sensitive information within, shipping records and such. I'd be breaking my client's confidence if I allowed just anyone to look," he stuttered in response.

"Well, we aren't just anyone. This is a matter of the law, good sir, this ship is associated with a possible crime," I said back. Anthony stood behind me looking menacingly at the dockmaster, seemingly old hat at these kinds of interrogations.

His eyes rolled. "Right, yes, the law. Of course, follow me." Grudgingly, he led us towards the small building in the centre of the harbour.

The 'office', if one could call it that, was more like an outhouse that had a table shoved into it. A large record book lay open with an inkwell and quill next to it. A bucket had collected rainwater that dripped in through the roof and had yet to be emptied. The records contained the comings and goings of ships, the names of their captains, and a short form shipping manifesto.

I scanned the book, looking for anything that might lead to our quarry. As expected, the name Hyacinth didn't appear at all in the records going back a week. I knew what I was looking for though, and found the last arriving ships the night Jennifer had vanished. As Baker had explained, only one had logged Shanghai in its manifest. "This one, the *Sugar Chaser*, that's the ship. Pier 7. This says it was bringing in tea and silks, but it doesn't match the manifesto we found on the ship's Captain at all," I said. I turned to start looking for the pier, but Elly was way ahead of me.

"Over here!" she called, pointing down a pontoon between two small vessels. Baker and I shared a surprised look for a moment before heading down the slippery dock. I stopped at pier seven. It was empty of people, and half a dozen small barges were moored on the right. On the left was a ship that was unmistakably the same ship from Stewart Street.

"This is it, I'm certain." I felt a bubbling in the pit of my stomach, as if some rancid beast was crawling out of a swamp. This was the closest I'd been to finding Jennifer. What if she wasn't there? What if I never found her?

What was an apprentice without a teacher? There was no one else in the entire city that I could go to—I barely knew any other alchemists beyond a brief meeting. But Jen was so much more than a teacher—I'd have given anything to see her stupid grin again. I swallowed hard and pushed the feeling down. There had to be something there, something to point the way. I had to believe that.

I walked to the gangplank and checked it was sturdy with my boot. "Stay close, Elly. Inspector, you might want your pistol."

The harbour master was aghast. "His what? You best not be planning on shooting up my docks."

Baker glared at him. "You'd be best keeping your mouth shut, lest I arrest you for aiding and abetting. What's the punishment for assisting in shipping fraud?" he said. The man shrank down even smaller and skulked away.

As I stepped onto the deck the ship creaked and groaned, like a sleeping giant waking from a long nap. The deck was very slippery, and the sails rustled in their bindings from the wind. I put a hand on the side of the ship and waited for Baker to ascend. Elly slipped on the deck and grabbed hold of me to stop from falling, and wouldn't let go. "I should have mentioned I'm afraid of boats."

"Well, this is a ship, nothing to worry about," I said, glibly.

"Very funny."

Towards the back of the ship was a raised platform, where the wheel was mounted, below which was a cabin of some kind. I pointed it out to Baker and said, "After you, Inspector." I had no such fear of boats, but I wasn't going to walk down into a dark cabin first.

Baker nodded and moved to the cabin. He was surprisingly steady on his feet as the ship swayed back and forth. I figured he might have served in the navy before he joined Bow Street, and later the Met. He had one hand inside his coat, no doubt on the flintlock he carried, and pushed open the cabin door. It was unlocked, but darkness pervaded beyond.

I followed him in and dug out a match and candle from my satchel of supplies. The orange glow formed a small bubble of light around us, but the much of the room was still in shadow. I could make out the shape of a desk and a bed, but nothing else. I stepped forward, lighting candles that were mounted on tables and cabinets as I went. Baker was moving round the opposite side of the room. I was about the reach the desk when I heard movement.

"Charlotte, get down!" Elly shouted, pushing me to the side, causing us both to tumble. I turned in time to see a silhouette in the doorway, before it leapt down the steps to the cabin, a flash of steel in their hand.

"Anthony—" I began, but Baker was already in motion. As soon as the mystery assailant had hit the deck, the officer's pistol cracked. The attacker grunted and slumped to the floor.

In the moment of calm that followed, I finally realised Elly was lying on top of me. Her face was illuminated by the muted overcast light when Baker pulled a curtain to. Looking into her eyes, I almost forgot about the man with a fresh bullet hole in his skull. She seemed taken in as well, until she laughed and said, "I assume that's your pistol poking into my leg, or have you been keeping secrets from me?"

I pushed her, rather unceremoniously, off of me, and then helped her up. Baker held his firearm at the ready and approached the body. I sidled up next to him and said, "Good shot, Inspector. Let's see who this was." In the dim light, I could make out the face of a young man with porcelain skin, not at all a sailor or dock worker. He was wearing simple, but finely made clothes, and he seemed unremarkable.

Except, for the black orbs that sank into his face where his eyes should be. Obsidian tendrils bled from the sockets, tracing the man's veins, and the blood that seeped from the wound on his head was black as well. Elly knelt down beside me, a look of curiousness on her face. "What is this? I've never seen anything like it—look at the burns around his nostrils, those are fresh."

"I have a suspicion," I said, before pulling the man's sleeves up and revealing the markings on his arm, along with an Arcane tattoo of a wolf. "Another of Bryce's classmates, we're on the right track." I checked his pockets, and found a small pouch, just like the one Timothy Waters had, and inside was about an ounce of Black Ember. "Something tells me we got very lucky, else he might have gone up in flames and taken us with him."

"He's clearly emaciated," Elly said. "If he didn't have those eyes, I'd be certain he was an opium addict."

"Black Ember is derived from opium, so that fits," I added, before turning to the inspector. "Well, at least we know it's the right ship. Might I suggest you keep this one quiet? The press have been running wild with stories this week."

"Aye, I'll see to it," Baker responded.

We threw a sheet over the body, and then I went about searching the captain's desk, which was strewn with papers and ledgers. "Here, two manifest copies, one matches ours and the other matches the dock's." The real manifest, which recorded the vast quantities of raw ingredients used to make Black Ember, was stamped with the familiar seal of Sparrow and Son's Trading Company. "This is interesting," I said, picking up another piece of paper.

"A money order?" Elly asked, plucking the paper from my hands. "I've signed dozens of these for Father. This is quite the sum, and it says it's from a Baron Cranley?"

I made a thoughtful sound, then looked to Baker, "is that a name you've come across?"

"Cranley is in Surrey, correct? I assume he's a peer," the inspector replied glibly.

I rolled my eyes sardonically, "Oh yes, of course, why didn't I think of that." Baker was off by a set of stairs leading down into the bowels of the ship. "Cargo hold?" I asked.

"Aye, grab that candelabra." Baker walked down the steps and pushed the door fully open. I followed him and came up to his side, holding out the light source ahead of us. Another pair of doors lay behind the stairs we came down, presumably to the crew sleeping quarters and such. I couldn't see far into the cargo hold, but the area around us was empty. "The size of this ship, and how much they were importing, what could they possibly be planning with all that Black Ember that isn't selling it on the streets?" I asked.

Inspector Baker said nothing and began walking up the length of the ship, his pistol in hand. It gleamed in the light of the candle, solid steel in construction, with what looked like an ivory hand grip. It was a fine piece of gunsmithing and not at all a standard issue warrant officer's sidearm. I followed behind him, sweeping my arm to illuminate the sides of the cargo hold as we walked.

As I suspected, the ship was almost empty, but something very curious caught my eye as we reached the bow. In a pile of sail cloth, nets and other supplies, something glimmered. A brass button reflected the light from the candles, and as I got closer and saw the rough outline of a brown long coat, my heart stopped. I walked in on far too many dead bodies that week already, and I could mercifully take another breath when I realised it was just a coat. But not just any coat. Elation, panic, confusion, and excitement wrestled for prominence inside me. I almost didn't want to believe what I was seeing.

As sure as I've been of anything in my life, it was Jennifer's coat, and beside it was her satchel. I dropped the candelabra and pulled the coat tight into my chest. Candles scattered across the floor, some going out, others clinging to life. I could smell the warm spiciness of Jennifer's perfume, and the acrid smell of her lab. Before I knew what was happening, I was slumped on the floor, sobbing quietly. The wicked voice in my head cackled with glee. She wasn't there, and maybe if I hadn't gone prancing around with Bryce I could have got there in time.

Baker collected up the candles, and then I felt a hand on my shoulder. Elly knelt beside me and rested her head on my shoulder. She didn't need to say a word. I let out a shuddering sob before wiping my nose on my sleeve. "She was here," I said meekly.

"That's good, right? It means we're on the right track," she said.

"But why leave her things, unless…" the idea haunted me. "Unless she was killed or captured."

"She's not dead till we find her dead, Charlotte," Baker said, full of certainty. "Your mentor is a tenacious bitch on the best of days. No way she'd go out like those candles."

"Maybe she's left us something, a clue, that's what I would do," I said. I got up and carried the precious finds to the captain's cabin and piled them onto the table there. Elly and Baker gave me looks of concern, but I ignored them and looked at the only evidence of Jennifer's whereabouts I had.

"You all right, sweetheart?" Elly asked, and I shook my head. "What do you want to do?"

"I don't know. Could you two give me a minute? I need to think."

They looked at each other and nodded. Baker then took off his hat and ran a hand through his hair. "I should be having a word with the dockmaster and see about getting this body moved." He walked up the steps to the deck and Elly followed him, sparing a glance back at me to see if I was sure.

Jennifer's coat was soft and damp in my hands. The heft was unexpected and uneven, the dozen or so extra pockets haphazardly added filled with trinkets. A pocket watch, a few vials, a money purse and paper cartridges, scraps of paper, blunt pencils, and a flask of gin. Good gin.

It should have made sense to me. Each item had a story that I well knew, but I couldn't make the connections. I was spent, exhausted, and it was all too much. Jen had told me to write everything down, so I pulled out my notebook and turned to a new page.

Her coat was still damp.

The pencil hovered at the end of the words, awaiting a command that wouldn't come. What did it mean? What did any of it mean? Why couldn't I work out something that should have been so easy?

The watch had stopped, ten pm the day she went missing. Not long after we arrived at the warehouse.

There were drops of water on the ivory face of the watch and the brass shell with its gold filigree. Was it water? Or were they tears? Had I been crying the whole time? It was too much.

Everything was just too much. Baker's muffled voice came in through the open cabin door. I walked over to it and slammed it shut—but not before catching sight of Elly stood in the rain outside. I needed to focus. Why was it so hard to focus?

I'd thrown myself too deep into something I couldn't begin to understand, and it was like a riptide had swept my feet from under me and dragged my head beneath the waves. It should have been so easy; I should have been able to do this. Everything I needed was right in front of me, but it felt like it was a thousand miles away. Something was holding me back, a weight I'd carried for as long as I can remember.

Hadn't I done everything right? I made plans and lists; I wrote things down and took my time. I had everything I needed and all that remained was to put my brain to work, and I just… couldn't. I stared at Jennifer's things piled on the desk, at the unopened satchel and the still damp coat, and I couldn't focus. Was it fear that clouded my mind? Fear of failure, fear of the truth behind Jen's disappearance, fear of myself?

I was doing everything right, what everyone had told me my entire life. Pull yourself together, pay attention, shut up and do it. Everyone else can manage. No one else struggles as much. This is the way it's always done. If it works for them it should work for me. Right?

When did I start believing those lies over my own instincts? I could hardly remember a time when I didn't hold myself to the standards of everyone but myself. Every time I failed, I told myself it was because I didn't play by their rules, and every time I succeeded, I told myself it didn't count. After so many years of being punished—of punishing myself—for going with my gut; is it any wonder I'd become so reliant on external validation? Who was there that could tell me I was on the right path?

I needed Jennifer—but goddammit, she needed me more. Isn't that the great irony of it all?

It would have been so easy to give up—to hand the pile of things over to Inspector Baker—go back home and sink into the void of my mind. I almost did, I'm ashamed to say. But Jennifer didn't need Baker, she needed me—my brilliance, my talent, my way of leaping across a chasm of logic and reason and finding the answer that no one else could.

There was a primal part of my brain—those deep, wild instincts that gave me the power to do all those brilliant things— that I never felt I had control over. Like it'd been stolen from me and kept just out of arm's reach, to be loaned back on a whim or a lark. But occasionally, when everyone around me was in a panic, or lost, or frozen in fear, something would click into place, and I'd know exactly what to do. I don't know if it was a coincidence, or if I managed to wrest back control through sheer force of will, but it happened. I was in control.

Jennifer's coat was damp from the rain, but it didn't smell like river water; she hadn't gone for a dip, meaning she was probably captured at the warehouse. One thing was missing from her pockets, because Jen wouldn't have wanted it to get wet, which was her notebook. If I knew Jen, she'd have taken any chance she got to leave me a clue in that notebook. I cleared space on the desk, briefly noting that, of the vials from Jen's pockets, one contained a dark red liquid I didn't recognise. It had a filament of something black that snaked around the bottle and didn't disperse when I shook it. It was also a distraction, so I put it aside.

Jen would have stashed the notebook in her satchel, which was made of a heavy-duty canvas with a sealskin lining, very waterproof. The inner fabric had a strange lustre to it, and when I shined some extra light into the bag, I saw something that did not make any sense. Despite being a very ordinary size for a satchel, inside it was massive, at least five times bigger than it should have been. I stared blankly into the voluminous space and was convinced it must have been an illusion of sorts. But, as I reached in a hand to pull out the first item I found, it really was bigger on the inside.

I had to consciously stop myself from trying to work out how it was bigger on the inside, else I might have spent the rest of the day just staring at it. Whatever enchantment, portal, Arcane material or fucking pixie dust was making this happen, wasn't important at that particular moment in time.

I steadied myself and started cataloguing the contents of the bigger-on-the-inside-than-the-outside bag. The first and most obvious item was Jennifer's ornate sword, which had been stored in a sheath that was belted in the inside of the satchel. I vividly remembered how, at the warehouse on Stewart Street, Jen had seemingly pulled the blade from nowhere. Around thirty inches in length, I'd been told repeatedly that it was a small sword, not a rapier. Rapiers were long and heavy, apparently, and no one used them anymore except in bad romance novels. The blade was straight, with a single cutting edge and a sharp point. The hemispherical guard looked like a delicate weaved basket of gold, but on inspection I realised it was in fact gilded steel and quite strong. Much like Jennifer's pistols, I suspected that the construction had been infused with some form of alchemical amalgam, but I couldn't be sure from a visual inspection.

Speaking of the pistols, the twin to the one I'd been carrying with me all week was nestled in the bag. A cursory look suggested it was in working order, and it still had that tell-tale scent of the air just after a lightning storm. With it were several syringes, most of them empty, except for one which contained a curdled, greyish liquid I suspected to be an expired shield potion.

Finally, beneath a jumbled pile of papers and raw component jars, I found what I was looking for. Jen's notebook had seen better days, and I was honestly surprised it still held together at all. My heart soared as I brushed my hand over the faded black cover, a relief I hadn't felt in days. There was a piece of ribbon that served as a bookmark, which revealed things Jennifer had written.

Two pages of notes lay before me, dated the day she went missing. The first looked to be an unfinished formula. It was hastily sketched; rings, pentagrams and intersecting lines forming a complex glyph of apparatus and ingredients, and it was accompanied by a sketch of the potion with the black, snaking tendrils. It was an order of magnitude more complex than even the shield potion, and I hadn't the faintest idea what it might do. At first glance, it was filled with Jennifer's trademarked audacity; she'd included Mercury, Sulphur, and

Salt, all the three base elements of Alchemy, where usually you would only use one. Whatever it did, if it did anything, it was powerful, and would result in one hell of a hangover.

Among the scant notes on the other page were the words, "Billy Parker, July, not suicide." Jennifer had known about Billy Parker; Bryce had said there was no investigation. Was he lying or was there something else at play? There was one other thing, too, an address for a factory or workhouse, on the south bank of the river. Shock, anger, and worry ravaged for prominence within me. Jennifer knew so much more about this case; she'd gleamed so much that I'd struggled to uncover. She didn't tell me any of this, despite how important and potentially lifesaving it could have been. There were signs of something much bigger and much more sinister at work that I had even begun to imagine, and I was woefully unprepared.

A thought struck me like a rampaging bull, a faint memory of something one of the 1735 Club members had said. Rumours from south of the river. Could this factory, Billy Parker's death, Timothy Waters and all the rest of it really be connected? Jennifer had clearly intended for me to find out.

Chapter 28

I burst out onto the deck of the ship, having stuffed all of Jennifer's things into the satchel. "I know where to go!"

The rain had started again, and Elly was huddled under a lean-to shelter on the dock, as Baker questioned the dockmaster. They both looked at me in surprise and moved to meet me at the end of the gangplank. "Found something then?" Baker asked.

"Yes, an address, a factory or something. It's in Lambeth," I explained.

"You think Jen might be there?" Elly said, putting a hand on my arm.

"Maybe, maybe not, but it's important. Her notebook, Elly, she mentioned Billy Parker."

Baker spoke in a puzzled tone, "Billy who?"

"Billy Parker, he was a mage, someone Bryce knew who died a few months back. I think Jen investigated his death and thought it was suicide. This address is linked to him, and he's linked to everything else."

Baker looked unsure, probably worried I'd run off and do something rash like Jen. After a moment's pause, he nodded, and said, "I'll fetch you a cab. I need to take the dockmaster back to the station. You keep a good eye on her, won't you, Dr Chynoweth?"

"I'll do you one better and keep both my eyes on her," Elly responded. "Thank you, Inspector." Baker then walked off to wrangle us a cab, and we parted ways with him and the now very nervous-looking dockmaster.

I settled opposite Elly in the four-wheeler, and her smile seemed to rub away at the edges of my mood., "Sorry, for getting all weird."

"Just now, or is that a longer-term apology?" she joked. "You don't need to apologise for who you are.

It was nice seeing you work, despite the circumstances. You can be kind of brilliant."

"You're kind of brilliant, too." She reached over and put a hand on mine. The space between us was small enough that I could almost kiss her. I wanted to hold her close, let the warmth of her body take the aches away from mine. But we had a job to do. Jennifer was out there, and we were one step closer.

***

The weather turned from bad to worse, and we made slow progress from London Docks to Lambeth. There was a mixture of apprehension, impatience and dread sloshing around in my mind as I tried not to focus on the possibility that we were chasing a dead end. Elly watched me for a while before speaking up. "What's the plan, Charlotte?"

"It reassures me that you think I have a plan," I said back, surprising even myself.

"Not funny," she said, a note of sternness in her voice that reminded me of Mr Chynoweth.

I sighed, more annoyed than I should have been. "I'm working on the information we have. I don't know what we'll find, so I can't make a plan. Don't worry, I'm good at improvising."

"Improvising got you stabbed, Charlotte," she said, worriedly.

Frustration flashed within me—she was right, I didn't have the best track record so far. "I know! I know. Please, I'm just trying to trust my gut right now. I know I'm being impulsive and reckless, but it's what I know. Just let me do things my way for once." I regretted the words as soon as I said them, and Elly looked away obviously hurt.

"I'm trying to help."

"Fuck," I said with a deep sigh. "I know. I appreciate it, I appreciate you. It's just—No, no just, I shouldn't have snapped, I'm sorry."

She turned away and started biting her lip. I looked out the window in time to see the old, decaying Blackfriars Bridge, and before long, the cab rolled to a halt at the address we'd given. Elly got out, still intermittently chewing her lip, and surveyed our apparent destination.

A large grey building of fairly plain construction stood before us, cordoned off by a stone wall and a set of large wrought iron gates. Two large chimneys belched out smoke and soot, and a sign proclaimed "CRANLEY MANUFACTURING" on the side of the building. People of all ages were moving around a courtyard, all wearing simple clothing and looking bedraggled and malnourished. A worrying realisation came to me, and Elly must have realised too.

"It's not a factory," she said, "it's a workhouse." Proposed as a way to get the poor and vagrant off the streets and give them the opportunity to work off their debts and re-enter society, the workhouses that were springing up around the city were a new form of indentured servitude. Rich, powerful groups and people financed these hell holes, where the poor and inconvenient were forced to live, some from birth. You couldn't leave a workhouse once you entered, and your debts would only grow as you use precious food, clothing and supplies necessary for your survival.

"That changes things." I had no idea how to get into the building, and certainly no idea how to get out again. I didn't even know what we would be looking for when we got inside.

Elly, however, finally stopped biting her lip. "I have a plan. Follow my lead."

"What?" was all I managed to say, before she started striding confidently to the gates. "Follow your lead on what?"

"Be quiet," she said, walking up to a man who appeared to be a porter of some sort. "Good day sir, how goes it?"

He looked at us suspiciously. "A miserable day, ma'am, but I shouldn't complain. What's your business here?" The porter's voice was low and grouchy, but he didn't look as poorly looked after as those in the exercise yard.

"Eloise Chynoweth, Chynoweth Mining and Materials," she produced a business card of some sort from a pocket. "This is my secretary, Miss Price. We're here in my father's stead to speak with your Governor." Elly's delivery was flawless.

Even I would have had trouble spotting the lie. Somehow, she'd changed her whole demeanour and presented the form of a completely respectable businesswoman.

"Chynoweth? Not heard of it. Have you got an appointment?" the porter said, but it was obvious he was merely exercising what little power he had in the situation. I suspected he found the two confident women before him rather intimidating.

"Do you want to go and check if we have an appointment, and leave us in the rain while you do?" Elly asked rhetorically.

"Oh, no ma'am, my apologies. Please, I'll show you in and alert the Gov'ner." He opened the gate with a large key and alerted the attention of a number of the residents. A dozen or so pairs of eyes fell on us as we crossed the yard and entered the main building by way of a set of oak double doors. These also needed to be unlocked by the porter.

Inside, a small foyer opened up into a set of stairs leading to the upper floors, and small hallways split off beyond. The interior was simply decorated; plain wood flooring and panelling, with little in the way of furniture where we stood. The sound of machinery echoed off the walls from some distance away, and the smell of general human occupation clung to every surface. The porter asked us to wait and quickly moved up the stairs to find the governor.

"Your secretary?" I asked. I was more than a little impressed by the subterfuge, and my earlier panic was beginning to subside.

"Quite, just stay quiet unless you are spoken to. I'll try to get as much information out of the governor as I can." Elly kept looking around, uncertain.

"There's something fishy going on here, why would Jennifer lead us here?"

"Somehow I doubt she knew, but you're right that something is odd," Elly noted. She was nodding to herself, as if she had just worked out a puzzle. "Place like this should be teeming with people. Where are they?"

Before I could answer, the porter emerged at the top of the staircase, accompanied by an elderly gentleman. He was stick-thin, almost bald and covered in liver spots, and he wore a colourful waistcoat and jacket. As he descended the stairs, he placed a bowler hat on his head.

"Miss Chynoweth?" he said. His accent was refined, but it grated against the shrill, scratchy tones of his voice.

"Actually, it's Dr Chynoweth," Elly corrected, putting the governor on the back foot almost immediately. She was good at this, as nervous as she seemed. "A pleasure, my secretary Miss Price." I nodded, and kept my mouth shut.

The governor regarded us both, clearly unsure of the situation. He'd stopped a few steps up the staircase to maintain the high ground, I thought. "I'm afraid you weren't expected. Usually I wouldn't make the time for such guests, but I recognised your father's name."

"We weren't expected? I was certain an appointment was made," Elly said, stepping up onto the staircase so she would be mor level with the man. "Charlotte, are you sure you sent the letters I asked for?" She looked at me with clear disappointment, and I reacted like a rabbit in the eyes of a fox.

"I… Well… Yes?"

"You should get yourself some better help, Miss Chynoweth,"
the governor said.

"Doctor."

"Yes, Doctor, my apologies." Somehow, I suspected he wasn't sorry at all. "To what do we owe the pleasure of Cornwall's finest?"

Elly took another step up the staircase. "My father is looking to expand his investments in the city, which you would have known about had you received my letters. We heard of this establishment and wondered if you were looking for more financing."

The governor looked deep in thought for a moment, before waving away the porter. "We have been running low on funds recently. Allow me to show you to my office."

"Actually," Elly interjected, "I was hoping we could see the work floor first. I find it's always better to see where the work is done before seeing where the papers are signed."

"Do you, now?" The old man stepped down so that now he and Elly were eye to eye, and he held his gaze longer than was comfortable to watch. "This way," he said, eventually.

He walked past me, and in the moment, he wasn't looking at us. I turned to Elly and mouthed "What the hell?", to which she responded, "I have no idea."

And I'm the one with the improvisation problem?

We followed the governor down a long corridor and were heading in the direction of the echoing mechanical sounds. We passed by a number of rooms where the off-shift workers huddled together to stay warm. Elly was right, though, there weren't nearly as many people here as I would have expected. I nudged Elly and gestured that she should ask some questions.

She looked confused for a moment, then caught on, "right, yes. Governor, could you tell us when this institution was founded?"

"1832, ma'am. Or, rather, that was when construction was completed and we accepted our first paupers," he responded. He sounded sickeningly proud of his position.

"And you've been in charge since then?"

"Indeed, I have."

"How many residents do you have living here?"

"Two hundred, currently, but we've capacity for eight hundred. We work them on two shifts, and they receive two meals a day before and after they work." Two meals a day sounded horrific, and I suspected it wasn't the most nutritious food—then again, I wasn't known for eating well or regularly. "We currently produce textiles, but we hope to expand our output once we have more residents."

More prisoners, more like.

"Well, textiles are an area we are interested in," Elly said. "Could I inquire to your current turnover?"

Before the governor could answer the question, he pushed open a set of doors that lead to a wide, open room, and the sounds of work reached an almost deafening level. Inside, the sound of voices added to the din, people yelling and barking orders, or discussing the work at hand. There was something else as well, underlaid in the noise that I couldn't pinpoint; something almost rhythmic.

The machinery in the place was a marvel. Cotton or wool was being stretched and spun by one large banks of machines. Elsewhere, large sheets of fabric were being woven on power looms. Above me was a mess of spinning pipes, cog wheels and drive shafts coming down to the individual devices, maybe a hundred in total. My mind boggled as I watched the machines being operated by their minders. Small children ran the lines, checking that the spindles were set and not snagging, while the adults operated the machines themselves and carried finished products to the far end of the factory.

"Here we are," the governor yelled above the racket. He led us down a row of machines. The people here looked as worn down as those outside, and they obsequiously bowed their heads as we passed. Elly walked close to the governor's side, so she could continue questioning him, but they became too quiet under all the noise.

As we walked, I noted several men watching over from above. They wore dark blue uniforms, but they did not look like the regular sort to be managing a work floor. They were scruffy and unkempt, their uniforms ill-fitting. Wouldn't a workhouse keep better standards for its staff?

Something else jumped out at me as I watched those at work. At first, I thought I was seeing things, mistaking a flash of colour for something it wasn't. But then I saw it again, on the arms of those workers around us. Every single one of them, as far as I could tell, was a mage. Their brands had been exposed deliberately by slashed open sleeves, and some had scars and welts across them. A workhouse just for mages? Was that what Jen wanted us to find?

The strange rhythmic noise finally made sense to me; it was coming from the mages around me. Those that could were working to time, repeating their actions to a beat only they could perceive. They murmured wordless verses, and I realised I was seeing Worker's Cant on a scale I never imagined. Cant had emerged as a way to make work go faster from those that had no formal training in magic. I'd heard that a mage working a loom could work twice as fast with the right verses, but I never quite believed it. Looking around, I wondered if I needed to re-evaluate that belief.

Billy Parker must have found out about this place, or even escaped it. Rumours then reached the 1735 club, and poor Billy was probably killed to keep him quiet. The pieces were starting to fall into place. I was about to pull Elly back so I could share my thoughts, but someone got to me first. My yelp was muffled by a hand, not I would have been heard over the noise, anyway. I struggled against the hands holding me tight, and looked in horror as Elly kept walking away, unaware of my predicament.

Chapter 29

I was dragged between two mechanical looms, and my ears felt like they were going to explode from the noise. I managed to get an arm free from the grapple, and I drove an elbow into my would-be captor. I turned and regained my balance and was surprised to see a familiar face. The young man was winded and collected himself before holding up his hands in a gesture of surrender.

"Caspar?" I said, shouting to be heard over the racket of the looms. The mage with the dark skin and friendly smile I'd met at the 1735 Club had seen better days. He'd gained a black eye and several fresh cuts up and down his arms.

He shook his head and gestured to his ears, then he put up two hands as if to tell me to stay put. From a pocket of the work trousers he wore, Caspar produced a handkerchief; he took my hand in his and wrapped the cloth around them both. His lips were moving the whole time, but I couldn't make out anything of what he was saying, except that he was repeating himself. There was an almost imperceptible change in the air pressure around us, and I could suddenly hear what he was saying. "Share a secret, I'll share mine; and we'll keep them safe for all of time. There, that should hold for now. What are you doing here?"

I tried to work out how much to tell him, and where Elly had got to. "It's complicated, but it's about those fires, and a lot more. What about you, what happened?"

He looked forlorn. "Got snagged after that meeting. I managed to get out safe but didn't have nowhere to go. Blue coats stuffed me in a cell last night, and this morning I was bought here."

"Fuck, I'm so sorry. It was my fault what happened at the club," I said, but it seemed to bring him little comfort. All too aware that we could be found at any time, I had to press him. "What do you know about this place? Anything you've learned could be useful. How is this even legal? Surely this goes against magical labour laws?"

"Don't know nothing about the law. All I know is no one leaves. They're doing something here, some kind of experiment. You need to get out if you can," he said, his voice turning conspiratorial.

"What kind of experiment? Is it anything to do with Black…?" I started to say, but he shoved his hand back over my mouth.

"Don't say that; don't let anyone hear you say it. That was the first thing I learned," he said. A shout called out from nearby, and Caspar looked at me in shock before running.

"Fuck," I said. I tried to follow him, but he was lithe and scrawny, and able to squeeze through a gap in machinery that I couldn't. I went back to where he grabbed me, and to my shock, I couldn't see Elly anywhere.

At one end of the row of looms, one of the uniformed bruisers was stalking toward me, and I had no other choice but to leg it. Hoping that Elly was safe, I sprinted down the length of the work floor, and tried to spy a way out. Another of the guards tried to cut me off, but I had a trick up my sleeve I'd been waiting to use. I pulled a small vial from my pocket, filled with a pale green liquid. I hurled it ahead of me, where it smashed on the ground before the man blocking my way. He took a deep breath of the fumes released from the vial and slumped to the ground, unconscious.

Valerian and nightshade. "Thanks, Jen," I said under my breath, before leaping over the slumbering body. There was a set of double doors, above which the tangled mess of pipes and driveshafts met and led through the wall. If there was a steam engine there, there would need to be an external access for all the coal to be delivered.

I kicked open the door and ran in, turning quickly to pull over a stack of crates off to the side. Coal and boxes collapsed down in front of the door, blocking off the guards, and my way out. The room was filled with steam and a great black iron steam engine chugged away in its centre, a boiler next to it, glowing red around its door.

One corner of the room was taken up by an array of large boxes, and the worktable beside them was strewn with blueprints of some sort. I jogged over to see what they were, but couldn't make heads or tails of it. A device of some sort, with a glass chamber and symbols I thought could be Arcane. Loud footsteps echoed over the din of the engine, so I stuffed the blueprints into my bag before I could study them further.

I turned and a man I didn't recognise was coming down some stairs from what appeared to be an office. He wore an expensive looking embroidered waistcoat and smoking jacket, and carried a cane topped with a raven's skull carved from ivory. It was an Arcane focus for certain, used to intensify magic. "Miss Price, I presume?"

"How do you know my name?" I said. I began walking to the side, trying to maintain my distance. The way I'd come in was cut off by the stranger, but I spotted another door across the room, one used to bring in coal.

"Word travels. We know all about you," he said. He was cocksure and arrogant, but I could tell he was no older than twenty-one. Arrogance was expected, and I could work with that.

"'We'? Is that the elusive Hawkins, or this Baron Cranley I've heard so much about?" I asked. My left side still ached where I'd broken my rib, so I did my best to keep it turned away from the man. Something told me it wouldn't do a lot of good.

"You've been of interest to a number of parties. Miss Price," he said, smirking.

Both, then, I figured. He carried himself with the sense of smug satisfaction that oozed from a superiority complex, and I didn't need the cane or a brand to tell he was a mage. "You know my name, what's yours?" I asked.

"No one of any such importance in the grand scheme of things." He was toying with me, and that pissed me off. I did my best not to rise to the bait. I just needed a way out, and to find Elly.

"Just another guard then, another pawn thrown off to die.

Let me guess, one of the missing University students?" I said, "Is it worth it, oppressing your own kind?"

That hit a nerve, "You haven't the faintest idea, you insignificant welp," he snarled. I grinned, wryly, and watched the man recompose himself. I wasn't far from the door, I just had to pull the right strings.

"You know, what I don't get is why your peers were so eager to die for all this," I posited, "A workhouse? That's what all this has been about?"

"My employer has a vision much grander than this, I assure you," he said.

"Enlighten me. What vision?"

He cackled. "Power, influence—the right kind of people have never been beholden to attempts to restrict our abilities," he said. "The rabble of the lower classes believe they have some right to the Arcane, an absurd notion."

"So, only the rich and powerful can use magic? You do realise that when people say that magic has a price, that doesn't mean you can buy it up?" I wasn't far from the door, I just had to keep him talking long enough.

"An infantile response from an infantile mind."

We locked eyes. I took one more step and lunged for the door. Before I could reach it, I was hit by a wave of invisible force that drove me back a few feet. Despite the intensity of the spell, the mage hadn't even spoken a word, and I looked up to him holding his cane out, the raven eye sockets glowing white.

"Let me give you a taste of that power," he said. He reached into his pocket and pulled out a tobacco case. He placed the cane on the ground, and it stood upright under its own power. From inside the case, he took a pinch of black opalescent powder—thin wisps of smoke rose from his fingertips and the skin turned red.

Black Ember, I was fucked.

He inhaled the powder up one nostril, and within seconds his eyes went blacker than the night, and his veins began pulsing over his face. He picked up the cane again, and the world seemed to warp around it as he spoke a deep word of power. There was a thunderous rush of energy, and he sent me careening into the back wall of the room.

"Ah, fuck me!" I said as I tried to pull myself from a pile of broken crates and coal.

"True power, Miss Price, so few can handle it," he said, and then laughed like a madman.

I pushed myself up. "Like Monica? She couldn't handle it. Do any of you know your limits?" He stopped in place, and I saw my opening. I whipped out my pistol and fired it towards the mage.

He raised the cane and spun it in an arching motion in anticipation, and for the briefest of moments, a shell of magic formed around him. The round ricocheted off a bubble of force, which barely reacted to the attack. "Your mundane weapons are nothing compared to my power," he said, calmly returning to his overconfident stance.

Well, shit. There must have been something I could use to level the playing field—just long enough for me to get out and find Elly. I'd been so focused on the mage that I'd almost tuned out the immense racket being made by the machinery all around us, but a sudden shuddering noise to my right gave me an idea. "Oi, prick," I said, "how's this for power?" I levelled the unloaded pistol at the mage long enough to bait a reaction from him, then pivoted on my heel and fired at the huge, iron boiler. The bolt of Arcane electricity lanced out of the barrel and into the pressure vessel. The lightning jumped around the shell of the boiler, letting off sparks that cascaded around the room. A second later there was a deafening whistling sound, and every pressure gauge in the room had spun to max.

The boiler buckled, then cracked open like a chestnut with a wild, rending screech. Steam, scolding water, and iron shrapnel burst force from the exploding vessel. I dived for cover just in time and got behind a stack of crates. The force of the explosion was still enough to lift me off my feet, but I was protected from the deadly debris. I was thrown through the door that led out to the yard and found myself sprawled in the thickening mud outside. I managed to pull myself to my feet, and I looked around desperately for a way back to the work floor, back to Elly.

A trail led round to the right of the building, and after a few moments of following it, I managed to make out the main gates and the entrance to the workhouse. I made a run for it, but only made it halfway. The air roiled like the ocean as another wave of invisible energy crashed over me and I was hurled off my feet. With no wall to stop me, I hit the muddy ground hard—sharp pain lanced down my side from the already broken ribs.

The mage cackled wildly, the kind of unfettered hysterical laugh that only the truly mad could make. "It's too late, Price! Now you die!" he shrieked at me.

Unfathomable energy rippled around his body, and black ooze, almost like tar, poured out of his eyes and down his face. The white glow around his cane flared as bright as the sun, and the mage's laughed grew more and more hysterical. This was it; the moment where I died, or he lost control.

I tried to stand again but couldn't pull my boots from the mud. He lifted the cane, and I braced myself for whatever came next. When he spoke the word of power, with all the discordant glory of an out of tune orchestra, a blinding flash whited out the world around me and I expected to be blasted to pieces.

There was a hard, resounding thud, and the ground undulated. The unnatural light faded and, as my eyes adjusted once more to the dwindling daylight, the horrific form of the mage's crushed body came into focus. He writhed in the mud, his limbs and spine broken beyond recognition. With his last breath, he screamed as the unfettered Arcane energy incinerated his mortal form.

I struggled to pull myself from the mud, my whole body ached. I had one thing on my mind: find Elly, and get out of there. I never should have left her alone. Who knows what could have happened? As I wrenched myself up from the sodden ground and limped toward the front door, I steeled myself to rescue Elly from whatever danger my foolishness had put her in.

Shadows appeared in the light coming from the factory entrance, and the door burst open moments later. Elly—thank goodness—leapt down the steps from the open door before she turned on the spot and delivered the meanest right hook I'd ever seen to the guard on her tail.

Maybe she was in less danger than I thought.

Three more guards appeared in the doorway, but they hesitated at the sight of Elly standing over an unconscious man twice her size. I aimed my pistol at the sky and pulled the trigger—the crack of the Arcane lightning echoed all around us—and the guards staggered back.

"Time to go," said Elly, as she ran over to me and grabbed my hand. She had a look on her face that was equal parts relieved and excited—Jennifer would have been proud.

Those few moments before the guards gave chase were enough for us to reach the gates, where we skidded to a halt in the mud. Locked—we were trapped. At least, that's what I thought until the scrawny form of Caspar Smith rounded the perimeter wall with a set of keys in his hand. "How did you—?" I asked as he jammed a key into the lock.

"No time to explain, see you around Charlotte Price!" he responded, before he set off at a sprint away from the workhouse. For such a scrawny kid, he was fast, and headed away from where we needed to go.

Elly tugged on my arm, and without another moment to lose, we ran toward the river. My heart pounded in my chest, and I had pains in muscles I didn't know existed.

Chapter 30

Wet, terrified, and exhausted, we moved with the crowds of people the left the surrounding factories. I was too scared to stop and wave down one of the four-wheelers roaming the roads and kept looking over my shoulder to see if we were being followed. My heart thumped away in my chest like a horse in a steeplechase.

We walked south along the bend in the Thames, hoping to find a bridge to cross back onto the north bank. The rain was so heavy that the river was close to bursting its bank. The refuse of a million inhabitants threatening to spill back over into people's lives.

We reached the Battersea Bridge and the crowds had started to thin. The old toll taker on the bridge nodded kindly as we paid to cross, and I felt myself begin to calm. "I don't think we're being followed," I said, letting out a sigh of relief. "Remind me never to get on your bad side. You might have broken that man's jaw."

"He deserved it. What happened back there? I heard the explosion and just started running. Where did you go?" She sounded terrified, and I couldn't blame her.

"I was grabbed, the kid who got the gate. He was in the 1735 and recognised me. Next thing I knew, the guards were chasing me," I said as we walked along the old bridge. Iron railings roughly four feet high served as a barrier between foot traffic and the river, and I stopped halfway across to lean against them and catch my breath. The orange light of the gas lamps sputtered in the rain, casting strange shadows on the river below.

Elly placed a hand on the small of my back, and I turned away from the dark waters. Little droplets glistened on her cheeks like stars and ran down her neck to her chest. She was safe, we both were, even for just a moment. I stared longingly into her eyes—the rings of azure around her pupils like the clear sky through a hopeful break in the clouds—and I desperately wanted to kiss her. Truth be told, I was more afraid of that than I had been at any moment in the workhouse. What if I pushed her away again?

But she wasn't moving away; Elly reached up to brush a strand of wet hair from my face, and then she pulled me closer. Before I knew what was happening, she kissed me, with all the sweet tenderness I imagined she would. When at last she stepped away, she put a hand over my heart and said, "Promise me that you won't pick any more fights with wild mages. Who was he, anyway?"

"No idea; one of them, whoever they are. He was mad." My mind raced, trying to make sense of what I'd seen. Each time I felt like I'd made sense of things, another mystery reared its head at me. "He found me in the boiler room, huffed some Ember and… well, you saw the result. I don't get it, he could have crushed me regardless, why take the risk?"

"He wanted to feel more powerful, maybe? He could have felt like he needed it," Elly said.

I shook my head. "He didn't sound like an addict wanting his next fix, he was arrogant—completely convinced of his own righteousness. Black Ember has been a death sentence for every mage that's used the stuff, and all of them, bar Timothy Waters, have been willing to die for something—or someone." An image from that night in the warehouse; the sharply dressed mage with a pointed beard. I shuddered and fought back the despair that flooded my chest. "Whoever is behind this has convinced these mages that they can control something that no one is capable of controlling… Well, no one except—"

"Bryce."

"Bryce. What makes him so different? Why isn't he burned to a crisp like the rest of them?" I put that thought aside, it was no use speculating on Arcane mechanisms in the rain. "You spotted it, right? All the mages there?"

"The governor was very proud of it, in fact." Elly leant back on the railings and crossed her arms. "I couldn't get him to explain why any of it was allowed, though. Your little distraction saw to that."

"Bugger, sorry." I looked down to the river again and collected my thoughts. So much still didn't make sense. It was like having all the pieces of a puzzle, but without the box to see what picture it made. It couldn't be as simple as wanting to stuff mages into workhouses. They could do that already; they just couldn't exploit their magical talents. But why did they need the Black Ember? Caspar was almost afraid of it when I tried to bring it up. Were they planning to use it as a means of control?

"Let's get out of the rain, shall we?" Elly asked a few minutes later. We were both soaked, and it'd be a tad ironic if I was bought low by a cold after everything that had happened. We hailed a cab once we got off the bridge, and soon found ourselves back at The Potent Solution.

Bryce was pacing outside the front door when we got there, and he was looking rattled, but curiously sober. His black hair was a matted mess, and his shirt was soaked from the rain. "You're back," we said at the same time, and then stood in awkward silence for a moment.

"You're hurt, and Miss Eloise, you look positively water-logged," Bryce said. I waved him out of the way so I could unlock the door, and we bundled into the cool, dry air of the shop. "What on earth happened to you two?" he asked.

"A lot, we'll explain upstairs. We should get a fire going." The three of us hurried up to the office and Bryce made short work of lighting the fireplace. I stripped off my outer layers, and Elly went to fetch some towels from the washroom. "What's going on?" I asked Bryce, "You're pacing."

He let out an anxious sigh. "I have been followed all day, Hawkins' muscle. I managed to lose them, but it has me on edge. Where were you? I have been here for an hour already."

I filled him in on what we'd learned from the Hyacinth, Jennifer's notebook, and the mysterious strawman companies. He listened intently, more so than I'd noticed him do in the past few days. He really was sober. I started to tell him about the workhouse, and he turned pale.

"The rumours," he said, pensively. "People disappearing, that kind of thing. I didn't believe any of it, there was nothing to believe, really."

"Well, it's true, and I ran into another of your peers while we were there. Young man, full of himself, had a cane topped with a raven."

"Grayson," he said. "A bright young kid, full of himself, as you said. He was old money, older than me even. How did he get tied up in this?"

"Tied up is putting it lightly. He bought into whatever Hawkins was selling whole hog. He was mad, going on about power and what the working class deserved, and now he's dead." I sat across from Bryce, meeting his eyes. "I'm wondering why you aren't pushing up metaphorical daisies yourself."

"I wonder that every day," he responded. "I should be, I used more of that poison than any of my classmates. The trick was always to taper off, let the high mellow out. You can go for hours if you have the supply, and someone to watch over you."

"So now, someone is supplying them, and feeding them these megalomaniac ideas about mage superiority?" I asked. He just shrugged in response. "You're a big help."

"Your sarcasm is noted," he said, melancholically. It was like talking to a brick wall. Talking to myself was more useful.

I got up and dug the blueprints out of my satchel, which made Bryce cock an eyebrow at the apparent mismatch between the amount of papers and the size of the bag. I left him puzzled and laid out the main diagram on the coffee table. "Found this at the factory, in the engine room. What do you make of it?"

Bryce's face tightened with a growing sense of horror as he looked over the pages. The diagram appeared to be of a large glass chamber. It was around twelve feet high and four feet wide, cylindrical with a domed top, with a hatch, around two feet across and high, near the floor. "My God..." said Bryce, as something dawned on him, "They're going to put people in this thing."

"You can't be serious," I said, but the more I looked over the designs, the more I was convinced. We were looking at a boiler, of sorts; a pipe connected to the bottom of the chamber would carry heat through a reservoir of water and create steam. That steam would be used to power an engine. Just like any steam engine, really, except instead of burning coal…

Another diagram provided details on a mechanism to disperse an unnamed fuel inside the chamber. "No prize for guessing what this is," Bryce said. Black Ember—a near endless supply to keep the mage inside burning as long as possible. He riffled through the rest of the papers, more careful drawings of complex pieces of machinery. "Look here, that's an alchemical formula, correct?"

The formula wasn't all that complex, a way to treat glass to have a high degree of heat resistance. "I suppose," I began, horrified at the words that came out of my mouth, "that if the chamber were made of steel, like a normal boiler, you wouldn't be able to see the… occupant."

Bryce stepped back from the table and let out a ragged sigh. "This is all my fault."

"That's ridiculous," I said.

"Is it?" He walked over to the window and looked forlornly out onto the street. "Grayson and the rest of them, I introduced them to Black Ember. I convinced them to try it, and I helped find the best ways to use it. They're dead because of me, those plans exist because of me."

"Don't give yourself so much credit. Hawkins and this Baron Cranley—whoever they both are—are the ones behind all this." I stood next to him and leant on the cold glass so I could meet his verdant gaze. "We're going to find them, Bryce, and we'll put a stop to this." He looked down at me and I suddenly realised that there was now very little space between our bodies. It was like the night we met, in the rain, when I'd been a little too taken in by his charms. All too aware of my rising heart rate, I bumped my fist against his shoulder and said, "What about this professor of yours? Carrington. Did you have any luck tracking him down?"

"Right, yes," Bryce said, shaking off his daze. "That's why I was here actually, I've arranged a meeting."

Elly came into the office a moment later, carrying a tray of tea along with the towels. The three of us huddled around the fire, and Bryce filled us in on his plan.

Chapter 31

"You want me, to accompany you, the son of a member of the House of Lords, to a ball hosted by your father, so that we can have a clandestine meeting with an old professor, while we are both being followed by assassins and mages?" I said. Not only was it utterly preposterous, but the idea of mingling with London's upper crust was so far outside my idea of a good time that I was determined to find any way out of it.

Bryce hesitated; he was nervous but one look at Elly gave him the encouragement he needed. She agreed with him, the traitor. "Yes, it makes perfect sense. Professor Carrington was going to be there anyway, and it's not out of the ordinary for me to go to a family function, despite my strained relations." He took a sip from a cup of tea that Elly had brought up with her and looked at me. He was clearly hiding something.

"Why is he going to be there?" I questioned.

He gulped and, for a brief moment, looked like a puppy about to be kicked. "My father invited him. I told you, they're friends. It's the perfect cover, no one will have a second thought about us going to have a private chat with Carrington, and it makes a lot more sense for me to bring company to these sorts of events." He had a strange look in his eyes. He was avoiding looking at me directly, instead opting to look at the bottom of his mug.

"What kind of events?" I pressed. I wasn't going to agree to anything unless I knew every detail.

"Social events, soirées, parties!" he dodged.

"What. Kind. Of. Events?" I poked him in the chest. He was determined, I'll give him that, but that was only making me angrier.

"Introductions," he offered as an utterly meaningless explanation.

"Introductions of what?" I was getting frustrated. Bryce held his tongue, and I knocked the mug of tea out of his hand. Thankfully it was empty. "Introductions of what? Bryce. What are you getting me into?"

"Introductions of young, eligible bachelors and bachelorettes. It's when the Lords and Ladies show off their children to each other in the hopes of finding good matches."

"Good matches, Bryce? Well fuck, that's the finest compliment I've ever received," I scoffed, the sarcasm so thick you could cut it with a knife. "Why the hell do you need me there?"

"First, because this is your case, you're smart and resourceful, and second," he hesitated. "Second, if I go without company, my father will spend the entire night trying to palm me off on some hapless lady-in-waiting."

"This is ridiculous." I looked at Elly, who had so far tried to make herself quiet in the corner of the room, "Tell him this is ridiculous."

She looked at me, "Is it? We both saw that workhouse. What other plan do we have?"

"Why can't we meet Carrington literally anywhere else?" I said, getting desperate.

"He's on business in Surrey right now," Bryce answered. "This ball will be the first time he's back in London."

I huffed and threw my hands in the air. I hated everything about this. I hated being ganged up on, and I hated being put in a position where I was just some kind of decoration. "This is ridiculous! I'm not going to go to a ball and pretend to be some noble girl you intend to marry. Besides, I have nothing to wear," I stated confidently, hoping it would shut him up.

Elly giggled, "Actually, there's a dress in Jennifer's closet." I knew the dress Elly meant, Jennifer bought it for a party last year, it was ridiculous.

"Jennifer has half a foot on me, it'll never fit." Elly grinned, cocksure like I'd never seen her. "Don't you dare."

"I know enough about dress making that I can adjust it," Elly said. "I'll just have to take your measurements."

"Charlotte, I need you there, please," Bryce said.

A low, frustrated growl rumbled in my chest. "You better have a good plan," I said, pointing at him. "I can't just show up to a high society ball." I sat down in the armchair and resigned myself to my apparent fate.

Bryce explained his plan nervously, and obviously hoping I'd approve. It seemed to me that he had spent a lot of time thinking about it, and when it came to share the details of the fake persona that he'd devised for me, he got far too excited. The whole idea made me sick to my stomach, but as much as I tried, I couldn't find a flaw in his reasoning.

The ball was to take place the next evening. I would pose as a Miss Elizabeth Banbridge, of Cambridgeshire. Apparently, my time at university would be enough to convince the London Elite that I'd lived there a time. My father was posted in Africa, hence why nobody knew him, while my mother manages the estate. I have no siblings and hope to move to London to live with an uncle before finding a suitable match for myself. I met Bryce at a gallery opening, and we had been courting for a number of weeks. It was a solid cover, and I hated it.

We would arrive late, as Bryce had a tendency to do, and wait for Professor Carrington to arrive. Then, we would retire to the gallery upstairs, which Bryce assured me would be unattended, and discuss the case and the missing students. It was a sound enough plan, and honestly, the worst part was the idea of making small talk with the upper classes, something I'd learned to avoid during my time at university. There's a world of difference between the sons and daughters of the landed gentry and me, who grew up playing in an alley.

I finished eating as Bryce wrapped up telling me the plan. "I hate you," I said after an uncomfortable pause, "But I don't have a different plan, so I guess we're doing this one." To be honest, I was tired, I was done with running up and down the city looking for clues and finding nothing. Once again, my mind felt like mashed potatoes, all I wanted to do was curl up and not have to make any more decisions.

Bryce could tell how I felt, he put his hand on my shoulder and said, "This'll work, Charlotte. We'll find the rest of my classmates and who's behind all this, and then we'll find your mentor. I know it'll work."

Still thoroughly unconvinced that this was a good idea, as opposed to just an idea, I began to work out how to keep myself safe. "I'm taking my gun," I said after regarding Bryce for a moment. "Do ladies take bags to these things? Or am I going to need a thigh holster or something?" Bryce brushed off the comment, saying something about how I should use my best judgement. I tried to press him for more information, but he made his excuses to leave, promising to be back at seven PM the next day.

"Come on, let's get you measured," Elly said, snapping a measuring tape she produced from somewhere in her hands. She took me upstairs to Jennifer's bedroom, a wide, open space that took up most of the second floor of the building. One wall was lined with yet more bookshelves, but I knew most of these tomes to be esoteric philosophy and works of literature, the latter mainly being made up of speculative fiction and romance novels. There was a reading nook by the big bay window, with a well-worn armchair and a tea table. The décor was mostly dark, earthy tones, but splashes of colour from rugs, curtains, and paintings balanced things out. Much like the rest of the Jennifer's home, the bedroom was a mess, but I was sure Elly had already done some surreptitious cleaning.

I opened the closet and pulled out a waist length coat, filled with extra secret pockets like everything Jennifer owned. It was black, with a velvet lining, and had a small tail in the back. Luckily, Jennifer and I shared the same size feet, so I found the least offensive pair of leather shoes I could. Finally, I looked at the dreaded dress.

It was cream coloured and had an off the shoulder neckline with lace trim that came down lower than I liked. The sleeves were ruffled and featured outrageous plumpers around the shoulders. The waistline was tiny, Jennifer tended to wear a cinched waist, but this would be tight even on her. I winced at the thought of squeezing myself into it. The only redeeming feature, in my eyes, was that the skirt was fairly gracefully cut, unlike the petticoat puffed monstrosities I had seen recently around town.

I was ready to write the whole thing off as the dullest thing I'd ever wear—until I noticed the pattern in the lace. Little round birds, perched among leaves, were expertly laid all along the neckline.

Little round birds, with a rather distinctive crown around their cheeks and eyes. I could picture her stupid grin, walking around in polite company, waiting for someone to notice her great tits.

"It's nice," Elly said, "A little out of fashion, but I figure you can just say that's what people in Cambridge are wearing these days."

"I hate it," I said in response. "What are you and Bryce getting me into?" The question was rhetoric. I knew exactly what they were getting me into, and it was a cream-coloured death-trap.

Chapter 32

Elly was lighting some candles, which filled the room with soft orange light. I was surprised by how calm she had been through everything that had happened. Even now, while I waged a war with my fears, Elly kept a stalwart and soothing demeanour about her. She smiled at me and giggled softly before saying, "I'm going to need you to get undressed."

My heart skipped a beat and I stood there flummoxed for a moment. "I'm. What?" were all the words I could manage. I felt a hot flush in my face and looked away.

"To take the measurements, I need you to get undressed," Elly said again, firmer this time. She took a few slow, deliberate steps toward me, exaggerating the sway of her hips and wrapping the measuring tape around her hand.

My mind snapped back to some semblance of awareness, and I said, "Right, yes, the measurements." During my argument with Bryce, I hadn't noticed the light, slender dress she 'd changed into from her wet clothes. It was pale blue and cut a flattering line around her shoulders. She had her hair up in a bun, and the light from the candles danced off her freckled cheeks.

I started fumbling with the buttons of my waistcoat, which I was sure hadn't been so fiddly when I put it on in the morning. The room also felt warmer than I remembered, and before I realised what was happening Elly was helping me slip the waistcoat off my shoulders.

"I was a little jealous when I saw you and Bryce the other day," Elly said as I unbuttoned my shirt. "Absurd, I know, you were clearly wounded, and I saw all the lab equipment. But for a moment, seeing you, no shirt, with a strange man. I thought I'd scared you off or something."

"Elly, I…." She cut me off with a finger to my lips before

I could finish. I was on the back foot in a way I never had been before, totally enraptured by her and waiting with bated breath for her desires. I liked it.

She brushed the hair off my face and tucked it behind my ear, sending a wave of warmth through my body with every touch. "I nearly didn't knock on the door that day. I wondered if it would have been easier for both of us if I just went back to Cambridge. I didn't know how you'd react when you saw the real me. Or how I'd feel about it."

I opened my mouth to speak, but it was as if every word of the English language suddenly lost all meaning. I wanted her, more than I had realised, and I felt like my body was being drawn in by an unseen force. She placed her hands on my hips and drew me close, leaving a space between our lips as an open invitation. Her lips tasted of sweet summer wine, the kind we drank when we were young, and foolish. She pulled away and I tried to follow.

"You were never satisfied with one of anything," she said, and gestured for me to take off my shirt. I did so, and then undid the laces of my stay and dropped it to the floor , exposing my breasts to the cold air.

"You really could have done this with my shirt on," I noted, tongue-in-cheek.

Elly looked up at me and held up the tape measure. "I could have, yes. May I?" she said. I nodded, and she passed a hand around my back, tenderly stroking across my spine as she reached for the tape measure in the other hand. She pulled it tight around my middle, taking note of my waist size, before moving it up just under my chest. I shivered each time her hands brushed against me.

"Is it getting warm in here?" I said, trying to break the tension. Elly responded by pulling the tape tight, a muttering a number under her breath.

"Breathe all the way in, then all the way out," she said, and then slid the tape so it sat just on top of my nipples, sending a little pulse of sensation through them. My breath came out as a shudder and I stared at the roof, far too embarrassed to look

Elly in the eyes. She didn't seem to mind, and let the tape measure fall, before reaching up to bring it around my shoulders.

"Now," Elly said, stepping back and looking at me with a devil-may-care smile, "Take off your trousers. I need to take hips and leg measurements." She bit her lip, and I flushed a deep crimson. I fumbled with the lace on my britches and pulled them down, then hesitated before doing the same with my underclothes.

She studied me, running her eyes up from my feet, over my knees and thighs to the slight curve of my hips. She took a step towards me again and wrapped the tape measure around my hips, letting her hands linger on my cheeks. She dropped to her knees and then took a measure down my leg. Her fingers moved with slow, agonising precision, as if she was inspecting every inch of my flesh, from my hips to my ankles. Inside, I was begging for more, and every second she took served only to prolong my anticipation.

Finally, she worked her way back up on the inside of my leg. I gasped as her palm brushed my inner thigh and begged with my eyes. She dropped the pretence—along with the tape measure—and her fingers entwined themselves in my crotch. I was quivering and wet in moments. Elly knew exactly where and how to touch me. A physician's practiced knowledge, no doubt.

She slipped a finger inside me, and I moaned in delight. I was desperate for more, desperate for her, and desperate to escape into passionate bliss. Unable to contain myself any longer, I whispered into her ear, "fuck me." I tried to kiss her but found myself helplessly following her lips as she pulled away, literally wrapped around her fingers. She kept me waiting one moment longer, and with a seductive and wicked smile, she pushed me back onto the bed.

She climbed onto the mattress beside me, one hand going back to my quim, and the other to my breasts. Overwhelming waves of pleasure crashed over me, and I cried and begged for more until she had taken me to the point of absolute ecstasy. I pulled her face to mine and tasted her sweet lips, and as I came, she bit down on my neck with ravenous glee.

Elly slowly removed her fingers and lay down beside me. She wiped her fingers on her dress and leant in to kiss me on the forehead. Her lips were soft and warm. I wanted to kiss her back, but my body was too shaken to follow my thoughts. I curled up into her chest, lost in a serene afterglow. "Can I do anything for you?" I asked, my voice more timid than I'd ever known it.

She stroked my hair and said, "You've done so much already. Besides, I can't stay."

"What?" I asked, looking up at her. "Why not?"

"I have dress alterations to make, and my sewing kit is at home," she replied apologetically. "I'm sure you can manage till tomorrow afternoon by yourself?"

I nodded and rested my head back down, sleep beginning to creep up on me. "I'm sure I'll find something to keep me busy," I yawned.

"Good, get some rest first, though."

Too tired to protest, I watched her gather her things and leave before slumber finally took me.

October 15th, 1834

A Dance Façade

Chapter 33

I had the best night's sleep since this whole ordeal started. I awoke in Jennifer's bed, bleary-eyed and rosy-cheeked, and feeling invincible. Without really realising it, I got myself up and dressed, and fetched food for the day and the morning papers from the grocers down the road. My good mood survived a whole hour until I sat down to read the headlines.

"EMERGENCY DEBATE on WTICHCRAFT ACT in COMMONS," read The Observer. "Yesterday evening the Prime Minister Lord Melbourne bowed to cross party calls to table a debate on the Witchcraft Act of 1735. Despite strong objections from the government that it was considering any changes to the legislation, which pertains to the use of magic in public life, recent events have sent fury through the back benches. Two grizzly deaths, believed to be caused by misuse of a drug known as Black Ember, followed by the attack on Piccadilly, had been brushed aside by the Minister of the Interior.

"'The only thing unusual about these events is that mages had been involved. Tragically, suicides happen all over the city, as do assaults on our streets. The fact that these tragedies were caused by magic instead of firearms or knives is immaterial to wider issues. Crime is down across the city, thanks to the stellar work of the London Metropolitan Police,' the minister said yesterday morning. But events later in the day caused the government to backtrack, leading to the emergency debate being called in the late hours of the evening.

"This paper understands that a group of radical mages has been behind events of the last week, known only as the 1735 Club. No representative of the organisation could be reached for comment. The incident that tipped the scales for the Prime Minister, was an attack on a Workhouse which resulted in the explosion of a steam boiler, and the death of one of the institutions employees. The perpetrator of the attack, a young man by the name of Caspar Smith this paper has been informed, is believed to be a member of the 1735 Club. He was remanded in the custody of the institution on Monday, following the incident on Piccadilly.

"While the full details of the motivations of this man, and the organisation he represents, are unknown. It is clear that the fates of all mages in the nation are to be brought into question by his actions. As we approach the centenary of the partial legalisation of witchcraft, this paper must ask if we are stepping in the right direction."

I dropped the paper on the table, took a large swig of my tea, and muttered, "Bugger." Everything I'd done since Jennifer disappeared had seemed to make the situation worse. It was me that led the assassin to Piccadilly, after insisting on getting Bryce involved, and I was the one that caused the explosion at the workhouse. The only thing Caspar Smith had done was be in the wrong place at the wrong time, twice. Worse still, there was nothing I could do about it. The inner machinations of Houses of Parliament being what they were, my only hope was to find out who was really behind everything and expose the truth before it was too late.

And I couldn't do that, not until Bryce and I met with Professor Carrington. I had itchy feet, but every time I sat down to read up on Witchcraft law, ball etiquette, or anything else related to the case; my brain just shut down. I had a whole day ahead of me—surely an hour or two in the lab wouldn't go amiss? I did owe Elly a favour, after all.

An hour or two. I was optimistic. It's not like I intended on spending the whole day in the lab, it's just that once I got started, there was never really a good time to stop. Somewhere in the back of my mind, I think I hoped that I wouldn't need to do anything else—that Jen might just walk in the door, and I could avoid going to the ball.

I'll be honest and say I didn't entirely know where to start on the potion for Elly. What she had wanted was something that, to my knowledge at the time, had never been attempted before. A wholesale transformation of the human body, to realise an inner truth. Maybe I was already mad to even try.

My morning was spent researching the many alchemical, arcane, and historical volumes in Jennifer's extensive, if poorly organised, library. Proper research techniques in experimental alchemy were something Jen always said she would teach me, but I never took much in, except, "Find the right books and look for related attributes and formulae." I trusted my instincts to guide me, however, and by lunchtime had a plan forming in my mind.

My first experiment was to prepare a Ceration of Iron, performed by melting a bar of the metal in a crucible, and slowly adding linseed oil and crushed fluorite til it forms a malleable, almost flowing putty. Iron embodies the traits of Mars: war, strength, ambition, and, importantly, masculinity. The transmutation achieved by the Ceration softens the metal, and so too do the Arcane properties soften. Or so I hoped.

Next, I dissolved Copper in Oil of Vitriol, producing a deep blue liquid. Copper embodies the attributes of Venus, the chief attribute in concern being femininity. I attempted to Multiply the Copper, by boiling the liquid and gradually adding more Copper and Oil of Vitriol, in the presence of an Arcane power source, of course. I used a tuning crystal made of Aquamarine that Jennifer had acquired from the island of Lesbos. It seemed appropriate.

My third task was to inject a little mythology into the formula. I'd failed to find any inspiration in contemporary writings on magic and alchemy, but the myths and legends of ancient civilisations do have kernels of truth within them. Those stories may be fantastical, but this is simply a case of sufficiently advanced magic being indistinguishable from miracles.

There was a tale about an oracle of Apollo, in ancient Greece, who came across two mating snakes. The oracle killed the snakes, according to some tellings, and the Goddess Hera came down to punish him. His punishment, loathe as I am to use that word, was to be transformed from a man to a woman. He got better, apparently.

Jennifer had some preserved vipers in jars, don't ask me why, and I removed the venom glands from one male and one female snake. I burned the sacs separately till they turned to ash and added them to the other two Transmutations. The ashes of the male gland were added to the Iron wax, and the female I added to the multiplied Copper.

Nothing had gone explosively wrong, which was good, and the tuning crystal was getting warm, which I hoped was good. The last step was to combine everything together and add a base ingredient. Salt was the obvious base. I wanted the potion to change Elly's body, after all. I dissolved the iron in more oil of vitriol, which it did so readily and produced a deep crimson liquid.

I boiled the two liquids together until all that was left was a fine, purplish powder, to which I added crushed salt and dissolved in water that I had soaked the tuning crystal within. There was a violent bubbling and hissing sound from the solution, and I dived under the table, fearing the worst. The worst never came, however, and when I returned to my feet, I found a pleasant smelling violet tincture.

I had no idea what the effects, side-effects, longevity, or really anything at all about the potion. But it didn't explode, and it had definitely undergone a magical transformation. The only way to know, of course, would be to test it. I had a good feeling that the potion wouldn't kill me—you get a feel for that sort of thing after a few accidental poisonings—but a good alchemist always tests a new potion themselves. If I survived and the side effects weren't too bad, I'd make another batch for Elly to try. After a moment's hesitation, I downed the bottle—it tasted of snake guts and iron filings.

I didn't die, obviously. Nor did I feel any different. Perhaps the potion simply didn't take? Or maybe the quantities of reagents were wrong, I had underestimated them after all. I waited for around ten minutes in the lab to see if anything would happen. When nothing did, I shrugged, noted down the negative result, and went to relax in the office.

Elly arrived shortly after I settled on the couch, bearing

a box that undoubtably contained the modified dress, and a roasted pheasant. "You are covered in soot! What have you been doing?" she exclaimed when I let her in the front door.

"I've been quite busy, actually," I said, and proceeded to fill her in on my experimentations. "Sorry to say I had no success this time round, but I'm not ready to throw in the towel just yet. What are you wearing?" She had on a black suit, with a tailcoat and top hat, cut in a lady's style, with a floral waistcoat.

"Don't worry about that now, you're a mess." She sighed and rubbed her forehead. "Go draw a bath, I'll help you get cleaned up. We need something to get all this gunk out of your hair."

She went on for a while, picking out each thing I needed to do on a long list before I could possibly be allowed into public. All the energy and enthusiasm I had earlier in the day drained out of me, and I soon found myself reluctantly hauling buckets of hot water up the two flights of stairs to the washroom.

I bathed with a rose scented soap from Jennifer's collection, which we both agreed was appropriate for the evening. Elly then helped to wash my hair, which I wouldn't have minded if she had stopped telling me how healthy and luscious it was looking.

When I was deemed sufficiently clean, we moved to the bedroom so I could get dressed. Elly was blushing the entire time, but despite that, she watched me with a hint of curiosity in her eyes. "This is a lot more awkward with you watching me," I said when I caught her doing it.

"Sorry, I guess I just haven't seen you cleaned up in a while," she responded, but I sensed there was something more to it. As soon as I started to contort myself into the corset I was being forced to wear, she leaned forward as if to get a closer look at me.

"What?"

She sat back quickly, as if she'd been caught by a teacher, "Nothing, really, I'm sorry I don't know what's come over me." Her face had turned crimson, and she averted her eyes. But only for a second.

I dropped the bodice and threw up my arms. "Seriously?"

"I don't know what to say," she said. "I thought I was

just seeing things, but there's something. Different. About you," her voice was calm and kind of soothing in the way a person speaks to an angry alley cat.

"Different? I don't feel any different. Stop being silly and help me get this damn thing on," I said, grabbing the corset from the floor and chucking it at her. She shook off her strange attitude and started to help lace me into the torturous undergarment.

She was tightening the laces around the top of the corset, when she suddenly lost her balance and toppled into me like she was being pulled forwards. "What the hell?"

"My apologies, Charlotte, I—" I turned to face her, and her jaw dropped. "I was pulling the laces, and they pulled back. Because your tits just got bigger."

"Holy shit." She was right. I couldn't be sure how much bigger, but they were definitely bigger. I moved over to the mirror and finally saw what had Elly so enraptured. The changes were all subtle, except the bigger tits, but there was no doubt that I looked different. More feminine.

My hair was softer and shinier. My skin was smoother than it had been since before my teens. My figure had changed to a slightly more hourglass silhouette. Even my facial features had been altered, I had fuller eyelashes and lips, higher cheekbones, and a softer jawline.

"I thought you said the potion didn't work," Elly said, her voice sounding slightly hopeful.

"I didn't think it did."

"Will it do that for me?"

"I have no idea."

"Bryce is going to freak out."

"Fuck Bryce, I'm freaking out." Not only did I have to dress up like a doll and prance about in front of a bunch of aristocrats, now I had to do it looking like fucking Aphrodite herself.

"Why? You're gorgeous," Elly said, like I was some ungrateful child.

"I know I'm gorgeous, I'd fuck the hell out of me right now," I said, exasperated but honest, "But my one sense of comfort for tonight was hoping that none of those ennobled pricks would want to fuck me."

"The lady doth protest too much," Elly said, because of course she'd quote fucking Shakespeare at me while I was having a crisis.

"Exit stage left, pursued by bear!" I responded, pointing at the door. There was a tense moment of silence before we both started laughing. Laughing in a half-tied corset hurt, however, so it didn't last long.

Once the bodice was finally in place, I put on white stockings and the petticoat, before slipping into the cream-coloured dress itself. The plump sleeves were uncomfortable and made me feel like a ridiculous balloon. I was surprised to find pockets in the skirt, with enough space for my various vials, bottles, and syringes, which was one saving grace of the ensemble.

"A little blush, powder, and something fancy with your hair, and we'll make a lady out of you yet, Charlotte Price," Elly said with a sly grin. I yielded what little resistance was left in me about the whole ordeal and allowed Elly to make up my face and hair. The make-up was very light, which Elly assured me was the correct style, and we settled on braiding my hair into a fairly elaborate bun that Elly finished with a white rose she'd acquired.

Looking in the mirror felt like looking at someone else. I cleaned up good, magical enhancements aside. Never again, though, I hoped.

We retired to the office, and I flumped onto the couch in a mountain of fabric. We ate, very carefully I might add, so I didn't drop any food on the dress, and not long after the clock struck seven, Bryce arrived.

Chapter 34

"You're not driving us," I told Elly as she buttoned up her coat.

"I am. I may not be able to go to the ball, but there's no way I'm leaving you two on your own while I'll wait here for you to stumble back full of holes." The suit finally made sense, and I even recognised the white gloves Elly produced as belonging to her father's driver.

Bryce made a thinking noise and said, "Oddly, I agree with Charlotte here. You'll be much safer here."

She popped her hip to the side, and looked us up and down. "I don't need either of you telling me what's safe, thank you very much. I'm perfectly capable of taking care of myself." The image of Elly clocking the guard at the workhouse in the chin played in my mind, and for a moment, I almost relented.

"No, absolutely not. I'm putting my foot down," I said.

There was a moment of tension and I felt like I was staring down another mad mage about to explode. Elly frowned, bit her lip, and said, "You're putting your foot down?"

Ten minutes later the three of us had set off in a two-wheeled gig, with Elly sat in the driver's seat, and I tried to work out what the hell I was doing. A week of stress, fallbacks, and mistakes, not to mention near-death experiences, must have completely fried my senses. Bryce's plan grated on me for reasons I couldn't explain. Something felt off about it, too convenient, too easy. Not to mention that I hated parties, I disliked upper class snobs, and I wasn't exactly fond of Bryce, either.

Something about the whole evening felt off to me. The invitation had come so suddenly, it was much too convenient for Bryce's old Professor to show up right when we needed him. Why had he been in Surrey in October, when the academic term at London University College would have only just begun? I put my concerns aside, as nothing could be gained by dwelling on them with incomplete information.

Bryce hadn't mentioned how different I looked when he arrived to, but I was all too aware of the way he had been looking at me. I had made no mention of his cleaned-up look either, to be fair. He'd worn a crisp black suit with a high collar, red silk cravat, and black top hat. He had slicked back his usual messy mop of black hair and carried a somewhat dandy gentlemen sense of charm with him. Dare I say it, he may have looked somewhat handsome for the first time since I'd known him.

The two-wheeled gig was all black, with a seat big enough for the two of us set back from where Elly sat. The hood was up to cover us from the misty drizzle of the evening. Bryce's horse was a dappled grey mare, which trotted along contently.

"I never asked where your estate is," I offered up as conversation.

"My father's estate, not mine. We're going to Kensington, where the family home is," Bryce said in reply.

"The family home? You don't live there?" I said.

Bryce looked pensive and thoughtful and said, "Not for a few years. Father and I have disagreements if we spend too much time in close proximity."

I furrowed my eyebrows at him quizzically. "I couldn't imagine, being away from father is one of the hardest parts of my day. I didn't see him for months at a time when I was in Cambridge, I missed him a lot."

He looked at me and smiled. "Then consider yourself very lucky that you still have each other. After everything that happened at university, he nearly cut me off completely; if not for my mother…"

"Bryce?" I said.

"My Mother. She died a long time ago, an accident on the river." Bryce's tone was matter of fact and guarded.

"I'm so sorry," I said, and put a hand on his arm.

"Don't be. It was a long time ago." He smiled again and put his hand on mine. "She was very fond of me, and suspected father would try to be rid of me. She had her own income and left it to me in her will. Caused quite the stir, but the courts ruled in my favour." That's how he was able to afford to fund the 1735 and get away with it.

"I never knew my mother. She died in labour," I said. "It's hard. Father remembers her so fondly, but for a long time I just felt like I had this shapeless hole in my life that she was meant to fill."

"I guess we have that in common then," Bryce said.

There was a reason behind my questioning. I needed to know just who I might meet at this ball, and if Bryce was going to pass me off as some romantic companion, I should be informed. "What about the rest of your family? Any siblings?" I asked next.

"An older brother, Daniel, and one younger brother, Edward, and then Caroline, my older sister." Bryce's mood lightened as he spoke. "Caroline won't be at the ball; she lives with her husband in Derbyshire. I expect Daniel and Edward will be though. Dan can be a stuck-up prick sometimes."

"Says you!" I interjected.

Bryce narrowed his eyes but didn't rise to the bait. "Eddy, however, is good fun. You'll like him."

"Please don't set me up with any of your brothers. Take Elly instead."

Elly looked back from the driver's seat. "I would, but I don't have anything to change into now. Besides, I'm not looking for a husband."

Bryce laughed a full-belly laugh. "Trust me, Charlotte, I wouldn't inflict you on anyone except my worst enemy."

I feigned a scoff and turned away from him. "Well, I never!"

"That's a lot of siblings," Elly said, when she'd stopped chuckling. "Your house must have been utter chaos when you were children." Bryce nodded and laughed again, but there was a melancholy about him I couldn't quite place.

"Are any of them, you know?" I asked and pointed to his arm.

"Marked? No, and thank God, as far as I know it's not hereditary," he held up his hand as he spoke, "This little thing is the root cause of a lot of my father's grief with me. I wouldn't wish that on any of them." There it was. At the mention of his father, Bryce withdrew into himself. I decided not to press any further. I'd learned enough, and Bryce deserved some peace. We spoke for a while about Cambridge, Elly and I working out a patchwork of our experiences into a believable identity, and eventually descended into chatting about the weather.

My attention drifted away from the conversation as the gig passed down alongside Hyde Park and Kensington Gardens. I gazed wistfully into the parks and thinking about times Jennifer and I had spent there. Had Jennifer filled that hole in my life left by my mother, or did it seal itself? I asked myself. I never really considered Jennifer as a mother figure, she was my mentor, my friend. But I certainly didn't feel the longing I felt as a child. I don't remember growing out of it, if that's what happened.

It must have been sometime before Bryce interrupted my thoughts by saying, "Charlotte, are you alright? We're nearly there."

"Oh, yes, what?" I responded before my brain could catch up from being left in the parks.

"You've been wrapping that ribbon on and off your fingers for nearly fifteen minutes," He pointed at my hands and just as he said I had a ribbon from my dress twirled around my index fingers.

I let out a stunted snicker and put the ribbon down, "Sorry, 'Off with the Fairies', that's what father always used to say. Don't worry about me and my thoughts," I said, trying to reassure him. "Explain to me why we're doing this again, why all the pretence of going to a ball?"

"It's going to be safer meeting Carrington here than anywhere else—there's too many people for Hawkins to risk sending in thugs," Bryce said patiently. "This way, we look like two normal people going to a party and having a private meeting with an old acquaintance. No one will suspect anything untoward."

I raised an eyebrow and looked at him suspiciously. "It's frankly bizarre that you would find any of this normal, Bryce."

"Says the woman with robins on her dress."

There was a brief moment of silence, where I seriously considered taking the higher ground—then I asked myself what Jennifer would do. "They're tits, actually," I said, and all three of us burst out laughing.

Not long after we pulled up outside a modestly sized home, built in a neoclassical style, on the road leading towards Kensington Palace. The front façade was flanked by roman columns, with four rows of wide windows. The din of chatter and music came from inside the home, and many other carriages and gigs were parked along the road.

Elly pulled the horse to a halt and turned in her seat to look at us. "I'll be out here if anything goes wrong. Be careful, both of you."

"No need to worry, Dr Chynoweth," Bryce said as he hopped off the gig. "Nothing bad ever happens at a society ball." I squinted at him as he walked around to the door on my side. "What? It will be fine."

"Don't you dare open that door for me."

Bryce puffed out his chest and let out a short laugh. "This door?" he asked, grasping the handle.

"I don't need you to help me out of the gig."

"Are you sure? It would be improper of a gentleman such as myself not to offer assistance." He was beaming, and I turned to see Elly stifling a giggle as well.

I put my hand on the door to keep it closed, and leaned over to Bryce. "I have a pistol strapped to my thigh, and it'd be very improper for me to shoot your hand off."

Bryce held up his hands and stepped back. "Right you are." He looked at Elly, smiled and said, "I'll give you two a moment."

Elly slapped my arm. "That was mean."

"I'm going to have to pretend to be a prissy high society girl all night, that's mean," I said. Elly's face went from amusement to concern before she turned away from me. "What's the matter?"

She took a deep breath to steady herself, and then said, "Promise me you'll come back."

"Elly, everything will be fine, you don't have to worry."

"Promise me."

Against my better judgement, and all the fear I had about what might happen, I took her hand and said, "I promise I will come back." I only hoped it was a promise I could keep.

I hopped out the gig, rather ungraciously, and waved to Elly as she drove the gig somewhere more suitable to park. Bryce then took my arm, smiled, and led me to the front of the estate. A flight of stairs led to the front door, large and painted black. It had finely polished brass fittings, and a pair of oil lamps hung on either side. Standing by the door was a kindly man in his late forties or early fifties, wearing a red and black servant's uniform, complete with top hat and tails.

Bryce strode up the stairs with his arms out in a welcoming gesture. "Malcolm! It's good to see you," he said to the servant, who bowed before shaking Bryce's hand.

"Young Master Rosehouse, so, good to have you back at the estate sir, it's been too long," he said in a raspy voice. "Shall I inform your father of your arrival?"

"No, I'm sure I'll run into him eventually. Malcolm, this is Miss Banbridge of Cambridgeshire, my accompaniment for the evening. Elizabeth, this is Malcolm, he's been with the family for many years," Bryce said, cheerfully introducing the two of us and helpfully reminding me of my fake name. I shook Malcolm's hand and smiled in a way what I hoped was dainty.

The door opened and revealed a grand foyer with stairs leading to an upper level in the centre. The floor was white marble, with a mosaic depicting a rose surrounded by thorns at the bottom of the flight of stairs, the family crest, I assumed. The walls were divided with oak panelling on the lower half and painted white on the upper half. Numerous portraits of family members lined the walls, and the roof of the foyer featured a fresco of an idyllic landscape, all greens, and blues.

The wash of colour and majesty almost took my breath away. "No wonder you like art so much, Bryce, growing up in a house like this," I said, as I turned on the spot in the centre of the foyer.

"This is nothing, you should see the gallery upstairs," Bryce said. He waved away a servant carrying a tray of wineglasses and indicated I should move away from the door. "Oh, and you should call me Mr Rosehouse, while we're here. You don't want to come off as too familiar."

I brushed him off and wandered over to a painting that had caught my eye, one of those heavily posed family portraits. "This is your family, then?" I asked, but those green eyes were unmistakable, even on canvas. I tried to imagine the Bryce in the portrait, no older than eight or nine, stood for hours as his essence was captured. It was so unnatural and stiff that I had to look at the real thing stood next to me to ground myself.

"I always hated this one," Bryce said softly. When I asked why, he sighed deeply and pointed at the rendering of himself. "Look where they had me stand." The boy in the painting wasn't stood with his siblings—two boys and a girl, all in their morning fineries—he was separated from them by the seated figure of their mother. She was posed as if she were turning away from Bryce, so slightly that it wouldn't be noticed at a casual glance.

Behind them all stood the imposing figure I had to assume was the Viscount Kidderminster himself. He had jet-black hair and a short beard and moustache and wore the ceremonial robes of the House of Lords. As calm and serene as Bryce's mother looked, his father was nothing but fierceness.

Reluctantly, I pulled myself away from the painting. I could already feel the eyes on me from the few people gathered in the foyer, like they already knew I didn't belong there. "What shall we do, now, B—Mr Rosehouse?" I asked, in my best attempt at a Cambridgeshire accent.

Bryce looked to be enjoying himself a little too much at my discomfort. "We shall attend to the ballroom, Miss Banbridge." He led me down a hallway off the foyer and my heart slowly made its way up my throat.

There were no candles or oil lamps hanging from the walls; rather, dancing, ephemeral lights that were tethered by some invisible force to chandeliers lit the way down the hall. They cast peculiar shadows and moved in time with the echoes of distant music. I never expected for magic to be so plainly on display, but the rich and powerful played by their own rules in matters Mundane, why not the Arcane as well? I wondered who had weaved the spells and under what arrangement—how many working-class mages had been punished for doing the exact same thing?

People filled the halls, all dressed in finery. There seemed to be a split in styles for the male attendants, where the younger among them sported colourful suits with large cravats and frilled sleeves, while the older gentlemen chose a more muted black or grey suit.

The women mostly wore white, with large petticoats and ridiculously plumped sleeves. Some chose to flaunt a little colour, but these were limited to pastel shades of blue or yellow. There were those who strayed from these norms, of course, but the exceptions were few and far between. I was reassured, slightly, that Jennifer's dress was not so wildly out of fashion.

The reassurance did me little good, however, and I soon developed an unwelcome sense of foreboding. The house was loud, and the marble floors carried the distant music through the house in strange, discordant echoes. The voices of the guests blended together, and even in the foyer, I felt like everyone was watching me. I'd never liked parties, and crowded parties were the worst.

"I can't do this," I said and took a reflexive step backwards. "This was a bad idea."

"It's going to be fine, just follow my lead," Bryce replied in a reassuring tone. He put his hand on my shoulder to stop me from walking into the door.

My heart started to pound in my ears, and Bryce's hand felt like a hammer ready to strike me against an anvil. "I can't. No, I can't do this. There's too many people." My breath turned short, and my eyes widened.

"Now is not the time—" Bryce started to say, but I was starting to back away.

My eyes darted back and forth, searching for a danger I was convinced was there—another assassin waiting in the shadows, a prideful mage high on Ember, or a creature of myth with teeth like daggers. "We need to go, we need to leave," I said, but my body was frozen in place.

Bryce pulled me aside by the arm, and whispered angrily in my ear, "This is our one chance at ending this, Charlotte. I want this to be over as much as you do, and you don't see me panicking. Pull yourself together."

Panic turned to anger. Anger turned to fury. Pull yourself together. The words echoed in my mind, in a hundred voices, each more patronising than the last. I was allowed to be scared; I was allowed to think this was a bad idea; I was allowed to make my own damn decisions—even if they were based in emotion instead of reason. What right did Bryce have, did anyone have, to tell me otherwise?

I slapped him. "Don't you dare talk to me like that," I barked. "We're not friends, Bryce. Do not think for a second that you are in charge here, or that you get to dictate how I think or feel."

"I was just—" he tried to say before I interrupted him.

"I know exactly what you were doing," I snapped, before turning to walk away. "I need a drink."

Chapter 35

I found a servant giving out glasses of wine in the next room. It was a ballroom with an arched ceiling that was decorated in white plaster roses. There was a dancefloor made of dark wood, varnished to a perfect sheen. A balcony looked on the dance floor from above, and a great chandelier made of crystal hung in the centre of the room. More of the floating lights danced around its arms, making the crystals shimmer and gleam.

The dancefloor was filled with free-flowing pairs of dancers, accompanied by the elegant performance of a trio of musicians; a pianist, a flutist, and a violinist. The music was joyful, and the couples swept around the room like a murmuration of swallows, all somehow aware of the movements of everyone else. Many of the dancers were young, some even still in their teens. I wondered how many of them chose to be there and chose their partners.

From above, the hawk-like eyes of opportunistic parents carefully watched their children. How many of them would ruin their child's life for an ounce of influence, for the steady income of a healthy dowery, for the chance to offload a burden on their resources? I watched them all with barely concealed disdain from the edge of the ballroom, sipping from a second glass of wine I'd acquired after downing the first. It was all I could do not to fall again into a panic.

I needed to occupy myself, so I decided my time would be well spent trying to gather information on the mysterious Baron Cranley. I had no intention of asking anyone directly, but many small conversations were happening throughout the ballroom, all I needed to do was listen. I started to drift, keeping from making eye contact with anyone that might be enticed into my company. Snippets of conversations tickled my ears as I walked.

"Did you hear that Anne Lister of Shipton Hall has wed another woman? Could you imagine?" said one button-nosed lady.

"Man-bats, they say, living on the moon! I almost believed it, had I not heard from Sir John Herschel himself that it was fiction," explained a pot-bellied young man.

"These fires are just horrific," said a blonde woman in her mid-forties, and my interest piqued. I took up an inconspicuous place beside a table near the group she was talking with, and pretended I was waiting for someone. "I heard two more were discovered today, one in Chelsea, at a school, no less. The other was a factory in White Chapel, just terrible."

"Drugs the papers are saying, and radicals," the woman's daughter said. The papers had been pushing the story much harder than I'd realised.

"Why doesn't anyone do anything about it? How can they be allowed to practise such dangerous arts?" a third woman said.

"Well," the older woman said, "You didn't hear it from me, but the debate in Parliament today was fierce, and then some. The Prime Minister will be forced to act, no doubt."

"I wouldn't attribute any weight to any such rumours, mother," a young man in a colourful suit said. "Despite these incidents, there's not nearly enough support in the Lords for such a response."

The group drifted away from me, and my thoughts began to percolate. Whatever plan was at work was accelerating, and it was clear to me that turning the public perception toward mages sour was one intended goal. The 1735 Club had turned out to be the perfect scapegoat, and I was an unwitting pawn in exposing them. I lost myself in the endless possibilities, trying to find a solution to the problem that wasn't there just yet.

All that to say, I had no hope of noticing that the man approaching me from a buffet table a few yards away wasn't Bryce. "I'm not talking to you until you find our man," I said, remembering I was angry at him. But when I turned, the man I made eye contact with was a stranger. I fought the urge to roll my eyes, and instead meekly apologised.

He made a thinking sound and cocked a perfectly plucked eyebrow at me. "Well, that's certainly a first, someone who does not know me. Miss?" His voice was low and smoky, and his smile shone out from his dark brown lips. The light from the chandelier danced off his dark skin, like the last glow of the sun before the night. He held out a big hand, and I shook it tentatively.

"Oh, my apologies. Banbridge, Elizabeth Banbridge. Everyone here is dressed so similarly I must have thought you were someone else." I must have blushed, and my face suddenly felt hot. The man was outrageously handsome and acted like he knew it. He had a powerful build, tall and broad, but with an undeniable grace in his movements one might expect from a dancer or a boxer.

He laughed merrily and said, "And to think, I usually stand out so well. Arthur Remington." He flashed that smile again, and it promised comfort and joy. "I came over because I didn't recognise you, and I make a point of knowing everybody. Everyone worth knowing, anyway."

I laughed nervously and tucked my hands into my pockets. "I don't think I'm worth knowing, to be quite honest," I responded, flustered, but also wary of his intentions.

"Nonsense, you are perhaps the most unique and peculiar person here." I wasn't sure how to take being called peculiar by the man, but before I had time to think, he put a hand on my arm and ran it down to my wrist. Gently lifting my hand out of its pocket, he cupped it with both of his and asked, "Would you care to dance?"

Not only was I flummoxed by Mr Remington's confidence and audacity in his proposition, I certainly didn't have the first idea about dancing. "Dance?" I asked, battling the urge to laugh, "I couldn't possibly."

"Come now Miss Banbridge, it's a ball. Dancing is what we are all here for, isn't it? Or do you not want to dance with me, in particular?" he pouted in jest before smiling again.

"Yes, I do, but, um, no. Sorry," I stammered and pulled my hand back. "It's just, I'm here with someone else." I began looking around for Bryce, wondering where he had got to.

"Someone else? Who is the lucky devil? I might want to

duel them for your honour." His smile turned into a smirk and then a deep belly laugh that caught the attention of some nearby ladies. Frankly, I'd have duelled him myself if it meant not having to dance.

I felt a hand on my shoulder and a familiar voice came from behind me. "I shouldn't think that would be necessary, Mr Remington." Bryce stepped beside me with all the swagger of a pirate captain, holding a large glass of red wine in one hand and placing the other confidently on the small of my back.

Arthur's smile dropped, replaced with a grimace that was part fear and part disdain. I'd seen that look before, from those who take "abhor the witch" as a central tenant of their beliefs. Always coupled with furtive glances at the wrist. Bryce, I imagined, must be very used to seeing it. Remington didn't need scare stories and propaganda to fuel his hatred, it clearly ran deep and old.

Mr Remington spoke to Bryce through gritted teeth, "That's Lord Remington to *you*, Rosehouse."

"My condolences, m'lord," Bryce said without a hint of respect. Arthur said nothing more and turned his back on us to stalk out of the ballroom.

"How can you come to these things if that's how they look at you?" I asked, turning to look at Bryce. He was unfazed, encouraged even, a wry smile creeping across his lips.

"Hah, Arthur couldn't keep me away even if they tried. I learned long ago not to give them an inch, lest they take a mile." He turned from watching Arthur's back to looking down at me. "Do you ever wonder why I wear my mark so openly in public? It's to get those looks out of the way. Everyone here already knows, hence the nice jacket for a change." He drank from his wine and removed the hand that I didn't notice had moved to my waist. "You look wonderful, by the way," with the same look he was giving me in the gig.

I pursed one corner of my lips at the compliment, and said, "I'm still mad at you, don't think you can charm your way out of it."

Bryce smiled and bowed in front of me. "Well then, Miss Banbridge, allow me to apologise for my earlier uncouthness. My comments were unwarranted and unhelpful, and I regret them deeply."

"You practiced that," I replied.

"From the moment you stormed off."

I took a drink and pursed my lips again. Bryce shrugged in response and leant back on the table next to me to look at the dance floor. Leaning into him conspiratorially, I asked, "So, where's our guy?"

"Not here yet, I checked with Malcolm before I came after you. He'll likely arrive later, but don't worry, we'll know when he does. Apparently, he's been ennobled quite recently, so there will be an announcement when he enters. For now, we just need to blend in." He drank from his own wineglass and smirked at me.

"Blend in how?" I asked in an accusatory tone.

He put a hand on his hip and looked at me like I'd never been in public before. "We drink, we mingle with the other very eligible young attendees, enjoy some nibbles, and we dance."

"I'm not dancing."

Bryce looked at me unsympathetically. "You'll need to dance. Not right now, try to watch the others, and later we'll hit the floor. It will be noted if we don't."

"Noted by who? I don't care what I bunch of snooty nobles think," I objected.

Bryce put a finger to his lips and said, "Not them, there's no telling who else might be here and who they might be working for."

I sighed. Of course, nothing that had happened in the past week had been simple or easy. Of course, Hawkins or Cranley were going to have eyes in the ball. Of course, Bryce and I were just bumbling through a half-cooked plan as if we had the faintest idea what we were doing.

"You didn't say there would be dancing." It was about the only thing I could think of saying.

"It's a ball, I thought it was implied," Bryce said with a chuckle.

"I can't dance. I've never danced." That wasn't entirely true, I danced in taverns when drunk, when coordination wasn't important.

Bryce, cocksure and overconfident, simply said, "that's why I'll lead." I shook my head in response, but knew this was another battle I'd lose, anyway.

It wasn't long before Bryce was in full mingling mode, drifting between groups of old friends and new faces. I mostly stayed quiet, only speaking when asked a direct question. I thought it best, so I didn't make up too many unbelievable stories about my fake identity.

Watching Bryce talk with his peers was an odd experience in juxtaposition. The party goers respected him as the son of the balls' host, but their conversations were distant and curt. With only a few exceptions, people did not talk with Bryce long. Many more glances like the one I saw on Arthur's face were made, but Bryce never let his stride falter.

"Curious," Bryce murmured during a lull in the mingling. I asked what he meant, to his apparent surprise that he spoke out loud. "I know many of these people, and they are no friends of my father, politically speaking."

"Is that unusual?" I asked.

"No, but it means he's planning something, trying to sway people. But what for?"

I looked at him quizzically. "You haven't seen the papers, have you?" Bryce shrugged, as if it was an absurd thing to ask. "The Lords are voting on something tomorrow, something related to those plans we found."

"You think my father is involved?"

"I don't know what to think anymore."

Just then, a young man with a familiar-looking face approached us. For a moment I stood dumbfounded, the man was the spitting image of Bryce. He was dressed like quite the dandy, however, with a lilac-coloured waistcoat under his suit jacket, white pantaloons, and a pair of polished black riding boots.

"Eddy!" Bryce said, walking up and clasping his brother's forearm. "You look good."

"As do you, Bryce. Changed your hair," Edward Rosehouse replied. "And who is this lovely lady?" He turned to me with a beaming smile and lifted my hand up to kiss it.

"Of course, Elizabeth Banbridge, my brother The Honourable Edward Rosehouse. Eddy, this is Elizabeth, we met last year when I visited Cambridge. Can you believe she's never been to London?" Bryce was good at lying to his family, I could tell, better than he was at lying to me. At least, if Edward could tell Bryce was lying, he didn't let on.

"Miss Banbridge, it is a pleasure that you would choose our family home as your first outing into London's social circles," Edward said. "Are you enjoying your time? I hope my brother hasn't been boring you with arcane theory."

"Oh, it's wonderful. Big fan of the wine," I said with a light laugh. "I'm sorry, I have to ask. I knew Bryce had siblings, but he didn't say he had a twin?"

Bryce and Edward laughed jovially, in on some old family joke. Bryce spoke first. "Edward is three years my junior. A stroke of luck that we both inherited the same handsomeness."

"You're not the first to ask though, I once spent a week in university lectures pretending to be my brother until someone ask me to demonstrate a spell," they laughed again, and I was struck by how at ease Bryce looked all of a sudden. Since I'd known him, he'd always been on guard, nervous, or putting up a front of swagger. But all that melted away as he spoke with his younger brother.

Edward told us about his latest business venture, opening several new fashion boutiques throughout the city. Apparently, he'd been inspired by a recent visit to Paris, and paid for a well-known suit maker to come to London and train new apprentices. I expected he could talk for hours about fashion, but before we could let him, the music changed.

"Ahah!" Bryce exclaimed. "Edward, I would love to listen to all your wonderful plans, but a Waltz is exactly what we've been waiting for." Before I could protest, Bryce pulled me towards the dance floor. He stopped and twirled towards me, annoyingly dashing, and took my left hand in his right and held it high. His left hand settled high on my waist—modest and respectful—and sent a jolt of pain through my chest.

I carefully slid his palm down toward my hips. Bryce raised an eyebrow, with a smile that was dangerously close to flirtatious. "I cracked my ribs, remember—don't go getting any ideas."

He pulled me closer, his hand on the small of my back and the warmth of his body pressed to mine. "Wouldn't dream of it," he said, and I couldn't tell if he was joking or not. What the hell was he doing? What the hell was I doing?

The panic I'd tried my best to ignore reared its head again and played a percussive solo on my chest with my heart as its instrument. My feet all but turned to stone and the perfect sheen of the dancefloor looked like ice—a thousand ways of falling and breaking my ankles flashed across my mind.

"Trust me," he whispered in my ear—his voice like a rugged growl—and a shiver ran down my spine. "This is a simple dance, we just go around in circles and spin a little. Right hand on my shoulder." For some ghastly reason I couldn't fathom, I did as he said without hesitation.

"I hate you. This is a bad idea. I hate you. Why did I agree to come here? I hate you," I said, which only made things worse. Why was he grinning so much? My chest went light as a feather, and I dearly hoped it was just another stage of panic. "I hate you," I said, for the last time.

Bryce rolled those dazzling emerald eyes of his and said, "You can tell me all about how much you hate me later."

Other couples joined us on the dancefloor, about two dozen in total, we all stood in a circle. The pianist played a gentle introductory trill, before the flute and violin joined in on a light, playful melody. Bryce led and we moved around the room. I did my best to watch his feet, match his movements and not fall over, but it was hard. I kept stepping on his feet or tripping over my own.

Bryce encouraged me with kind words, chuckled when I stepped on his toes and praised how well I did when I managed a few steps in a row correctly. He was every bit the gentleman, and I could feel his charm slowly working away at the walls I had up. It was all over for me the moment I cracked a smile; Bryce pulled me closer, and we started to move as one.

Somehow, that clumsy, drunken fool I'd dragged into my life had turned into a graceful, elegant beau. Or maybe this was who he'd always been. No doubt he could have had his pick of anyone in the room to dance with—would he have chosen me in a different time and place? I couldn't help but notice all the eyes on us. "Bryce, everyone is looking."

"Good, that was the point," he said. "There's a twirl coming up, are you ready?"

"No, but apparently I have no choice," I answered. Moments later the steps stopped, and I did my best effort and spinning under Bryce's hand. I stumbled, of course, and Bryce caught me and swept me back into the motion of the dance. As the music came to its close, Bryce led me into a backwards dip.

He smiled down at me, our eyes meeting for an age. My breath strained against the corset, and I could feel his heart thumping against mine. For a moment, the world stood still, and I saw Bryce in a new light. The handsome, mysterious gentleman, with a heart of gold and a tough exterior, a more perfect dance partner one could only dream of.

The music faded away, and the dancefloor began to rearrange for the next number. Bryce led me by the hand, kissed it softly when we reached the side of the room, and said, "You continue to surprise me, Charlotte Price."

"I'm full of surprises," I said. I thought of the night we met, looking into the eyes of a man in any other circumstance, that I might have fallen for head over heels for. Maybe it was the excitement of the dance, or the wine, or something else entirely, but I found myself really quite fond of Mr Rosehouse and his dashing smile. "Bryce, I…"

"Not here," he said, softly. "Besides, what would Miss Eloise think?"

Before I could begin to imagine the taste of his lips and made a face Elly could spot from a mile away, Bryce excused himself to the call of nature. Not a moment after I started to think that everything might just go to plan, Arthur Remington stepped to my side and cleared his throat.

Chapter 36

"He's not the sort a fine lady like yourself should consort with," Remington said, his voice as smooth as brandy, and as poisonous as nightshade. "Bryce Rosehouse is dangerous."

I regarded the young Lord with obvious disdain. "I'm more than capable of recognising dangerous men." I looked around the room, hoping to see where Bryce had gone, and where I might run to if it came to that.

Remington took another step closer, and I had to fight my instincts not to react. "He's an addict and a drug dealer, it's astonishing his father even allows him to move in society. You would do better to leave."

People around us had begun to stare, and I had a sinking feeling that my cover story might not hold up if I punched Remington in the face. Bryce had been gone too long, there was no telling what might be holding him up, or who. "Where is he?"

"No need to worry about him. Bryce Rosehouse isn't worth it. Come with me, I'll keep you safe," Arthur said before taking my hand.

I pulled my arm away from him. "Don't touch me, I don't need your help. Where is Bryce?"

Arthur laughed and smiled jovially. "Clearly the young lady has had too much to drink." The crowd sniggered and feigned looking away in shame. "Come now, I'll take you somewhere quiet. You can trust me, Charlotte."

I scowled at Arthur and said, "I wouldn't trust you with my boots. Where's Bryce?" He regarded me with a crooked smile, holding out his hand. My head was feeling fuzzy from the wine, and suddenly the fullness of what he said caught up to me. "How do you…?"

Arthur grabbed my wrist and locked my arm behind my back. The crowd gasped, but they didn't stop watching. "I think it's time for you to go." The jovial, friendly veneer collapsed in that moment, revealing a visage of rage. "Bryce will have his hands full when his guest arrives. Ah, speaking of which."

I managed to twist myself free of his grasp, but now found myself surrounded by lords and ladies, with Arthur Remington confidently standing in front of me. I was about to run when I noticed the commotion at the entrance to the ballroom. Malcom, the old butler, was standing beside a man blowing a horn, and behind them I saw a vision from my nightmares.

"Ladies and gentlemen!" the crier called, "Presenting Professor George Carrington, Baron of Cranley." My heart stopped, and the ballroom filled with rapturous applause.

Professor Carrington. Baron Cranley. An older man with a pointed black beard laced with a touch of silver-grey hair, fierce bushy eyebrows, and high cheekbones so sharp they could cut steel. He was the mage from the warehouse. They were all the same person.

The world around me felt like it was crashing to the ground. Bryce was nowhere to be seen, and the memories of my last moments at the warehouse were flooding back to me. Across the cavernous expanse of the ballroom, the man from my nightmares locked eyes with me through the crowd, like a hawk spotting its prey. I realised then what I should have known all along. This was a trap, and it had already been sprung.

Remington had had enough of my gawping and made a move to grab me. To my left were a pair of dainty women in overly puffed dresses, and I figured they'd be my easiest route. Arthur and I stood off for a moment before I broke into a run and shouldered past the women, knocking them to the ground. I looked back briefly to find Arthur struggling to get past the mountain of petticoats.

"Bryce! Bryce, run!" I yelled as I ran, hoping beyond hope that he was somewhere nearby, and he could make it out. I barrelled through a side door and found myself in a smoking room of sorts, a dozen nobles set around in a cloud of cigar smoke and stared at me quizzically. I didn't hang out long enough for them to respond, however, and ran to the next door.

A long, white hallway stretched out before me, lined with doors. I kept moving, trying to get my bearings, but the echoing sound of my shoes on the wooden floor broke any chance I had at focusing. Each door I passed offered the possibility of escape, of finding Bryce, of safety, but I was paralysed by choice. It wasn't long before I reached near the end of the hallway and footsteps came up behind me.

Arthur, flanked by two servants who looked oddly familiar, smiled at me confidently. "What's this about, Remington? Who are you? Who are you working for?" I questioned, holding out one hand in a stopping gesture and slipping the other into a pocket in my dress.

"You're a fool Miss Price, thinking you could come here unnoticed." He pulled something out of his pocket. It glimmered in the dim candlelight, but I couldn't tell what it was from that distance. "You can make this easy you know, just come with me for a talk."

"Christ on a fucking bike. I'm so sick of you stuck up twats. No, I won't come with you. Where is Bryce?" I had two vials of Valerian in my concealed hand. It'd be as simple as uncorking one and throwing the contents in my assailants faces to knock them out. I just needed them closer.

"Such foul language from such a pretty girl. Get her," Arthur said, pointing at me. The servants broke into a run down the hall. As they closed, I placed their faces, both of them had been in the warehouse that fateful night on Stewart Street. I started putting the pieces together in my head. This entire night had been a setup. Carrington, or Cranley, or whatever he was called, had known what we were up to the entire time, and Bryce was in even more danger than I had imagined.

The servants were close. I pull my hand from my pocket and uncorked one of the vials. I swung my arm in an arc, sending the green liquid into the face of the larger of the two attackers. They fell to the ground with a thud and began to snore through a bloody nose. The second stopped in his tracks and put his fists up in a guard.

"You'd hit a lady?" I said and winked at him.

"Consider it payback for when you shot at us last week," he snarled in an east London accent.

My heart was pounding. I knew I couldn't take a hit from this guy without a shield up. Thinking fast, I grabbed a candelabra from a nearby table and hurled it at the servant and then ran towards him. He failed to deflect the burning projectile and with his guard down, I tackled him at the waist to bring him to the ground.

I poured the remaining vial of Valerian onto his face, having to pull up my skirt to cover my face from the fumes. He passed out in seconds, and I got back to my feet.

Arthur laughed. He'd cleared about half the hallway at a gentle stroll. The object in his hand was a dagger, a simple thing with a steel blade and leather wrapped handle. He flipped it in his hand as he walked. "You know, I'd think most men would be happy to collapse under a lady's skirts."

"Oh yeah, you want to be next?" I said between heavy breaths. "I don't tend to prefer the male sex, but you do seem like a fun tumble."

"Have you ever considered that running your mouth will only get you in more trouble? My employer asked for you unharmed, you wouldn't want me to disappoint him, would you?"

"I couldn't give a flying fuck what your employer thinks, frankly." I was trying to find a way out, I'd been pushed to the end of the hall to keep my distance from Remington. There was a window behind me, but I didn't fancy jumping through it. Back the way I came, through Arthur, was the ballroom and I couldn't escape that way. I had to find Bryce as well, I couldn't leave him here.

I bumped into a table at the end of the hall, and Arthur was getting close. Thoughts rattled around in my mind, trying to figure out what to do, what Jennifer would do in my position. I had to deal with Remington, else he'd just raise the alarm and have the entire manor looking for me. Fighting him would be risky, but I trusted the shield potion in my pocket to keep me safe. Besides, if it didn't, that knife might be the end of me, and I'd already had enough of a taste of being stabbed.

"Fuck it," I said, pulling the heavy syringe from my pocket and jamming it into my arm.

The sudden pain shocked me in my core, but I pushed through it and injected the potion. The cool sensation of the protective magic flowed through me, and I opened my eyes just in time for the knife to come down at my face. I outstretched my hand and the blade caught on the shield; its point just shy of a barleycorn from my skin. I smiled at Arthur, and we stared at each other for a brief moment at the cracked forcefield began to reform.

I used the shield's grip on the dagger to twist it in Arthur's hand, and it clattered to the ground. I tried to feint past him, but he stepped on my trailing skirts, and I stumbled. He shoved me into the wall, knocking the wind out of me, but it didn't hurt as much as I'd expected. A fist flew at my face and the shield fractured as it absorbed the force, but it didn't prevent my head from whipping around.

I threw up my arms to guard my face as the shield reformed, but Arthur used the opportunity to pick me up by the waist and throw me to the ground. I looked down over myself. I looked like I was wearing a bodysuit of broken glass.

"Fucking magic. It's always fucking magic," Arthur snarled angrily. "You'd best hope Carrington kills you, because the rest of your kind will be wishing for it."

"What—" I managed to say before Arthur dragged me up into a bear hug, trying to crush the air out of my lungs.

"If I had it my way, we'd get rid of the lot of you, but Cranley has other plans," he said through gritted teeth. "At least this way there's some benefit to leaving your kind alive—with a leash around your neck instead of a noose."

"You're mad," I gasped. Talking was hard, but the shield was giving me enough room to breathe. I sneered at him, and Arthur cocked his head, "And you're an idiot."

"What are you talking about, witch?" Arthur growled.

Straining to speak, I explained his error. "Well, first, I'm not a witch." Arthur looked down at my bare arm and saw that I had no Brand. "Second, I have this." I found the grip of my pistol in the holster I'd strapped to my thigh. There was a crack and a scream, and blood and ichor exploded from Arthur's right leg.

I dropped to the ground but managed to stay on my feet. My dress was completely ruined, the skirt had ripped in the struggle, and blood stained the petticoats. The shorter of Remington's two accomplices looked about my size, so I stole his trousers and jacket, and tore off the tattered fabric around my waist. Remington was writhing on the floor as I did. I gave him a pitiful look and a loud sigh.

As I moved my supplies into the ample pockets of the servant's garb, I held up one of the vials, "This is a healing draught, it'll patch up that wound nice enough and stop the bleeding." Remington reached up and flailed weakly. "No, you can have it if you tell me where Bryce is."

He groaned and said, "You common folk have no respect for your betters."

"My betters? Have you ever considered that running your mouth will only get you in more trouble?" I moved closer to him and then pressed a foot into the bloody ruin of his shin. "Big place like this, a party with loud music, could take someone quite a while to find you."

Remington screamed again. I was slightly worried the sound would carry farther than I wanted but needs must. "He's upstairs! In the gallery!"

"Thank you," I said as I released his leg. I walked away and placed the vial on a table about twenty feet from Remington, before turning and positing the question, "Why are you working with Carrington? He's a mage, what do you gain from siding with him?"

Remington crawled along the ground, pausing to say, "He's a means to an end, one step in a much grander plan. Carrington will have his day soon enough."

I let out a short, amused interjection and said, "That's a shit excuse." With that, I left Remington to crawl his way down the corridor and snuck back the way I came.

Chapter 37

It didn't take long for me to find a servant's staircase and make my way up to the second floor of the residence. This part of the house was surprisingly quiet, I only had to hide from a maid once as I navigated the halls. I moved quickly and as silently as I could, straining to keep myself focussed on finding Bryce, and getting to safety.

The house was like a labyrinth of oak-panelled walls and gold filigree. I hadn't a clue where I was going, and I'd risk getting caught if I started opening doors at random. I stood in the middle of a long corridor, baffled at the idea that anyone would choose to live in a place like this. I turned, and turned again—it was so dimly lit that I couldn't tell which way I'd come from—every which way looked the same. I let out an audible, "Fuck," to vent my frustrations, and then my blood went cold.

"Is someone there?" came a voice that was almost familiar, and footsteps along with it. I panicked and tried the nearest door, it was locked. I was well and truly fucked and convinced that my best bet now was to throw myself out the nearest window. But then a light came around the corner and my heart skipped a beat.

"Bryce?" I said. His colourful clothes gave away my mistake. I was relieved all the same. "Edward!"

"Miss Banbridge? Was that you I heard cursing? Why are you dressed so strangely?" he said as he regarded me, his voice a mix of concern and puzzlement.

"It's very difficult to explain, and frankly I don't think you'd believe me if I had the time," I touched his arm in a gesture of reassurance. "Please, Bryce may be in danger, and I need to find him."

"Danger? What danger could he possibly," he stopped mid-sentence when he saw the duelling pistol in my hand.

"Miss Banbridge, you're armed!"

"Shh, please, I need to find the gallery. It's on this floor, correct? For Bryce's sake, I must find it," I implored.

Edward looked wearily at me; a mirror of the same look Bryce's had given me a dozen times before. My instincts urged me to trust him, Bryce obviously regarded him well, and I needed friends in this dangerous situation. After a pause, Edward pointed down a hall and gave me directions to the family gallery. "It was always Bryce's favourite place in the house until…"

"I'm sure that's a very interesting story, Edward, but I need to go. Thank you."

"Elizabeth, please, tell me what's happening, why is my brother in danger?"

I held up my hands in a shrug. "Politics, magic, crime. A day in the life I imagine, and it's Charlotte by the way. Please go back to the party. Bryce will be able to explain everything later." I left him standing befuddled in the dim corridor.

The gallery was the largest room on the second floor, the entrance to which was a large set of mahogany double doors. The moulding around the panels was detailed in thorn patterns, as was the outer door frame. The doorknobs were cast bronze, in the shape of rose heads. The orange light of a wood fire flickered under the door and inside were the sounds of muffled conversation.

"Where is she?" someone said.

"The Lord Remington went after her, m'lord," another replied.

I drew my pistol and pulled back the hammer slowly. With a tap on my leg with the barrel, I tested my shield for reassurance. The forcefield shimmered momentarily, and I took a breath to steady myself. With not a moment left to lose, I opened the door quickly and levelled the pistol.

The gallery was huge, about half the length of the ballroom directly below us. A large fire burned in a hearth on the far wall, casting the room in dancing shadows. The floor was covered in overlapping Persian rugs, on top of which sat a chesterfield suite upholstered in a faded yellow.

The walls were covered in a cacophony of portraits, frescos, landscapes, and more. Hundreds of paintings, some hung directly over others and in dozens of different styles assaulted the eyes of anyone who looked upon them. The ceiling too was not spared. Murals of passed lords and ladies scattered the plaster, surrounding an unfinished piece of a large rose entangled in thorns which took centre stage. It was incredibly distracting.

One corner of the room looked to have been recently redecorated and was taken by a large floor-to-ceiling bird cage. An exotic plant of some kind branched along the walls and grasping at the bars around to the top was a scaled, bat-like creature with sharp claws and a long-barbed tail. Another wyvern, I realised, but this one looked scrawny and malnourished.

There were four people in the room. Bryce had been tied to a chair, unconscious. A young woman in servant's clothing stood closest to the door, and by the fire were two men in evening suits.

On the left was the unmistakable face I now knew to be Carrington. His suit jacket was split up the forearms, revealing the Brand on his right arm. He carried with him the same cane topped with a crystal ball he had used in the warehouse. Seeing him up close for the first time, I noticed the wrinkles and grey hairs that gave away his age.

The last man leant on the right side of the mantle with one foot resting on the basket of pokers by the fire. He had a glass of whisky or brandy and stood taller than even Carrington. Clearly aged from the portrait, Lord Rosehouse was still an imposing individual. His hair had greyed on the sides, leaving a streak of black across the top of his head. What struck me the most were his eyes; I'd half expected he'd have the same emerald irises as Bryce, but the Viscount's were a stark sable, flecked with darker browns. He flicked his fierce gaze between his son and me.

The woman in the servant's uniform rushed at me, drawing some kind of cudgel from her belt. I didn't hesitate and shot her in the shoulder before she could reach me and kicked the club away from her body. I loaded another round with practiced precision, locking eyes with the mage and then the lord.

"Miss Price, how nice of you to finally join us," Carrington said, his arms open wide. His voice was cold as ice and filled with disdain.

"I hope I didn't keep you waiting, I was held up by one of your friends," I had the pistol pointed at Carrington, and began to circle around to the right side of the room so I could keep my eyes on both of the men. "Lord Rosehouse, Viscount of Kidderminster, I presume, we haven't had the pleasure."

"We still haven't," Rosehouse responded. His voice was rich, gravelly, and filled with authority. "Did you really expect you could break into my property and maim several of my employees?"

"Technically, I'd argue I've only maimed one of them so far," I said, gesturing at the woman cradling her shoulder.

"I was speaking of our warehouse, where you and your accomplice interrupted a very important shipment. Then there's the incident at the workhouse in the past few days," he said matter-of-factly.

I looked at him, puzzled. Cranley owned the warehouse on Stewart Street, and the workhouse. I'd worked that out. How was Bryce's father involved here?

"Tell me, where are the plans you stole from me and my associate?" Lord Rosehouse asked.

"What plans?" I responded as nonchalantly as I could. My brain was working nineteen to the dozen. What was I missing here? All this time I'd thought he was working alone with Hawkins. How had Jennifer missed the involvement of one of London's premier lords?

"The designs you stole are patented, and very important in advancing the nation's industry," Carrington interjected.

"Industry?" I exclaimed back at him, unable to contain my indignation, "You mean the burning people alive industry?!"

"Then you do know what we are referring to, where are they?" Lord Rosehouse said.

"We have a very important demonstration coming up, you see, slightly delayed due to your continued interference," said the wizard with a shrill laugh.

By now I had rounded half the room and stood with the sofa between me and the two nobles. Bryce was still out cold, in an armchair across the room from me. He had a nasty bruise coming in around his right eye, but he was otherwise unharmed.

"Sorry about that, people have always said I'm too nosy for my own good," I said. "Perhaps you should have stressed to your employees not to use your product. Black Ember is nasty business after all."

"On the contrary, Miss Price, I find Black Ember a very useful means of control over troublesome individuals," Rosehouse replied, lazily gesturing towards Bryce.

"Control?" I said and then realised what he meant. "You hooked him on that poison in the first place, didn't you? What kind of sick parent does such a thing?"

"Oh no, my dear, it's Bryce who is sick. He doesn't know his place," Carrington said. "He could have a privileged place in the natural order of things, yet he insists on consorting with the wrong influences. Alas, he will have to be dealt with like the rest of the abnormalities."

"Abnormalities? They're people," I said dismissively.

"You just don't get it, girl, do you?" the Baron sneered. "For centuries the rabble could be trusted to regulate themselves. Fear and doctrine kept the number of mages under control, with only those in appropriate positions able to wield the power of the Arcane. Now, other methods are required to maintain order and balance. If we allowed just anyone the freedom to use magic, it would be a danger to ordinary people."

"And who has the privilege of deciding who has the right to bare that brand and who is an abnormality, Carrington?"

"A role I regrettably take upon myself, a true sacrifice you must understand," he said, without a single shred of honesty.

"It's for their own good, girl. The poor and the feckless must be kept in line, lest modern society collapse around us," Rosehouse explained.

"That's absurd. Mages have always existed, and society hasn't collapsed. This isn't about control or stability. What you're doing is slavery. It's murder."

Rosehouse rolled his eyes. "Legal words with legal definitions. We're simply ensuring that any changes to the law are made in the best interests of the public. My son's little band of radicals wanted more rights to work. We're giving it to them. If I need to make certain troublesome elements disappear because they've found out too much—well, magistrates are easily paid off."

The puzzle pieces finally started to fall into place, and I understood what I'd been missing. The Black Ember, the warehouse—even Billy Parker—it would take someone with a lot of power and influence to keep all of that hidden. Someone with connections to the law, who could even arrange a noble title for a university professor. In a moment of clarity, I turned the pistol on Rosehouse, "I'm sure you don't have trouble making all sorts of things disappear—Hawkins." The anger in my voice began to boil over, and my composure started to drop.

"Very clever, my dear, very clever. A shame your mentor isn't here to congratulate you," Rosehouse said calmly. A wicked smile crept onto his face, born from a sadistic joy in inflicting pain on others.

"Where is she?" I snarled.

He just stared at me and took a sip of his drink.

I yelled, "Where is she?!"

The door to the gallery opened, a young servant came in and said, "My lord, word from Westminster, preparations are underway," before stopping and looking dumbfounded.

"They have the plans?" Carrington said, and the servant nodded nervously.

Rosehouse looked at me with a sense of intense self-satisfaction. "Well Miss Price, your role in this dance is complete. Foolish of you to leave your shop unprotected. The only thing left is to dispose of you."

The plans. I'd left them at the shop, not realising how important they may have been. I couldn't believe how foolish I'd been. I'd walked headlong into a trap, and left the one piece of leverage I might have used behind. My mind started to replay the last few days over, trying to find where I might have done things right, things I should have said. I was paralysed by the enormity of it all, by the endless possibilities of every step I took, all leading to a monumental cock up.

In the next few moments, several things happened. First, Bryce bolted awake and looked at me in horror and shock. Second, Carrington flicked his cane into a level grip, with the crystal orb pointed right at my chest. Third, my instincts took over, and I shot Lord Rosehouse.

The glass in his hand exploded, and a gush of blood splattered on the mantelpiece from his hand. Bryce spoke a word of power and the ropes tying him down burnt to cinders. Then, as I turned to fire an empty chamber at Carrington, he drew a rune in the air and let loose a torrent of lightning that struck me square in the chest.

The shield took the bulk of the magical energy, but Carrington was incredibly powerful. I held up my arms and grimaced as my muscles seized up, and it felt like my heart was trying to tear itself from my chest. The power Carrington had stored up for the spell ran dry, and the shield reverberated around me as it regenerated. When my senses returned to me, a flash of red and orange light dazzled me again, and the sound of an explosion filled my ears.

Bryce had one arm engulfed in flame, and Carrington rolled on the carpets trying to put out the flames on his suit. His face was badly burnt, and what was left of his hair was smoking.

"You always were a disappointment, Bryce!" Lord Rosehouse said. He'd fallen to one knee and was wrapping his hand in some torn fabric.

"Well, at least I'm predictable," Bryce responded. He walked over and punched his father in the face, knocking him to the ground. Bryce stood over the Viscount; his face twisted into a visage of absolute fury. Raw Arcane seemed to spark between Bryce's fingertips, and his words were like venom as he spoke. "Where are they? How many have you built?! How many have died already, you sick, twisted bastard!?"

The lord didn't answer, instead he looked at the servant still standing in the doorway. "Don't just stand there, get the guards!" he shouted. Bryce kicked him in the head, knocking him out cold, and probably breaking his nose.

"Come on, there's a back way out. If we go now, we can make it." He walked over to Carrington and stepped on the crystal ball of his cane, shattering it and releasing a whimpering few sparks that danced across the floor.

"What about Elly?" I asked.

Bryce crossed the room. He put a hand on my shoulder, which was still warm from the spell he'd cast. "We need to get somewhere safe and then we'll come back for her. She'll be fine."

"We can't just leave her here, if they find—" I said.

"Be quiet and don't say her name again until we get out of here. She will be fine, trust me," Bryce said confidently.

Trust. Could I trust Bryce Rosehouse? Did I have a choice? I trusted him when we walked into his family home, when he told me that Carrington would help us. I'd be wrong about so much. Maybe I was wrong about him, too. Maybe he was a radical mage, threatening the fabric of society. Or maybe he was just as broken as I was, just as prone to making mistakes.

"All right, I trust you."

"Good. Hold still, this'll feel weird," he said, and took my hand in his. He murmured a word of power that reverberated in my ears, and from a tattoo of an eye on his right arm, and shimmering wave of light engulfed us. When the light faded, I couldn't see Bryce, or myself. "Do not let go of my hand and move very slowly."

"Bryce? Are we invisible?"

Chapter 38

The world was strangely out of focus, and I felt seasick as the floor beneath me seemed to move and shift. I couldn't see Bryce, but he held tight to my hand and pulled me inexorably onward. He led me past groups of patrolling guards, armed with pistols and bludgeons, and dressed in servants' uniforms, down the stairs to the rear of the house.

After what felt like hours of slow, considered steps through the house, we came to a smoking room that was unoccupied by the unaware party guests. Bryce stopped moving and started counting under his breath. To my surprise, he then pulled aside one of the bookcases to reveal a set of steps spiralling into the darkness. We climbed down them, closing the entrance behind us, and emerged into a tunnel of sorts where the air was cold and damp. Bryce released my hand, and as the magic waned, I felt the sense of queasiness leave the pit of my stomach with it. In the darkness, I could just make out the form of Bryce becoming visible once more.

"What is this?" I asked.

"An escape route, it was built a few generations back in the days of the Protectorate. Apparently, my family didn't take kindly to Cromwell," Bryce explained. He was moving in the darkness, and I could hear his hands fumbling on the stone wall. A few moments later he spoke a quiet word of power, and light filled the tunnel from a wooden torch. "I found this when I was eight, not long after mother died and my father," he paused, looking melancholic. "It doesn't matter. This way."

I followed Bryce down the tunnel, all sense of direction having been lost to me. The glow of the torch reached out some twenty feet, and beyond that was blackness. Part of me wanted to take Bryce's hand again, out of some longing for comfort. I wondered if he felt the same.

"I'm sorry," he said after a long period of silence. "I was a fool to trust Carrington, I should to have realised what was going on."

"We both made that mistake, Bryce. I'm the one who should be sorry. I had all the pieces of this puzzle in front of me and didn't make the connection. Some detective I turned out to be," I replied dejectedly.

"I thought you were an alchemist?" he said. He turned around and flashed a smile at me, and I smiled back.

"You know when you said you were sorry, I thought you were going to say: 'for abandoning you to the hands of that sleaze, Remington.'"

"Oh shit, Charlotte," he said and stopped in place. "It all happened so fast, he didn't harm you, did he?"

"Just my pride, a little, don't worry though, I got him back much worse." I regarded him for a moment, and then asked, "What's the story between you two?"

Bryce's expression turned forlorn, and he started to walk again. I came up to his side and gave him a look that threatened to ask him a second time. He acquiesced and said, "I was engaged to his sister, Leeanna. He was never fond of me to begin with, his animosities go way back. But, when my trouble with certain substances and my expulsion from college became public, he forced her to break everything off. Whatever seed of hate within him sprouted, and he grew toxic toward people like me."

"Hate is easy, because otherwise you have to believe in the complexities of every person. Including yourself," I pointed out.

"You're probably right there. I should never have been surprised he'd fallen in with my father." He had a look of intense anger on his face, the kind of rage that was deep-seated and aged like a fine wine. "I should have killed him."

I didn't disagree. We walked a little further before the silence started grating on me. "Hey, why didn't you use that invisibility spell at the club?"

Bryce made a thinking sound, then said, "It's tricky to start with; and you saw how slow we had to move. We'd have been run down in the corridor."

"I guess that makes sense. One day you're going to have to fill me in on all your tattoos." Before Bryce could respond, something else that had bugged me popped into my head. "And why do you use Cant? Isn't that a bit common?"

He laughed. "Cant is useful for small, spur-of-the-moment spells. I picked up the way it worked from the club. What happened to your dress, by the way? You looked quite pretty in it."

I rolled my eyes. "Only quite pretty?" I said with a grin. "Remington happened; I swear if I see him again I-" Pain shot through my chest, and my words were cut short. I felt as though the floor dropped out from under me and I fell to my knees.

"Charlotte? What's wrong?" Bryce said in a panic.

"I can't breathe," I said. My lungs felt as if they were being crushed by an anvil.

Bryce grabbed me by the shoulders—he looked puzzled, more than anything. "What are you talking about? You're breathing fine."

Had I been in less pain, I'd have been furious with him, but all I could think about was the sensation of pins and needles on my skin, like a thousand angry bee stings. "Bryce. Bryce, do something, anything. God, my heart's going to explode. I can't breathe!"

His hand was on my chest, pressed hard to feel my heartbeat—it roared in my ears like thunder. "Your pulse is normal. What on earth has got into you, Charlotte? You're being hysterical."

"I'm dying, and you're calling me hysterical!? What part of, 'I can't breathe,' don't you understand?"

Bryce looked at me, completely aghast. "God, woman. As clever as you are, you'd think you'd know that you need to be able to breathe in order to talk so much!" I tried to pull away from him, but I took hold of my wrists and I felt too feeble to do anything about it.

Unable to move, my mind ran away with itself. "I'm going to die in a fucking sewer, and I bloody well deserve it. I've nearly killed everyone I've ever got close to, I've failed at everything I've ever put my mind to, and now I've apparently forgotten how breathing works—"

Electricity coursed through my veins, just enough to literally jolt me out of whatever mania had its grip on me. I took a series of long, deep breaths to steady myself, then reached out a hand to Bryce so he could help me up. "You shocked me!"

"Sorry, I suppose. I didn't know if it would work." He cocked his head and held the torch up to my face. "You look different."

I had to push his arm back to get the heat of the torch away from me, and then I tentatively touched my face. The attack, whatever it was, suddenly made sense; it was the side-effect of the potion I'd made before the ball. Scratch that one out of the formula book, there's no way I'd want Elly to go through that every day.

"I'll explain later, we need to keep moving, Frankenstein." I said dismissively and took off again down the tunnel.

"If I'm Frankenstein, doesn't that make you my monster?"

"I've chosen to believe a lot about you, Bryce, that some might think strange. But don't expect me to believe one second that you've actually read Mary Shelley."

"Right," Bryce mumbled. He took the lead again down the tunnel, and it wasn't long before we came to an iron ladder with a stone hatch above it. Bryce set the torch into a sconce and then climbed up the ladder. I followed, and we soon found ourselves in the cool night air, in the back of a stone building. Moonlight streamed in from the three open archways that lead into separate chambers of what I realised was Queen Caroline's Temple, in the middle of Kensington Garden's. I'd been there a few times with father, but I was always too busy reading the rude graffiti on the walls to notice the slight cut in the stone floor where the hatch was.

As I stepped out onto the grass my eyes were drawn upwards to the sky. The moon shone brightly, reflecting off the still surface of the Long Water, and the vast expanse of stars above twinkled with delight. I could have got lost in them, right then, and spent the night counting the lights of the heavens and drawing out the constellations. But, in an instant, my attention was grabbed to something else, a shape moving in the sky.

For a moment, I thought it to be a bird of some sort. A kite or buzzard, circling around on an updraft. But it was much too late for that. Bryce watched it too, his expression as puzzled as my own. The shape descended, growing larger in the sky, and blocking out more of the stars. As it did, I recognised the pattern of the wings, not feathered but bat-like. With a shrill cry that echoed across the park, the wyvern dived towards us with preternatural speed.

Bryce pushed me to the ground, and just barely got out of the way of the creature's talons himself before it took off again to the skies. Its tail had lashed against the ground, and I watched as the grass withered and died in seconds. "Watch out for the tail!" I called to Bryce, and he nodded in response.

My first thought, once I was back on my feet, was whether the shield potion was still active. I hadn't got the chills and fever that came when it did, but I wasn't about to take my eyes off the creature to check. It would be better, of course, to not get hit by the winged lizard at all.

I drew and loaded my firearm and watched the movement of our predator carefully. Bryce was moving around, but I dared not take my eyes off the wyvern to see what he was doing. Without warning, the wyvern dived again. Bryce unleashed a gout of flame to light up the night, but his aim was wide and didn't deter the creature's descent.

I levelled the pistol, took a breath, and waited until I could see the glint of fangs. The creature spread its wings wide at the nadir of its dive, and with but a moment to spare, I met the ear piercing shriek of the lizard with the crack of a gun. The wyvern let out a pained cry and tumbled to the ground. Something cracked when it did, and the lizard struggled to stand, awkwardly lifting the ruined mess of its right wing. The bullet had torn through the skin, and the bones at the wrist had splintered.

Bryce came up beside me and made motions to cast another spell. "Wait," I said, and held out a hand to protect the now pitiful looking wounded creature. This, I realised quickly, was a mistake. The wyvern, still lighting fast, took two bounding leaps towards us. Bryce was barrelled aside, and I fell beneath the creature, raked by talons and teeth. Thankfully, my shield hadn't run out.

As much as I struggled to kick the wyvern off me, it moved too unpredictably for me to find any purchase on its bony form. My pistol had been knocked from my hand and was lost in the darkness. The latticework of cracked Arcane energy covered my torso and arms, and I braced myself for its inevitable failure. Suddenly, the creature reared back and held a taloned foot to my throat before whipping its tail upwards to strike me.

The venomous barbs lashed towards me, and I pulled my hand up to protect my face. The tail struck the shield around my palm and glanced to the side, giving me an opening to throw the beast over with its own momentum. A second later, Bryce uttered another Arcane incantation and the air filled with the smell of burning flesh.

"Fuck," I said.

"Fuck," Bryce echoed.

I pulled myself up and brushed off the dirt and ash from my trousers. Bryce came beside me and looked me up and down. "You need to stop saving my life, it's becoming a bit of a habit."

"You've welcome," he said, with a little bow of his head.

My heart was racing, and I wasn't sure if it was just from the wyvern. Bryce had a self-assured grin on his face for some reason. "Thank you. Again. What now?"

"Find Miss Eloise. If things went to plan, she shouldn't be far," he said, with nothing else by way of explanation.

"Bryce, wait," I said, not too desperately, I hoped. A small pit formed in my stomach at what I was about to do. "We need to talk—about what happened."

He looked over his shoulder quizzically, but kept on walking. "We can talk about everything once we find Miss Eloise and get somewhere safe."

I ran a few steps to catch up with him and grabbed his wrist, and he came to a halt. "I don't mean all that stuff. I mean, we need to talk about the dance." I regretted the words as soon as I said them. I was being ridiculous—nothing had happened—and while I may have felt… something, I had clearly imagined any reciprocal feelings on Bryce's part.

Hadn't I?

It was quiet for far too long. Bryce's gaze drifted from me to his shoes, to the sky, and back to me again. Maybe he had felt something. There was a longing in his eyes, hidden under a layer of stoicism. "I'm sorry, Charlotte. We can't, we have to keep moving."

Perhaps I had imagined it then. At least that was easier to accept. I let go of Bryce's wrist, and we trudged through the muddy ground in silence. Before long, I saw the familiar shape of Bryce's gig, parked by a glowing streetlamp.

Bryce jogged ahead and called, "You got my message then?"

A familiar, lilting voice called back, and my heart soared with relief. "Message? You call having an old man tell me to drive off into the night down a strange street a message?"

"Well, I couldn't tell Malcolm what had gone wrong, because it hadn't yet." Bryce ran his hands through his hair and laughed. I caught up with him and smiled at Elly, she was still sat in the driver's seat.

"What the hell are you wearing?" she asked, and I rolled my eyes.

"I'll explain on the way. The shop's being watched, I figure we should go to Stepney instead. It'll be safe there." I climbed up onto the gig, and Elly grabbed my shoulders to kiss me. Bryce whistled, to which I could only respond, "Fuck you."

He put a hand on his chest, looked at Elly, and said, "I understand what you see in her, she's so charming." He climbed up to the gig and gestured for Elly to vacate the driver's seat. "What's in Stepney?"

"Just trust me," I said. Elly snuggled up next to me in the back seat, and I rested my head on hers. "Wake me when we get to St John the Evangelist Church." I yawned and closed my eyes, hoping for a shred of sleep.

<u>October 16th, 1834</u>
The Burning of Westminster Palace

Chapter 39

I was sweating profusely when Bryce woke me up outside the old chapel in Stepney. I directed him to the police station where Inspector Baker worked and prayed that the officer of the law was on duty that night. It was getting close to midnight when we rolled up outside the plain brick building, and a tired-looking constable perked up as I got out of the two-wheeler.

"Evenin' ma'am, afraid you'll have to wait till morning to report any crimes," she said. She was young and uncertain, and the dark circles under her eyes suggested she'd had a few too many night shifts. I climbed the steps, with Bryce waiting below.

"It's quite urgent, officer. Is Inspector Baker on duty?" I asked, ensuring to stay a step below the officer so as to not intimidate her. She gave me a puzzled look. "Big guy, quite jovial, clean shaven?"

"Ah, yes, Baker," she said, "I think he is around."

I let out a sigh of relief and said, "Thank you, constable, I know where the Inspector's office is." The constable nodded and pushed open the door to let the three of us inside.

Anthony Baker was having a kip in his office, and damn near fell off his chair when Bryce, Elly and I walked in. "Buh, Charlotte, what time is it?"

"Past one," I said. Baker rubbed his eyes and let out a yawn so mighty you might think a bear had awoken. "We need help, Inspector."

I watched as Anthony regarded Bryce carefully, "And who is we, Miss Price?"

Bryce prickled, and before I could answer myself, he held out a hand and said "Bryce Rosehouse, a pleasure."

"We meet at last, Mr Rosehouse, heard plenty about you. Are you aware there's a warrant out for your arrest?" Baker said threateningly, squaring up to Bryce and towering over him. I shot him a look of disapproval that went unnoticed, but Bryce was unconcerned.

"For things I rightfully deserve, no doubt, but there are bigger things at work. As I am sure you are aware." Given the night we had endured, Bryce gave off the perfect air of the landed gentry.

Both men relaxed, and after a moment's pause, I interjected, "The two of you done measuring your cocks?" They turned red, and Bryce let out a quiet chuckle. "Good. Inspector, a lot has happened."

"You best take a seat then, Miss Price," Baker said.

I did so; Elly sat beside me at the inspector's desk and Bryce set about making a pot of tea, while I regaled Baker with what we learned at the Rosehouse ball. "So, there you have it. After all this time, it was none other than Viscount Kidderminster himself behind everything. Smuggling the Black Ember, kidnapping Jennifer; and this Baron Cranley he's working with? Turns out that he is the recently ennobled Professor Carrington of London University—the mage Jennifer and I encountered on Stewart Street."

Baker let out a heavy sigh from his cheeks and leaned back in his chair. "Blimey," was all he could say.

I leaned forward and tapped my finger on a folded-up copy of The Times in the corner of the desk. "That's not all. I assume you read about the debate in Parliament. On the Witchcraft Act?"

The inspector got up out of his chair at this and ran his hands through his hair as he paced the small office. "Aye. Seems a bunch of tosh to me. No use separating out folks with magic and folks without, not these days. Crime is crime."

Elly spoke up, "I'm afraid it may be more than that. They want to make it legal to put mages into specialist workhouses. Places where their talents can be exploited, without running afoul of the Witchcraft Act."

"And they have a device of some kind," Bryce butted in having returned with the tea, "I've seen the plans. It's Arcane, and if I understand it correctly, it's what they intend to do with any mage that doesn't cooperate."

Baker looked puzzled, "I don't think I'm following, Mr Rosehouse, what does this device do?"

Bryce looked at me, full of contemplation, then he took out a match from his pocket. He held it up for Baker to see, muttered a quiet word of power, and the match burned away to ash in a second. "Turns mages into matches. One person could power an entire factory, if they get the balance of Black Ember right."

The room went quiet. Baker looked at Bryce with an unsettled expression. "Even if you are right, of which I cannot be certain without evidence, Parliament would never go for it. Such a thing goes against all the principles of law and order that I signed up to when I joined this force."

"The parliament that established the poor law in practically the same breath as it abolished slavery?" I said, sharply. "How many people have you and your officers sent to the workhouses already, Inspector? How is this any different?" Elly shot me a disappointed look; maybe it wasn't fair to snap at him like that, but he did make a choice every morning to put on that swallowtail coat. "They're planning something, Inspector, a demonstration of some kind at Westminster, tomorrow. Whatever it is, we have to stop them."

Bryce snapped his fingers, realisation dawning on him like the first day of spring. "They're going to test the device, at the palace. Of course, if they can show that it works, the last votes they need might just swing in their favour."

Baker sighed and sat back down. "Ever since we went down Stewart's Street, I keep thinking about what Jen would do. Alas, I never was able to see things the way she did—I have to do things my way, follow the law. I can't go arrest a viscount without evidence. It's your word against his."

He was right, of course. Despite the fact that Kidderminster had admitted it all to my face, I had no concrete evidence—at least, nothing that he couldn't have swept away with the flick of the wrist. Kidderminster needed to be stopped and maybe I'd always known that there was only so far that the law would go in helping me do that.

I thought for a minute and decided to ask for the one thing

I needed most, "Then, inspector, the only thing we require from you now is a bed." Baker and Bryce mirrored each other's cocked eyebrows, and I corrected myself, "Beds. We require beds."

***

Baker woke us before the start of the morning shift, ensured we were fed and sent us on our way before prying eyes could see. I nodded in and out of consciousness as Bryce drove the gig. A breeze blew in from the east, carrying with it the faint remnants of salty air. In my brief moments of wakefulness, I watched the breath rise from Bryce's nose, like little puffs of smoke from a sleeping dragon. Elly sat up front with Bryce, more awake that she had any right to be.

We travelled south of the river, crossing at London Bridge, and through the quiet morning streets of Southwark towards Westminster Bridge. Stacks of smoke rose from the factories throughout the city, threatening to blot out the clear pre-dawn twilight.

Bryce insisted on abandoning our vehicle as we entered Lambeth, lest there be some description that could be used to stop us. I made a mental list of the supplies I had with me; a pair of pistols, one syringe of shielding potion, a dozen or so paper cartridges, Jennifer's vial of mystery red liquid, a sword I didn't know how to use, a doctor, and a mage who walked too quickly. Somehow, we would need to break into the heart of the British government, find out where and when Bryce's insane father and his cronies intended on showcasing their incinerator, and stop them before they could enslave every mage that didn't fit their model of proper behaviour.

A day in the life, I suppose.

Dawn came with rosy fingers and warm tidings as we crossed Westminster Bridge, the hopeful orange light of the sun creeping down Birdcage Walk to the Palace to meet the cool autumn air. Bells rang out across the city, welcoming the new day. Little did they know that those bells also heralded disaster. The image of the Palace of Westmin-

292

ster that morning was wreathed in the glowing morning sun, almost as if it were ablaze.

The palace loomed over the river like an old haggard crone, a cacophony of conflicting architectural styles, where new buildings seemed to have been bolted onto old ones without any due care or attention. The old stone hall of the palace stood proud where it had for hundreds of years, but the additions of neo-gothic spires, neo-classical pillars and Palladian monoliths had ruined the once majestic façade.

I stopped about halfway across Westminster bridge and looked down at the river. The steady flow of the Thames had settled after the days of rain and carried with it a hundred miles of detritus. I tried to calm myself by focussing on the water, to quieten down the hundred voices in my mind and centre myself on that moment alone. Everything that had happened in the past week had led to this point. Ever since Inspector Baker arrived at The Solution with the mysterious death of Timothy Waters, I had been on an inexorable path that bore me to that bridge. I couldn't help but wonder if I'd done the right thing—if I was on the right path.

I pondered on the events that had brought me there, the choices I made, and the ones that were made for me. I tried to make sense, one last time, of the conspiracy I'd been an unwitting pawn in. There was one piece of the puzzle that still didn't fall into place in my mind. In the middle of it all an empty hole where Jennifer should be. Would we find her somewhere in the walls of the Palace? Or was she being held somewhere distant, where she couldn't interfere with the plans of Lord Rosehouse and Baron Cranley? Or was she dead after all, her body long since carried away by the currents below me?

Bryce cleared his throat, and I snapped back to reality. "Are we ready?" I asked without turning from the view.

"I have not a clue what to be ready for, Miss Price," he responded in a pensive tone. "The best I can offer you is on guard and somewhat alert."

"That will have to do," I said, "Elly?"

"If you ask me to stay out here, I will slap you," she said.

"Actually, I was going to ask if you can handle a pistol." I pulled out the twin firearms from the satchel and held one out.

Elly looked at it for a second, and then shook her head. "I'm a doctor, not a marksman."

"Noted. Stay behind me then." Bryce came up beside me and leant on his elbows on the parapet. I looked at him and conjured what confidence I could. "Whatever it takes, we end this. I won't let another innocent person die because of them."

There was a sense of surprise in his demeanour. "I was wrong to underestimate you," he said. "Whatever happens, I'll be beside you." We stayed there, looking into each other's eyes for a moment that has since stretched out in my memory. One of us, I don't remember who, broke the silence with a sigh and we turned our attention back to the labyrinthine monstrosity before us.

The foot traffic had started to pick up, and the morning comings and goings of members of parliament, clerks, servants, and pages were approaching their full swing. Before long, the carriages and cabs that carried the Lords to the palace for the coming debate would start to arrive. If the papers were to be believed, the proposed amendment to the Witchcraft Act would be defeated by a small margin, but whatever Viscount Kidderminster had planned would likely turn the last few votes he needs to ensure victory.

Bryce explained that he had attended the halls of Westminster a few times in his youth, but even in the last ten years there had been significant remodelling and renovations. To our advantage, however, was the fact that there were a limited number of places that would provide a private enough venue for a group of Lords to hold an inconspicuous meeting and be large enough to contain the device we had seen in the plans I stole.

We made our way across the rest of the bridge and then walked into the New Palace Yard. The wide, open paved courtyard occupied the space before the medieval façade of Westminster Hall, from the retaining wall of the bridge to the perimeter of the palace and stretching west as far as the Old Palace Yard on the other face on the complex. A well-worn path of cobblestones led to the mammoth sized entry way of the Hall, flanked by stone pillars topped with proud lions. Westminster hall had two large gothic towers on either side the vaulted roof, and a high arched window between them with stained glass reliefs of royal heraldry. A modest spire rose from the peak of the roof, topped with a wind indicator shaped like a bird of prey.

Small buildings had sprung up around the perimeter of the yard like mushrooms, filled with coffee houses, gentlemen's clubs, and smoking rooms. They took the form of tall slender town houses, small Tudor halls, and thatched roof public houses, and only added to the bizarre sense of juxtaposition.

It was only when I started to note the various people moving to-and-fro that I realised just how absurd we must have looked. Bryce was wearing the same unkempt white shirt, black waistcoat and trousers that had survived the night after the ball. I was still wearing the servant's uniform I'd stolen after ruining my dress, and Elly wore her driver's suit. Without a care to the looks of passers-by, I ditched the jacket of the uniform on the ground and retrieved Jennifer's long coat from the bottomless satchel. The coat was definitely cut for Jen's height, not mine, but it didn't drag behind me on the floor at least.

We walked with purpose towards the hall, determined to look as much like a group of individuals going about our usual business as we could. The huge doors of the hall were open, and as we came inside, I was struck by the sheer majesty of the space. The vaulted clear span roof was supported by arched oak timbers that almost defied the laws of gravity. The floor had a wide-open space that took up most of the length of the hall. A counter ran along the length of the hall down the left side, where young workers were busy organising books and papers, while on the right there were raised viewing boxes and ground level seating areas that looked upon the dais at the far end. Upon the dais sat a grand throne, and several smaller raised judges' boxes, from which the various courts heard cases and delivered their judgements.

We were able to move surprisingly freely, and Bryce led

the way down the long hall, and through a side passage that he said would lead to the Cloisters, and then the two Houses of Parliament. Strangely, I noticed that it was Bryce who was distracted that morning. He moved somewhat aloof, occasionally losing himself in the architecture, and deep in thought about where we might head. I kept my apprehension to myself, for the moment, and trusted his instincts to guide us.

We came to a small vestibule in the gothic style, decorated in all the British Empire's majesty with heraldry and gallant stained-glass mosaics. The vaulted ceiling had small buttresses that flew out into the open space above us, and the smell of incense filled the air. One small door to our left opened onto the rear of Westminster Hall, where the dais sat, presumably where the justices of the courts entered. To our right were the mighty doors that led to the House of Lords.

Stood in stony silence before the doors of the House was a gentleman dressed in black ceremonial uniform, trimmed in gold and with a navy collar that rose up to his chin. In his right hand he held an ebony staff topped with a golden lion, which rested on his shoulder. The Black Rod, as he was known, was the ceremonial keeper of the doors and sergeant-at-arms within the House of Lords.

The man moved so little that I thought for a moment he might have been blind and not even known we were there. If not for the subtle shifts in his grip on the staff, and the way he softly re-centred his balance as we approached, that is. Bryce bowed in respect, which I copied in the hopes of not offending the living gargoyle of a man. "Does the House sit, Black Rod?" my companion asked.

"It does not for some hours yet, Mr Rosehouse. Your father, I'm sure, will be in attendance." The Black Rod's voice was as stony as his demeanour, and he didn't move to look at Bryce as he spoke.

"Yes, quite right. My thanks, Sir." Bryce said, before bowing again and leading me away.

"Black rod?" I asked when I was certain we were out of earshot. But Bryce didn't deign to respond to the question. "Where are we going?" I followed up with, but again, Bryce seemed much more concerned with walking than talking. "Bryce?"

Eventually I had to grab his arm to stop him, and he turned to say, "We're almost there," before heading off around another corner. "Here," he said before I could object further. "Father's office, we might find some clues as to where he is. He doesn't use it much, from what I recall, but maybe we'll be in luck." Bryce tried the door, but it was locked. He tried to force the door a few times, then stepped back and shrugged.

Elly stepped forward and pulled out a pin from her hair. "I learned this little trick in Cambridge after you left, Charlotte," she said, before jimmying the lock open. "Easy," she boasted, and pushed open the door.

Lord Rosehouse's office was spartan, to my surprise, with a simple mahogany desk and chair, and very little in the way of pomp and circumstance. The carpet was worn and in need of replacement, the desk sagged with its age, and the windows were coated with grime and black mould. Quite how much of a state the office was in took me by surprise—surely it would require explicit orders for it not to be cleaned. That was my first hint that Bryce was on the right track, his father didn't want anyone else in here, not even the palace staff.

One wall had a line of dusty bookshelves, but they were barren except for a few volumes on property law and an old bible that clearly hadn't been read in years. The desk had an oil lamp in one corner, a small stack of papers, an ink well, and an ashtray.

Bryce let out a disappointed sigh. "Typical. He never was one to leave a trail."

"Don't be so sure," I said. Everything we needed was right there on that desk.

I was drawn first to the ashtray; it was sterling silver, tarnished in the corners and dented in several places. It was formed, much like the rest of the good Lord's aesthetic taste, to look like a rose in bloom. The smell of tobacco smoke lingered in the air, and I was intrigued to see that the stubbed-out end of a fine Havana cigar still had a few faint wisps rising from it. A few stray flecks of cigar ash were scattered across the table, landing clearly on top of the older layers of dust.

The lamp, too, showed signs of recent use; the glass was warm to the touch, and the reservoir of oil had run mostly dry. Above the lamp, black soot had stained the ceiling. All indications that Lord Rosehouse, or someone else who had access to his office, had been working here not long ago.

The papers on the desk, on closer inspection, revealed to be perhaps the most important find. I sat down in the creaky chair to read them and as I did, I was overcome with waves of relief and dread. The first paper had a Metropolitan Police letter head, and detailed the charges against one "Jennifer Morton, Carnaby Street," and included breaking and entering, burglary, murder, manslaughter, and conspiracy to commit high treason.

"What is it, Charlotte?" Elly asked.

"This whole time, she's been here." I gave her the papers, and she scanned over them. "Held without trial, on manufactured charges."

"There's witness statements here," Elly said, "signed by Arthur Remington? It looks like Bryce's father was the one that had her held here, look." She held out another leaf of the documents for Bryce and me to see.

"I'm going to kill him," I stated. "He's a monster."

Bryce exhaled sharply through his nose and said, "You've only known him for a week."

I kicked the desk in frustration, which disturbed the dust that lay across it. As I watched it drift through the air, I noticed at the foot of the desk and tracking through the office a trail very fine, very light ash, the kind you get from burning paper. It was also discernibly different from the cigar ash in the tray, and it had been trodden into the carpet ever so slightly where it might have been carried in on the sole of a shoe.

"Your father's been at this for years, smuggling, people trafficking, assassination, political machinations, you name it," I put to Bryce in a moment of clarity, the words coming as fast as the thoughts connected in my mind. "All those things have a paper trail, all that evidence had to go somewhere. Every time he bribed a judge or signed a false manifest or wrongfully imprisoned a political opponent. Someone signed something. Where did it all go?" The puzzled look on my companion's face indicated that he wasn't following, so I spelled it out for him, "Where would your father go to burn documents?"

Bryce thought for a moment, then snapped his fingers in excitement, "Of course, below the House of Lords! There are these bloody great big furnaces, and plenty of room for Cranley to set up their demonstration. Oh, Charlotte, you are brilliant, do you know that?"

I rolled my eyes to hide my embarrassment, and said nonchalantly, "Of course I know that, my dear companion. Now is not the time for compliments, however, we have a demonstration to attend. Lead the way."

Chapter 40

Before long we found ourselves at the top of a flight of stairs. I could smell the faint scent of burning wood and paper, and voices echoed up the stone walls. I gave Bryce a knowing glance and drew out the last syringe of shielding potion from my satchel. The familiar, all-encompassing coolness of the alchemical creation washed over me, and I felt a renewed sense of confidence knowing that I was safe from harm. Or safer, at least.

The three of us locked hands, and Bryce spoke the word of power that conjured forth the veil that hid us from view. The lower levels of the Palace of Westminster were not as grand or chaotic as the floors used by the lawmakers and aristocracy. The wood-panelled walls gave way to much simpler stone and plaster, and the carpets were replaced by bare floorboards. I could smell the faint scent of burning wood and paper, and voices echoed up the stone walls.

The doors to the basement were open, and we slipped to the side of the frame unnoticed. The room stretched out beyond my vision into darkness and was filled with the low rumbling sounds of the furnaces that heated the House of Lords. Stood in the centre of the room was something that I could only understand as a nightmare made real. The mage furnace stood roughly twelve feet high, held together by bands of brass and lined with copper piped that coiled around the structure like snakes. Its cylindrical form domed at the top, and a fluted pipe spouted off like the top of a distilling flash, which connected to a small boiler and miniaturised version of a stream engine.

The Viscount Kidderminster, Lord Rosehouse, was stood back from the crowd, his wounded hand bandaged and resting in a loose sling. His red robes of office were stark in the firelight, and I noted that he appeared unarmed. In the dim light, it was hard to make out his features, but his posture was haggard and tired. Nevertheless, it was clear he still held a commanding presence around his peers, who looked at him occasionally in a sycophantic display of obsequiousness.

Cranley stood by the chamber; his face marred by swollen blisters and burns. He reminded me in that moment of every tired, old professor I had the misfortune of being lectured by. His delivery was monotone and dull, in stark contrast to the horrific nature of what he was explaining to the group of assembled peers, "As you can see, my Lords, the chamber is specially designed to contain Arcane energies. We utilise an Alchemically treated glass that creates a resonant frequency with the occupant. This ensures that the indentured workers use their abilities to their full, ah, potential."

"My Lord, I fail to see why this is necessary," said a tall, broad man with greying mutton chops. "Mage or no, surely sending them to the workhouses with the rest of the poor is enough."

"You would certainly hope so, my Lord, but as we have seen in these past days, some branded individuals are far too dangerous to be contained within the structures of a common workhouse. Specialist institutions are necessary, which will require changes to the law to operate fully." Cranley grinned with barely contained disdain, and the rest of the Lords nodded in general agreement.

Standing to one side, leaning on a cane with his leg bandaged, was Remington. He looked pompous and full of himself, despite his injury, and was nodding along to Cranley's explanation with self-assured satisfaction.

As I scanned the room, I almost didn't see the last person present, as they were on their knees in the shadows behind Lord Remington. I almost let go of Bryce's hand and broke the invisibility spell as my heart tried to leap from my chest. If he hadn't gripped me hard and pulled me back, I'd have spelled doom for us all. Jennifer was alive.

A torrent of heartache and relief surged through me. There she knelt, my awe-inspiring thunderstorm, with all the wind and rain drained from her. How I longed to see that flash of brilliance in her eyes, how I ached to be drenched to the bone by her wonder—how I raged at the carnage she'd left behind. I wished there were a dozen of me, so that I could do all the things I'd dreamt of doing from the moment she vanished. Hold her close, kiss her forehead, slap her across the face, berate her stupid decisions, tell her it was all right, unleash every shred of grief and fury and love that kept me going, and—most of all—try my hardest to forgive her.

My fingers twitched around the grip of my pistol; it would have been so easy to take it out and place a bullet between the eyes of The Viscount Kidderminster. I hesitated. I'd been acting on instinct, trusting my gut for so long that something in my mind seemed to pull back ever so slightly. Jennifer would have done it and dealt with the consequences down the line. But—I realised, with no small effort—that was how we ended up in this mess in the first place. *...shoot first, leave no one alive to question.* I didn't need to fight Kidderminster, or Cranley. This had all begun with one peculiar case: a case with a solution.

I noticed the muttering of voices die down, and Cranley cleared his throat to get the attention of Kidderminster. Bryce's father stepped towards the huddled group of peers and smiled wickedly. "My Lords. We stand on a precipice. Today we make a mark on the history of this great nation, and we choose whether to bow to the unknowable, unfathomable desires of those poisoned by Arcane blood, or to stand true to our ideals of reason, truth, and God's will on this Earth. Left untethered, the branded will continue to multiply, and with them, they will bring untold horrors. The events we have seen in the past week are but a ripple compared to the tidal wave of destruction that magic can reap.

"I ask you, my Lords, how can we stand by when our great nation is turned to rot from the inside out? When radical groups, such as this 1735 Club, plot to overturn the mechanisms that barely keep their kind in line. As it stands, there is nothing the laws of this land can do to prevent disaster, to deter criminal use of magic, or to protect those that would be in the most danger. When the architects of the Witchcraft Act of 1735 put their bill to the house, they gave the mages in this nation an inch, and now they wish to take a mile. It is clear now that the restrictions on work and business with magic are not enough to deter violent crime, and at the same time, they prevent honest businessman from fully utilising their work forces.

"I asked you here today, my Lords, in the hopes of convincing you that there is another way. As Baron Cranley has explained to you, a new system of specialist workhouses, and this remarkable device gives us a new option. A hope for a glorious future. No longer will mages be free to abuse the Arcane, no longer will they be able to threaten our families, our society. Under our proposal, mages will be controlled, and they will become productive members of society. Vote with me today, and I assure you, no magical misdeed will go unpunished, and a new dawn for Britain's industry will rise."

There was a pregnant pause as the Lords around Bryce's father absorbed his words. The something in my mind holding me back released its grip, but my hand didn't go to the pistol in its holster. I found myself pulling out the little blue notebook Jennifer had given me, the one that I'd somehow filled with pages of notes that I don't even remember writing. I let go of Bryce's hand, allowing the invisibility charm to fade, and I stepped into the stark light of the basement.

"It's a good speech, my Lord, I wonder when you found the time to practise it," I said, an eerie sense of confidence filling me. "My apologies for interrupting, my Lords."

There was a chorus of gruff utterances from the robed crowd, until one of them spoke, "Who are you? This is a private meeting."

"Charlotte Price, The Potent Solution, at your service."

"Miss Price, how unfortunate to see you again, and you've bought my son too. Were you not content with breaking into my property and maiming myself and Lord Remington?" The Viscount Kidderminster spoke with uncontained disdain, each of his words dragging on the ear like a venomous talon.

"Not content at all, my Lord," I replied. "I find it interesting, my Lords, that you've chosen to hold this meeting in the basement, and not one of the many available rooms in the palace above. Hiding something, are we?"

"This is preposterous," Remington blurted out. "We should have her arrested."

Bryce put a hand on my shoulder. "Shut it, Remington, lest I burn your tongue out." The young lord stepped back, aghast, but it was clear he had no standing in the room for anyone to care.

"Bryce, what on earth are you doing?" asked his father.

"Standing up to you." Bryce regarded his father with contempt, and then turned his attention to the rest of the group, "My father speaks of truth and reason, yet his argument contains little of either. He is fuelled by hate, and deceit."

"Lord Kidderminster, explain this at once," said one of the lords.

"What is there to explain? You all know my son is a delinquent, and this woman is a violent miscreant in league with her treasonous employer."

"High praise from the most prolific criminal in the city," I said. I was trying to get a rise out of him, to find a crack in his armour and peel away the layers of aristocratic refinement.

"An absurd allegation."

"Have you told the lords about the large quantities of opium you've been smuggling into the city? That's used to create a dangerous drug known as Black Ember."

"These are baseless—"

"The same Black Ember that was found in the possession of one Timothy Waters, who died from supposed spontaneous combustion on the night of the 7th of October?"

"I had nothing to do—"

"The same Black Ember that you will use to placate and subdue the mages you intend to put into that furnace behind you? The very same substance that you admitted to providing to your son, with the intent of removing him as an obstacle from your plans. What about the strawman companies that your accomplice, the recently and conveniently ennobled Baron Cranley, has been using to establish infrastructure ahead of the approval of your sick plans? What about the girl that you sent to her death to burn down the warehouse on Stewart Street in an attempt to ferment hatred and distrust against mages and cover up your crimes? The assassin you sent to kill Bryce and me when you realised that I was on your trail? The wild misrepresentation of the 1735 Club?"

The armour cracked under the barrage of questions, just like it did when Jennifer had interrogated Bryce. Except I didn't need a truth serum. "You worthless, indignant bitch. Cranley. Kill her."

I had my pistol levelled at the Viscount before the rest of the room could react. "Move another inch, professor, I dare you."

"You forget, girl, that I bested your mentor, and I taught Bryce everything he knows," Cranley said in his weaselly, conniving voice. From a pocket in his robe, he drew a small, ornate rod, tipped with a cut ruby—a casting focus, not as grand as the one Bryce had smashed.

"At the warehouse, you mean. Where you bested Jennifer?" I said.

"With ease."

"So, you admit it? You were at Stewart Street the night of the fire?"

"I…" he stumbled.

"Of course, it was your property after all. Why wouldn't you have been there?" I held up the little notebook for the lords to see. "Everything they've told you has been a lie, all the stories in the press situations of their own making. A conspiracy to turn this nation against mages, and justify—not progress, or industry, or God's fucking will on this earth—but genocide and slavery. The proof is all in here."

The small group of men muttered words of doubt, their loyalty to Kidderminster faltering by the second. No one spoke. No one was brave enough to step forward. But it didn't matter. I could tell by the look on Kidderminster's face that he knew he needed to act now or lose everything. He started clapping, which echoed off the cavernous walls, and walking forwards. "Very good, Miss Price, very good. There is but one flaw in your deduction."

"Try me," I said, and in a moment of stupidity and over-confidence, I dropped my guard.

"No one will care when you're all dead." Kidderminster had a pistol, a tiny pocket thing barely bigger than his hand. It was no wonder I hadn't seen it. Unphased by the threat—he didn't know I had a shield up—I didn't react immediately. But he didn't level it at me. He turned on the spot and pointed it straight at Jennifer. She moved as best she could in her bindings, but the shot found its mark on her lower back.

Chaos erupted.

Chapter 41

I screamed as I watched Jennifer's body hit the ground and a small pool of blood began to grow beside her. Inside my head I was clawing against myself, willing my body to move, to act, but the shock had frozen me in place. Bryce was behind me, forming a word of power, and moments later I felt the heat on the back of my neck. Every fibre of my being was crying, and it felt as if my heart had been ripped from my chest.

Jennifer was going to die. I'd come all that way and barely looked her in the eyes, and it'd all be for nought. She would bleed out on the floor of some ratty basement beneath the House of Lords and there was nothing I could do.

Things were happening all around me. Bryce was yelling for me to move as he deflected spells coming from his old professor, Kidderminster was fumbling with his pistol's loading mechanism, and the other lords were running for their lives. Elly ran past me. Her hair—which had been until that moment tied into a bun—was messily falling around her face and she had a blade of sorts in her hand. A surgical scalpel. Had she honestly used it to tie up her hair?

She dived to her knees beside Jennifer and started to apply pressure to her wound with one hand, and with the other, she began tearing at her shirt to form a makeshift bandage. My body finally caught up with my mind when I saw Remington stalking towards her. My hand whipped into place, and I shot Arthur Remington in the arm. He grimaced in pain and turned to see me staring at him down the barrel. In those few seconds, he seemed to weigh his options, and then exclaimed, "Fuck this!" before running from the basement.

Another shot echoed through against the walls and my head was cracked to the side by the force of Kidderminster's pistol. I rolled the stiffness out of my neck and turned toward him; half of my face obscured by the latticework of the Arcane shield. Bryce and Cranley were facing off beside us, and I could tell they were both exhausted. Kidderminster ducked behind his ally and began to fumble with his pistol again.

We split, Bryce going left to draw Cranley's attention, while I went right towards Jennifer and Elly. Cranley threw a bolt of lightning my way before Bryce could distract him, however, and I dived to avoid it. The spell crashed into a pile of firewood as I loaded my pistol and fired at the wizard. With a flick of his wrist and a guttural word of power, the shot deflected, but it was enough for Bryce to unleash a gout of draconic flame at Cranley, casting him to the ground.

I skidded to my knees beside Jennifer and was relieved to see her eyes open. "How is she?" I asked Elly.

"I got the bullet out, but she needs stitches, or she'll bleed to death. I don't suppose you have anything in that bag of yours?" she replied, a frenetic tone in her voice that I didn't recognise. I shook my head at her question, but stuffed my hand into the satchel anyway, hoping to find something.

Jennifer put a hand on my knee, which almost made me jump out of my skin. "Charlotte, you brilliant fool, what are you doing here?" she said, wearily.

"Looking for you," I said, brushing a stray bit of her fringe from her face. "I've looked over the whole bloody city."

"And you found me here. With friends. I'm sure it's all a fascinating tale and I can't wait to hear it, but I think we have bigger problems right now." Jen pointed behind me, where Bryce was facing off with Cranley.

"I'm not leaving you. Not again," I said, tears rolling down my face. All the while my hand was fumbling around in the too big bag, rattling against the empty vials and the scabbard of Jen's smallsword. "I can't. I don't have anything. I gave the only healing draught I had to Remington, because I'm a fucking idiot apparently…" I stopped mid-sentence as my hand fell on a tiny, unopened vial in the bag. I could feel the liquid moving inside it. The little red potion practically glowed in the light of the furnaces, the black substance within still snaking around of its own volition.

A mix of things, Jennifer had said. *I'll show you the formula when we get back to the shop, but you won't believe when you see it.* That formula, with all three prime elements, the insane diagram in Jennifer's notebook. "Charlotte, no!" Jennifer said as I opened the vial and downed the potion. It tasted like iron, sea water and raw meat.

The world around me stopped. Jennifer and Elly, Bryce and Cranley, and somewhere Viscount Kidderminster, all froze in place. I turned and a bolt of lightning arced from Cranley's wand, and realised that the world was moving, just incredibly slowly.

"Charlotte, listen to me." The words came into my head and at normal speed, it was almost like I was processing the world at two different paces. "Firstly, you're an idiot and I taught you better. Secondly, that potion has a very short lifetime and afterwards you are going to feel like hell, so stop gawking and do something!" Jennifer stopped talking and suddenly the world crept to a near halt again. I moved faster than I ever had in my life, but at the same time I perceived it at an almost glacial pace, I was able to fine-tune each of my movements as I made them.

The mages yelled at each other, their voices layered over my perception in a bizarre, disjointed way, like two orchestras playing the same music at different speeds. "You were a brilliant pupil, Bryce," Cranley said as he pushed back against Bryce's onslaught. "Such a shame you never had the vision for greatness."

"It wasn't vision I lacked, Professor, it was greed," Bryce spat back. "We both saw the world changing. Only you and your pets were determined to stop it." They were both yelling over the sounds of wild magic. There was a crack of lightning, the roar of flames, and a chorus of words of power. The lights danced between the mages as they deflected and returned each other's spells, at moments causing the air itself to ignite into glowing orbs of energy that burst into dancing motes of ball lightning.

I pulled the sword from the satchel and held it awkwardly.

I cleared the distance between myself and Cranley in a few strides, slamming into him and casting him to the ground. Then Kidderminster stepped out from behind the towering mage furnace, pistol levelled at his son. I put myself in the line of fire and absorbed the shot into my shield before I leapt toward the Viscount and drove the sword into his chest.

I forced my mind back into the normal flow of time and said through gritted teeth, "It's over."

"Wrong again, Miss Price. As long as poison runs in the veins of the nation, it will never be over." He coughed up blood and pulled my wrist towards him by driving the blade clean through his back. "Besides, I'm not the one you should be worrying about."

Twisted, maniacal laughter echoed down the basement. I wrenched the sword free from Kidderminster's chest and he collapsed onto the ground, dead. Baron Cranley floated a few feet above the ground, raw golden arcane energy dripping from his fingers like sap. Where his eyes should be, were two deep, black voids of nothingness. The blackness—a deeper, blacker, more sickening blackness I had never seen—bled out into the veins of his face, as if his blood were the made of the night sky.

My immediate reaction—which was so immediate that it came to me like a greyhound sprinting on a bolt of lightning—was, "Shit."

The spell, if you could call it that, hit me like a tidal wave. The unrefined Arcane split and morphed between the base elemental forms as it coursed through the air. A quintet of wild energy—scorching fire, freezing water, battering earth, ferocious winds, and pure force. I held my ground, the un-natural strength and speed from Jennifer's potion giving me the edge I needed. The skin on my forearms began to char as the Arcane glass of my shield superheated and fragmented away. My sense of pain must have been dulled, because could barely feel the uncontained magic tearing away at my flesh. It was then that I had a moment of clarity.

The realisation hit me as hard as Cranley's spell. There wasn't a single doubt in my mind that Cranley was the type of mage who could survive an overdose of Ember and walk away unscathed—so I had no choice but to put him down. This would only end in one of two ways—he could go out like Timothy Waters or bring down all of Westminster like the warehouse on Stewart Street—just as Bryce had said, *an irresistible force meets an immovable object*. Either way, I couldn't risk Elly, Bryce or Jennifer being there when I found out which was stronger. The crazed wizard drew the power for another torrent of magical destruction, which I narrowly managed to avoid—even with my enhanced speed—and I knew I only had a moment to act.

"Bryce! Get them out of here! I need to end this."

He looked at me like I was mad, which was an entirely valid perspective, all things considered. "What about you?" The damned fool. What did he think he was playing at, getting all concerned about me? It was almost endearing, the way his eyebrows lifted at the mere suggestion that I'd put myself in danger.

As powerful as Cranley's spells were, he had no control over them; all he could do was open and close the floodgates. The raw, incandescent surge of Arcane that coursed from his hands bored through a support pillar; it crumbled to the ground and the roof began to crack. He cut the spell off, and the pure golden light of unrefined magic dripped from his fingertips—that would have to be my opening.

I took Bryce's hand, the vibrations from my body jolted through his arm, and pleaded with my eyes. "Just trust me. Get to safety and raise the fire alarm. I'll hold hell at bay as long as I can." I backed away from him as words of power formed a new verse behind me. "Go!" I ordered, and Bryce didn't need telling again. With strength I didn't know he had, he heaved Jennifer off the floor and led Elly to the stairs.

With a steady grip on the hilt of the small sword, I faced Cranley. Aether seemed to manifest from thin air, like a thick mist rolling and rushing to his outstretched hands. It was now or never; I rushed at him one last time, closing the gap before he could let loose another spell, and slashed the blade across his chest.

The flesh under his skin bubbled and roiled—as though his blood had turned to magma—and the raw magic erupted from him in two wild beams. One burned through the roof with such unstoppable fury that I caught a glimpse of daylight through the vast chamber of the Lords above us. His other hand cast a wide arc around the basement. The magic struck the great furnaces, which exploded with thunderous force. Shrapnel and burning debris slammed into me, but my shield held fast, as did I.

With an unnatural scream, Cranley wrenched back control. His eyes bled with thick black tar. When he opened his mouth, not a word of any human tongue echoed around the chamber, but even the sonorous, dark speech itself exerted power enough to throw me off balance. The foul, deep incantation pressed against my eardrums like hot iron rods and came in waves with every syllable. My chest was crushed by the onslaught, splinters of pain shot through me as my ribs broke one by one.

I fell to my knees and cried out; scarlet darkness crept in from the corners of my vision, as the sorcerous baron loomed over me. He stepped on cushions of air; his feet bobbed as the distance between us closed once again. I might have died had he stayed still—if he hadn't been an arrogant narcissist. But then, it was being an arrogant narcissist that got him where he was. He ceased the onslaught of crushing death and seized my hair in a fist—pure globules of Arcane trickled down my neck; it was surprisingly cool, and I even shivered—behind the inhuman visage that looked down on me, befouled by the Ember that seeped from his veins, was the look of a man who thought he'd won.

"Power, Miss Price, is something you will never understand. Any last words?" said Professor George Carrington, Head of the School of Arcane Studies at London University, Baron of Cranley, who, some say, was one of the greatest living mages in the country. His words echoed in my ears, my perception of the world still a blend of two different flows of time.

If I were a dishonest person—well, perhaps more dishonest than I already am—I would say that I looked the Baron in his oil-shot eyes, and said, "The thing about power—*my Lord*—is it makes you miss the small, important details: like the gun strapped to my thigh." Unfortunately for my ego, I am not a paragon of well-timed wit, and only thought of that blistering rejoinder three weeks after the fact.

In truth, what I said was, "Go fuck yourself, *my Lord*," before I shot him in the gut.

A bubble of superheated air blossomed from the point where the lightning from my pistol struck Cranley, which I watched expand in agonisingly slow motion. The force of the explosion blasted me toward the staircase, the last gasp of my shield being all that stopped my back from breaking. A wail of horror came from the Baron's hunched over body, as unfettered magic bloomed forth from under his skin. Lights of every colour danced across the walls and ceilings, as if—at that time of year, confined to that very basement—the great auroras of the north had graced us with their presence.

The mage's skin began to melt around his eyes, his chest burst with ethereal flames and there was a sickening sound of bones cracking open as the marrow cooked from within. I watched in terror—my breath held as I watched the mortal form of the old man be consumed. With his death, the roaring flames came alive, and they licked across the ground to find purchase in something, or someone.

I, for one, was not going to hang around while he opened a portal to the fucking fire dimension. So, I ran.

***

My escape from the Palace was a blur—between the disorientation caused by Jennifer's miraculous potion, the pain that leeched through my entire body, and the panic that settled in once my blood had calmed. All I know is that I ran. Flames liked at my heels through the winding corridors, and I could hear the distant cries of, "Fire! Fire!". When I emerged out onto New Palace Yard, I was struck by the eerie calm of it all. Everyone was still going about their business, unaware of the horror that had been unleashed beneath the House of Lords. None of them mattered though. Nothing did, because just as soon as my lungs filled with fresh morning air, Jennifer collapsed onto the cobblestones.

"Jen!" I yelled, trying to get to her, but suddenly feeling like my whole body was moving through treacle. "Jennifer!" I dropped to my knees as my joints began to lock involuntarily, and I tried to struggle my way towards her.

I felt a hand on my shoulders, someone holding me back, and then I realised people were talking. "Hold her still Bryce. She'll only get in the way. Jennifer? Ms Morton, can you hear me?" It was Elly, she was kneeling over Jen's body and tearing a long piece of fabric from her dress. "The bleedings started again—shit, she's lost a lot of blood." She pushed a new wad of fabric into Jennifer's wound and pressed hard. There was a gasp, and Jen's eyes opened, but there was no conscious thought, only shock. "Bryce, I need some thread, or string, or something. Anything I can use for stitches once this bleeding stops." She then proceeded to pull a needle of some kind out of her the folds of her clothes. "Now."

I felt Bryce take his weight off me, and he started looking around the square, before taking off at a run. He was yelling at someone, but I couldn't hear what he was saying. I reached out towards Elly and lost consciousness. For the next few minutes, I dropped and rose from deep slumber to hyper-awareness of my surroundings. I tried desperately to stay awake and only caught fragments of Elly's desperate attempt to save Jennifer's life.

"Fishing line? It'll have to do," Elly said.

"I think the bleeding is slowing."

"We shouldn't stay here much longer," Bryce noted.

"How's Charlotte?" Jennifer asked.

I forced my eyes open and saw Jennifer sitting up, holding the bandages to her side. She looked concerned, but smiled when she saw me watching her. I rolled over onto my back, relief overcoming me for just a brief moment and the partial paralysis beginning to fade. Smoke began to fill the sky.

Chapter 42

The fire started in the chimney stacks of the House of Lords. The heat from the furnaces below was so intense that it melted the copper lining of the flues, and as the flames grew, they drew ever more oxygen into the furnace chamber, creating a violent feedback process. It was so hot from the inferno below that the floor of the Lord's chamber began to smoke. Before long, the wooden structure of the chimneys ignited, and thick black smoke began to rise from the roof of the House. As the superstructure of the building began to weaken, the floor of the chamber gave way and collapsed into the fire below. The rush of fresh air and fuel caused the rapid expansion of the fire, and the roof of the house exploded outwards with terrifying force.

In less than thirty seconds, the entire palace complex south of the Cloisters were consumed in an incandescent blaze. The flames tore through the maze of buildings that connected the two houses of parliament, bursting free from the windows and coursing onward with preternatural intent. Black smog choked the sky and turned it red. The bells tolled out across the city, calling the small private armies of firefighters to the conflagration to throw away their lives in the hopes they can stop the flames from spreading into the city at large.

When the unnatural inferno reached the House of Commons, it licked at the walls like a hound tasting its prey. With tentative, almost loving caresses, the fire found purchase in the window frames and doors. Unlike its first victim, the fire took its time with the second, breaking apart every beam, every pillar, and every floorboard with the preciseness of a seamstress. As if it were some damned souls to be flayed alive, the House of Commons groaned as it buckled under the strain of the blaze but held on with Promethean unwillingness. The fire roared in victorious rage as the wooden supports of the lower house finally gave way, and the walls collapsed inwards with a pathetic sigh. The flames rolled through the palace and reared up with exalted fury. They reached toward the ancient gothic hall that had stood for so many centuries and poised to strike at it with all the power and incendiary force the Arcane could fathom.

The blaze was coiled like an ethereal viper, ready to slither into the ancient structure of the hall. The flames batted against the majestic towers and spires, trying to find purchase in the oak beams of the grand roof—and were beaten back. Like tiny ants battling to save their hill, the firefighters moved with practiced precision, pushing back where the flames threatened to dig in. The easterly breeze rolled down the Thames, as if the river itself was giving its life's breath to save what remained of the Palace.

The fire brigade cut away the wooden beams in the roof that connected the Hall to the already ablaze Speaker's House and soaked the Hall floor to ceiling. The fires blazed for hours, but they never took hold in Westminster Hall. It wasn't until late that night that the inferno dwindled down to pathetic embers.

The next day, the reports claimed that the House of Lords, the House of Commons, Speaker's House, the Courts of Law and the attached libraries and committee rooms were all destroyed in the blaze. Where just days before the headlines had read about the danger of mages running wild, they now read about the heroism and bravery of London's Fire Engine Establishment and mourned the loss of the heart of the empire.

I watched the blaze from Westminster Bridge, tired beyond all reason. Elly had insisted we leave so she could treat everyone's wounds properly, but Jennifer refused, adamant that we stay. It was as if we were in a dream, almost, or a nightmare. Trapped in an unfathomable limbo of awareness—a liminal space where lucidity was forever beyond our grasp. There was nothing any of us could do but watch in languid torpidity. When we finally left, taking a cab in Lambeth on the long roundabout journey to Carnaby Street, it was as if the flames had burned themselves into my eyes. We had borne witness to what few could comprehend as the eldritch will of the Arcane itself.

October 17th, 1834

Rest and Restitution

Chapter 43

I fell asleep almost immediately, finally giving over to the days of exhaustion. To my relief, my friends were all still there when I woke. Elly was nudging me awake and gesturing out the window of the cab—we'd stopped a few yards down from the Solution, and it had seen much better days. The patchwork windows and door were broken in, and the squared circle above the door was cracked.

I dragged myself through a sleepy haze and the turned over tables of the shop floor and made my way up to the lab. Jen was in rough shape and staying on Westminster Bridge had not been one of her best ideas. The lab had been ransacked; the stacks of shelves had been pushed over, spilling on the floor the wild and unnatural Arcane ephemera used in the creation of potions and poultices. Good thing was, I could make a healing draught in my sleep, and if I didn't know better, I would have said I did. She was surprised when I bought the potion downstairs inside a syringe, but the results spoke for themselves.

"I wrote a damn paper on those syringes, and here you are innovating in ways I couldn't imagine," she said as her wound knitted close.

"You take risks when you've been stabbed," I responded. The world rocked around me as a new wave of tiredness hit me, "Oh, I would love to spend hours talking but," I yawned, "can we sleep first?"

***

I passed out before I got an answer to my question, but the next day I found myself huddled on the bed with Elly in my arms, and Jennifer snuggled up behind me in the huge bed of the second-floor bedroom. At the foot of the bed, Bryce was curled up, at peace for the first time in days.

I extricated myself from the pile of sleeping bodies and caught a glance of myself in a mirror. I was a fucking mess. I was bruised head to toe, with strange lighting pattern scarring along my arms. Two days old make up had smeared in my eyes, giving me the look of a sullen skeleton. My hair was a tangled bush, flecked with blood, dirt, and soot. I sighed at myself and found solace in the fact that most of the bruising would fade in a day or less. The same couldn't be said of my broken ribs, which had doubled in number at least and sent a sharp stab of pain through my chest when I threw on a dressing gown.

When I returned with a tray of tea and biscuits, the others were stirring awake. Elly got up first and came to sit with me on the chaise. She rested her head on my shoulders and quietly said, "You came back."

I smiled. "We came back at the same time. No need to act so surprised"

"Shut up and let me have this," she yawned meekly, then poured herself a cup of tea, dropped in two lumps of sugar and took a chocolate biscuit.

"I'm sorry for putting you in so much danger…"

"But you got us out," she interjected. "All of us."

I rested my forehead on hers and time seemed to melt away. The warmth of her skin on mine, the soft breaths on my cheeks, and the gentle touch of our intertwined fingers were all that I needed. All the pain and hardship, it had all been worth it for that warm, quiet morning, and the knowledge that everyone I cared about was safe.

Elly looked into my eyes, like she was studying them for something, and I was transfixed by those crystalline irises—blue as the morning sky. She asked me, casting her gaze away for just a moment, "Do you know what the hardest part of all this was?"

I shrugged and said, rather flippantly, "Being stabbed and nearly bleeding out on Regent's Street."

"Fine, yes, I expect that was very hard on you," Elly said. "I meant for me—numpty. From the day I walked into the shop, you looked like you'd lost your shine." She stroked my cheek, and I kissed her palm. "I didn't understand where that brilliant, splendid girl I'd known all my life had gone."

"Splendid, was I?"

"I would go as far as to say splendiferous," she remarked with dimples from her grin. Elly sighed, and her smile faded, but not into sadness—she had that wistful, nostalgic look of someone who was homesick. "I saw you doubt yourself, blame yourself and hold yourself back—and I didn't know how to help you."

My chest was as light as a feather, and I realised just how utterly lost I was in her eyes. "You helped just be being here."

Elly shook her head and pursed her lips, as if I'd just mispronounced a word and she'd found it all too funny. "Darling, you didn't need my help. I watched you pull yourself up, time and again, and that shine—that splendiferous brilliance—it came back all on its own."

I was speechless—shocking, I know—so I simply leant in, and kissed her. Her lips tasted of too-sweet tea, and she leaned into me with a gentle eagerness.

Someone cleared their throat behind us, and I turned to see Jennifer sitting up with a sly half smile on her face. "You have a room downstairs."

I snorted out of laugh and said, "It's a mess."

"It's always a mess," she quipped back. We locked eyes and there was a tense moment of silence before we both broke into a brief fit of giggles. Jennifer got out of the bed and sauntered over to Elly and me, her night shirt swaying as she walked and the silhouette of her body showing slightly as the morning sun caught her through the window.

She made herself some tea and I regarded her intently. She was a little gaunt and ragged, with heavy dark circles under her eyes and a new minor crook in her nose. She had a few cuts and bruises, miraculously no one of them looked fresh from the day before. If that was luck or skill I couldn't say. I noticed once she sat down that she was giving me the same treatment I was giving her.

"What do you see?" I asked.

She grinned with pride, "You've been fighting nearly

every day, and you managed to brew up more of my shielding potion. Impressive." Jennifer leaned back in the armchair she'd perched in, "You were stabbed, left torso. The wound is healed but you've been carrying your weight differently and wincing when you turn. Scratches on the forearm match the ones I got fighting that wyvern, so I suspect Kidderminster or Cranley had a second one of those beasts.

"You're wearing make-up, but not much, probably done by your new friend here. Hello dear, thanks for not letting me die. Be with you in a moment." She was just showing off at this point, "Your hair was styled, and those trousers you were wearing weren't yours. You, Bryce, the trio of Lords were all tired from lack of sleep. Was the party nice?"

"It was a nightmare," I said, "and a trap. Viscount Kidderminster and Baron Cranley set the whole thing up to get Bryce and me in one place where they could 'dispose' of us."

"You never did say what happened to the dress," Elly asked.

"Knife fight," I said nonchalantly.

Jennifer held up her hands. "Wait, you wore a dress? As in, a full-on ball gown? And you trashed it in a knife fight?"

"Not just any dress," I said into my teacup, and then side eyed the open wardrobe across the room.

"You…" she said, "Not my dress? How did you even get it to fit? That was expensive." She looked more annoyed than angry and let out a dejected sigh as she looked at the empty space in her wardrobe.

Remorsefully I said, "Sorry, Jen. Elly refitted it the day before last, and I had a run in with that young lord, Remington, at the party."

Jen shrugged it off in a moment. "No worries, my dear, there's always another dress. Now, I suppose we should talk about what happened." There was a pause, and she added, "At the warehouse?"

I knew what she meant, and honestly, I'd been trying not to think about it. It took a heartbeat for that furious grief to bubble its way back into my gut, for all the pain and anger to find its way back to the forefront of my mind. I remembered that brief crystal-clear thought I had, sitting on the floor of the shop after Baker had told me about the fire on Stewart Street—and I slapped Jennifer across the face.

"Charlotte!" Elly exclaimed.

Jen recovered quickly, holding her nose in case it started bleeding. My hand throbbed, and I would bet her face felt even worse. "I suppose I deserved that," she said.

I screwed up my face, biting back the tears in my eyes. "You drugged me. What the fuck were you thinking? Were you even thinking?"

"I realise that may not have been my best decision," Jennifer said. She leant back, out of my immediate reach, and put on a placating tone. "I had to get you out. I was scared for you."

"That wasn't your decision to make," I said bluntly. The hurt ran deeper than I thought, right the way to my core. It ached and wept inside of me.

"You're my apprentice, Charlotte—" ("I'm not a child!" I protested), "—and I'm responsible for your safety," she said. Jen looked at me with concern and leaned forward to put a hand on mine. "I'm sorry I hurt you. I did what I thought was best. I was wrong."

The pain and the words started to flow, like a river un-dammed. "I trusted you! You kept me in the dark and threw me into a life-or-death situation. I was terrified, and you *fucking* drugged me."

"I—I thought you were ready for all that, and when the mage showed up, I—"

"How could I have been ready? You weren't telling me anything." I got up and paced the room, desperate to keep myself from crying. "Even if I was, even if you had told me everything you were planning up until that point, it still wouldn't make a damn difference to the fact that you *poisoned my brain with magic.*"

Jen seemed to consider her words very intently. Beyond the weary tiredness on her face, I could see the pain in those eyes like drops of gold—their lustre had been dulled by the knowledge of just how catastrophically she'd fucked up. "For what it's worth, I regretted what I did every minute since it happened—and I will spend every minute of my life trying to make that up to you. I was stupid, foolish, and downright pig-headed. I should have trusted you more, I should have seen your brilliance for what it was, and I should have treated you far better than I did."

I was so angry at her, so hurt and frayed, inches away from tumbling down from the razor-sharp edge of fury I found myself walking. As much as I hated what she did and the way she made me feel, I hated *hating* even more. When she reached out a hand to me, I took it without hesitation—not out of forgiveness, because I knew that would take time—but out of a desire to forgive, when I was ready.

I squeezed her hand in mine, and the tears finally made a bid for freedom down my cheeks. "I want to trust you again, Jen, I really do. You need to promise that you won't hide things from me anymore—don't keep me in the dark, even if you think it's for my benefit."

Jennifer nodded. "Done."

"And burn that formula, the suggestion potion," I added. "I meant it when I said you crossed a line with that one. I don't ever want to see it again."

"All right, consider it gone."

"Good. Thank you." The river slowed into a stream, and then a trickle. A dull ache in my chest found a comfortable spot to rest. I knew I'd carry that ache for a while yet, before it healed, like a broken rib, a broken heart takes its time. "What happened after I left?"

Jen looked as though she wasn't ready to change the subject, but relented after a moment of silence. "Cranley put up a good fight, but I was wounded as you'll remember. He managed to knock me out with a sleep spell, and his goons took me hostage on the ship. I awoke around the time they set the warehouse on fire. I managed to stash my bag, hoping you'd find it, and when we docked, I was taken into custody and imprisoned at Westminster. I didn't even know it had a jail."

Elly piped up, "Lord Remington signed a false statement

implicating you for treason. Though I doubt it would have held up in court."

"Treason? That's ridiculous." She took a sip of her tea, flashed her devil-may-care smile at me, and said, "I do have to apologise for my apprentice's dreadful manners, by the by, you saved my life, and she hasn't even introduced us yet." Elly and Jen laughed as I turned a deep shade of red.

"I hate you both. Jen, this is Dr Eloise Chynoweth, my oldest friend. Elly, this is Jennifer Morton, my mentor and professional pain in the arse."

"Chynoweth? You're that old friend, I see. You know, from Charlotte's tales of her time in Cambridge, I pictured you being taller," Jennifer said jovially. Elly blushed and smiled and went back to quietly nibbling on her biscuit.

"We should wake Bryce up," I said, looking at his huddled form on the bed. "But he looks so peaceful."

Elly sighed, "Is he going to be all right? I know he had a bad relationship with his father, but…"

"But I stabbed him in the chest after he tried to kill us all, and then we left his body to be consumed by ethereal fire?"

"Yeah. That."

"I can hear you," said a dry voice from beneath the blankets.

I winced; probably shouldn't have mentioned the stabbing. "Bryce, I…"

He rolled out of the bed, and I'd be lying if I said my heart didn't skip a beat when I saw he was shirtless; his tattoos extended across his chest and emphasised his trim physique. "If you hadn't stabbed him, I'd have incinerated him. He deserved it. Like you said, he was a monster."

"Still, I—Do you need anything?"

"A stiff drink." He stretched and found his shirt from among the pile of discarded clothes, "Elly, Ms Morton, pleasure to see you both up and well."

I realised that, for the first time in days, there was no pressure over me, no imminent danger, no impending doom. There was no beast lurking in my unconscious waiting to tear my heart out or assassin around the corner, waiting to tear my heart out. There was just… us, in that room. I was filled with an unfamiliar sense of tranquillity, utterly content with the world.

I was naïve to think it would last.

The doorbell rang, which was strange because we left the shop in such a state that no one would want to come by for weeks. I looked surprised, and a little expectantly, at Jennifer. She sighed a faux annoyed sigh and got up, saying, "Fine, I guess I'll get it."

Bryce fixed himself a cup of tea and sat where Jennifer had been. "Can you guess the weirdest thing going through my mind right now?"

I smiled and bit my lip, "I'll tell you the same thing I told Remington. I don't usually swing your way, but I make exceptions." Elly pinched my arm, and I yelped at her, "What's that for?" She just laughed, and it was like music to my ears. I could have listened to her laugh all day.

Bryce cleared his throat, apparently less phased than my flirtation than I expected. "Actually, I was thinking about how, with my good-for-nothing monster of a father dead, my older brother inherits the title, making me his heir. Until he has children, at least.

"That is weird," I said. "Fucking aristocracy."

As if on cue, the door opened at the very moment, and Jennifer entered the room, accompanied by one such member of the fucking aristocracy.

"Prime Minister!" Bryce exclaimed, and Elly and I practically jumped out of our night clothes.

Chapter 44

Lord Melbourne, Prime Minister of the United Kingdom, was a white man in his fifties, with salt and pepper hair that fell in gentle locks, mutton chops on his jowls, and a small mouth that bore a solemn expression. He wore a fur coat over a black suit, with a gold chain dangling from a breast pocket. A blue neckerchief was wrapped around his collar, and what I could see of his white shirt was dirtied with soot.

"Can I offer you some tea, Prime Minister?" Jennifer asked, while the rest of us sat in silence, aghast at the presence of the nation's premier.

"No, thank you, I won't be long," he said, before looking around the room and choking back a sneer at our arrayed stages of undress. "Imagine if you will my surprise when, as I watched the seat of our government burn to the ground, the Gentleman Usher of the Black Rod approached me to explain that the son of The Viscount Kidderminster was skulking around the palace merely half an hour before the fire broke out. Add to that detail that Mr Rosehouse had in his company an oddly dressed, unidentified woman—" rude, "—with whom he fled the palace, also in the company of one Jennifer Morton, who was being held; not in an actual jail or prison, but the disused cells in the law courts—on charges of high treason. This was after a throng of terrified peers apparently shouting about a terrible fight happening in the furnace room beneath the House of Lords."

"Prime Minister, we can—" Bryce began to say, but the stern Lord cut him off.

"Explain? I hope you will, Mr Rosehouse. But not to me, not now. I've come to inform you that there will be an inquiry, and you will all be called as witnesses." He cleared his throat, and pulled out a wad of papers. "We have already prepared your statements. Memorise them, do not stray or the consequences will be dire."

Jennifer took the papers and skimmed the first page. "This is all lies."

"Yes," Lord Melbourne said.

"You want us to lie to a royal inquiry?"

"Yes."

"About how the fire started and who was responsible?"

"Yes."

"And not mention anything about the conspiracy concocted by members of the House of Lords to implement a draconian policy of enslavement on mages?"

"Ms Morton, allow me to be very clear. Despite the carnage wrought last night, the nation has escaped disaster. There is no telling what might have been unleashed if Kidderminster and his followers had succeeded. This fire has presented an opportunity to sweep this whole ordeal under the rug." The Prime Minister was cold and stern. This was a man thrust into the premiership in difficult times, a man of the old guard struggling against the reforms that had seen so much change in the political structure of the nation, a man that barely held a grip over the government before the fire. He needed this. He needed us. Corruption of the scale that we'd found, the decades of criminal activity by a prominent peer, the lies and deceit. It would destroy him.

Lord Melbourne didn't strike me as a man who wanted to be Prime Minister, but here he was, trying desperately to hold on to it. Why else would he have come out here, apparently alone and in secret? He hadn't really noticed me regarding him—he was much more focussed on Jennifer and Bryce—and he almost jumped when I spoke. "What about us? What happens to us?"

"Nothing."

"By nothing, I assume you mean we aren't all going to be arrested for who knows what—breaking and entering, assault, murder, arson. But what would stop us—any of us—from telling people the truth, anyway?" I asked the pointed question, knowing I wouldn't get an answer. "I'm tired, my Lord. Tired of a lot of things, but the thing I'm most tired of is pompous, upper-class twats, coming into my life and telling me what to do."

"Charlotte!" Jennifer exclaimed.

I ignored my mentor's protests and stood up as tall and confident as I could make myself. "Two-thousand, or we go to the press," I stated bluntly.

"Pounds? Are you mad, girl?" Melbourne responded, half stunned, and half impressed at my gall.

I turned to Elly. "Do I look ten years younger than I am or something? Why does everyone keep calling me girl?" She shrugged, and I continued, "Yes, two-thousand pounds. More than enough to repair the damage caused by Kidderminster's goons when they ransacked the shop, replace the very expensive materials used in the course of my investigation, and contribute to assuaging the very serious emotional harm that we have all sustained. Consider it a speaker's fee for the inquiry."

Jennifer gasped at my diatribe, "Charlotte, this is really not—"

Melbourne interrupted her. "Done."

"Really?" all three of us asked at once.

The old man very nearly cracked a smile before assuming the proper composure and replacing his hat on his head. "You will hear from my offices when the formal inquiry takes place. Until then, I bid you good day."

Melbourne left without another word, and after Jennifer had shown him out, we all sat around the coffee table in stunned silence. I was shocked that it had worked, and impressed with myself, truth be told. I felt uneasy about not sharing the whole story with the public, but something Melbourne had said struck a chord with me somewhere in my mind. Kidderminster would never have stopped with his mage furnace; his bill would have been just one step in instigating government sanctioned hate against mages.

The thing about hate is it's always hungry. No matter what you feed it, it will always demand more. You tell people that mages are dangerous and the hate nibbles away at the public consciousness, so they agree to put the dangerous people somewhere else. But it's never enough. Soon the hate demands more, and it's not mage furnaces anymore, it's pyres in the streets. What happens then? How do you satiate the rage permeating society? Who is next on the platter? Hate doesn't stop when you say it stops. If people knew what happened, that a mage was responsible for the fire, or if Kidderminster's plan had worked and the fear of magic was stoked; the hate would have found its roots and never left. So, I knew we had to keep it secret, at least until the world was ready for the truth.

"That's it then?" asked Bryce after the dust had settled. "We just pretend it never happened, carry on like everything's the same." He looked weary all of a sudden, as if the wind had been taken from his sails. How could we pretend like nothing had happened? Things had changed, whether the Prime Minister liked it or not.

"No," Jennifer said, "but we play by their rules. For now, at least. Charlotte, where's your notebook? We should collate all the evidence and write up a report of sorts. In case we need it."

"In your coat, I think. Fourth pocket down on the inside left."

Jen rummaged through her coat for a minute and then produced the little blue book. She smiled when she saw how much I'd written. "This is good, very thorough." She stopped on a page a third the way in and gave it a puzzled look, "Charlotte, what's Heart's Remedy Tea?"

I gave Elly a furtive glance and answered, "Ooh, it's a commission piece, it's not finished yet. I really don't think you need to worry—"

"Transformational?" Jennifer said, not paying attention to my protestations. "Trying to enhance feminine characteristics—" ("Jen, it's still experimental"), "—Ah, I see you've relied on Roman symbolism, interesting. Nice touch with the tuning crystals—" ("I really think we could discuss this"), "—Oh God—" ("What?"), "—please tell me you didn't use viper's venom in this without something to counter-balance the side effects?"

The room went dead silent, and three pairs of eyes stared at me, expectantly. "Are you asking me that question because the venom would likely result in catastrophic heart failure as an Alchemical side-effect? Perhaps in the middle of a life-or-death escape from a wild magical creature?" I said straight-faced.

"You idiot."

November 8th, 1834

Epilogue

Chapter 45

*Destruction of the Houses of Parliament: Report of
the Privy Council – The Observer*

"Says here that some fool was burning old tally sticks in the
furnaces below the House of Lords," my father said from behind the broadsheet. "Seems mighty careless, if you ask me."

"Yes," I answered nonchalantly. "Very careless indeed. I
need to be off, Dad; I'll see you this evening. Six O'clock, remember?" He pretended not to hear me and stuffed eggs into his
mouth. "Father?"

"Aye, yes, six O'clock, I'll be there."

"You know as well as I do that Mr Chynoweth likes to
get an early start on the brandy, so if there's any chance of a
polite conversation, I need you to be on time."

"I will be there, Charlotte. Don't you worry about me."
He was going to be late—which is why I told him six, despite
Elly inviting us over for dinner at seven.

It was an important evening; between fixing up the shop,
giving statements to the inquiry, and working late with Jennifer on my new formula, I still hadn't had a chance to see
Mr Chynoweth since Elly had arrived back in London over a
month ago. He also didn't know the two of us were involved
yet. It wasn't that we expected him to take it badly—quite
the opposite, really. He'd always been supportive of my rela-
tionships regardless of the sex of my partners—but it felt more
proper to tell him in person. He'd had one big change in his
life recently already, so a gentle touch was needed.

I kissed father on his bald spot and grabbed my new coat
from the rack. It fit perfectly; a long black riding coat, tapered
at the waist and flared at the hem—giving it a very satisfying
swoosh as I walked. Paired with a woollen waistcoat, black shirt

and trousers, and my sturdy boots, I actually grinned when I caught a look at my reflection. I looked good, and I wasn't covered in bruises. I'd taken Jen's advice and cut my hair shorter, not above my ears as she did hers, but short enough that it wasn't in the way with enough length I could still tie it up.

I took another look at my father before I left, he was once again engrossed in the morning paper. "Love you, old man," I said from the door.

He didn't look up from the paper, but I could hear the smile in his voice, "and you, you little rascal."

***

"...the other seven are still missing," I heard from inside the office as I climbed up the stairs of The Potent Solution. It was Bryce speaking, somewhat more refined than when I first met him. "Do you think you can find them?"

I had a moment of pause as I put my hand on the door, a short stab of panic that had followed me for the last few weeks. I couldn't shake the feeling of loss and loneliness I'd felt when Jennifer had first gone missing, and now anytime I went looking for her there was always a second that hung in time. I could open this door, and she wouldn't be there—I was terrified that she wouldn't be there. But then my mind would catch up with me. I'd hear her voice or smell her perfume, and everything would feel right with the world.

Jennifer responded in the affirmative, before realising I was at the door. "Come in, Charlotte. We'll have to speak with Home Secretary, see what they have on Baron Cranley's holdings and contacts. This is a loose end. I don't think they'll want ignored."

I walked across the room, dropping my coat across the couch and perching myself on the arm. "The rest of your classmates?" I asked Bryce.

"Indeed, they still haven't surfaced. I figure there's three possibilities: Cranley indoctrinated them as well and they are biding their time. They refused to work with him and were killed as a result, or they are on the run and unaware of Cranley's death." Bryce replied. He was wearing a sharply cut suit and was clean shaven for the first time in a while. I even thought I could smell some cologne on him.

"I prefer the last one," I said. "You have a romantic rendezvous."

"What?" he said, acting surprised. "How did you… No, definitely not. I'm just seeing the family."

Jennifer gave me a grin that confirmed she'd come to the same conclusion. "What was the girls name you told me about Charlotte? Leeanna?"

Bryce's eye twitched and his fingers flexed, but he acted nonplussed. I cocked my head at him, "I don't suppose Remington is very happy about that."

"Remington has taken to staying in his country estate. Something about the hustle and bustle of the city not being good for his injury."

I let out a soft giggle and said, "I hope it goes well."

He relaxed a little bit and let out a soft sigh. "I don't want to jinx anything. She's agreed to go on a walk through the park, that's all. Just don't tell Miss Chynoweth or I will never hear the end of it."

"Mr Rosehouse, do you really think so little of me that I would share details about your private affairs?"

"Yes."

"No need to be so blunt. My lips are sealed."

Jennifer clapped her hands. "Hallelujah, peace and quiet."

I shot Jen a wounded look before we all cracked up and laughed. Bryce made his excuses to leave and before long, Jennifer and I were going about tidying the shop floor before opening. She must have noticed the involuntary way I kept glancing over to see if she was still there, and when we stopped to have some tea, she put an arm around me.

"Are you alright? You've been a little skittish these last few weeks," she said warmly.

"No," I responded in an uncharacteristic moment of honesty, "but I will be."

I took a moment to breathe and collect myself. The thoughts didn't all come at once, I had to pause and let them crystalise before committing them to words.

"I was—just—so—lost without you; I think maybe I've always been lost. My whole life I've been waiting for someone to find me and fix me—like I'm some unfinished work of clay—and until recently I thought that person was you.

"I'm afraid you'll disappear again, and I won't know what to do.

"—and I'm afraid you'll hurt me again—and don't promise me you won't. No promises.

"It's stupid—I know—I'm a grown woman. I shouldn't need you as much as I do—

"—and I know I'm capable of taking care of myself.

"I think—I think what I'm finally starting to realise and learn is that…

"…I have to be the one to find myself, and that's terrifying. But that doesn't mean I don't need you. Because I do; I need all of you; I'm still looking for myself—there's this whole journey ahead of me—and you are my map. Elly is my compass. I can't do it alone."

Jennifer ran a hand through my hair—she was always so loud and so grand. It made it hard to see how tender she could be. I rested my head on her shoulder and melted into her warmth. "You can be very profound sometimes," she said.

"I had a good teacher," I said.

Acknowledgements

I started writing this book halfway through a six-month internship that I had already mentally checked out of. It started small, an opening chapter that grew from the backstory of a tabletop RPG character I played in a recently finished campaign, hastily typed into a poorly formatted word document on my phone during my two-hour train commute. It wasn't great, but it was a start. All told it took a little over six years for The Potent Solution to find its home, and there was no way I could have done this alone.

I should start by thanking the person who has been by my side throughout those six years, and who has been my biggest fan that entire time—despite steadfastly refusing to read a single early draft. Sarah, I love you, tremendously so, and I am so grateful for everything you do for me. Now please, read the book, I finished it for you.

The fact that this book got over the line at all is down to my agent, Laura Bennett. I was honestly almost ready to give up on finding an agent when Laura and I connected during a pitch event on Twitter, despite, and I quote, "I'm a bit full on urban fantasy at the moment. [pensive face emoji] So right now I'm very unlikely to take any on." Laura's edits were like a ten-thousand grit whetstone used to refine the edge of a sharpened blade, and her support and encouragement kept me going in the dark times when the book was on sub. Laura, I cannot thank you enough—the best I can do is get you the next book.

Some of my favourite parts of this book came from working with my amazing development editor, Megan Records. I feel so immensely privileged that Megan picked my book to work on when I entered the 2021 #RevPit contest. From making Charlotte a driving force of the plot and fleshing out the worldbuilding, to deepening the romance between

Charlotte and Elly, she knew exactly how to breathe life into this book and make it shine. Thank you, Megan, for helping me get inside Charlotte's head.

To Ren, I am endlessly grateful for the feedback you gave me and all the advice you shared, you were one of the first people to say you loved my book and I will treasure that always.

I have to thank my friends and fellow players who adventured with me in the campaign that brought Charlotte to life in my mind. To Pete, I honestly can't believe you let me get away with making a simulacrum of a Solar Angel—let this be a reminder to never give a power gamer a Scroll of Limited Wish. To Amy, George, Jimmy, Laura, Lawrence, and Rae, those evenings we spent rolling dice and doing silly voices were some of the most fun I had during our time at the OU. And to Rhian, thanks you to you especially, I hope I did Bryce justice, I simply couldn't leave him behind when I plucked Charlotte out of Korvosa and dropped her into London.

To Emma, Morag and James, my love for you all is boundless. So much is said of the polyamorous experience on how hard it must be to love multiple people—but I'm just here wondering how I got so lucky to have multiple amazing people love me back.

To my family. To my Mum, for standing by me and helping me become to woman I am today. To my Dad, for instilling in me a love for all things sci-fi and fantasy. And to my brothers, for the happy memories of Lord of the Rings marathons and quoting Anakin Skywalker.

To my fellow alums of the #RevPit class of 2021, I will cherish the memories of our journeys together, and I wish you all the success in the world for your wonderful books.

Lastly, to all the people who listened to me rant about my writing, gave advice and feedback, read early drafts or just said nice things: Patti Thatcher, Matthew Grierson, Christina Greer, Ash McAllan, Luke Jordan, Aoife Deane-Scott, Natalie Garrett, Izzy Garland, Kaja Franck and Anne Tibbets.

About the Author

Ashley Nova is a sci-fi and fantasy author and professional astronomer. When she isn't studying the intricacies of galaxy evolution and artificial intelligence, she's plotting out and writing character driven speculative fiction at the intersections of queerness and neurodiversity.

Ashley enjoys picking up and putting down heavy objects at the gym, playing table-top RPGs, and she developed a taste for going to raves at the age of thirty.

Excellent LGBTQ+ fiction by unique, wonderful authors.

Thrillers

Mystery

Romance

Literary

Young Adult

& More

Join our mailing list for new, offers, and free books!

Visit our website for more Spectrum Books

www.spectrum-books.com

Or find us on Instagram @spectrumbookpublisher